STAR CRUISER TITAN
C.G. MOSLEY

SEVERED PRESS
HOBART TASMANIA

STAR CRUISER TITAN

WWW.SEVEREDPRESS.COM

ISBN: 978-1-925711-83-7

CHAPTER 1

Jake Crosby spent the evening in what had become his customary position. With his hands laced behind his head and his feet kicked up on the desk, it was all he could do to keep his eyes open. When he'd joined the Space and Aeronautics Military Alliance (S.A.M.A.) three years prior, he'd done so with aspirations of space exploration and a strong desire to do his part for the betterment of mankind. He knew that his dreams and aspirations were simply not going to be enough as it was well-known that S.A.M.A. was an extremely hard organization to gain acceptance into. He'd made the grades, and kept his nose clean all through grade school and when the time finally came to take the Tactical Acceptance and Placement exam, or TAP test, Jake was more than ready.

Out of a possible score of 350, he'd scored a 285, which just happened to be the minimum score required to gain a place in the most elite military organization on planet Earth. His parents were beyond proud, and the small town he'd grown up in had a parade in his honor before his departure to boot camp. His test scores showed that, although he excelled in reading comprehension and technical knowledge, he scored very low in social skills. This ended any possibility of him becoming an infantryman, and seriously put a damper on his chance of becoming a pilot—though his technical knowledge and mathematics scores made him a viable candidate.

Unfortunately, his repeated attempts to get into the pilot training program had been denied and so far, Jake was forced to a desk job. He'd decided that if he was going to have to sit behind a desk and grind out more time until he gained acceptance, he'd do so on an off-earth station. There were multiple colonies on Mars, and between the Saturn moons of Titan and Enceladus, there were another four more. Jake fought hard for a job on Titan's secretive Discovery station. Discovery's mission was simple: search and monitor deep space for signs of life.

The surface of Titan surrounding the Discovery station was peppered with military bases designed to respond at a moment's notice if alien life was discovered and turned out to be hostile. In the ten years since Discovery's creation, the sky had been monitored on a continuous basis, and so far, nothing had been found in the vast cold darkness of space. Jake often played out in his mind what he would do and how he would react if something popped up suddenly on the radar. When he'd been assigned the position, he'd been warned very sternly by his commanding officer that sleeping on the job would not be tolerated in any way. If he was caught sleeping, he'd immediately be shipped back to S.A.M.A. headquarters on Earth for trial. The trial would almost certainly lead to his dismissal from the program.

The thought of losing his job terrified him and what he had not anticipated was just how difficult it would be to stay awake. He was essentially left in a room alone with an array of monitors covering the wall in front of him. Coffee was the only beverage he drank, and he'd begun to wonder if he'd built up an immunity to caffeine. It seemed that the dark liquid no longer had any effect in keeping his eyes open. To combat exhaustion, Jake often jogged in place and even sang songs to himself to keep his blood pumping and his mind occupied. He never dreamed that such a boring position existed in S.A.M.A but he kept reminding himself that if it meant he could eventually earn himself a spot in the pilot training program, it would be worth it. He knew of other great pilots that had taken a similar path and he found himself wondering if they'd struggled as badly as he was.

This particular evening was still young, and so far, Jake's battle with sleepiness had not yet begun. A small monitor on his desk played the first hockey game of the season—a much talked about meeting between New York City and the first lunar colony on Earth's moon—Tranquility. The game was held on the surface of the moon, and a transparent oxygen-filled dome covered the open ice rink. The images on Jake's monitor showed a large crowd had gathered to witness the game in person, and as the camera panned around the rink, he caught sight of Earth looming beyond the moon's horizon. It was a beautiful sight and it made him momentarily long to be back home.

There were no hockey teams on Titan—at least not yet. Hockey had been around for hundreds of years and had claimed the title of oldest sport in history. In a different time, many years ago, sports like basketball, baseball, and football had been wildly popular. However, the appeal of all of them soon faded until all that remained was hockey. Jake was rooting for his hometown New York Lions though they were heavy underdogs. The Lunar Knights were the defending champions and were expected to repeat again. The anticipation of a few hours of hockey had Jake feeling wide awake and it was just what he needed to somehow push through until his shift ended.

Fortunately, the game turned out to be a real nail-biter with both teams knotted up at 3-3 midway through the third period. Jake stared at the television with his eyes wide. His heart raced as the seconds ticked by and he began to accept the possibility that maybe his team was going to be victorious despite their underdog label. As the game entered the final two minutes of play, an alarm suddenly beeped from one of the monitors on the large wall in front of him. At first, Jake didn't even notice it as the spell of the spectacular hockey game continued to unfold in brilliant high definition in front of him.

By design, the alarm was made to grow louder every thirty seconds until a button was pressed in acknowledgement. When the realization finally came to him that the alarm was sounding, Jake looked over at the monitor, his jaw slightly dropping open. The digital readout below the monitor indicated that multiple lifeforms were discovered all at once a few thousand miles away along with the exact coordinates. He then turned his attention to another monitor in the center of the wall. It was the largest of all and the picture it showed was provided by a large mechanical telescope fixed on top of the Mithrim Montes mountain range—the tallest point on all of Titan.

Jake quickly punched in the coordinates he'd read into the keyboard in front of him and the telescope changed its focus in response. Within seconds, the high-powered lens concentrated on an eerie sight that made Jake's heart race much faster than the hockey game he'd suddenly forgotten all about. In the center of the screen, with a black and starry backdrop behind it, a massive space craft travelled at a high rate of speed. It wasn't a saucer like countless U.F.O. sightings through the years had been described. To Jake, the shape of the ship he was looking at reminded him more of an almond. The small end of the "almond" seemed to be the front and its sleek design clearly boasted a level of speed that no ship on earth was capable of. The ship was heading straight for Titan and there would be little time to react.

With his anxiety level at an all-time high, Jake reached over and punched a green button located near the top right corner of the control panel in front of him. Within seconds, a six-inch holographic figure of a man's head appeared in front of him—it was General Harry Hightower. The image had a defaulted green hue, but otherwise was incredibly life-like.

"I trust this is important," the middle-aged Hightower said with a yawn.

"Y-yes sir," Jake stuttered. He took a deep breath trying to regain his composure. "Sir, the moment we've been waiting for has arrived. I've got an unidentified flying object approaching at a high rate of speed. I have visual and I have confirmed it's not anything of ours," he stated in as calm a manner as he possibly could.

General Hightower's face perked up considerably. His eyes widened to the point they reminded Jake of ping pong balls. For a moment, he said nothing. It was as if he were trying to decide if he was really awake or not.

"Very good Crosby," he said finally. "Does the incoming object appear to be hostile in nature?"

"There is no way to tell," Jake replied excitedly. "The U.F.O. is moving towards us with a high rate of speed...I anticipate an E.T.A. of half an hour."

"Half an hour?" Hightower asked, his voice raised an octave in disbelief. "Crosby, keep your eyes on that object and be prepared to call out the exact coordinates when requested. I'll be back in touch with you in a matter of minutes."

Hightower was just about to disconnect, when Jake suddenly shouted for him to wait.

"What?" Hightower hissed. "We have absolutely no time to waste!"

"Sir it stopped," Jake said, his eyes still locked on the monitor.

"What? What do you mean it stopped?" Hightower asked. He wasn't sure whether to be relieved or annoyed.

"It's just hovering now," Jake explained.

"And you're absolutely sure that this object isn't one of ours?"

"Yes sir," Jake replied, nodding. "I've never seen a ship stop that abruptly ever before. None of our ships are capable of that."

General Hightower took a moment to stroke his chin as he considered the new development. "Crosby, be ready with those coordinates," he said finally, and the holographic image immediately vanished.

***

Roger Stellick had just completed his daily exercise routine and was wiping sweat away from his forehead when he noticed the gym manager jogging in his direction. She was young, very attractive, and the last sort of woman Roger would ever expect to show interest in him. She was very athletic, and he estimated she was at least ten years his junior. Her hair was long, blonde, and pulled into a pony tail. Roger, on the other hand, was balding and only in the gym because General Harry Hightower had forced him to. In his words, Roger was getting "a little fluffy" and was in danger of getting grounded if the trend continued.

"Commander Stellick," the woman said excitedly as she came to a halt in front of him. "General Hightower is on the phone wanting to speak with you immediately."

"Hightower?" Stellick asked, tossing the towel aside. He glanced at his watch. "He's usually asleep at this hour." He glanced up at the woman. "Lauren, did he say what it was about?"

As expected she shook her head and he found himself wondering why he even asked the question.

"Alright," he said as he rose from the padded bench. "I'm assuming I can take it at your desk?"

Lauren nodded and motioned for him to help himself. As he walked away, she bent over to pick up his sweaty towel and to check on some of the other military personnel using the gym.

As Stellick reached the desk he took in a deep breath and let it out slowly. He then placed the phone to his ear, expecting the worst.

"This is Commander Stellick," he said, speaking into the receiver.

"Stellick, it's Harry," the gruff general replied. "Listen, I don't have a lot of time to explain, but I need you in a fighter in half an hour and in the air in forty-five minutes at the most."

Roger felt his jaw tighten. "What is going on?" he asked.

"It's the moment we've been waiting for…and the moment you've been training for," General Hightower answered. "A legitimate U.F.O. is hovering near Saturn's ring…I need you up there to intercept it. We need to find out real quick if this thing is hostile."

Everything Hightower was saying made Roger feel as if he were in a dream. Nothing about it seemed real. "Alright," he said in an almost robotic tone. "I can be at the hangar in ten minutes…I'm assuming they'll have a Comet ready?"

"Already ahead of you," Hightower responded. "By the time you get at the hangar, a Comet fighter will be fueled and ready for take-off. All I need is for you to get your butt over there."

"Be there in ten," Roger said, but General Hightower had already disconnected.

CHAPTER 2

Each base of operations on the Titan colony was comprised of numerous domes—enormous domes that were temperature controlled and also sourced the precious oxygen needed for human survival. Human beings had the ability to venture outside of the domes without the need for a pressurized suit, however, the air was unbreathable and dense clothing would be necessary to combat the extreme cold. Each of the domes on Titan's surface were connected by various tubes, and within some of the tubes a railway system provided quick transportation when necessary.

Many scoffed at the idea of installing a railway as the primary means of transportation on Titan as it was seen as an antiquated and subpar option. S.A.M.A. researchers were quick to point out that the railway system was astronomically cheaper than other more technological ideas, but even more importantly, it was the most reliable option. There was little room for failure in any capacity on a distant colony near the outer edge of the Earth's solar system.

Roger Stellick made use of the railway system to quickly travel from the main military hub of operations to the large hangar where the Comet fighter planes were housed. The moment he stepped off the train, he was greeted by the deck crew chief, Tim Reed. Reed was a large, muscular, African-American man in his early thirties. The man was well respected by crewmen and pilots alike. To Roger, he was also a close friend.

"About time," Tim said as he began shoving Roger's flight suit and bright yellow helmet in his face.

Roger snatched the suit away and flashed a sideways smirk. "I see you've been in my locker," he replied as he paused to push a leg into the gray suit.

"I just do what I'm told," Tim replied very matter-of-factly. "The only man on this rock that truly scares me is General Hightower. If that man tells me to break into your locker, grab your gear, and wait on you to get off the train...well, that's what I'm going to do."

"I see," Roger said as he pulled the zipper on the front of the flight suit upward. "Did he bother to tell you what's going on?"

"Only that you're going to intercept a U.F.O.," he replied. "That true?"

"That's the rumor," Roger answered as he reached for the helmet. "How's my bird...are we ready to go?"

"I'm surprised you'd even ask," Tim said as he shook his head. "We've even punched in the exact coordinates the Discovery station provided on the craft's current position."

Roger paused as he was about to secure the helmet over his head with the chin strap. "It's still hovering?" he asked. "It hasn't moved at all?"

Tim shook his head and shrugged. "Hasn't moved since it stopped," he replied.

"Well that'll make it easy to find," Roger said half-heartedly, and he turned toward the hangar. "The general here yet?"

"Nope," Tim replied. "He's on the way…he said for you to get in the Comet and he'll radio you once you're out of the atmosphere."

Roger jogged into the hangar and was surprised to find many other pilots there suited up and waiting on him.

"Bout time commander," a young man said as Roger entered the building. It was Christian Smith, call-sign Sabre. "They're not allowing us to go with you," he added gruffly.

"No need for that right now," Roger replied as he began to climb the ladder leading into the cockpit of his Comet fighter. "I'm gonna ease over to them and see if they're looking for a fight—and if they are, well then you'll get your opportunity."

Sabre coughed and ran his fingers through his sandy-blonde hair. "It seems to me that we should be there to back you up in case something goes wrong," he said.

Roger eyed him for a moment and could see that his head was covered in perspiration.

"You feeling alright?" he asked as he began pulling the cockpit straps over his shoulders.

Sabre wiped the sweat away from his brow with the back of his sleeve. "I'll be alright," he said, a bit of annoyance in his tone. "I woke up with a fever, but I'll be good to go if I'm needed."

Tim Reed walked up and began to remove the ladder.

"Tim, please see to it that Smith here gets checked out by the doc as soon as possible," he said as he began flipping switches on the console in front of him.

"I said I'm fine," Sabre snapped. "Probably just something I ate."

"If it were something you ate you'd be in the bathroom right now," Roger said. He looked at Tim again. "I mean it, he doesn't go up until he sees the doc."

"He won't," Tim replied, but he was looking at Sabre.

Tim Reed's size made him a difficult man to argue with. Sabre huffed and turned away to make his way toward the infirmary.

"Anybody else you want to ground before you leave?" Tim asked as he scanned his eyes over the other pilots in the hangar.

"Nah, not unless there are more that are sick," Roger quipped as the canopy closed over him. He then signaled for Tim to remove the wheel chocks and in seconds the Comet fighter was rolling.

Roger guided the large spacecraft toward the nearest launch bay. A massive door rolled upward, and the Comet fighter entered and then came to a smooth stop in front of an even larger door. Roger sat patiently as the door behind him rumbled closed. Once it did, he pushed the radio button located on the yoke.

"Launch bay is sealed," he said.

"Roger that, launch bay is sealed," a voice crackled back at him. "Opening exterior launch bay door in three, two, one..."

The large door in front of him cracked open in the center and then both sides slowly swung open. Roger had complained for quite some time that he felt the doors opened much too slowly and that something needed to be done to speed it up. So far, his complaints had seemed to fall on deaf ears.

Once the door had fully opened, Roger again lurched the Comet fighter forward and onto the long stretch of runway before him. Bright blue lights zipped along both sides of the concrete path and it was a noticeable contrast against the yellowed soil of Titan's crust. Roger glanced to his left and through the thick and hazy atmosphere he could see the ominous view of Saturn over the horizon—or at least most of it.

With his spacecraft finally clear of the hangar, Roger gave the fighter throttle and within seconds the Comet was airborne. He rocketed toward the looming planet that he'd peered at before he'd left the surface of Titan. Somewhere just off the rings of Saturn, a mysterious alien space craft was hovering in place for unknown reasons. It would be up to him to try and discover not only why the craft was there, but also if they were going to pose a threat to the colony. Surprisingly, this seemingly dangerous undertaking had not rattled him. Roger was as cool as a cucumber and extremely focused. The Comet fighter was the most advanced military spacecraft that had ever been developed and it was a big reason why he felt as comfortable as he was.

The Comet was fitted with twin laser cannons—one on each side of the nose—and an electrical ion drive for powerful propulsion. The spacecraft was twelve meters in length with a wingspan of 23 meters. It was fitted with a titanium skin painted white in color trimmed with black. On average, the Comet fighter weighed over 40,000 pounds, depending mostly on its payload. The Comet was capable of carrying a nuclear warhead and though he hadn't asked, Roger was almost certain he was carrying one into space now. Suddenly, the radio crackled to life.

"Commander Stellick, this is General Hightower, over."

"I hear you general," Roger replied. He glanced at one of the digital readouts on the console in front of him. "I've got an E.T.A. of eight minutes before I rendezvous with the U.F.O."

"Very good," Hightower said. "Now I'll make this quick. You've got a warhead behind you and if this thing goes haywire, your orders are to use it."

Roger allowed himself to smile as he considered the general's timing since he'd just been thinking about the possibility that he was carrying a warhead. "Roger that," he answered. "How do I need to engage the target?"

"You do it by the book," Hightower responded quickly. "You approach them head on and once in range, try to contact them by radio."

"So, you're assuming they speak English?" he asked with a chuckle.

"No, but it's what the protocol requires you to do—as I said, we're doing this by the book."

"Alright, alright," Roger replied. "And if they don't respond?"

"Then you turn on all your landing lights and we'll wait to see if they respond in kind," Hightower explained. "Keep in mind that while you're doing all of that, we're going to be monitoring the airwaves down here. I've got a language expert right here beside me and if we hear any chatter from that ship we'll immediately work to see if we can make any sense at all in regard to what they're saying."

Roger huffed. "That doesn't sound real promising, sir."

"Well it's a start, and for now, it's all we've got."

"10-4," Roger replied. There were a million other questions that he wanted to ask but he refrained from doing so. He trusted General Harry Hightower with his life and at the present time, he could not remember a moment where his faith in the man had been tested so heavily. Whatever bad scenarios Roger could think of—and he'd already thought of several—he knew Hightower had thought of them too and had a contingency plan to address them.

As he piloted the Comet fighter within several hundred miles of the outer edge of Saturn's rings, a glint of sunlight reflected brightly off the metallic shell covering the mysterious spacecraft ahead of him. The ship was large—much larger than he'd anticipated it would be. There had been no time for him to get a visual of the ship before he'd left Titan, and as he scrambled to intercept it, it seemed the sense of urgency was not necessary.

For whatever reason, the craft remained in a stationary position and seemed unconcerned with his approach. Roger knew that, for better or worse, he was severely outmanned and outgunned. It was S.A.M.A.'s belief that it was a necessary stance to make it clear that the humans were peaceful. This moment was something Roger Stellick had been training for since he'd become the captain of the Titan squadron seven years ago. His unwavering commitment and diligence to his job had effectively destroyed his marriage and had put a strain on his relationship with his teenage daughter, Samantha. This was his moment to make it all worth it.

"Commander Stellick, provide an update please," General Hightower said suddenly, shattering Roger's thoughts.

He glanced at the console and said, "I'm only a couple of hundred miles away. The ship is very large and covered in shiny metal…so shiny that the reflection of the sun is pretty substantial."

"Has the ship moved?"

"That's a negative," Roger answered. "The craft is still stationary and appears to be all metal…I don't even see a window."

Roger reversed thrusters and brought the Comet to a slow approach. "I'm going to attempt to radio them now," he said as he flipped a switch.

"Unidentified space craft," he began, his voice strong and direct. "This is Commander Roger Stellick, a pilot with the Space and Aeronautics Military Alliance of planet Earth. I want to make it very clear that we are a people of peace and wish you absolutely no harm."

Roger released the mic and awaited some sort of response. The silence was long and unsettling.

"Please acknowledge," he urged.

The silence continued and just as Roger was about to turn on his landing lights, the radio suddenly crackled to life.

CHAPTER 3

"Greetings Commander Stellick," a voice responded.

Roger was taken aback. The voice that had replied to him was male, spoke in English, and appeared to be a man.

"Greetings," Roger replied cautiously. "Please identify yourself."

"I am Malcolm Steiger, Captain of the S.S. Pinnacle," the voice answered. "You say you come from a people of peace?"

Roger cocked his head and sighed. The moment was surreal. "That's correct," he replied, doing his best to sound calm. "We are a people of peace and as I said, we mean you no harm."

There were a few seconds of silence, and then, "If that is so Commander Stellick, then why are you carrying a powerful bomb on your ship?"

Roger winced as he realized that his task of appearing peaceful had just become a much harder sell. It was also unsettling when he considered the fact that somehow his payload had been discovered with ease. Clearly, as suspected, the technological advantage on the foreign ship was far superior to anything the humans currently had.

"Captain Steiger, my payload is standard issue and should not be taken as a threat," Roger said quickly. "I assure you, I—humans, we come in peace."

There was another long pause.

"Commander Stellick, I and my crew come in peace also. There is a matter I need to discuss with your people. Are you their representative?"

"Affirmative," Roger replied. "Tell me what you want."

"I'm afraid I'd prefer to do that in person," Malcolm Steiger replied.

Roger chewed his lip and contemplated his next response. "Captain Steiger, I'm sure that can be arranged. Can you give me time to contact my superior office on Titan and—"

"Commander, I'd prefer to speak with you," Malcolm interrupted. He sounded anxious.

"And I'll make sure that happens," Roger said. "All I need is to make arrangements for you to land and we can discuss whatever it is you want to talk about…just me and you."

As Roger said the words, he was very cognizant that General Hightower was listening to the entire conversation. He wasn't sure if he'd approve of the promises he was making to Malcolm or not, but at this point he felt that he had no other choice. The radio crackled to life as Malcolm spoke again.

"We won't be landing…at least not yet," he said.

Roger could feel his anxiety level rising and the cockpit suddenly felt very warm. Perspiration beaded up on his forehead. "What are you proposing?" he asked.

"I'd like to invite you to join me on the Pinnacle," Steiger replied.

Roger's heart rate picked up. He knew that his vitals were being monitored on the ground as well and strangely he felt a bit embarrassed at how rattled he'd suddenly become.

"I'm not sure if that's a good idea," he said finally doing his best to sound calm.

"I sense that you don't trust me," Malcolm answered. "I assure you that no harm will come to you."

Roger chewed his lip as he pondered his next move. "Allow me a moment to think it over," he said, and he immediately flipped a switch that would allow him to speak with General Hightower.

"What do you think?" he asked.

"Absolutely not," Hightower replied. "It's much too dangerous. You tell him that he can land here and then we will consider sending you on board the ship."

Roger took a deep breath and then exhaled slowly. "This guy isn't going to budge on this sir, and I think you know it."

"Well if he refuses, then we'll have no choice but to consider them hostile," General Hightower said defiantly. "We will then respond accordingly."

"Meaning what?" Roger asked, now annoyed. "You'll order me to use the nuke?"

There was a pause.

"Roger," Hightower said with an exasperated sigh. "I'm ordering you to use your best judgement right now."

"That's exactly what I'm going to do."

Roger flipped the switch back. "Captain Steiger, tell me how to board your ship."

"Fly to port side and you'll see the landing bay," Malcolm explained. "Enter the ship and fear not, because there will be oxygen for you to breathe. By the time you get out of your ship, I'll be there to greet you."

"I'm on the way," Roger said as he gave the Comet thrust.

As he piloted closer to the Pinnacle, Roger felt himself becoming more anxious. In comparison to his Comet fighter, the ship was enormous. He estimated it was at least 200 meters long and probably

150 meters tall. He looked closely for any sign of weapons, but saw none. The outside of the ship was sleek and looked almost seamless. After circling the ship once, he spotted the landing bay entrance. It was an odd sight as it seemed the rectangular opening just suddenly appeared. The bright illumination originating from the interior of the ship shone brightly into the blackness of space and almost beckoned him to enter.

Roger carefully piloted the Comet toward the opening and he soon got close enough that he could see beings walking around inside. As he entered the landing bay he noticed a loud humming noise and bright light coming from the ship's hull, just below the outer metallic skin. Roger soon deduced that there must have been some sort of forcefield that he'd just flown through to protect the interior of the ship from the cruel vacuum of space.

Once inside, he saw two humanoid beings directing him to land on an illuminated strip in the center of the landing bay. The beings were covered head to toe in black armor and they carried ominous looking rifles. No sooner had the Comet rolled to a stop, the armored beings immediately began motioning for Roger to exit the vehicle. For a moment, he feared he'd made a terrible mistake.

He remained in the cockpit and looked around in all directions for any sign of someone friendlier. Captain Steiger had assured him he'd be there waiting on him when he arrived, but so far, he saw nothing.

"Commander Stellick, would you mind exiting your ship?"

It was Captain Steiger.

"I thought you said you'd be here when I landed," Roger replied, unable to hide a bit of annoyance in his tone.

"I said I'd be there by the time you get out of your ship," Malcolm countered. "My ship's protocol doesn't allow me to meet you until my men make sure that you're not a threat. Please exit the vehicle so that my men will see you mean no harm."

Roger clenched his jaw and shook his head. He contemplated jetting out of there before things got out of hand. However, when he glanced over his shoulder he was dismayed to see that the opening he'd flown through just minutes earlier was now gone and replaced with a solid wall. With reluctance—and no other choice—he opened the canopy and stood up. He showed his hands so that the soldiers watching him would know he had no weapon.

"Step out of your ship," one of the soldiers commanded.

Roger quickly did as he was bade and was then carefully searched.

One of the soldiers then held up his wrist to his mouth and said, "It is safe to enter."

The sound of an automatic door opening to his left made Roger look over; two more guards and another man dressed in what appeared to be a military uniform of some sort. The suit was dark blue in color and decorated with an arrangement of shiny buttons and what Roger believed were possibly military medals. There was no hat on the man's head, only light brown hair cut short. His eyes were a striking gray color and bright with life.

"Commander Stellick," the man said as he flashed a wide smile. "Welcome to the Pinnacle."

Roger returned a smile, though his was less enthusiastic. There was still an uneasy feeling that he was having trouble shaking.

"Captain Steiger I presume?"

The man nodded and cocked his head slightly. "Commander Stellick I get the feeling that my appearance is not what you were expecting."

The smile on Roger's face did not fade. "You're very perceptive," he said. "I wasn't sure what to expect, but for you to look like…" he paused as he considered his next words.

"Human?" Malcolm asked, attempting to ease the tension.

Roger nodded and raised his eyebrows. "Yeah…exactly," he said.

Malcolm laughed. "So, you and your people think you're the only humans in the universe?"

Roger shook his head, and felt his face redden. "I didn't mean that to come across as an insult."

Malcolm's smile seemed to brighten even more. "Relax Commander Stellick," he said cheerfully. "I realize this must all be very confusing."

"That's an understatement," Roger replied. "Your ship suddenly shows up in our solar system, you all speak English, and you all appear to be human. How can that be?"

"We are indeed human," Malcolm answered. "Most of us have learned your language because we've been preparing for this moment for a very long time. Our fates have been intertwined for quite a while, but I must admit I didn't anticipate our meeting happening this soon."

"Wait," Roger said, as he raised a hand to scratch his head. "Are you saying you've been watching us?"

Malcolm nodded. "For a long, long time, yes."

"Why?"

"To the best of our knowledge, the humans of Earth are the only other human race that we are aware of. Once we discovered your existence, the leaders of my world began to plan for the moment that we would reveal ourselves to your race."

"I see," Roger muttered in awe. "So, you said that you didn't anticipate this meeting happening so soon...what do you mean by that?"

Malcolm crossed his arms and for the first time his smile began to slowly fade away. Even the light in his eyes seemed to dim slightly as if Roger's question had somehow conjured storm clouds to roll in and overtake his spirit.

"Commander Stellick," Malcolm began. "My people are in grave danger—danger so great that we were forced to leave our home world."

Roger cleared his throat and took a breath. "Are you saying that you're looking for somewhere to provide you safe harborage?"

Malcolm considered the question and furrowed his brow. "Not exactly," he answered. "Though any safe harborage your people are willing to provide would be greatly appreciated."

"Well, obviously it's not my call alone," Roger replied. "But I know that the leaders of my world would be very interested to hear your story."

"And I'm more than willing to tell it, but I'd like you to be the one to hear it," Malcolm said.

Roger stared at him a moment and then looked to the armed guards. They were quietly listening to every word of the conversation. Their helmets were perhaps blacker than the rest of their uniform and encased their entire heads. Their eyes were covered with round, bubble-like glass tinted so dark that Roger wondered how they could see through it. He assumed they were as human as Malcolm Steiger but part of him wondered if there was something much more sinister hidden from view.

"The guards are perhaps unnecessary, I know," Malcolm said, as if he were reading Roger's mind. "Again, our policy is to always err on the side of caution. However, I think it's clear that you're friendly and mean us no harm." He paused and looked to the guards. "We need to have a private discussion, thank you for your support."

The guards all looked at Malcolm, and then slowly at each other.

"I assure you, I will be just fine," Malcolm assured them. "I'm going to take Commander Stellick to the observatory where we may speak in private."

The guard closest to Malcolm nodded, and then motioned for the other soldiers to disperse. Malcolm then motioned for Roger to follow him.

"I'm putting a lot of trust in you," Roger said. "I hope that counts for something."

Malcolm smiled and put a hand on Roger's shoulder. It was the first physical contact that had occurred between the two men. "Once you hear what I have to say you'll understand why it's not in my best interest to harm you, Commander Stellick."

Malcolm then turned and headed for an arched doorway. The door had retracted into the interior of the wall and allowed the two men entry into a wide hallway. There were multiple doors on either side of the hallway, all of them still closed. Roger took note that each door had its own signage that was undoubtedly a label depicting the purpose of each room. Unfortunately, the words were scrawled in a language that Roger did not recognize. It didn't look like anything he'd ever seen before and was a glaring reminder that he was no longer among earthlings.

"Your ship is amazing," Roger said as he casually walked beside Malcolm. "Your technology seems to be more advanced than anything we have."

Malcolm smiled, but it wasn't out of arrogance. "Our civilization is much older than yours…we've had plenty of time to develop it."

Roger opened his mouth to reply, but closed it quickly. But not before Malcolm saw him.

"What were you going to say?" he asked. "Please feel free to ask any questions you'd like."

Roger sighed. "Well, it wasn't going to be a question," he said. "I'm just anxious to know what this is all about. Clearly, your ship is far superior to anything we have. You say that your people are in grave danger. Clearly, we can't offer anything technologically better than what you already have. What could you possibly want from us?"

Malcolm stopped abruptly and faced Roger. "Are you speaking for your entire race, or is this just a question you yourself has?"

Roger scrunched his face as he wasn't sure if he understood the question. "I'm not here to speak on behalf of my entire race, but I'm sure my question would be asked by the leaders of my world."

Malcolm again smiled widely. "It seems as though you all underestimate your value. As I've said repeatedly, we are not here to start a war Commander Stellick. We are here in hopes that you will join us."

"Join you?" Roger asked, confused. "Join you where?"

"You still don't understand," Malcolm said, and for the first time it was his turn to sound confused. "We are here for one reason and one reason alone. We are in desperate need of your help and I'm prepared to beg for it."

CHAPTER 4

Roger's curiosity peaked once he began to fully understand that Captain Malcolm Steiger's primary interest in the humans of Earth seemed to be based on a desperate plea for help. Though he wanted answers immediately, Malcolm was adamant that they discuss the matter in more detail once they reached the ship observatory. Roger followed him through the brightly lit corridors of the Pinnacle until they finally reached a circular doorway. He noticed a seam that ran diagonally across the metal door and no sooner had Malcolm stepped in front of it, the seam parted, and the doorway opened to reveal a tiny room. Roger guessed that it must have been an elevator.

"You're my guest," Malcolm said as he gestured for Roger to enter ahead of him.

Though Roger still felt a twinge of skepticism, he took a leap of faith and stepped through the opening and was relieved to find that Malcolm immediately followed. The tiny room did indeed turn out to be an elevator of some sort, but it was unlike any that Roger had ever been inside on Earth. There did not appear to be any cable system of any kind to propel the car in either direction. He felt the sensation of moving upward but it was extremely smooth and eerily quiet. Within seconds the door opened to reveal a sight that made Roger's knees go weak and his jaw drop.

Malcolm immediately walked into the ship observatory, but Roger could only remain where he was and stare. His legs simply would not allow him to move. Malcolm walked over to a small round table in the center of the room and pulled out a chair. He cocked his head to the side and the straight line of his mouth curled slightly.

"Are you alright?" he asked.

Roger took a deep breath and took one step out of the elevator. The room he now found himself in seemed to be comprised of nothing but glass. The ceiling and all the walls were completely transparent, revealing an incredible display of a star-speckled blackness, highlighted by the majestic presence of Saturn and its trademark rings. The glass— at least that's what Roger thought it was—seemed almost nonexistent. It was so clear that for a moment his mind attempted to convince him that he'd somehow been led into the harsh vacuum of space. The ship observatory appeared to be on the top-center of the Pinnacle.

"How is this possible?" Roger asked, unable to contain his awe.

Malcolm took a seat at the white table, crossed his legs, and scanned his surroundings. "How is *what* possible?" he asked. He seemed genuinely confused.

Roger's eyes moved around the room until they finally found Malcolm staring at him. "It's almost as if we're outside the ship," he said. "I don't understand. I flew around your ship and I saw no windows. It appeared to be covered in metal."

Malcolm took a deep breath through his nose and then chuckled. He seemed to be very amused by Roger's sudden child-like interest in a room that he'd taken for granted for as long as he'd captained the ship. "The ship's outer skin is a bit of an illusion," he explained. "On the exterior it certainly appears to be nothing but metal, but inside the presence of windows are evident and plentiful throughout."

"So, this is nothing but a large window?" Roger asked, looking over his head at a bright star.

"Think of it as a large dome," Malcolm explained. "I assure you the material that makes up the exterior of this ship—including this dome—is much stronger than anything you've got on Earth. We are completely safe here. I often come here to think and relax."

"Is this room used for any other purpose?" Roger asked curiously.

"Oh, of course," Malcolm replied. "When in battle, I send spotters up here to monitor the positions of other ships. They can obviously see everything but what is underneath us...and if you're wondering, we have an observatory on the bottom of the ship also."

Roger shook his head in disbelief. "You're telling me that as technologically advanced as your race seems to be, you don't have other means of monitoring the surroundings of your ship?"

Malcolm shot him a look that suggested he was unsure if the comment was meant to be an insult or not. "Of course, we do," he replied. "But no matter how much technology one has at their disposal, it is—and will always be—people that are behind the success of that technology...and sadly, its failures too. No technology will ever be perfect. A live person that can look and call out information in real time is just as valuable, if not more so, than any technological benefit this ship has. I hope this is a lesson that the humans of Earth have already learned."

Roger sighed and scratched the back of his head. "I wish I could say that was always the case," he answered meekly.

Malcolm frowned, undoubtedly surprised by the reply. Roger quickly tried to veer the conversation back on track.

"You said you came here looking for help?" he said as he sat at the table in the second chair.

Malcolm's eyes narrowed, and he nodded slightly. "Yes, I'm ashamed to say that is true."

"Ashamed?" Roger asked, confused by the declaration.

Malcolm frowned, though he looked as if he were trying hard not to. "Yes," he said quickly. "I think it's clear to the both of us that my race is more technologically advanced than yours. That fact makes it shameful and difficult to ask for assistance."

Roger closed his eyes and shook his head in disbelief. He fully believed that Malcolm had no intentions of sounding condescending, but alas it was hard not to take his comment that way.

"So, what do you need from us?" he asked, ignoring the comment.

Malcolm drummed his fingers on the table and sighed as if he were trying to conjure up the gumption to spit out his request. "Are you familiar with the Ara Constellation?" he asked, staring at Roger.

"I've heard of it, yes," Roger replied. He closed his eyes and thought a minute. "That's a long, long way from here," he said finally.

Malcolm nodded and suddenly his eyes lost their once lively appearance. "Yes, it is certainly a long way from here. Fourteen light years in fact."

Roger whistled. "How long have you been travelling to get here?"

"The Pinnacle travels at light speed so—"

"Fourteen years?" Roger asked in disbelief. "You and this ship have been traveling here for fourteen years?"

Malcolm yawned as if hearing the lengthy amount of time triggered more exhaustion. "Yes, and it feels like every bit of it," he said. "You have no idea what the relief was like when we picked up the Titan colony on our radar. The entire ship has been celebrating since we've stopped."

Roger ran his fingers through his hair. "You guys must have been pretty confident that we weren't going to try anything."

Malcolm smiled. "Again, this ship is much more advanced than anything you humans have."

Roger rolled his eyes. "Yeah, you keep reminding me of that."

For the first time, Malcolm seemed to realize how his words came across. "My apologies," he said, his eyes widening with embarrassment. "I'm much humbler than I'm sounding right now."

Roger cleared his throat and smirked. "Captain Steiger, forgive my manners, but I've got a lot of people anxiously awaiting my return on Titan. Can we get on with what this is all about?"

Malcolm nodded and then turned his gaze upon Saturn, looming just to the west of the Pinnacle. "We come from a solar system in the Ara Constellation, which as you probably know is found in the heart of what your race refers to as the Milky Way Galaxy. The planet we are from is called Kalo."

Roger listened intently as Malcolm continued.

"About thirty years ago, an asteroid crashed into one of Kalo's moons, Jara. It really had no effect on Kalo, but the scientists of my planet were curious and could not help themselves." Malcolm paused, and Roger watched as the features on his face tightened. This part of the story apparently angered him. "Jara had always been a barren moon, much like the moon of Earth. There was no life of any kind to be found on its surface," he said, sounding somewhat agitated. "There was no reason for us to be concerned with an innocent asteroid on Jara. However, as the scientists continued to monitor the area, they began to notice lifeforms."

Roger felt butterflies in his stomach. He had to constantly remind himself that he wasn't dreaming. "Lifeforms?" he said softly. "What sort of lifeforms?"

Malcolm shook his head and smiled, but there was a sadness behind it. "At first, they were thought to be harmless," he said still gazing at the stars. "The scientists think that the asteroid may not have been an asteroid at all, but an egg of some sort. An egg travelling aimlessly in space until it crashed upon a surface where it could hatch. I suppose we were very fortunate that it didn't land on Kalo or you and I may not even be having this conversation."

The butterflies in Roger's stomach slowly disappeared and was replaced with rumbling bees. The anxiety he was feeling was building.

Malcolm continued. "I just wish we'd have stayed off Jara," he said with disgust. He then looked back at Roger and seemed to realize he was beginning to ramble. "They resemble a species of insect from your planet...the mantis I think," he explained. "Only the ones that landed on Jara were the same size as me and you."

Roger leaned back in his chair and crossed his arms. "Wow...guess you need something more than the heel of your boot to deal with those," he said in amazement.

Malcolm leaned forward across the table. "Commander Stellick, they are monsters...horrific monsters. They are not invulnerable, but their exoskeleton is like a suit of armor. It takes heavy fire power to penetrate it."

"But they're contained to Jara, right?"

Malcom pulled back from the table and frowned. "I'm afraid not," he replied sadly. "They probably would have remained there if we had not decided to send a crew to Jara to study them."

Roger shook his head as he began to understand.

"The crew never stood a chance against those monsters," Malcolm said. "There was only one survivor and he just barely managed to get off the moon before he too was killed. Unfortunately—and unbeknownst to him—some of those things managed to travel back to Kalo with him."

"Oh no," Roger whispered.

Malcolm popped his knuckles and shifted in his chair. "They multiply quickly. And they grow fast too."

There was a long silence where neither man said anything. Finally, Roger mustered the courage to ask a question.

"How bad is it?" he asked somberly.

Malcolm smiled, but the sadness was still there. "Bad enough that we decided to finally make our presence known to the earthlings that we've known about for hundreds of years. Bad enough that the leaders of my world put me in charge of making the long voyage here to beg for Earth's help in dealing with this scourge before my race is wiped out completely."

"I see," Roger replied. "So, I assume you've been in contact with your home all this time? I mean I'm not sure if Earth is willing to help or not, but before they would even consider it, obviously they'd need to know if you even have a home to go back to. Fourteen years is a long time."

Malcolm looked away toward the stars again. "We lost contact with them two years ago," he said. "But that doesn't mean they're dead."

Roger raised his eyebrows and took a deep breath through his nose. "Really? Because it doesn't sound good Captain Steiger."

Malcolm snapped his head around to face Roger again. "Commander Stellick, things were bad, but they were holding their own. We lost contact with them but there could be other reasons for that. We've never travelled this deep in space before."

Roger chuckled. "Are you saying all your technological advancements may not be as good as you thought?"

Malcolm sighed, and his eyes narrowed. He didn't find any amusement in Roger's jest.

"So, what do you want from us?" Roger asked, though he believed he knew the answer.

"We need your help in fighting them. We want to destroy them completely."

"So, to be clear, you want our boots on your ground?" he asked. "You want Earth to send our soldiers over to fight for your world?" Roger paused and stood from the table. He walked toward Saturn and crossed his arms, staring. "Why would the people of Earth do that? What is in it for us?"

Malcolm slid his chair back and stood to join him. Once he was standing beside Roger, he reached over and put a hand on his shoulder. "Have I mentioned that our technological achievements dwarf your planet's?"

Roger looked over at him and found his new alien friend was smiling. "You're saying that if we help you, you'll share all of your technology?"

Malcolm nodded, but said nothing.

Roger sighed and looked back toward Saturn. "Assuming that the leaders of Earth will decide to help you…" he paused and looked over at him. "Captain Steiger, it took you fourteen years to get here. With another fourteen years to get back…" his words trailed off and he shook his head.

Malcolm smiled widely. "Commander Stellick, the hard part was getting here. The trip back will only take a matter of minutes."

CHAPTER 5

"You've got to be kidding me?"

General Hightower scowled as he said the words and Roger couldn't tell if he was angry or amused. He was a hard man to read. The decorated veteran took a deep breath and then used his hands to smooth out the front of his navy-blue uniform, before finally taking a seat at the head of the long wooden conference table among the other military leaders on the colony.

Harry Hightower had joined the Space and Aeronautics Military Alliance as soon as he'd become old enough. He was a textbook example of what a good S.A.M.A. soldier could and should be. His sixty-year-old face was weathered and in fact made him appear even older than he actually was. His hair had all but disappeared, evidenced by what remained around his ears and along the back of his skull. He'd once worn glasses, but a recent surgery had corrected his vision to what it had been in his youth. Though the picture of the world through his eyes had become crisp and clear, until his eyes fully healed there was one drawback. Roger had never timed it, but he estimated that the man had to place medicinal drops in both of his eyes at least every twenty minutes.

"You're telling me that with all their fancy bells and whistles they somehow need *our* help to deal with their little pest problem?" Hightower asked as he unscrewed the cap off his eye drops.

Roger sighed and cleared his throat. "I know, whatever you're thinking, I was thinking the same thoughts when I heard it too," he said. "The problem must be pretty severe."

"And if it's that severe, we don't need to get involved," a middle-aged British man named Merrill Madigan said. He was a S.A.M.A. colonel and second in command on Titan.

General Hightower snapped his head around to look at Colonel Madigan. "Merrill, that doesn't sound like you," he quipped. "You're usually leading the charge to help those that need it."

Though Madigan had once had a head of full red hair, in the past couple of years it had lightened significantly due to age. He blushed and seemed embarrassed at Hightower's observation, his color almost matching the hue of his hair. "I still will lead that charge, Harry," he replied. "I'll always lead the charge to help any humans that need it. These..." he paused as if he were pondering the right word to use.

"These…people—they're not from Earth. We have no responsibility to them."

Suddenly there were murmurs from the other officers at the table and Roger began to feel a sinking feeling in his gut.

"Captain Steiger made it pretty clear to me that their situation is dire," Roger said. "His entire race could be driven to extinction if we sit back and do nothing. And then there is the matter of the technology."

General Hightower held up a hand to silence him. "We cannot base our decision on that," he said firmly. "You say that this man is telling you he fears his race will be driven to extinction. Well what about our race Stellick?"

"Exactly," Colonel Madigan said, and he nodded his head enthusiastically. "We must stay out of this."

"You gentlemen forget that ultimately it isn't up to any of us," a woman said. It was the senior medical officer Dr. Phoebe Holtz. Holtz was in her mid-thirties and easily the most attractive person in the room. Her dark, curly locks ended just above the line of her shoulder and her green eyes sparkled brightly no matter which direction she looked.

Roger peered over and shot her a slight nod and smile. He was glad she voiced what he was already thinking.

"Yes, Dr. Holtz," General Hightower replied, slightly annoyed. "Though Earth's government has the final say, I feel I should remind you that I have a close relationship with the president of the United West."

Phoebe's face immediately contorted into a look of disgust. "General, are you saying you're going to use your personal clout with the president to get him to side with you?"

Hightower's jaw tightened, and he clenched his fist. "That's exactly what I'm saying doctor. It's my job to keep Earth safe and I intend on doing just that."

"So, what are you going to tell President Callahan?" Roger asked.

General Hightower snapped his attention to Roger. "What do you mean?" he asked. "I'm going to advise him not to help the aliens."

Roger nodded slowly and drummed his fingers on the table. "And how are you going to do that sir?"

"Careful," Colonel Madigan warned him.

Roger shot the colonel a dumbfounded look. "What are you talking about?" he grumbled. "It's a legitimate question." He returned his attention to General Hightower. "Sir, with all due respect, I just find it hard to believe that President Callahan would not only immediately dismiss helping a friendly alien species that is in danger of being eradicated, but also completely disregard the opportunity to gain tremendous technological knowledge. Unless…"

"Unless what?" Hightower asked. He clasped his hands on the table and leaned forward eagerly.

Roger nervously cleared his throat. "Unless you somehow bend the truth," he said.

He heard Phoebe gasp and someone else in the room whispered something he could not quite understand.

"I oughta have you locked up," Colonel Madigan growled. He then glared over at Hightower. "Harry, just give me the order."

General Hightower shook his head slowly and closed his eyes. "That's not necessary Merrill," he said softly. He then opened his eyes and looked at Roger. "Commander, we've known each other a long time and I have a tremendous amount of respect for you and the pilots you've trained."

"Thank you, sir," Roger said.

"And that is why I'm going to ignore your insubordination," Hightower continued. "I understand that you've met the alien. You've spoken with him at length and clearly you believe everything that he is telling you."

"That's right sir," Roger said quickly. "I do."

"Quite frankly, it's disappointing that you'd be so quick to believe an alien you just met, and then less than two hours later accuse me, your commanding officer, of conspiring to lie to the President of the United West."

Roger felt his face flush red. "Sir that's not what I—"

"You'd insinuate that *I*," Hightower continued, "a man you've known for twenty years, would essentially tell lies to the president."

Roger bit his lip and cleared his throat. He wanted to argue his point further but decided against it.

"I think we should give Commander Stellick the benefit of the doubt, sir."

It was Lieutenant Hayden Carter. At twenty-seven, he was the youngest officer in the room. His blonde hair formed a perfect crewcut and his blue eyes were only second to Phoebe's in beauty. The man was usually quiet, but known to be extremely intelligent and very wise beyond his years. Roger's only gripe about him was that he had a nasty smoking habit. What he did have going for him was the fact that for some reason that Roger hadn't figured out, General Hightower was quite fond of him.

"I agree," Hightower replied so swiftly that it almost seemed rehearsed. He kept his gaze on Roger and said, "Commander, let's not quibble over things that have not even happened yet. But for what's it worth, I assure you that anything I tell President Callahan will consist of nothing but truths."

Roger nodded and accepted the proverbial olive branch that was being presented to him.

"Let's discuss the technology a moment," Lieutenant Carter said, turning his attention to Roger. "Tell me more about this gateway Captain Steiger told you about."

Roger scratched at the back of his neck and took a deep breath. "There's really nothing else to tell outside of what I've already said," he replied. "Basically, he told me that now that they've made the long voyage to our solar system, they can assemble a gateway in Saturn's orbit that would essentially give them the ability to jump back to their world within a span of less than two minutes."

"Did you see any of the materials he says will be used to assemble this gateway?" Hightower asked.

Roger shook his head. "No. I was just eager to get back and share all this intel."

"But you believe him?" Hightower asked. He was clearly intrigued.

"Yes, I absolutely do," Roger answered.

"That's incredible," Lieutenant Carter said. "That would be a very useful tool."

"And it still can be," Colonel Madigan said. "Whether we help the aliens or not."

Carter and Hightower looked over at him simultaneously. "What do you mean?" the general asked.

Madigan smirked at him. "Well I'm pretty sure if we turn them down, they'll just put together their little gateway and head back home," he replied. "I don't exactly see how they could take it with them."

"That's a good point," Phoebe said. "The gateway is one piece of technology we'd get our hands on whether we help them or not."

"Yes, but you're assuming we could figure out how to use it," Carter countered. "And if we did use it, and we travelled over to their world...what then?"

The room fell silent for a long moment and General Hightower was just about to speak when the large screen on the wall at the front of the room suddenly illuminated to life. Everyone immediately sat up straight and turned their full attention to the screen. The picture in front of them materialized to show the face of a man that appeared to be similar in age to General Hightower. The man had deep crow's feet around his gray eyes and his cheek bones were prominent. His hair was dark gray in color. Roger immediately recognized him to be President Britt Callahan of the United West.

The camera panned out a bit and revealed another man seated beside him. This man was smaller, though he appeared to be similar in age. He was Asian, and, despite his age, his hair was a deep black color. His brown eyes were framed with large horn-rimmed glasses. Roger assumed the President of the United East probably spent a great deal of time dying his hair.

A deep voice off camera introduced the two men as President Britt Callahan of the United West and President Akagi Hiro of the United East. The voice then quickly debriefed the two presidents of all the events that had unfolded between Titan and Saturn, except for any details surrounding Roger's visit with Captain Steiger. When the person was finished, he then announced the com-link was now open for dialogue.

"Good evening Mr. Presidents," General Hightower said as soon as he'd become free to do so.

"Good to see you again, Harry," President Callahan replied with a cheerful smile. "Tell us your version of what the hell is going on over there."

The general cleared his throat and then stood from his seat. "Sir, it sounds as if you've been briefed well on the situation. Basically, we have an alien spacecraft hovering near the rings of Saturn. As you know, we've been training for a scenario such as this for as long as this colony has been operational on Titan. Commander Roger Stellick, whom I consider to be the finest pilot in the entire S.A.M.A. fleet, was ready and willing to intercept the spacecraft to find out what exactly they want. He did so, and the entire ordeal went off without a hitch."

"Well, I'm glad to hear that," President Callahan said. The man remained remarkably calm for someone that had just received confirmation that humans were not alone in the universe. He turned his eyes toward the direction where Roger was seated. "Commander Stellick, thank you for your bravery."

"It's my honor," Roger replied.

"Sir, the aliens want our assistance with an issue on their home world that threatens the extinction of their race," Hightower said, clearly trying to keep the conversation on track.

"What sort of *issue*?" President Callahan asked.

General Hightower sighed and crossed his arms. "Well, it seems that they've been invaded by some sort of deadly alien creature," he replied firmly, as if he were trying to convince himself that it was the truth.

Roger looked on as President Hiro leaned forward and seemed to show great interest in the revelation. He also noticed that the man seemed to be eyeing him specifically.

President Callahan looked confused. "Clearly, they have a technological advantage over us," he said as he shook his head. "If they can't handle this threat, what makes them think we would be able to make a difference?"

"That's exactly how I view the situation," Hightower said anxiously. "In my opinion it is too great a risk for us to get involved."

"However," President Callahan continued, seemingly ignoring Hightower's statement, "I also understand that if we provide some assistance they are willing to share their technology with us?"

"That's correct," General Hightower replied. Suddenly, he seemed less enthusiastic.

"General Hightower, thank you for your insight," President Hiro said suddenly. He kept his eyes on Roger. "Commander Stellick," he said with a slight smile. "I'd appreciate it if you'd be willing to answer a few questions."

Roger nodded and immediately stood up. He looked over at General Hightower who suddenly appeared slightly worried that he was now being overlooked. The general reluctantly sat down.

"Of course, Mr. President," Roger said. "What would you like to know?"

"I'd like to know more about Captain Steiger," Hiro said. "Tell me about him."

"Okay," Roger said, and he paused to ponder the question a moment. "Well, he—and everyone else on the ship for that matter—looked just like us. In fact, the captain told me that they are humans, just like us. They know our language and probably know a lot more about us than they let on. Captain Steiger suggested that they'd been watching us for quite some time."

"Do you believe that they are indeed as friendly as they portray themselves to us?" President Hiro asked.

Roger nodded. "Yes sir, I do," he answered. "They treated me well on board their ship, and I never felt like a prisoner."

Suddenly, General Hightower stood again. "Mr. President, though the aliens may indeed be friendly and cordial, I still strongly believe that it's in the best interest of the entire human race to stay out of their affairs."

For the first time, President Hiro turned his head away from Roger and to Hightower instead. "General, I have a tremendous amount of respect for you and your opinion," he said with a toothy grin. "But I also recognize that you are not the man that actually sat down and had a discussion with Captain Steiger. That was Commander Stellick. I'd appreciate it if you'd allow me to finish questioning him so that I can form my own opinion."

President Callahan shifted uncomfortably in his chair as he noticed Hightower's face flush red. Despite the fact that the distance between Titan and Earth was 886 million miles, the tension in the room easily transcended time and space. Without another word, General Hightower slowly sunk back into his chair, and proceeded to apply another round of eyedrops. Colonel Madigan snorted and crossed his arms.

"I'm tired of referring to them as aliens," President Hiro said as he returned his attention to Roger. "I understand that you learned the name of their planet?"

"Yes," Roger answered. "They come from a planet called Kalo, located in the Ara Constellation."

"Then from now on can we all agree to refer to them as Kaloians?" Hiro asked, glancing over at President Callahan.

"I think that would be respectful," Callahan agreed.

Roger briefly looked over at Hightower and could see that his jaw was clenched tight.

"Commander Stellick," President Hiro continued. "Do you think we could realistically be of any assistance to the Kaloians?"

Roger shook his head. "Sir, I'm really not sure. I don't think it's a decision that any one man should make. It could have terrible consequences for Earth if we make a wrong decision."

"True," Hiro agreed. "But it could also reap tremendous benefits. In addition to the technology, Earth would have new allies. We've long suspected that there were other sentient beings in the universe and it would be foolish to think that there aren't more beyond the Kaloians. Perhaps they could provide more insight on this?"

Roger nodded. "They may know of other alien species," he said. "Aside from the creatures that are currently attacking their home world, we did not discuss the possibility of other worlds and races beyond their own."

"So, the creatures that are invading their world," Callahan chimed in. "They're not intelligent beings, correct?"

"That's the way I understood it," Roger answered. "Captain Steiger described them as insect-like. He said they were like the mantises of Earth, just much larger...the size of a man in fact."

Hiro nodded and seemed even more intrigued. He then looked to President Callahan again. "Britt, I think we should put this to a vote in

Congress. We should call an emergency session, present the facts, and get an answer on how to proceed very quickly."

"Yes," Callahan agreed, and he glanced over at General Hightower. "And to be clear, a vote to help the Kaloians will still require a great deal of planning and gathering information. We will not rush into anything, and if any new information suggests a greater danger, it will require another vote. Is that clear?"

"Yes, Mr. President," General Hightower replied. "What should we do with them in the meantime?"

Callahan looked over at President Hiro for a reply. "They may remain in Saturn's orbit until we reach a decision," Hiro said. "As I said, we will have that answer very soon. I don't think it will be wise to allow them to land on Titan until we know how we're going to proceed."

"I agree," Roger said, and he was pleased to see that General Hightower was nodding.

"Commander Stellick," President Hiro continued. "I want you to remain the sole representative of the humans for now—meaning, I want you to be the only person communicating with that ship." He turned to Callahan. "Is that a reasonable request Britt?"

President Callahan nodded in agreement. "Commander Stellick, you may bring Captain Steiger up to speed and please thank him for his patience," President Callahan said. "Plan to meet back here in three hours."

At once, the screen went black and the presidents were gone.

CHAPTER 6

Jake Crosby snapped to attention as soon as Commander Roger Stellick entered the room. He'd heard a lot about the legendary pilot and his respect for the man had only grown when he watched in awe as Stellick bravely flew into the strange spacecraft, completely disregarding his own safety.

Roger gave him a nod and gestured for him to relax. Crosby immediately offered his hand.

"Commander Stellick," he said, awestruck. "I've looked up to you for years...you're one of the main reasons I joined S.A.M.A."

Roger shook the younger man's hand, and though he thought Jake's behavior was slightly inappropriate, he was not about to correct him.

"It's P.F.C. Jake Crosby, am I right?" Roger asked as he released his grip.

Jake nodded enthusiastically. "Yessir, that's right." He glanced over his shoulder at the vast array of screens on the wall and the knobs and buttons on the counter. "I'm here to assist you in whatever capacity you need, otherwise, it's all yours."

"Thank you," Roger said as he pulled the padded rolling chair back and took a seat. "You know this is exactly how I got my start too," he added as he flipped a couple of switches.

"Really?" Jake watched Roger work and suddenly felt more encouraged than ever.

If Commander Roger Stellick started in communications...then there's hope for me, he thought. Jake seriously considered asking him what his T.A.P. score had been—or worse yet, how many times he'd been rejected before he'd gained entry into the pilot training program. Fortunately, he considered the matter long enough to talk himself out of it before verbalizing the question. During this thinking, General Harry Hightower approached behind him.

"Keep this communication all business," the general barked, as he drew near Roger.

General Hightower's distinctive voice startled Jake. He immediately snapped to attention again and his star struck demeanor vanished. Though it was the first time that he'd met Commander Stellick, he'd met General Hightower many times before. Jake was terrified of the man. He always tried hard to hide it, but he was certain Hightower could still sense his fear.

"Relax Crosby," Hightower said, barely acknowledging his presence.

Jake exhaled slowly and slunk away into a darkened corner in a desperate attempt to disappear.

Roger pulled the headset on and adjusted the microphone close to his mouth.

"Captain Steiger, this is Commander Roger Stellick, do you copy?"

There was a long moment of static, when finally...

"I hear you Commander Stellick," Malcolm replied. "You have news?"

"Not really," Roger said. "Our leaders on Earth are discussing how to proceed. We should know something very soon."

"You were unable to convince them," Malcolm replied, disappointment evident in his voice.

Roger looked over at General Hightower.

"Don't give them false hope," Hightower said.

Roger cleared his throat and glanced at the monitor that was focused on the Pinnacle. "I don't know yet," he said. "They're discussing the matter and will let me know something very shortly. In the meantime, is there anything you need?"

Hightower glared at him with a scowl. Clearly, he didn't appreciate the question.

"No, we are fine," Malcolm answered. "I'm wondering if I should make a plea to your leaders...maybe they will listen to me."

"You may get that opportunity," Roger replied. "First, let's see what they decide."

"Do you think our odds are good?"

Roger took a deep breath through his nose and again glanced over at General Hightower. "I'd say 50-50."

General Hightower tightened his brow, showing his displeasure. "This conversation needs to end," he grumbled. "Tell him that he will hear from you again once the decision has been made."

Before Malcolm had a chance to reply, Roger said, "Captain Steiger, I'm going to break off now, but I will reach out to you again as soon as we have a decision. If you need anything, please reach out to us."

"Thank you, commander," Malcolm answered. "I trust you."

General Hightower snatched the headset from Roger's head and tossed it aside.

"What the hell are you doing?" he asked.

Roger looked up at him and for the first time in a long time he noticed a fury burning in the general's eyes.

"Sir, things are very friendly right now and I'd like for it to stay that way," he replied. He then pointed to the monitor at the Pinnacle. "That ship is capable of destroying this entire colony if Captain Steiger feels it's necessary."

Hightower stood up straight and huffed. "If what you say is true, *they* are the ones that are vulnerable right now. They need our help."

Roger was taken aback. *"If what I say is true?* Do you think I'm lying?"

The general snorted and tightened his jaw. "Of course, not Stellick," he snapped. "What I'm trying to make you understand is that if their desperation is great enough to travel through space for fourteen years, then I seriously doubt they'd be so quick to destroy this colony. If the situation on their home world is so dire, then they do not have another fourteen years to search for more help."

Roger pushed back from the counter and stood. "Sir, I thought you made it very clear that you have no interest in helping them?"

"I don't," he answered. "But I also recognize it's not up to me. I'll carry out whatever orders we are given, but I'll also do it with extreme caution. I also took an oath to protect planet Earth at all costs. If I get a sniff of anything off kilter, then we are prepared to respond accordingly."

Roger opened his mouth to speak, but then closed it as if he'd thought better of it. Hightower noticed it and smiled.

"Stellick, say what's on your mind. I want to hear it," he urged.

Roger remained tight-lipped for a moment as if he continued to contemplate the right words. "Sir, I'm just curious what the next step will be if we refuse to help them."

General Hightower glanced over at Jake Crosby standing over in the darkest corner of the room. He'd almost forgotten he was there. "Crosby, give us the room," he ordered.

Jake nodded and immediately exited so quickly that it was apparent he was glad to do so.

"If the decision is made to not assist them, the protocols that have been written would require the aliens to either leave peacefully at once, or we will be glad to give them safe-haven assuming they'd meet certain conditions."

Roger raised an eyebrow. "What conditions?"

"Nothing unreasonable," Hightower replied. "Their entire crew will be required to undergo a medical evaluation and will have to remain in quarantine until completed. They will be forced to hand over all the technology they have and obviously share all the information about their home world."

"And then what?" Roger asked.

Hightower looked over at him, unsure what he was getting at. "Then they can live peacefully among us."

Roger crossed his arms and smirked. "They won't be imprisoned?" he asked, skeptically.

General Hightower looked away. "As long as they comply…no."

Roger paced the room a few times as he considered what Hightower had said. The general's brown eyes followed him, unblinking.

"How do we respond if they refuse any of the conditions?" he asked, finally stopping.

"Then they will obviously be asked to leave our solar system at once," Hightower answered matter-of-factly.

Roger walked up to the general and stopped in front of him. "And what if they refuse to leave?"

The muscles in Hightower's jaw tightened again along with his brow. "You know the answer to that question," he growled.

At once, he turned and exited the room without another word.

***

Tim Reed tossed the open-ended wrench into the tool box beside him and then reached for the rag hanging out of his back pocket. As he wiped the grease and oil away from his large hands, he turned to the mechanics that had been working with him.

"All clear?" he asked.

One of the men was tall and skinny with a mop of blonde hair. His face was streaked with grease and he shook his head. "All clear, chief," he said. The young man was Charlie West.

Reed and his men had been tasked with combing over the Comet fighter that Roger Stellick had used to board the Pinnacle. General Hightower was concerned that perhaps the fighter could've been tampered with, or worse yet, something harmful could've been placed aboard the ship to be brought back to the Titan colony.

"Alright," Reed said, satisfied that the job was done correctly. "I'm going to report my findings to the general, but I want this ship looked over again to ensure that she's ready to fly again when needed. We've poked and prodded on her so much I want a pre-flight checklist completed, and then I want it done again. That understood?"

Charlie looked at his counterparts and then back to Reed. "Understood sir," he said unenthusiastically.

Tim Reed stuffed the dirty rag back into his pocket and then spun on his heel to leave the hangar. On his way out the door, he was met by

Christian Smith. Sabre seemed nervous but appeared to be in better condition than the last time Tim had seen him.

"Feeling better?" Reed asked, pausing to speak to the pilot.

Sabre shoved his hands in his uniform pockets and looked away sheepishly. "Doc says I got mumps."

Reed smiled widely, revealing his bright white teeth. "Mumps?" he asked, doing his best to stifle laughter. "How in the world did you contract the mumps?"

Sabre shook his head. "Not important, chief. What *is* important is that she gave me a shot and said I'll be good to go by tomorrow morning."

"I hope you got some paperwork for Roger," Reed said.

Sabre pulled a piece of crumpled paper from his pocket and held it up. "I've got my clearance," he said. "Stellick ain't grounding me."

Tim Reed laughed. "If the man wants to ground you, he'll ground you no matter what that paper says," he said as he walked away.

Sabre rolled his eyes and continued into the hangar. He eyed the crewmen going over a checklist next to Commander Stellick's Comet fighter.

"Charlie," he said as he approached.

Charlie West was holding a clipboard that he immediately passed over to one of his counterparts.

"Kinda busy right now," he said as he walked toward Sabre.

"Do you know where Lauren is?" Sabre asked.

Charlie cocked his head slightly and eyed him suspiciously. "Why are you looking for my sister?"

Sabre narrowed his eyes and glared at him. "You know why I'm looking for her. Now do you know where she is or not?"

Charlie sighed and crossed his arms. "I thought I asked you to— politely mind you—to stay away from her."

Sabre stared at him in disbelief and then burst out into laughter. "Charlie, I really don't have time for this. Lauren is a grown woman and can see whomever the hell she wants. I never agreed to stay away from her."

Charlie felt his blood pressure rise and fought to keep his composure. Regretfully, he knew he was no match for Sabre in a fight. "Everyone on Titan knows you're not faithful to anyone," he said angrily.

Sabre shook his head slightly and did his best to appear hurt. "I've never cheated on Lauren," he said defiantly. "Charlie, I got no problem with you and quite frankly I don't think I deserve this. Can you please just tell me where she is...it's important."

Charlie rolled his eyes and bit his lip before finally saying, "She got off work early today. She's probably in the marketplace shopping."

Sabre reached over and patted Charlie on the shoulder. "Thanks bud," he said, turning to walk away.

"I'm not your bud," Charlie called after him. "This changes nothing!"

"I thank you anyway," Sabre replied. "You'll be the best man at our wedding."

Charlie's jaw dropped, and he cursed under his breath.

CHAPTER 7

Roger Stellick was becoming increasingly anxious. It had been four hours since President Callahan had told him that a decision would be made very *soon* and now he found himself wondering how long soon was going to be. General Hightower seemed to believe the decision would be reached in a matter of hours, but Roger was not so sure. In his mind's eye, he pictured the leaders of Earth bickering about what the right decision would be. Something in his gut told him that the majority of them would be leaning toward doing nothing. Roger knew fear was the driver of this position, and though he certainly understood it, he would stop short of excusing it.

He'd spent most of his time since he'd last conversed with Captain Steiger pacing in the lobby that led into the communications room. General Hightower had returned to his office with Colonel Madigan. Jake Crosby had walked into the lobby on more than one occasion but had stopped short of actually saying anything. Roger could tell the young man was somewhat star struck with his presence and part of him felt guilty for not taking the time to talk to him. Just as he'd decided that it was time to head back to his apartment, Jake Crosby again entered the room.

"Commander Stellick," he said excitedly. "General Hightower just called the comm room looking for you. You're needed back in the conference room."

Roger felt his pulse quicken a bit. "Well it's about time," he said. He began to walk away but paused and looked back at Jake. "What do you think they're gonna say?"

Jake looked around as if Roger had been speaking to someone else. "You're asking me?"

Roger chuckled. "Of course, I'm asking to you. There isn't anyone else in here."

Jake Crosby felt his face redden with embarrassment. "Oh…right," he stammered. "I think they're going to help them."

Roger was surprised. "Really? What makes you think that?"

"Well why wouldn't we?" Jake replied, surprised that Roger seemed to feel differently. "The aliens treated you well. They travelled a long way for help and they've got a lot to offer the human race if we help. I think it's a no-brainer."

"Sure, they've got a lot to offer," Roger replied. "But at what cost?"

"I feel like the cost is even greater if we do nothing," Jake countered. "Whatever is bad enough to drive them all this way to ask for help could possibly reach us too. Or maybe something else is out there that will put us in a similar position. We need allies."

Roger pursed his lips as he mulled over what Jake had said. The young man was much wiser than he'd given him credit for.

"Jake, I heard you're interested in being a Comet pilot," he said finally.

Jake's eyes immediately lit up. "Yes sir, it's why I joined S.A.M.A."

"So, what's stopping you?"

Jake cleared his throat and suddenly seemed nervous. "Well, I uh...I've applied for the pilot training program a few times, but I keep getting denied."

Roger crossed his arms and gave him a puzzled look. "Okay Jake, here is what I want you to do. Fill out another application and then I want you to hand deliver it to me along with your T.A.P. scores. Can you do that?"

Jake's eyes widened, and his mouth hung open. "Absolutely," he muttered just above a whisper.

"Very good. I guess I better get going," Roger said. "Get to your station, you may be called on very soon."

Jake nodded and looked on as Roger exited the room. Once alone, he fell backward against the wall and then slowly slid down it as the realization of what Commander Stellick had suggested set in.

***

As Roger approached the double wooden doors that led into the conference room, he noticed Dr. Phoebe Holtz had arrived at the same time. She paused when she saw him.

"Commander Stellick," she said as he stopped beside her. "Whatever happens, I want you to know that I'm in support of helping the Kaloians however we can."

"I know that," Roger replied. "I could tell you were on my side earlier and I appreciate it."

Phoebe shook her head. "It's not about taking sides. This is a historic moment in human history and I want to make sure that it's handled correctly. I didn't appreciate the general's suggestion that his personal relationship could play into any decision that is made. This is much bigger than that."

"We agree on that," Roger said, and he motioned for her to enter the room first.

Phoebe flashed a brilliant smile and pushed the doors open. General Hightower was standing at the front of the room. Colonel Madigan, Lieutenant Carter, and other senior officers were already seated at the table. It seemed Roger and Phoebe were the last ones to arrive. With everyone seated, Hightower cleared his throat and reached for a file folder lying on the table in front of him.

"They've made a decision," he said as he opened the folder. He paused to apply some eye drops and then glanced over at Roger. "As Presidents Callahan and Hiro eluded to earlier, there won't be any rash decision. After much debate, the council ultimately decided that more intel is needed before we risk the safety of Earth."

"So, the answer is no," Phoebe said. She sounded disappointed.

Colonel Madigan flashed a broad smirk in the direction of Roger.

"Not exactly," Hightower said.

The room fell very silent as the weight of Hightower's words sunk in.

"What does that mean Harry?" Colonel Madigan asked. His smirk had suddenly been replaced with a scowl.

General Hightower's expression was determined and solid. He had the look of a man that was used to taking orders, whether he agreed with them or not. Roger sensed that the news he was about to deliver was not what he himself preferred.

"The council is not closing the door on helping the Kaloians," he said. "However, as I said, they feel that more intel is needed in regard to how much help we are going to give."

"And how are we supposed to gather that intel?" Lieutenant Carter asked.

"We'll have to detain Captain Steiger and get it from him," Madigan suggested, glancing up at Hightower for confirmation.

The general said nothing, but he shook his head.

"Then how?" Phoebe asked. "Are we going to question the crew?"

Again, the general shook his head. "No, relying on anything the Kaloians are telling us is not good enough for the council."

The room again fell silent as it seemed everyone was trying to mull over what the general was getting at.

Hightower sighed and looked over to Roger. He seemed to be reluctant to speak to him, but it seemed obvious he didn't have a choice. "Commander Stellick, this gate you mentioned," he began. "The one that will provide a direct path back to the Ara Constellation…did Captain Steiger happen to mention how long it would take to assemble?"

"No, he didn't," Roger replied. "But I got a sense that it would not take long."

"Alright," Hightower replied. "Well that is a piece of information the presidents want at once. The plan is for us to send a ship with our own people on it through the gate to see this foreign world for ourselves."

There were momentary gasps in the room.

Roger shrugged and asked. "What ship, sir?"

"I'm curious about that as well," Lieutenant Carter chimed in. "We don't really have a space craft that is built for deep space exploration at this time."

General Hightower slowly looked over to Colonel Madigan. Madigan read his eyes and knew what he was thinking. "Well, that's not entirely true," Madigan said.

Everyone in the room turned their attention to the colonel.

"Please explain," Phoebe urged. "What do you mean 'that's not true'?"

Madigan looked back to Hightower and again the general locked eyes with him.

"Tell them," Hightower said, and then he glanced around the room. "And I expect each one of you to keep this confidential."

Roger and the other officers nodded. He could see they were all as perplexed as he was.

"For the past three years a top-secret project has been underway to build a large spacecraft unlike anything we've ever seen before," Madigan said. "In fact, the ship is only slightly smaller than the Kaloian ship, Pinnacle," he added proudly.

The room was thick with tension and disbelief. There was a long silence when Hightower continued. "It's called Project Shooting Star," he said. "The ship is in the final stages of completion now."

Roger shook his head in disbelief. "How is that possible?" he asked. "How could S.A.M.A. possibly keep a ship that size a secret?"

General Hightower rubbed at his eyes and paused to apply more drops. "Commander Stellick, it's been a challenge to say the least. The only place feasible to take on such a challenge in secret is on the dark side of Earth's moon."

"So, if I'm understanding you, the council wants us to use this ship to enter through the Kaloian gateway and explore their galaxy?" Roger asked.

"That's pretty much the plan," Hightower confirmed.

Colonel Madigan drummed his fingers on the table and shifted uneasily in his chair. "The crew will need a captain and a crew," he said, glancing up at the general.

"Yes, it will," Hightower agreed. "President's Callahan and Hiro have appointed myself as captain and you as executive officer," he added, staring back at Madigan.

The expression on the colonel's face was a cross of bewilderment and astonishment all at the same time. Roger could not tell if he was exactly happy about the appointment or not.

"Furthermore," Hightower continued. "Commander Stellick, Doctor Holtz, and Lieutenant Carter have also been appointed as additional officers. Other crew members will be assigned over the next two weeks."

Roger immediately looked over at Phoebe and could see the concern on her face.

"Sir, I assume this is a direct order?" Roger asked.

Hightower glared at him with an icy stare. "Of course it's a direct order Commander. Are you suggesting that you're unwilling to join us?"

Phoebe glanced over at him, her eyes wide. She immediately realized he'd asked the question for her benefit.

"No sir, I'm not suggesting that at all," he said. "I just want everyone in this room to be sharp and focused on this mission. If someone doesn't want to be there, I feel that maybe some consideration should be given to replacing that individual."

General Hightower crossed his arms and breathed in deeply through his nose as he scanned over the room. He seemed to take Roger's words to heart. "Is there anyone in here that opposes their appointment?"

The officers in the room slowly looked around the room at each other. The room was extremely silent. Phoebe crossed her legs and looked away at the wall. She was visibly uncomfortable.

"Alright then," Hightower said when he was satisfied no one was going to speak. "Since it seems we're all on the same page, there will be another briefing tomorrow. Are there any other questions?"

"Yes," Roger answered. "What are we going to tell Captain Steiger?"

"The truth," Hightower said immediately. "And part of this plan hinges on whether or not you can convince him to share some of their technology."

Roger clenched his jaw and shook his head in disbelief. "I told you that the deal required our assistance before any technology is shared. That's the terms we were given."

For the first time the general smiled. "Well I guess you need to renegotiate the terms," he said. "According to Captain Steiger, the Pinnacle can travel at light speed. We need our ship to be able to travel at light speed also."

"I think that's a reasonable request," Lieutenant Carter said. "If they truly want our assistance, they should be willing to bend a little and give us what we need to meet in the middle, so to speak."

Roger gritted his teeth and popped his knuckles as he felt perspiration begin to form on his forehead. Suddenly it seemed a lot was riding on him. "I'll do what I can," he said finally, obvious concern in his tone.

"That's all we ask," Hightower replied. For the first time he seemed sympathetic to Roger's uncomfortable position. "Let me know if I can help," he added thoughtfully.

Roger looked up at him and gestured his thanks.

"What's it called?" a young officer called out from the other end of the room.

Hightower cocked his head and stared at him, confused.

"The ship...what's it called?" the young man clarified.

"It's a Star Cruiser...SC Titan is what they named her," the general replied. "She's named after the very soil you're standing on now. So far, the colony here on Titan is Earth's greatest achievement. The SC Titan should be the first of many other Star Cruisers and since she is the first, what better way to commemorate what we've done here so future generations will remember."

There were murmurs in the room, but the general consensus seemed to be positive regarding the vessel's name.

"Let me remind you that what you've been told thus far is confidential. I better not get an inkling that anything that was just told to you is leaked beyond the doors of this room. If I do, the consequences will be severe. If there are no other questions, you all are dismissed," Hightower said.

Everyone rose to their feet and began to file out of the room at once. Roger was one of the last to stand and as he approached the door, the general called after him.

"Not you Roger," he said.

Roger turned to see the general motioning for him to sit back down. Colonel Madigan had remained where he was seated.

"I require a few more minutes of your time," he said.

Roger sighed and watched as Phoebe winked at him as she shut the door.

CHAPTER 8

"As commander of our Comet fleet, you will be third in command aboard the Titan," Hightower explained just as Roger sat down.

"That's a big responsibility," Colonel Madigan said, and he held out a hand. "Congratulations to you."

Roger shook the colonel's hand and smiled. "I—I don't know what to say," he said.

"The SC Titan will have a landing deck for a fleet of forty Comet fighters," Hightower said, seemingly keeping the conversation all business. "I want you responsible for those pilots and it'll be your job to relay my orders. It's your responsibility to see that those orders are followed."

Roger nodded. So far this was nothing different from his current responsibilities.

"Obviously, if anything happens to myself and Merrill, you will become captain of the ship," Hightower continued. He then held up the file folder that had been in his hand during the entire meeting. He gently tossed it across the table. It slid across the slick surface and came to a stop right in front of Roger.

"What's this?" he asked as he picked the folder up.

"That's the orders from the presidents," the general answered. "And there is also schematics and a lot of general information about the SC Titan. I want you to read every word in the file and then read it all over again. Merrill and I will be doing the same. We need to know that ship inside and out."

"Of course," he replied. "I'll start tonight."

"In addition to that," Hightower continued. "I need you to compile a roster of pilots you think will be up to the task. We don't know what we'll get into once we cross through that gate and I want the best pilots available. All I want at this point is names. Merrill and I will have the final approval, but we'll almost certainly agree with your choices. Once we are all in agreement, we'll discuss the mission with each one individually."

Madigan nodded in agreement, then said, "Seeing how there are only twenty Comet pilots on Titan including yourself, you'll obviously need to look at who is available on the Mars and moon colonies, as well as Earth."

"And don't feel that you have to use all twenty pilots here on Titan," Hightower chimed in. "We want the best, and if the best isn't here on Titan, then find it elsewhere. Understood?"

Roger swallowed and nodded. "I understand," he said.

"That's really all for now," the general concluded. "I don't want to overwhelm you with anything else. Complete the tasks I've assigned and we'll meet back again tomorrow. I'll communicate the time with you later. Dismissed."

Roger stood and headed for the door. He felt as if he were in a dream. It was as if he were walking through a fog that he could not find an end to.

"And Roger," Hightower called after him.

He looked over his shoulder. "Yessir?"

"Nothing we just talked about will matter if you can't convince Steiger to work with our engineers to get our ship ready."

Roger frowned, and it felt as if the fog he was in just grew thicker.

"I'm headed to the comm room now," he said.

"Record the entire conversation. When the opportunity presents itself, give him clearance to come to the base," Hightower said. "He may bring a small crew of his own men if he sees fit. However, this time Merrill and I will join you. And the meeting must occur in the empty silo on the outer edge of the farming district. I won't risk having them near our people."

"Alright," Roger replied. "I'll be in touch."

The general nodded, and Roger finally disappeared into the hallway.
***

Sabre stepped off the railcar and immediately marched through the automatic doors that led into the marketplace. The dome housing the building was set up in a similar fashion to a twentieth century mall. The marketplace was enormous and ultimately the largest dome on the Titan colony. The railway encompassed the entire facility and there were numerous stops where patrons could gain access to a variety of store fronts to meet their every need—including grocery. Much like the malls the marketplace was modeled after, one of the main attractions consisted of the food court. There, pretty much any food imaginable was available in the fifty plus restaurant fronts that lined both walls. The tile floor in the center space was covered with tables of various sizes. Among the tables there was a variety of plant life; everything from palm trees to rose bushes. The ceiling was constructed of mostly glass, exposing the tangerine hue of Titan's later afternoon sky.

Sabre knew of Lauren's fondness for Mexican food and he had a hunch he knew exactly where to find her. As he walked along the restaurant fronts that lined the eastern wall, as he approached the midway point, he spotted her. She was seated alone among the hundreds of other patrons. Lauren was watching the news on one of the pop up digital screens that rose from the center of the table and was completely oblivious to him watching her. Sabre briskly approached from behind and quickly placed his hand over her eyes.

As she startled he said, "Guess who?"

She smiled and said, "Well, since I only know one man that uses lavender scented hand soap, I'm guessing you're the one and only Christian Smith."

Sabre immediately pulled his hand away and smelled his palm. "Holy crap," he said with genuine surprise. "The smell *is* quite strong, isn't it?"

Lauren laughed. "Yes, it is. What are you doing here?"

Sabre sat down across from her and grabbed a corn chip from her plate. He took a bite and then gave her his best sad face. "You don't want me here?" he asked theatrically. He then looked around in all directions. "Are you meeting someone else here or something?"

Lauren rolled her eyes and sighed. "I'm out of bread and you know I can't resist this place," she said, glancing over at the bright neon signage over the Mexican restaurant.

"Yeah, I figured as much when I heard you were over here," Sabre replied as he reached for another chip.

"Who told you I was here?" Lauren asked as she plunged her fork into the small pile of fried rice on her plate.

"Charlie did," he answered.

Lauren immediately dropped her fork. "What?" she asked, sounding half panicked.

Sabre smirked and raised an eyebrow. "Oh, come on," he groaned. "He's your little brother, not your dad."

Lauren crossed her arms and her smile disappeared. "No, my dad is dead and so is my mom," she snapped. "I'd appreciate it if you didn't remind me of it."

He slowly stopped chewing and leaned across the table, reaching for her hand. She didn't exactly reach for him, but she didn't pull away as he grabbed her either. "Hey," he said softly. "I'm sorry."

Her eyes drifted away from him and down toward the table. A collection of stray blonde hairs fell over her eyes as she lowered her head.

"Lauren, I just don't understand why what he thinks is so important to you," he added, and he took a moment to brush the hairs out of her face. "I've got nothing against Charlie, but he seems to have something against me."

She returned her eyes to meet his. "He constantly tells me that you've got a reputation of breaking hearts," she replied. "He's trying to protect me. And I care a lot about what he thinks. He's all I've got left."

Sabre slowly pulled his hand away and sunk down into his chair. He picked up a napkin and dabbed at his mouth. "Okay, it's true," he said, sounding defeated. "I do have a bad reputation and a lot of what he's told you about my past is true. But please believe me when I say that you're not like other girls. You're the first woman I've ever met that I can truly picture spending the rest of my life with."

Lauren blushed and her smile returned. "Really?" she asked with a silly grin. "We've only been seeing each other six months."

Sabre nodded and suddenly sat up straight again as he realized he'd regained the upper hand in the conversation. "Yes really," he said. "And six months is the longest I've ever been in a relationship..." he paused and looked up as he seemed to be in thought, "...by at least five and a half months," he finished.

Lauren rolled her eyes, but it was a playful response. "I don't know," she said. "Sometimes I don't know if I can trust you."

Sabre gasped—again for show. "What?" he asked. "How can you not trust me? I have complete trust in you and you're hanging out with muscle bound good looking guys all day at the gym."

"That's because it's my job," she snapped back.

"Sorry," Sabre quipped. "I'm just insecure...it's been a problem since I was a child." He closed his eyes for a moment and then opened one to look at her. "And it's not helping my insecurity by having the one woman I love doubt my affection for her." He then snapped his eye shut again.

Lauren laughed again. "Okay, I believe you," she said.

He opened his eyes widely and smiled. "About time," he replied.

"But," she cut in, "you've got to convince Charlie that you're a good guy."

"Oh, for crying out loud," he groaned.

"I mean it," Lauren said, and her tone was serious. "If we're going to work out, you've got to get Charlie on board. I know that sounds terribly unfair, but I'm just telling you the truth. My little brother is the other man in my life and it's important to me that you both get along."

Sabre crossed his arms and bit his lip. "Oh, alright," he said, sounding exhausted. "I'll make him see what a good guy I am if it's the last thing I do."

"Good," she said, and she again returned her attention to the fried rice.

"I suppose I better get back to work," he said as he thought again about the U.F.O. Commander Stellick had intercepted almost ten hours ago. It was still a secret to the civilians on the colony, but he was unsure how long that would last. He wanted to tell Lauren badly, but knew how severe the consequences would be if he did.

"Seems that's all you do is work," Lauren said as she chewed a mouthful of rice.

Sabre raised from the table and leaned over to kiss her on the forehead. "It's the life of a Comet fighter pilot, honey," he said as he leaned over and kissed her on the forehead. He turned to walk away and then stopped dead in his tracks as something suddenly occurred to him. He spun on his heel and leaned close where only Lauren could hear him.

"Sweetheart, I almost forgot," he whispered. "You need to go to the medical ward when you leave here."

Lauren's eyes widened as she looked over at him. "Okay," she said, worried. "Why?"

He stared into her eyes. "Because I'm afraid you now have the mumps."

**

Roger could not shake the overwhelming feeling of dread as he put on the headset and prepared to give Captain Steiger the news. Jake Crosby was more than happy to leave the room upon Roger's request for privacy. Once alone, he'd taken a few minutes to rehearse what he was going to say and how he was going to say it. He knew it was cliché, but for the first time in his life, Roger truly felt the weight of the world on his shoulders. So much was riding on him convincing Steiger to agree to Earth's terms without actually committing to helping them. When he was finally satisfied that he was ready, Roger flipped a switch in front of him and spoke into the microphone.

"Captain Steiger, this is Commander Roger Stellick, are you there? Over."

After a few seconds, there was a chatter of static followed by Malcolm's familiar voice.

"I'm here commander," he said. "You have news?"

Roger drummed his fingers on the counter and thought, *Boy do I ever...*

"Affirmative," he replied. "The leaders of Earth have made their decision, and though it may not be exactly what you were wanting to hear, I believe it's a good starting point to both of our races ultimately getting what we want."

There was a long awkward silence that spoke volumes before Malcolm said anything at all. Finally, he said, "Very well. I'm listening."

"Captain Steiger, first I want to remind you of my race's unusual predicament. Only hours ago, we discovered that we are no longer alone in the universe. Though we've always suspected it, having it now confirmed is a lot for us to process. You may see this as a weakness, but I tend to believe it's one of our greatest strengths. It's allowed us to take our time and think this through before any rash decision is made. With that in mind, please understand that Earth *wants* to help you. But to do that, we need more evidence to confirm that everything is exactly as you say. We are a cautious people and we want to do what is in the best interest for humanity."

"I see," Malcom replied without any hesitation. "You do not trust me?"

Roger winced. This was the response he was expecting. "If you're referring to me specifically, of course I trust you," he said.

"Then are you saying your leaders do not trust *you*?" Malcolm asked.

Roger suddenly felt a headache brewing. "No, that's not what I'm saying," he replied. "I'm saying that the people of Earth want to help, but we just want a clear picture of what we're getting into first."

There was a long moment of silence as Malcolm seemed to mull over what Roger had said.

"Alright," he said finally, and his voice sounded slightly annoyed. "What sort of evidence do you want?"

"Well," Roger replied, his pitch rising slightly. "Earth would like to send a crew over to the Ara Constellation to verify your claims."

Malcolm chuckled. "To *verify my claims*?" he said. Roger could picture him scowling. "Very well," he continued. "It will take my crew less than two days to construct the gateway and we will take a crew of your choosing back to Kalo. Since I'm sensing growing distrust between our races, I'm willing to leave some of my own men in your people's custody until we return to ensure the safety of your crew."

"That's not necessary," Roger replied. "We are willing to send our own ship and crew."

Roger hoped the statement sounded more like a favor Earth was willing to provide, than a condition that they required. He waited anxiously for a reply to see if his calculated choice of words worked.

"You have a ship capable of such a journey?" he asked, skeptically.

"We do—or we almost do," he said. "There is a ship in Earth's fleet that we feel will be perfect for such an expedition, however, there are technological advancements that your people have that would be very beneficial to its completion."

"You have a ship that isn't even finished?" Malcolm asked with even more annoyance dripping from his words.

"We're very close," Roger replied. "But what we're hoping is that you can provide an engineer from your crew to help us develop a propulsion system that will allow us to travel through space as swiftly as the Pinnacle."

"I see," Malcolm said, and he sighed. "Sharing our technology with you was not supposed to occur until you agreed to help us."

"I know," Roger said, almost apologetically. "And I said earlier, Earth wants to help you. We just need to be sure we can."

"And that I'm telling the truth," Malcolm quipped.

Roger started to reply, but thought better of it. He decided to let the request linger a little longer. The silence lasted for almost a solid minute before Malcolm finally spoke again.

"Very well," he said finally. "I don't have a great deal of time to debate this matter. We will need to set up a meeting between my engineers and the scientists of Earth to see how quickly we can resolve this matter."

Roger perked up, unable to believe what he was hearing. "So, you're saying you'll comply with our conditions?"

"I don't feel that I have a choice Commander Stellick," Malcolm replied, sounding defeated.

"Thank you Captain Steiger," Roger replied. "At this point I'd like to invite you and some of your officers down to meet with my superiors here on Titan."

"I was beginning to think you'd never ask," Malcolm replied, and he suddenly sounded more like his old self again. "I've been on this ship for fourteen years. I'd like to take any opportunity I can to get off of it even if it's for a short time."

Roger smiled as he began to feel the proverbial weight on his shoulders lighten substantially.

CHAPTER 9

It had been a long and exhausting day. Roger felt as if he'd accomplished more in the current day than he had in any other day in his entire life. He took the rail car back to his apartment and wanted nothing more than to collapse into his bed as soon as he entered the room. He knew, however, that there would be no way he could sleep until he took the time to crack open the file General Hightower had given him and take a peek at the schematics of the SC Titan. He sat down on the edge of his bed and opened the folder

The cover page was nothing more than a white sheet of paper with the words **TOP SECRET** stamped across it in red. The first page behind the cover consisted of a list of specifications for the ship. The first impressive stat that jumped out at him was that the SC Titan was built for a crew of 500. That was way more people than Roger thought the ship could hold and it was his first indication that the vessel was much larger than he'd initially thought. He read on and just as Hightower had said, the ship was capable of holding 40 Comet fighters.

The SC Titan essentially had five decks. The top was by far the smallest and was mostly comprised of the ship's bridge, conference room, and observation area. The second deck was made up of the captain's quarters, officer quarters, medical ward, two laboratories, and the armory. The third and fourth decks were filled mostly with sleeping quarters and bathhouses. Roger was impressed to see that every member of the crew would have their own room. The third deck was also flanked with two launching bays that extended the length of the ship on either side. Twenty Comet fighters would be housed in each bay and at the front portion of the third deck there was a briefing room that connected the two bays. In addition to the sleeping quarters on the fourth deck, there was also a large cafeteria and recreational area that had everything from a gym to a bar. Engineering made up the fifth and lowest deck on the ship.

Roger flipped over to the third page and found very detailed drawings of the ship. The shape of the vessel resembled that of a handgun turned backwards. The long *barrel* portion of the "gun" contained the upper three decks along with the launching bays. The fourth and fifth decks were considerably shorter, slightly angled backwards, and made up the *grip*. The drawings gave Roger a much clearer picture on the size of the engines and he wondered how much of that would change once the *Pinnacle* engineers got their chance to modify them to travel at light speed. Where the third and fourth decks came together, either side was flanked by rather large twin engines. The fifth deck was flanked by smaller engines that angled downward slightly, their purpose seemingly to provide vertical lift.

As Roger continued through the file, he finally found numerous documents signed and authored by President Akagi Hiro. He seemed to be a major driving force for the project and was heavily involved from the moment he was elected into office. So involved he was, Roger quickly came to the realization that the SC Titan was more or less a passion project of President Hiro's. He came across photos of the president—with an orange hardhat on his head—visiting the site and checking on the progress of its construction. Roger found himself wondering what the original plans for such a large star ship must have been.

After going through at least half of the file, Roger yawned and realized he could no longer go on. It would be a big day tomorrow and the highlight would be Captain Steiger's arrival to the Titan colony. He would need to be sharp because part of him knew that the general would look to him to be somewhat of a neutral party. If somehow things began to spiral in the wrong direction, everyone would look to him to smooth it all out. As he considered all the "what if" scenarios, he couldn't help but chuckle. He had no idea that when he'd begun training years ago to be Earth's first representative to meet alien life that the job would take him so much further than the initial contact.

With reluctance, Roger tossed the file aside and allowed himself to collapse backward on to the bed. He stared at the ceiling for a long moment and replayed the day's events in his mind. As amazing and historic as the day had been for he and the leaders of Earth, he wondered how the rest of the population would react when the news broke out. Minutes later, Roger drifted off into a deep sleep.

***

General Harry Hightower woke up early. He glanced over at the clock and realized in total he'd only gotten about four hours of sleep. The previous day had been a busy one and today promised to be even busier. As he sat up on the edge of his bed, he reached over and grabbed the small bottle of eye drops. His doctor had told him it would take a couple of weeks before the itching and burning ceased, and the thought of dealing with the irritation for at least one more week made Harry cringe. He supposed it was a small price to pay to avoid total blindness.

Long term, the cybernetic implants were the only way to go but he never dreamed the healing process would be as hard to cope with as it was.

Once out of bed, Harry showered and shaved and began to ponder what he would say upon meeting Captain Steiger. It was obvious to him that Roger Stellick had placed a great deal of trust in the Kaloian. Harry had always trusted Roger immensely, but for some reason that he could not quite put his finger on, Harry could not shake an uneasy feeling about Steiger. Despite Roger's insistence that the colony had nothing to fear, Harry had given the command for the Titan military defense department to keep a warhead pointed at the *Pinnacle* and ready to fire at a moment's notice. It was his hope that today's meeting would allow him to put the uneasy feelings to rest so that they could move forward with a much-needed galactic alliance. After all, he thought, it seemed that the Kaloian was willing to bend a little on his stance to share his technology.

Surely that was a positive sign…

General Hightower's position allowed him luxuries that no one else on the Titan colony had; chief of which was the fact that Harry was the only citizen in the entire colony that had an actual house. It was nestled away at the back of the property where the soldier barracks were built. The house was not large by any means, but relative to most of the apartments, it was a mansion. Harry stepped outside and onto the rocky soil of Titan. He looked up at the massive protective dome several hundred feet above his head and watched as a raincloud moved over. It was a strange feeling as he watched the droplets of methane splashing against the glass, and then slide innocently away along the convex surface. The sight gave him a sudden feeling of home sickness as he tried to remember the last time he'd stood in the rain on Earth.

"Good morning Harry," Colonel Merrill Madigan called out from ahead.

"Good morning, Merrill," he replied cheerfully. "What's for breakfast?"

"Great question, let's go find out together."

As they walked along the path that led to the mess hall, Harry sensed why the colonel had been waiting on him. He'd seen the look in the man's eyes before. Clearly, he was troubled.

"What's on your mind?" he asked suddenly.

Madigan snapped a look at him. "What?" he asked.

Hightower smiled, revealing his coffee-stained teeth. "We've served together for twenty years, Merrill," he said. "I know when something's bothering you, so spit it out."

Madigan allowed the slightest hint of a smile and took a deep breath through his nose. "You know exactly what's on my mind," he grumbled. "I've got a bad feeling about this."

"Bad feeling about *what* exactly?" Hightower replied with a raised eyebrow.

Madigan gave him a skeptical glance. "The meeting with the alien, Harry," he grumbled, knowing full well that the general knew exactly what troubled him. "I don't trust him...something feels wrong about all of this."

Hightower nodded but refrained from voicing his agreement. "Well it's not up to us," he said. "We've got our orders, and if we're going to carry them out we've got to meet Captain Steiger and get some help from his engineers."

They finally reached the door to the mess hall and Hightower held it open for the colonel. Madigan stopped and looked over at him, obvious concern on his face. "This stinks Harry. I'll obey orders, same as you, but when an advanced race of aliens suddenly visits us telling us that they need our help..." he paused and shook his head.

"I know," Hightower said. "I know."

***

Roger had given Captain Steiger very specific instructions on where he needed to land his shuttle, and how to approach the launch bay. General Hightower desperately wanted the presence of the Kaloians to be kept a secret from the civilians on the base for as long as possible. For that to occur, it was imperative that the Kaloian shuttle's approach was low and from the western side of the colony. Much to Hightower's delight, Steiger's arrival happened as discreetly as he had hoped.

The Kaloian shuttle was rather plain looking, and nothing like what the human crew was expecting. It was essentially a box with a sloped front. There was a clear windshield on the front and small triangular wings on either side. Visually, nothing about the shuttle's appearance looked conducive to flight, but somehow it had managed to soar to the surface of Titan flawlessly.

As planned, Roger was the first man to greet Captain Steiger when the side door on the shuttle slid open.

"Commander Stellick, it's good to see you again," he said with a cheerful smile. He stepped onto the concrete floor and immediately shook Roger's hand. He then looked past him to see twenty other armed guards standing along the wall.

Roger noticed the momentary look of surprise on Malcolm's face, but nothing was said about the guards. "Welcome to Titan, Captain Steiger," he said.

"Thank you. It's good to stand on land again," he said wistfully.

"We're glad to have you," the general said, offering his hand. "I'm General Harry Hightower of the Space and Aeronautics Military Alliance."

"General Hightower," Malcolm said as he took his hand. "It's a pleasure to meet you and I must take this moment to extend my thanks for your generosity in inviting me here."

Hightower nodded, but kept the greeting business-like. He looked past Steiger as ten more men stepped out of the shuttle, five of them armed with some sort of military rifles.

"Captain, we've made arrangements to conduct our meeting at a remote location near the edge of the colony," Hightower said. "I appreciate your understanding regarding our desire to keep you and the other Kaloian's presence secret for the time being."

"Of course," Malcolm replied. "We are your guests and I respect your wishes."

"And I assure you that you'll be treated as respectfully as you treated Commander Stellick when he was in your custody," Hightower answered. "I want to be clear that you have nothing to fear from us."

Malcolm smiled. "I believe you general."

It was Colonel Madigan's turn to step forth and make his introduction. After doing so, he urged Captain Steiger to follow him to the awaiting rail car. The car was large enough to comfortably transport thirty people. To keep things as friendly as possible, Hightower had refreshments available for the short ride.

"Very interesting machine," Malcolm said as he stepped into the vehicle. He looked the railcar over and seemed genuinely interested. "It's quite a simple concept," he added.

"We try to keep everything simple here," Hightower said as he motioned for the Kaloian captain to take a seat. "We try to keep the possibility of any mechanical failure to a bare minimum."

Malcolm nodded as he continued to scan over his environment. He noticed a cart near the front of the car. On top of the cart was a deep tray, filled with ice and soda cans of varying colors. He picked up a red one and held it up to the light. "Is this something to drink?" he asked, and he seemed to direct the question to Roger.

"Yes," he answered, nodding. "It's what we call a soda. It's basically a mixture of carbonated water, sugar, and a flavored syrup."

Malcolm's curious expression morphed into one of confusion. He glanced over at one of the other Kaloian officers that joined him. The man shook his head.

"I wouldn't drink that," he said, his voice gruff.

The man seemed to be close to the same age as Captain Steiger. His hair was shoulder length and brown. His cheek bones were very defined, and as Roger studied his facial features he quickly began to realize the man was very thin. As he looked around the room at some of the other Kaloians, he noticed they too seemed thinner than Steiger. Roger found himself wondering how badly their journey to Titan had left them depleted of food.

"Don't be silly," Malcolm replied to the man with a carefree smile. "I trust Commander Stellick." He then took the can and turned it over in his hand, examining it closely before finally looking over to Roger, a puzzled expression on his face. "I'm ashamed to say I can't figure out how to open this."

Roger chuckled, as did General Hightower and Colonel Madigan. "Here, let me see it," he said, reaching for the can. He pulled the tab, and then returned the opened container.

Steiger shot him a look of gratitude before turning the can up to his lips. His face immediately contorted into a fashion that reminded Roger of someone that had just sucked on a lemon. "It's quite strong," he said with a slight cough. He held the can up and looked at it again. "Although, I admit it is also quite tasty."

There were more chuckles in the room again, but Roger took note that none of the Kaloian officers or guards found it as amusing as their Earthling counterparts. After a few minutes the railcar began to move and a short time later it arrived at the farming facility on the outskirts of the colony. Once the doors to the vehicle opened, Colonel Madigan led the party into a large building in the center of the dome. Once inside, he ventured down a long hallway that ended at a set of double doors. Madigan then opened the doors to reveal a rather large conference room with a rectangular wooden table in its center.

As everyone filed into the room, one side of the table seemed to fill up with Earthlings, while the opposite side filled with Kaloians. General Hightower took one end of the table while Captain Steiger took the other. The two stood there behind their respective chairs and waited for everyone to take a seat. Finally, Hightower made a gesture toward Steiger, seemingly a request for him to sit as well. As Malcolm took his seat, the general began talking.

"This is a monumental and historic day for both of our races," Hightower began, and he smiled as he spoke. Roger was impressed to see that it didn't even appear to be forced. "I want to begin by extending my thanks to Captain Malcolm Steiger and the men that have accompanied him. We're glad to have you here and it's my sincere hope that this is the beginning of a strong alliance between our races that will last forever."

Malcolm smiled and nodded slightly before humbly raising his hand as if asking permission to speak.

The general chuckled. "Captain, you're free to speak whenever you please. What's on your mind?"

Malcolm cleared his throat and shifted in his chair. "General, thank you very much for your hospitality. However, I noticed you kept referring to our race as if we're different than all of you. That is simply not true. We are human, same as you."

Hightower smiled again, though this time it *did* look forced. "My apologies," he said. "Forgive me, but can you elaborate on that? How are there other humans across the galaxy that we knew nothing about until now?"

"Well," Malcolm began. "I want you to know we have a brain, heart, lungs, cardiovascular system, and so on, exactly like all of yours," he said, seemingly taking a quick moment to make eye contact with every Earthling in the room.

"As far as why we've been separated by millions of meters of intergalactic space between our worlds...I have no idea how to explain that," he admitted. "I think now would probably be a good time to tell you that there are other planets in our galaxy with other human races too. Humans seem to inhabit this entire galaxy, but I'd be remiss if I didn't also tell you that there are other entirely different races of aliens found in other galaxies. Some are not friendly either."

Colonel Madigan stroked his chin as he listened intently. "Captain Steiger, these revelations you're giving us...they're a huge part of why Earth's leaders were somewhat reluctant to help you with your er...problem."

Malcolm looked over at the colonel, confused. "I don't understand," he said, as he then turned his glance back toward General Hightower.

Hightower sighed and placed his hands in his uniform's jacket pockets. "What the colonel is trying to say," he said, "is that the only way you could possibly know these incredible things you're telling us about other races of humans—and even other races of aliens in different galaxies—would have to be because the Kaloians are so technologically advanced that you have the capabilities to explore every sector of our galaxy and beyond. Any race of people with that much of a technological advantage would have to most certainly have the wherewithal to deal with threats to their way of life. It's just hard for us to fathom that we could be of much help to you."

Malcolm's eyes widened slightly, and he bowed his head. He seemed to have expected the conversation to take a turn in this direction.

"What you say is true," he said, still looking downward at the table top. "As I've told Commander Stellick, though we have a clear technological advantage, it means nothing if we don't have the manpower to use it. I'm simply proposing an alliance between the people of Kalo and the people of Earth. An alliance to deal with a scourge that is destroying my home world, and will no doubt one day become a threat to your home world as well."

Malcolm paused and looked up again. He scanned the environment, making eye contact with nearly every Earthling in the room. "Kalo is at your mercy. I'm begging for your help. I need it so badly that I'm willing to bend the original terms I laid out for Commander Stellick. I understand your cautious nature and if you want us to construct the gate so that you can cross over and see for yourself before committing, then we are prepared to help update your ships with the technology you'll need to do it."

"All we really need is some assistance with our propulsion system," Hightower replied. "We have a ship—a large ship that is suitable for just such an expedition. However, it is not capable of travelling at light speed as your ship the Pinnacle is able to do. We want to know if it's possible to get our ship that fast. We're not even sure how the skin on her hull would hold up to speeds like that."

Malcolm smiled and evidently had good news. "General, not only am I confident that we can get your ship up to light speed, I'm also confident that if the hull isn't already strong enough—and it probably is—that we'll be able to make relatively easy modifications to get it there."

"Modifications?" Colonel Madigan asked, cocking his head slightly.

"Yes, we have a material—what you call paint—that can be applied to the exterior of your ship. Once it hardens, handling light speed will be no problem at all."

"Very well," Hightower answered. "How long do you think the modifications would take?"

"That depends on how much you're willing to assist us," Malcolm replied. "And of course, we know nothing about the size of your ship."

"You'll get all the help you need to make this happen as quickly as possible…and our ship is slightly smaller than the Pinnacle," Hightower said.

Malcolm nodded and looked over to the Kaloian next to him with the shoulder length brown hair. "Tago, what do you think?" he asked him.

Tago took a deep breath and seemed to clench his teeth as he pondered the question. After a moment, he said, "Under those circumstances I would say an Earth month would probably be sufficient."

"A month? That fast?" Colonel Madigan asked, surprised.

Malcolm smiled. "Colonel, we have tools that you do not yet have. You supply manpower to assist, and we will get your ship ready."

Madigan looked at the general, and then they both looked to Roger. Roger shrugged. "A month is plenty of time for us to put together our crew," he said.

General Hightower nodded slightly and then said, "Captain Steiger, let's plan on five weeks. That'll give you a week to construct the gate, and a month to make sure our ship is ready to go. We can always adjust to add more time if we feel that we need it."

"No," Malcolm said. "The sooner we get back to my home world, the sooner you will see that we are in dire need of your help. Then hopefully you'll provide it."

Hightower locked eyes with Malcolm and then walked around the table to where he was. When he stood before him, he held out a hand. "You can trust us," he said.

Malcolm slowly looked down at the general's outstretched hand. After a moment, he smiled and shook it. "You can trust us too," he said kindly.

CHAPTER 10

"Commander, do I have permission to speak freely?" Sabre asked.

They were standing in the hangar among the fleet of Comet fighters. There was no one else within earshot.

"Of course, Christian, speak your mind," Roger urged, and he crossed his arms, ready to listen.

Sabre shifted his feet and looked at the Comet fighter nearest him. "You know that my answer is yes, but why the delay?"

Roger resisted the urge to snap at the cocky pilot. "You were sick when I began putting my roster together, I had to make sure you were well."

Sabre shook his head and smirked. "Commander Stellick, you've been putting the crew together for almost a month. The mumps is not a serious illness."

"Every illness is serious when you're a pilot," Roger scolded. "I will not allow one pilot to leave the ground if I don't feel they are one hundred percent."

There was a long awkward silence. Sabre kept looking back and forth between Roger and the nearby Comet. He seemed to be having a debate within himself on whether to continue the conversation.

"Commander, I have a hard time believing that your decision to wait so long to ask me was based solely on my health," he said finally.

Roger took a step forward. "You need to tread lightly, pilot," he growled.

Sabre took a step back and shook his head. "I'm sorry sir," he grumbled. "I thought I had permission to speak freely."

"You do," Roger snapped. "And I have the freedom to keep you off the roster if I feel your insubordination will be a problem."

"I'm not trying to be insubordinate," he said. "It just doesn't make sense. I'm one of the best pilots in S.A.M.A. and am more than qualified for this mission. Logically, it seems that I'd have been the first man on your roster and not the thirty-eighth."

"Well you're on it now," Roger said, turning away from him. "Keep your nose clean for the next week and you can stay on it."

Roger then walked away, leaving Sabre alone. The disgruntled pilot stood in silence for almost a solid minute before finally punching the Comet fighter he'd been standing next to out of frustration.

"What's wrong?" Lauren asked, as she approached him from behind. Her hair was in a pony tail and she was wearing a jogging suit. In her hands were two coffees.

Sabre spun on his heel to discover that she'd entered the hangar from the doorway on the opposite side of the building.

"Nothing," he said, still sounding disgusted.

"It doesn't sound or look like nothing," she replied, as she glanced over at the Comet he'd just struck.

"I think your brother is talking about me," he grumbled.

Lauren was taken aback. "What? Talking about you to whom?"

"Commander Stellick," he answered. He walked over to the Comet and leaned his back against it. "Stellick just told me I've been added to the roster of pilots—finally."

Lauren's face brightened at the revelation. "Well that's great," she said excitedly. "That's the news you've been waiting on."

"Yes, but I can't figure out why it took him so long," he said. "I think your brother has been bad-mouthing me to him."

Lauren shook her head. "Charlie barely has any contact with the Commander," she said.

"Well then maybe he's been talking about me to Tim, and Tim's been telling Stellick," he countered.

"You sound paranoid," she said, handing over one of the coffees. "It doesn't matter, you're on the ship...and I'm on the ship. This is great! It's what we wanted."

Sabre rolled his eyes and took the cup. "Yeah, I'm glad you're on the ship Lauren, but can you not see why it's a little demeaning that a fitness manager was chosen before the best pilot in three colonies and Earth combined?"

Lauren suddenly appeared hurt. "I'm sorry, you don't think my job is important?"

Sabre sipped his coffee and then walked over to Lauren, putting an arm around her. "That's not what I meant, I'm sorry."

She drank her coffee and refused to look up at him.

"Would you ask him for me?" he asked suddenly.

Lauren pulled away and turned to face him. "Ask who what?"

"Charlie," Sabre replied. "Would you ask him if he's said anything about me?"

Lauren's eyes narrowed, and she was clearly agitated. "No, I will not," she said. "You're acting like a child about this."

Sabre's jaw dropped, and he shook his head. "*I'm* the one acting childish? *You're* the one allowing your little brother to play a role in your love life."

He watched as the color in her cheeks turned a dark pink. There was a storm brewing behind her eyes that he was now very aware that he had caused. "I'm sorry," he blurted out as he immediately regretted what he had said.

Lauren blinked a couple of times and then slowly turned her head away from him. "We will talk later," she said, and then she stormed off without saying another word.

***

"This is everyone," Roger said as he handed over a file to General Harry Hightower.

The general opened it, took a seat behind his desk and scanned through the paperwork. It seemed that his eyes had finally healed fully and the need for eye drops no longer existed. His vision was the best it had been since he had been a young boy.

"Very good," Hightower said as he glanced over the final pilot's sheet. "Allow Colonel Madigan and myself to look over these this afternoon. I'm good with your decisions, but I need to make sure he has no objections. I'll let you know for sure in the morning."

"Thank you General," he replied with a salute. Roger was seated in one of the two cushy leather chairs on the opposite side of the desk. After Hightower saluted him back, he asked, "What's our progress on the ship?"

The question seemed to perk Hightower up. "Very well, actually," he said. "Captain Steiger and his crew have been a tremendous help. It seems that a lot of the original engine design was similar to what is on the Pinnacle, with a few major exceptions. Merrill tells me the engines should be ready to go by the end of the week. The coating on the hull has been completed already. If anything, we should finish ahead of schedule. It's all been very positive."

It was all good news and Roger was happy to hear it. It seemed that the general's mood had been much better the past few days, no doubt because of the reduced stress he'd been under.

"And how do you feel about the Kaloians *now*?" Roger asked.

General Hightower cocked his head to the side and allowed a sideways smile to part his lips. "I'd say I'm cautiously optimistic," he said. "As I said, Captain Steiger has been very helpful. He's gotten his hands dirty and has been involved in the manual work. I finally got comfortable enough to sign off on allowing him a temporary living quarters on the lunar colony. Everyone I've spoken to about him have had nothing but good things to say about the man."

Roger smiled. "I'm glad to hear that sir."

"Yeah, me too," Hightower replied. "I hope you understood my position and the reason why I had to be the most skeptical person on Titan when the Pinnacle first arrived."

Roger chuckled. "Yeah, I do, but I think Colonel Madigan may have had you beat on that."

Hightower nodded slightly. "Yes, Merrill is very opinionated, but make no mistake, he has no problem telling me when I'm wrong."

This surprised Roger. "Really?"

"Sure," the general said. "I put more trust in Merrill Madigan than any other man I've ever served with. I know that there are never hidden agendas. What you see is what you get with him. It's hard to find that in people these days."

"I can't disagree with that," Roger admitted. "The colonel and I are not always on the best of terms, but I certainly respect him."

"And he respects you," Hightower said, pointing toward Roger's chest.

Roger's smile remained but he said nothing. His relationship with Madigan had been very rocky and he wasn't sure if he believed the man respected him or not.

"We've had Tim Reed involved in the work on the SC Titan also," Hightower continued. "I had a conversation with him yesterday and he seems to have a very good understanding on the changes that have been made to get the Titan's engines to lightspeed. In fact, he understands it so well that he believes we can transfer the same technology over to our fighters—at least eventually."

"Wow, a Comet fighter at lightspeed?" Roger said, seemingly thinking aloud. "That's amazing although I could never see us using that during a dogfight."

Hightower shook his head. "No, of course not," he said dismissively. "But now that it seems our footprint on the expanse of space is widening significantly, travelling great distances in a relatively short amount of time will be an eventual necessity to our species survival."

"So, what are the odds of us actually helping the Kaloians if we get over there and find out that everything Captain Steiger has told us is the truth?" Roger asked.

"I'd say the odds are much better than they were three weeks ago," Hightower replied. "President Callahan seems to be really impressed with them and of course President Hiro is pleased with anyone that helps get the Titan built."

"Yeah, I sort of got the feeling that the Titan is a passion project of his when I saw all the pictures of his involvement in the file you gave me," Roger said.

"It should be," Hightower said as he leaned back in his chair. "He helped design it."

Roger sat up straight in his chair. "Excuse me?" he asked, wearing a look of shock on his face.

"Now you didn't hear that from me," the general said sternly. "That's top-secret information and Hiro is terrified that if the public really found out how much he was involved, they'd politicize it and turn it into a controversy."

Roger stared at him, confused. "Why would it be a controversy?" he asked. "Is he making money off the project?"

"Some," Hightower said. "But not nearly as much as people would think. I think the biggest issue would be how some of the general public would respond to the world's government using tax dollars to build a star ship in secret."

"Well I think they'd have a valid reason to be concerned," Roger said.

"I do too," Hightower agreed. "Which is why this new discovery of life outside our own solar system could not have come at a better time for President Hiro. It justifies his entire reasoning for the project and the need for such a ship."

"He wanted us to go looking for alien life," Roger said as he began to fully understand.

Hightower nodded. "Yes, he strongly believed that we needed to find alien life before it found us first. He felt that if we had the opportunity to observe other life forms maybe we would be able to prepare for a possible attack in the future." The general paused and shifted in his chair. It squeaked in protest. "I guess what he never expected was that someone out there was already watching us."

"We were lucky that the aliens that have been watching us were not only friendly, but human," Roger said.

"Do you believe that?" Hightower asked.

"Believe what?"

"That they're human."

Roger shrugged. "Sir, you've seen the same reports I've seen. The medical team that examined Captain Steiger documented that his anatomy is almost exactly the same as ours."

Hightower held up a finger. "That's right," he said. "They said *almost*."

"Their muscle mass is different than ours, but they chalked that up to all the time they've spent in space," Roger countered. "The only other difference is with their cardiovascular system and it's very slight. The makeup of their internal organs—including their brain—is identical to our own."

Hightower smiled and seemed to be enjoying the conversation. "Any slight or minor difference is still a difference, Roger," he said.

"Well, I think it's enough to classify them as humans," he replied. "Same as us."

"It seems ironic to me that though they seem to be more intelligent than us, we are physically stronger," the general said thoughtfully.

"Again, they think it's because—"

"I know, I know," Hightower replied. "Their time in space..."

Roger nodded. "I'm willing to wager that if we met other Kaloians that have kept their feet on the ground that their muscle mass would be more comparable to ours."

Hightower laughed. "But *comparable* is still not the same, Roger," he said.

Roger sighed and cleared his throat. "Only because I'm assuming the gravity on Kalo may be different from what we're used to on Earth. That would obviously have an effect on it."

Suddenly there was a knock on the door.

"Come in," Hightower barked.

The door swung open and Colonel Madigan walked in. When he noticed Roger, he paused and looked back to the general. "Am I interrupting anything, Harry?"

"Of course not, Merrill, come in," he replied, gesturing for him to take the other seat. "What have you got?"

"I'm afraid I've got some unfortunate news," he said as he took a seat.

"Go on," Hightower said.

"Well, it seems one of our men, and a member of Steiger's crew got into a scuffle today while working on the Titan," he said.

The general looked away disgusted while Roger shook his head.

"That's just great," Roger grumbled. "Was anyone hurt?"

The colonel nodded slowly and said, "Yeah, the Kaloian's nose was bloodied."

Hightower shook his head and rubbed at the stubble on his chin. "Well, if one of our men is going to be that stupid, at least he got the upper hand in doing so."

Madigan looked at him and seemed momentarily confused. "No," he said. "You don't understand, Harry. Our guy suffered a spinal injury."

The news made both Hightower and Roger sit up straight in their chairs. "What?" the general asked, and suddenly his mood darkened. "How did that happen?"

"Well," the colonel said. "He was thrown against the wall inside the launching bay on board the Titan."

Roger shook his head as if he were trying to wake from a dream. "How is that possible?" he asked. "All of the Kaloian's appear frail and not nearly strong enough to inflict that kind of damage."

"Well that's the strangest part of all," Madigan said, and he took a deep breath as he seemed to ponder his next words. Roger and Hightower eyed him anxiously. "First, I think it's important to point out that there was only one witness, but it was another Kaloian that strictly refutes what our man is telling us happened."

"And what is our man telling us happened?" Hightower asked.

"He says he was thrown against the wall, but he was never touched. He says the Kaloian seemed to somehow do it with his mind."

Roger slowly slumped back into his chair and looked around to see the general staring at him intently.

"I told you," he said. "Not human."

CHAPTER 11

Since the altercation had taken place on the Lunar Colony, most of the investigation was performed there under the guidance of General Porter Buchanon. General Hightower did his best to stay out of it, but was ultimately pulled in by Buchanon. Two days after the incident, a teleconference was set up between Captain Steiger and Hightower.

"Good day, General Hightower," Malcolm said cheerfully as his face appeared on the large conference room monitor.

"Good day to you as well," Hightower replied. He was flanked at the table by Colonel Madigan and Roger Stellick. "I trust all is still on track with the Titan?"

Malcolm smiled and nodded. "It is, I'm happy to report we are ready to go. We will return to Saturn's orbit with the Pinnacle this evening to get started on gateway."

"Very good," Hightower replied. He paused a moment and drummed his fingers on the table. "General Steiger, we need to discuss the incident that left one of our men with a severe spinal injury."

Malcolm leaned back in his chair and looked over to his right. The camera that had been focused on him zoomed out slightly to reveal that General Porter Buchanon was seated next to him.

"Our investigation has been completed, Harry," General Buchanon said. "From what we've gathered, our man initiated the fight...and I'm happy to report that the doctor treating him says he'll make a full recovery."

"Well that's good to hear, Porter," Hightower replied. "What exactly initiated it?"

Malcolm again looked to General Buchanon.

"We're still trying to piece that part of it together. It seems that there were some derogatory things that were said about the Kaloian by our man. The witness to the incident said that the Kaloian tried to diffuse the situation peacefully but things escalated. A war of words began and moments later things got physical."

"And it ended with our man getting the worst of it," Hightower said, cutting him off.

General Buchanon nodded.

"General Hightower," Malcolm said. "If I may, I want you to know that I'm taking the incident very seriously and there will be consequences for my crewman's actions. General Buchanon has assured me that he is taking a similar stance with the injured Earthling."

Hightower shot a disapproving glance over toward Buchanon.

"Our man has a spinal injury," he said. "I think that he's suffered the most from this altercation and his consequences should be minimal."

General Buchanon shifted uneasily in his chair. "Harry, I assure you that he'll be treated fairly and in accordance with S.A.M.A. regulations."

Roger watched as the muscles in Hightower's face tightened. He seemed to be choosing his next words carefully. He slowly turned his attention back to Malcolm.

"General Steiger, how do you respond to our man's report that your Kaloian crewman lifted him through the air and slammed him against the wall?" he asked.

Malcolm's eyes drifted downward and he slowly shook his head. His mouth became a straight line. When he looked back up, he said, "General Hightower, just ask me the question."

Hightower crossed his arms but remained tightlipped. Roger noticed that the colonel's body language was more of the same.

"Do your people have some sort of special ability?" Roger blurted out.

Hightower snapped his head around to look at him but refrained from speaking.

Malcolm eyed Roger and his expression softened. "Commander Stellick, I've read the statement from your injured crewman and I must say that I found it somewhat appalling that you all would even take it seriously. If you're all suggesting that we have telekinesis…well, that just couldn't be further from the truth."

Roger took a deep breath through his nose and ran a hand over his balding head. "Captain Steiger, the man that was involved in this…scuffle. I've read his file. He's a six-year S.A.M.A. veteran and has never been in any trouble of any kind. In fact, he is known to be a stickler for doing things by the book."

"So, what are you suggesting?" Malcolm snapped. "Are you suggesting that I am lying?"

"No one is suggesting that," General Hightower cut in. "We're just trying to figure out why one of our cleanest men would make up something like that."

Malcolm seemed to roll his eyes and turned his head slightly away from the camera, as if he were completely giving up on the conversation.

"Harry," General Buchanon said. "For what it's worth, I don't think the Kaloians possess any sort of abilities that are any different from Earthlings."

"We don't," Malcom said, still looking away from the camera.

There was a long awkward silence before Hightower finally said, "Alright then. Let's move past this. Captain Steiger, you deal with your crewman and we'll deal with ours."

"There is nothing I'd love more than to move past this, general," Malcolm said, sounding exasperated.

"Well let's start by discussing the upcoming expedition," Hightower replied, and his tone turned much warmer. "We have our crew ready and it sounds as if our ship is ready. Once the gate is constructed, we'll be ready to move into the Ara Constellation to investigate the happenings in your world. Please understand that we're going to observe only and will not be prepared to engage in any sort of war that your planet may be involved in."

"Yes, we've been through this and I understand," Malcolm said. "Once you see what is going on, you'll understand the need for planet Earth to get involved in this war. It's only a matter of time before it reaches your own solar system."

"The plan is for us to spend no more than forty-eight Earth hours," Hightower added. "That should be enough time for us to gather all the intelligence needed for the leaders of Earth to make an educated decision."

"Very well," Malcolm said, and he sounded satisfied.

"Harry, I'm going to personally bring the SC Titan over to you along with some of the crewmen you and your team have selected from Earth. It's also my understanding that there are a few pilots from the Mars colony we need to pick up along the way."

"That's correct," Hightower replied. "The files on every individual that will be a part of this expedition have been sent to your online dossier. If you have any questions—and if you have any input you'd like to add, please don't hesitate to reach out to myself, Colonel Madigan, or Commander Stellick. I want to personally thank you for your assistance in getting the SC Titan ready for interstellar travel."

"It was a pleasure to do so," General Buchanon replied. "See you tomorrow."

Hightower saluted and immediately the feed was cut, and the screen went black.

"I don't like this," Colonel Madigan said curtly. He raked his fingers through his reddish-gray hair grabbed a cup of coffee that had been sitting in front of him on the table. He took a long gulp and then sat the cup down hard enough to cause some of the dark liquid to slosh out.

General Hightower took a drink from his own coffee cup. "Something seems off," he said, seemingly agreeing with the colonel. "What do you think, Roger? Do you still trust Captain Steiger?"

Roger took a moment to replay the entire conversation through his head. Finally, he said, "I still believe him about his home world being in trouble if that's what you mean."

Colonel Madigan smirked and shook his head. "We're not talking about that right now, Stellick," he grumbled. "What about that business about the telekinesis?"

Rogers eyes widened as he thought about it. "I admit that it seems odd that a six-year veteran that's been on the straight and narrow all that time would suddenly get into an altercation with an alien and then make up a story about getting thrown through the air without being touched."

"So, who do you believe?" Hightower asked. "That is the question."

"I think it's important to note that General Buchanon doesn't believe they have any sort of special abilities," Roger said. "He's been involved with working alongside them for many days now."

General Hightower took another sip from his coffee and then put his cup down as hard as Madigan had done minutes earlier. "Stellick, I'm asking you what *you* believe."

Roger sighed and slumped back in his chair. "I don't know sir...I just don't know."

***

General Porter Buchanon and the new crew of the SC Titan were stunned and amazed at how flawlessly the ship had travelled from the moon to Mars. What had once been a year long voyage had miraculously turned into less than five minutes. It was an eerie feeling as the general stood on the bridge and watched in awe as the red planet quickly came into view ahead of them. Travelling at light speed had been something only possible in science fiction a month ago, and now...

"This is incredible," Buchanon said as the Titan entered Mars' orbit.

Lieutenant Hayden Carter walked up next to him to take in the breathtaking view. Carter had been chosen by Hightower to accompany Malcolm and the crew of the Pinnacle to the Lunar base. Hightower wanted someone close to him involved in the project...someone he could trust.

"It's a shame you're not able to go with us, sir," Hayden said.

Buchanon looked around at the young lieutenant. The general was nearing retirement and up until this particular moment, he'd been looking forward to it. "I've got a lot of fishing to do," he said, not letting on that there was a tinge of jealousy rising in him. "It's up to men like you Lieutenant Carter. Your generation is going to take space travel to the next level and beyond. I'm excited for you."

Once in orbit, the SC Titan's engines were shut off and it glided around the planet like a giant space station. General Buchanon ordered Hayden to meet with every officer on the ship to go over all the telemetry gathered from the Titan's maiden voyage. General Steiger's engineers had provided a manual for them to reference and provided instructions on how to make adjustments so that their travels would remain as swift and as safe as possible.

General Buchanon boarded one of the ship's two shuttles and piloted the small vessel himself toward the Mars colony's receiving hangar. Once safely inside, he exited the vehicle and was greeted by the deck chief and the general on duty, Mark Stroth.

"Welcome, Porter," General Stroth said.

Mark Stroth was the youngest of the colony generals at fifty-two years of age, but he looked even younger than that. His hair was thick and brown and there was hardly a wrinkle on his boyish face. He was a fitness buff, and his physique showed it.

"Thank you, Mark," Buchanon said, shaking his hand. He then handed over a file folder. "I trust you've got these fine folks ready to depart within the hour?"

Stroth nodded. "They're all in the mess hall getting a final meal here." He glanced at his watch. "Wasn't really expecting you for another half hour."

"My apologies," Buchanon replied. "We arrived a little sooner than I'd anticipated."

Stroth looked toward the sky wistfully, beyond the dome. He seemed to be straining to see any hint of the SC Titan orbiting above. "So how did she fly?" he asked with boyish curiosity.

"Mark, I'm certain one day you'll get your opportunity, and when you do, you better jump on it," Buchanon said. "Our universe just got a whole lot smaller."

General Stroth patted his older counterpart on the back and then led him away to the mess hall.

"Any input you can give me on these pilots I'm picking up?" Buchanon asked as they walked.

A smile appeared on Stroth's face and he seemed to be trying his best to fight it. "Well, two of them, Howard Scofield, and Tobias Bancroft, are sharp as a tack. They've both got hundreds of hours in space and I'd put them up against any other Comet pilot in the entire S.A.M.A. fleet."

"And the other three?" Buchanon asked, suddenly intrigued.

"Two of 'em are good, but I wouldn't call them elite," Stroth continued. "At least not on the same level as Scofield and Bancroft." Suddenly the younger general paused and Buchanon stopped with him. "And then there's Merissa Voight," he said, and he shook his head. "Her call sign is Banshee, and let me tell you, she earns it."

"What do you mean?" Buchanon asked, his brow raised with interest.

"I mean she's a hell of a pilot, but a handful to deal with. I've had to give her more non-judicial punishments than anyone on this base. She seems to have a real problem with authority. Truthfully, I'm surprised she was chosen for this expedition."

"Commander Roger Stellick handpicked every pilot," Buchanon said. "His choices must've been based on experience and ability. What kind of T.A.P. score did she get?" he asked as an afterthought.

Stroth chuckled. "Porter, you'll never believe me."

The two men began walking again. "Go ahead and try me," Buchanon said.

Stroth responded by thumbing through the file until he found Merissa Voight's information. He passed the document over to General Buchanon. "See for yourself."

The older general scanned over the document until he finally found the line that revealed Voight's Tactical Acceptance and Placement exam score. His jaw dropped.

"Well this explains why she was chosen," he said, looking over at Stroth with surprise.

"Yeah, she's smart as a whip. Out of a possible 350 points, she scored a 348. I don't know if that's a record or not, but I'm betting it is. She could've gone into any division she chose but seemed dead set on being a Comet pilot."

"That's incredible...hell, I thought I did great when I made a 299," Buchanon said.

"296 here," Stroth chimed in, raising his hand. "Banshee could easily be a captain herself one day if she'd just get her attitude in check."

"I can't wait to meet her," General Buchanon said as they approached the double doors that led into the mess hall.

At that moment the doors swung open and a small woman charged through them, her nose bloodied. She'd had a buzzcut and there was little hair to speak of on her head but what was there was brown. General Buchanon estimated the woman was in her mid-twenties and stood at around five feet, three inches tall. Her pink lips were plump—though he couldn't tell if they were swollen or naturally that way.

"Looks like you just got your chance, Porter," Stroth said as he stopped and crossed his arms.

As soon as Banshee spotted the two generals in front of her, she immediately paused and snapped a salute. They responded in kind, and then Stroth said, "Everything alright Ms. Voight?"

She opened her mouth to speak, but before she got the chance to say anything the doors behind her again burst open and an angry man stormed out. Buchanon immediately recognized the rage in his eyes and then noticed that his lip was bleeding.

"You stupid tramp!" he screamed as he spat blood. "If you ever…"

His words trailed off as he caught sight of the two generals standing in front of her. He too snapped to attention.

"What the hell is going on here?" Stroth asked. His friendly demeanor had all but vanished.

Both of them remained tight-lipped. Buchanon resisted the urge to intervene as he didn't want to disrespect General Stroth's position over them.

Stroth stepped forward and looked Banshee in the eyes. "What's going on Merissa?"

Her jaw was clenched tightly, and her eyes darted away from his. "Nothing sir…it's nothing," she said.

Buchanon noted that there was not a hint of fear in her tone. She remained confident despite the angry hulking man behind her.

Stroth stared at her a long moment before finally stepping around her and up to the soldier with the busted lip. "What is going on?" he growled.

The man's Adam's apple bobbed as he swallowed. "N-nothing sir," he stammered.

Stroth shook his head and then looked back to Buchanon. The older general allowed a slight hint of a smile and shrugged. He then looked back at the large man in front of him. "Private, get your ass to the barracks now. Your superior officer will be with you shortly."

The man saluted and immediately jogged away without saying another word. Stroth then sighed and made his way back in front of Banshee. "Lieutenant, did you punch Private Smith in the mouth?"

Banshee cleared her throat and then wiped the blood away from her nose with the back of her shirt sleeve. "Yessir," she muttered, her voice steady.

Stroth clenched his jaw and shook his head, clearly disgusted. "Do you want to tell me what happened?"

"I'd rather not, sir," Banshee replied.

Stroth inhaled deeply, his shoulders rising when he did so. He then pinched the bridge of his nose and closed his eyes. It seemed to Buchanon that he'd had a lot of discussions similar to the one he was having now. "Merissa, if it were not for the fact that you're about to get off this rock, I'd throw you in the brig until you decide that you'd like to talk about what happened."

Banshee kept her head held high and stared straight ahead. "Sir, he refused to tell you what happened too," she countered.

"And he will be dealt with by his superior officer," Stroth barked back. "You outrank him, Merissa. You outrank a lot of the soldiers based here. When are you going to start acting like it?"

"I have no excuse for my actions, sir," Banshee replied.

Buchanon noticed for the first time her eyes seemed to drift over to where he was standing.

"Get out of here, lieutenant," Stroth growled. "I want you to leave on that shuttle with General Buchanon and I hope the next time I see you that you've grown up a little."

Banshee bit her lip and nodded slowly.

"You're dismissed," he said, and she trudged away in the direction of the hangar without another word.

General Buchanon crossed his arms and watched her leave. "You say she's a handful, huh?" he asked, glancing over at General Stroth.

The younger man cracked his knuckles and shifted his feet as if he were trying to ease the tension that had quickly washed over his body. "You just saw the tip of the iceberg," he grumbled.

CHAPTER 12

"Commander Stellick, sir," Jake said meekly as he peeked his head in the door.

Roger had been in his office for over three hours going over the files on every crew member that was to join the expedition aboard the SC Titan. He really was not in the mood for company, but he also knew that he was in desperate need of a break. As he turned his vision away from the small print on the documents he was reviewing, he pulled his reading glasses off and squinted to see who was at the door.

"Ah, it's P.F.C. Crosby, right?" he asked, as he put the papers aside.

Jake smiled a toothy grin. He was pleased that Roger remembered him. "Yessir," he replied. "May I come in?"

Roger pushed back from his desk and leaned back in his chair. He gestured for the young man to come in and have a seat. He noticed that Jake had a file folder of his own tucked under his arm. "What can I do for you Crosby?" he asked, eyeing the folder.

Jake came in and cleared his throat as he sat down. He appeared quite nervous and fidgeted with the folder. "I, uh...I brought the paperwork you requested," he stammered.

Roger's brow tightened, and he turned his head slightly, confused. "Paperwork?" he asked. "What paperwork?"

Jake again cleared his throat and shifted in his chair as if he were sitting on a cushion of thorns. "You...you, ah...you asked me to fill out another application for the pilot training program...and you asked for my T.A.P. scores," he said nervously.

Roger nodded as he suddenly remembered. "Yes, Jake, I'm sorry, I completely forgot," he said apologetically. "That's been over a month ago, why are you just now getting this to me?" he asked as he held a hand out to receive the file folder.

Jake handed it over. "I know, I just knew that you had a lot going on with the preparations for the mission," he said. "I didn't want to bother you. Is it too late?"

Roger put his reading glasses on again and began looking over the application. Everything looked in order and it was evident that Jake had filled out multiple applications before. He then moved on to the T.A.P. scores. "No, of course it's not too late," he said as he scanned over the paper. "I see why you're having an issue getting accepted."

"Yessir," Jake said anxiously. "Please tell me what you see."

Roger placed the documents back into the folder and closed it. "It's your social skills, they're very low. You're classified as an introvert and almost every pilot that gets accepted into the program are outgoing extroverts."

Jake lowered his head slightly, looking defeated. "I see," he said softly. "So, you're saying I'm not a good candidate."

Roger pulled his glasses off again and tossed them on the desk. "No, you're not a good candidate Jake," he said.

"Okay," Jake said, and he reached for the folder. "I appreciate you looking at it, sir, really, I do."

Roger pulled the folder out of his reach. "I said you're not a good candidate, Jake, but that doesn't mean you just give up."

Jake slowly moved his eyes from the folder and up to Roger's. "What are you saying?"

"I'm saying that though your scores aren't helping you, they're still within the minimums required to enter the program. The problem you're having right now is that you simply don't have anyone to vouch for you."

Jake squinted his hazel eyes as he tried to understand. "Yessir?"

Roger shook his head and chuckled in amusement. "Jake, are you sure this is what you want? The program you're trying to get into, it's…"

"It's what I want sir," Jake cut in. "It's all I've ever wanted."

Roger nodded and looked down at his desk seemingly deep in thought. "Alright," he said after a minute. "Jake, I'll pull some strings and I'm gonna get you in, but I want 110 percent out of you. If you don't give 110 percent, I'll see to it that you're pulled right back out."

Jake's jaw dropped, and he stared at Roger in a moment of stunned silence.

Roger raised an eyebrow. "Are you alright, Jake?"

Jake nodded slowly. "Yessir, I think so…I just don't know what to say."

"How about, *thank you*," Roger said as he offered his hand.

Jake smiled. "Thank you, sir, I will not let you down."

"You better not," Roger said. "Now I'm scheduled to leave late tomorrow night, but I'll make a call to get you on the enrollment list for the next time the program opens. It's usually in late March."

"Thank you so much sir, I won't let you down," Jake said again.

"You're repeating yourself now, Jake," Roger said with a chuckle. "Get out of here, get to studying, and work on your social skills."

"I'll do that, sir," he said jovially.

Jake got up and nearly stumbled over the chair as he made his exit. Roger shook his head and stifled a laugh as he returned his attention to the files in front of him.

***

Merissa Voight, or Banshee as she preferred to be called, had taken it upon herself to explore every nook and cranny of the SC Titan during the 80-minute voyage from Mars to Titan. As soon as she boarded, a good-looking lieutenant named Hayden Carter greeted her and gave her a slip of paper with her cabin number and other pertinent information. Carter appeared to be the same age as her and he had piercing blue eyes that made her heart flutter when she looked at him. He was the type of man that she could not help but feel an attraction to, but she was also very cognizant of the fact that he probably had zero interest in her.

Banshee had a terrible upbringing, and it was one she spoke very little about. Both of her parents had died in a plane crash when she was only four and she'd spent the next twelve years of her life under the care of her aunt and uncle in rural Minnesota, U.S.A. Unbeknownst to her aunt, and practically everyone else that she'd ever met, her uncle spent almost all those twelve years sexually abusing her at least twice a week. Banshee never dared to tell anyone. It wasn't because she felt that her uncle would hurt her—although he might have. It had more to do with the fact that she was incredibly embarrassed. She could not help but feel that it was somehow her fault.

As she blossomed into a young woman, she ran away from the home she'd shared with her aunt and abusive uncle which led her to a brief period in her life that included drugs and crime. She'd found refuge with other troubled teenagers, all of whom seemed to be running from something in their past. Banshee probably would've died in a cold dark alley one night if she hadn't been arrested for shoplifting in a department store a few weeks before her eighteenth birthday. The judge took pity on her, and since she was a minor, she received leniency that some of her friends did not. She was essentially given an ultimatum. She could return to her aunt and uncle's custody where the abuse she'd endured would most likely begin again; or, she could speak to a military recruiter where she could potentially find real purpose in her life, and more importantly, a skill that would carry her forward. She considered her options, and as she'd come to hate everything about her world, she thought the logical direction would be the Space and Aeronautics Military Alliance.

The recruiter she was assigned to was young and attractive. In fact, as she thought about it, he reminded her a lot of Lieutenant Hayden Carter. Against her better judgement, she had a sexual relationship with the man that eventually ended badly. Strange as it was, it was only then that her real self-hatred began. Not with her uncle, as one might assume, but it was that recruiter. She'd felt dirty and ugly with her uncle, but the recruiter, someone that was supposed to be helping her move forward in life, had somehow managed to make her feel even more worthless than she already did. Fortunately, the pairing with him was not all bad, as he did give her the T.A.P. test where she went on to make the second highest score ever recorded. Her score being as high as it was, suddenly there was a lot of attention on her from officers much higher than the recruiter and she soon found herself far away from him and all the other terrors she'd experienced in her home state of Minnesota.

S.A.M.A. officials made it clear that any opportunity was on the table and that they'd have her full support no matter which direction she chose. Again, fueled by a deep longing to get as far away from the terrors she'd experienced on Earth, Banshee chose to enter the pilot training program where she could learn to fly Comet fighters. Soaring at high speeds through the vacuum of space appealed greatly to her and she thrived in the program, finishing at the top of her class. Banshee had been a pilot for almost five years now and should've moved through the ranks quickly, but unfortunately, she discovered that no matter how far away from Earth she got, she could not outrun the ghosts of her past. Someway somehow, they always seemed to catch up to her and bring out her worst.

Lieutenant Carter had given her a security badge that doubled as the key to her cabin. When she arrived at the metal door, she hovered the badge over a blinking red light. The metal door slid open, revealing an apartment that measured approximately 20 feet by 20 feet. In the corner there was a tiny bathroom, but no shower. It had been explained to her that there was a bathhouse assigned for all women on her level, but a private toilet would be available in her cabin. There was a small kitchenette against the right wall with a small refrigerator, sink, and stove top. On the back wall, there was a table that she noticed could be folded back into the wall and in front of that there was a sofa and television. On the left wall she found her bed and noticed that it too could be folded away into the wall, though she couldn't think of a good reason to do it. The cabin, she had to admit, was better than what she had expected, but what she was most proud of was the small round window that allowed her a view of space.

Once she dropped her bag on the bed, she walked over to the couch and turned it so that she would be facing that window. What was going on out there may have seemed bland and boring to many of her other shipmates, but to her, it was beautiful, mysterious and far more interesting than anything going on in her television. Banshee returned to her bed and unzipped the large military gray bag. Inside, she pulled a picture frame out and stared at it wistfully for a moment. As she looked at the man and woman in the photo she began to feel moisture welling up in her eyes. It was the only picture she'd managed to get of her mother and father. Her biggest regret was that they were not there to see what she was now achieving. She hoped they would be proud of her.

After unpacking, Banshee decided to explore the rest of the ship. Her cabin, along with all the other Comet pilots, was found on the fourth deck. The sleeping quarters made up only a small portion of the fourth deck and she assumed that it must have been reserved for pilots only. Being on the fourth deck was fine with her because as she explored the rest of it, she found that it was the place to be for rest, relaxation and fun. The cafeteria was found there, along with a bar, gym, and recreation room that included a small movie theatre. She paid particular attention to the bar because she was certain she'd be spending a great deal of time there. She was pleasantly surprised to find it was already operational with a bartender there to greet her.

"Welcome aboard ma'am," the man said in a southern accent. "I'm Rayford Compton, but just call me Ray." Ray was tall, thin, and had a healthy mop of dark hair on top of his head. He wore horn-rimmed black glasses with eyes to match and appeared to be in his late thirties or early forties.

She noticed him eyeing her head to toe. He seemed to be particularly interested in her buzzed haircut. "Alright, nice to meet you Ray," Banshee said. "I'm Merissa Voight, but I prefer you just call me Banshee."

Ray nodded and smiled. "Banshee, eh? You must be one of the pilots we picked up on Mars."

She nodded. "You guessed it Ray. Are you a S.A.M.A. member?"

"Oh, yes ma'am," he said with a serious nod. "It's my understanding everyone that will be on this ship is. I'm mostly an old pencil pusher, but I ran the bar on the Lunar colony. Must've done a pretty good job since they offered me this gig," he added with a chuckle.

"And this is all you'll be doing here?" Banshee asked, sounding surprised.

Ray grabbed a glass and began polishing it. "Well, not completely," he said. "You'll probably see me helping up in the cafeteria from time to time." He paused as he noticed her watching him polish the glass. "Hey, can I get you anything?" he asked proudly.

Banshee smiled. "No thanks, Ray," she said. "But I promise you I'll be back."

Ray nodded and looked on as she walked away.

After she explored the rest of the fourth deck, she decided to move up to the third deck instead of down to the fifth deck. She already knew the fifth deckwas comprised of nothing but engineering and figured she could check it out another time. Once on the third deck, she found that it was mostly comprised of more cabins, but what she really wanted to check out was the two launching bays that flanked either side. To her dismay, she found the doors locked and no one around to grant her access.

Once she arrived on the second deck, she found that it was where she could go to seek treatment if she became ill or injured. There were a couple of laboratories along with officer quarters, and the captain's cabin. She also noticed a sign painted on the wall with an arrow pointing toward the armory, but decided it probably would not be best for someone to find her mulling around there. She'd encountered a lot of crew members on the fourth deck, and almost just as many on the second. The only difference was that on the second deck, she truly felt out of place. The stares that many of the crew members, from both men and women, that were working the second deck gave her made her feel even more out of place. She quickly retreated to the elevator where she ascended to the top deck.

She was surprised to find that when the doors opened, she was on the bridge. There were numerous officers and other crew members scurrying about and all seemed to have some sort of task. In the center of the chaos, and staring out the large viewing port on the front of the bridge, she found General Porter Buchanon. He seemed oblivious to the organized chaos around him.

"Ms. Voight?" a man's voice called out from her right.

Banshee peered over to find Lieutenant Carter approaching. "Everything alright? Do you need anything?"

She licked her lips and nodded. "Yes, I'm fine," she assured him. "Just exploring the ship."

"Did you find your cabin alright?" Carter asked. He seemed genuine to her, something she wasn't used to.

"I did, thank you," Banshee replied. "It's very nice."

Carter smiled widely. "Yeah, I think they're quite nice myself." He paused a moment and surveyed their surroundings. "It's not always going to be like this," he said, leaning closer to where only she could hear him.

She nodded as they watched people continue to scurry around them in all directions. "I was wondering," she admitted.

"No, it's just like this because this is basically her maiden voyage. We are gathering all kinds of data so that General Harry Hightower will be able to review it with the engineers once we arrive at Titan."

"I see," she said. "Well, if there is anything I can do to help…"

"Have you met General Buchanon?" Carter asked, interrupting her.

She smiled again and nodded. "I have," she said.

"Well good," he replied. "Come on, let's go speak to him."

"Oh no," she said quickly, and took a step back toward the elevator. "I don't want to bother him."

Truthfully, she was embarrassed about how she'd met him back on Mars.

"Come on," Carter urged. "Look at him, does he look busy?"

The general continued to stand almost as still as a statue, just staring out into space.

"No, but he seems to be deep in thought, and I…"

"General Buchanon," Carter called out abruptly.

The general slowly turned away from the large window and looked over his shoulder to see Hayden Carter and Merissa Voight standing just outside the elevator entrance. He half smiled and then strolled over to them.

"Good to see you again Ms. Voight," Buchanon said and he held out a hand.

She shook it. "Good to see you too, sir," she replied.

"She's been exploring the ship," Carter said. "She seems impressed."

General Buchanon chuckled. "Aren't we all? Ms. Voight, would you mind walking with me? There's another part of this deck I'd like to show you since you're exploring."

Banshee really wanted to retreat to her cabin, but she did not want to seem disrespectful. "Sure, I'd be glad to," she lied.

"Good," he said, and he then turned to Lieutenant Carter. "Hayden, the bridge is yours until I return."

Carter nodded, and his expression turned serious. "Take your time sir," he said, and he then trotted over to the captain's chair and took a seat.

General Buchanon placed a gentle hand on Banshee's back and ushered her toward a corridor that circled around to a hallway behind the elevator. Neither of them spoke a word until they reached a metal door with the words **OBSERVATION DECK** scrawled on it in black paint. The general punched in a code on the electric keypad beside the door and it immediately slid open. Banshee strolled in and looked around her in amazement. On either side of the room, there were large, full-view windows that gave an outstanding view of the space on either side of the ship. In the ceiling, there was a large circular window so that a view from above was accessible too. As the ship hummed along at light speed, it was not possible to make out much of anything outside...there appeared to be nothing but blackness, and a slight hue of blue that enveloped the ship.

"We can't see anything," Banshee said as she looked outside.

"Not at light speed, no we can't," the general confirmed. "Once we slow for our approach on Titan, everything will then come into focus. We're travelling at a high enough rate of speed that we can't see anything out there, and no one out there would be able to see us."

"I know," Banshee said as she continued to peer out the window. "As we speak, we're nothing more than pure energy hurtling through the cosmos. We're doing what was considered impossible a short time ago."

"And how do you feel about that?" General Buchanon asked.

"I don't know," she replied. "But it feels wrong."

"It only feels wrong because for so long we did not believe it to be possible," he countered. "Now that we're here and it's happening...well, it's hard to process."

The two of them stood and continued to stare into the blackness for a few minutes without saying anything. Banshee began to sense that the general had not called her into the observation deck just to show her a whole lot of nothing out the windows.

"General, is there something you need to talk to me about?" she asked.

He smiled and nodded slightly. "There is actually," he said, turning to look at her. He motioned for her to have a seat on the large white couch in the middle of the room. She did so, and he took a seat beside her. "You remind me of someone Merissa."

She was unsure how to respond. "I do?"

"Yes," he said, and he didn't look over at her, he just kept staring into space. "My daughter is who you remind me of. The two of you look a lot alike...well, except for the..."

"My hair," she replied. "I know. I'm probably the only woman you've ever met that cuts all her hair off."

"Well, I'd be lying if I said you weren't," Buchanon confessed. "Having said that, there is nothing wrong with it. I think it suits you."

Now she was becoming *really* confused. "Thank you...I guess," she muttered.

"Look, I'm not trying to make you uncomfortable, and I apologize if I am," he replied, finally glancing over at her. "But I read over your file and I want to make sure you realize how incredibly gifted you are."

Banshee scoffed at him and shook her head. "I'm not more gifted than any other pilot here," she said.

"Forget about being a pilot a moment," he said gruffly. "Your T.A.P. scores are incredible, and I feel that you have more potential than you realize."

"Yes sir," she said, trying her best to sound polite. "I've heard all that before."

"Yes, I figured you have," Buchanon shot back.

"Then why are you telling me all this?" she asked, this time unable to hide the fact that the conversation was making her agitated.

The old general sighed, cleared his throat and patted both his palms on his legs. He seemed slightly nervous. "I'm telling you this because I'm trying to understand why you're wasting your life away," he said very matter-of-factly.

Banshee narrowed her eyes and glared at him. "What do you mean, sir?" she said, with emphasis on the word *sir*.

"You seem to be hiding from something, though I can't figure out what," he replied to her. "You've got a tough exterior, sure. But any woman your size that is going around picking fights with men is clearly trying to cover up something."

"Sir, I didn't start that fight," she said with anger.

General Buchanon smiled and held his hands up defensively. "Okay, I believe you," he said, and he genuinely did. "But from what I hear, it's been a common occurrence. Not only are you better than all these men you're picking fights with, by now you should not even be spending significant time with them. You should have a cushy desk job..."

"I don't want a desk job," she snapped. "I like what I'm doing now."

"I'm glad you do," the general answered. "And if that's the case then by all means, keep doing it!"

"Then what are we talking about sir?"

The general scratched at the back of his ear and shook his head. He seemed to be getting aggravated too. "Merissa, I just feel like you haven't been told that you're valuable enough so far in your life," he said. "I didn't know you until today, and I still don't, but you have all the signs of a young woman with a lot of emotional scars." He turned toward her again and poked a finger at her. "Don't you dare sell yourself short. You're meant for greatness and don't ever let anyone tell you different."

"Is that all sir?" she asked.

Buchanon stared at her and could see moisture building around her eyes. "That is all," he said. "I probably won't see you again, but I want you to know that if there is anything I can do to help you, I'm only a phone call away."

"Thank you, sir," Banshee said as she stood and turned for the door.

Once in the hallway, she frantically wiped the tears from her eyes.

CHAPTER 13

"This is just a minor setback," Colonel Madigan said, doing his best to calm General Hightower.

"I want that young man sent for a court-martial as soon as possible," Hightower growled. "How dare he refuse to participate on the very day that we are supposed to leave?"

"I agree, Harry," Madigan said. "And he will be punished to the full extent of the law, but you know as well as I do that if the man doesn't want to be a part of this mission, we don't want him aboard."

"It's communications for God's sake," Hightower groaned. "All he has to do is sit in a chair and be a glorified switchboard operator."

Madigan laughed. "You dug deep for that one...switch board operators haven't been around for well over a century."

Hightower looked at his soon to be executive officer and smiled. "Who have we got to replace him?"

"This short notice? The best man I know on Titan for the job would be Jake Crosby," Madigan said. "He's still pretty green, and he has aspirations of being a pilot. Stellick is trying to get him in the pilot training program...but that will have to wait. He's reliable and knows how to follow orders."

"Alright," the general said, knowing full well he was out of options. "Go get him and bring him up to speed. Tell him he's got only a few hours to handle his affairs before he needs to board."

Colonel Madigan saluted him and spun on his heel to go about the task.

"And I want that coward placed in the brig until we return. I'll personally see that he's delivered back to Earth to get the justice he deserves," Hightower called after him.

The deck crew chief Tim Reed suddenly appeared in the doorway, followed by a trio of armed S.A.M.A. soldiers. "Sir the shuttle is ready for us to board the Titan," he reported.

"I was planning on boarding with the executive officer Merrill Madigan," Hightower replied. "He's got some unexpected business to attend to before we depart."

Tim swallowed and looked at the soldiers beside him. "Sir, if I may, Commander Roger Stellick, Dr. Phoebe Holtz and some of the other officers are already on the shuttle waiting for you. It's my understanding General Porter Buchanon is still at the helm of the Titan and did not want to leave until your arrival."

Hightower leaned back in his chair and cracked his knuckles. "Oh, alright," he huffed. "Let Merrill know what's going on, please."

"Will do, sir," Tim replied with a salute.

When he arrived at the shuttle, Hightower found Roger waiting for him at the door. "Good to see you general...or I guess it's captain now," he said with a smile.

"You look like a giddy schoolboy, Stellick," Hightower said as he grabbed the handle next to the door to pull himself up. "Keep in mind, the seriousness of this mission."

"Oh, it's still in mind," he replied. "But if you're telling me you're not a little excited, with all due respect, I'd have to say you're a liar, sir."

Hightower stopped abruptly and glared at Roger. "Commander, have you taken leave of your senses?" he asked. He wasn't smiling, and his brow slanted downward.

Roger sighed and held up an apologetic hand. "My apologies, sir," he said.

Hightower snorted, shook his head, and turned back around to find a seat. As he did so, a wide smile cracked his face.

The shuttle pilot had the vehicle out of the hangar and into the yellow Titan sky in a matter of minutes. As they ascended higher, the sky quickly faded from yellow, to orange, and finally to black as the tiny shuttle broke free of the moon's atmosphere.

"See that?" Roger asked, as he leaned over Dr. Phoebe Holtz, who was seated at the window.

She peered outside and could see that he was pointing to a rather large circular object hovering in space. It was much larger than she'd originally anticipated, and the metal plates had strange engravings that she could not identify. It definitely looked alien in origin. "That's the gate I presume?" she replied.

"Yep, that's it."

Some of the other officers, including Captain Hightower, leaned toward the nearest window to see it for themselves.

"Do you know what the Kaloians call it?" Roger asked.

Phoebe shook her head, her dark curls moving with her.

"They call it a H.T.G.," he explained. "It stands for Hyperspace Teleportation Gate."

"And that thing is going to take us to another gate fourteen light years away from here?" Phoebe asked.

"That's the plan," Captain Hightower said.

As the shuttle drew near the SC Titan, all the passengers turned their attention to the majestic ship hovering next to the slightly larger Kaloian ship, Pinnacle.

"Wow, that thing is big," Phoebe said as her green eyes widened. "How many people will it hold again?"

"500," Hightower answered. "And 40 Comet fighters."

"What sort of weaponry?" she asked, clearly interested.

Roger pointed toward the lower, angled portion of the ship where the vertical engines jutted out. "Look closely between the horizontal engines that are below the launch bay, and the vertical engines below it. On the side you'll see a large turret."

"Oh, I see it," she said excitedly.

"That's the laser cannon," Roger explained. "There is another one on the other side that mirrors that one."

"There are other smaller turrets found along the outside of the hull above the launching bays," Captain Hightower added. "And we're carrying nuclear warheads too."

Phoebe shot a surprised glance over at him. Her sparkling green eyes suddenly showed concern.

"Just in case," Hightower said with a reassuring smile.

She then looked to Roger, but found no comfort from him. He stared out the window at the massive laser turret but appeared to be suddenly just as concerned as she was. When he saw her watching him, he forced a smile. "It'll all be alright," he said.

She smiled back, but inside a knot was forming in her stomach.

The shuttle made a smooth transition into the launching bay and finally came to a rest inside a depressurization chamber. Once the chamber was filled with oxygen, a bright green light illuminated in the ceiling and the crew could safely exit the vehicle. Captain Hightower then led them, single file, to a smaller door that opened into the hangar area. As soon as they were inside, cheers erupted for Captain Hightower. It seemed that every member of the ship's crew was there waiting for the commander's arrival.

Even General Porter Buchanon was there with a microphone in his hand. He began walking toward Hightower and pulled the microphone to his mouth.

"It's about time, Harry," he said rather playfully. He then paused and looked around the room as he waited for the applause to wind down. "Now I know not everyone is on board just yet," he said as the crowd finally quieted. "And that's a shame because folks, it's not often that you get to see General—excuse me, *Captain* Harry Hightower blush."

Hightower smiled and shook his head as he was indeed blushing at the reception.

The crew began laughing and clapping yet again. Buchanon raised his arms to regain some quiet. "In all seriousness, I want each one of you to know two things. First that every single one of you is important to this maiden voyage. Each of you has an important role and I trust that you will all perform that role to the best of your ability. And secondly, you've got a damn fine Captain at the helm that will be behind you one hundred percent!"

More applause erupted, and Roger swelled with pride as he took in the powerful moment. Harry Hightower had been a lot like a second father to him, and he was happy to see him getting the accolades he deserved.

"Now if his ego hasn't made his head too big," Buchanon continued, "I think it's time that your new captain says a few words." He walked over and handed the microphone over to Hightower.

The captain held the microphone tightly and waited for the next round of applause to die down. When it finally did, he said, "Crew of the SC Titan, I don't think I've ever seen a finer group of men and women gathered together in one place in my entire military career. As General Buchanon just stated, every single one of you is vitally important to the success of this maiden voyage. You were all handpicked for this because you are all seen as the best of the best. Some may say that title will be hard to live up to, but I say it's just another day at the office for us!"

More cheers and applause erupted.

"Now I want to make it very clear that I have one job on this ship and one job only," Hightower continued. "And that job is to see to it that each and every one of you is kept safe and sound and that we all return home exactly the way we left," he said. "To do that, I may make decisions and say things that will make you not like me very much…"

A bit of laughter began…some sounded nervous.

"But if that's what it takes to make our mission successful and to keep you safe, then it's a sacrifice I'm willing to make," he added. "I want to thank you all for the warm reception and know that my door is always open to any man or woman that has a need or concern on this ship. I expect the best from each of you…and that starts right now."

He then handed the microphone back to General Buchanon and the crew began to scatter away back to their work stations.

"Nice job, Harry," Buchanon said as he switched the microphone off.

"Thanks for all your help, Porter," Hightower said as he shook his old friend's hand.

"It was my pleasure," he replied. "The keys are all yours. I'll wait here and hold the fort down at Titan until you get back."

"I trust everything went well?"

General Buchanon took a deep breath through his nose and placed his hands on his hips. "Honestly, I couldn't have asked for it to go any smoother," he said. "When you're travelling at light speed, the ship doesn't even feel like it's moving. There was not a single mechanical problem that I'm aware of."

"That's amazing," Hightower said in disbelief.

"Yeah, I thought so too," Buchanon agreed. "Those Kaloians must really know their stuff when it comes to mechanics and engineering."

Hightower nodded, but did not reply. Buchanon watched as his younger counterpart craned his head around in all directions to observe the interior of the Titan.

"Why don't you head on to the bridge," Buchanon urged. "That's where you belong."

Captain Hightower smiled, revealing his coffee stained teeth. "Thank you again for all your help, Porter," he said. "Take care of Titan for me until I get back."

"It'll be running better than it was when you left," he replied with a chuckle. Buchanon turned to head toward the shuttle, then paused as if something had suddenly occurred to him. Hightower looked at him curiously.

"Harry," he said. "You've got a young lady on your crew; her name is Merissa Voight."

Hightower raised his chin and his eyes narrowed as he thought about the name. "Ah, yes," he said after thinking a moment. "She's a Comet pilot...smart as a whip."

Buchanon nodded. "Yes, that's her," he replied. "Do me a favor and go easy on her, will you?"

Hightower again stared at his old friend curiously. "Why? Is there a problem with her I need to know about?"

Buchanon chuckled and shook his head. "No, no problem," he said quickly, then he paused as if he were second guessing the statement. "I mean, she's a little rough around the edges, but I believe she's destined for greatness."

Hightower crossed his arms and shifted his feet. "Do you care to elaborate?" he asked, raising an eyebrow.

Again, Buchanon chuckled slightly, and seemed rattled. "She...she reminds me of my daughter," he said sadly.

"Oh," Hightower replied softly. He was very much aware that the general's daughter had died a little over a year earlier. It was well-known that her death had been difficult on him and had taken a toll.

There was a long and awkward silence before Buchanon finally moved toward the shuttle. Before boarding, he stopped and glanced over his shoulder at Hightower.

"Good luck, commander," he said.

***

Charlie West stood in the portside hangar of the SC Titan. It was eerily quiet and as he stared over the sleek and shiny Comet fighters, he wondered if he was just experiencing the calm before the storm. When he'd first learned of the expedition and the existence of the ship in which he was currently standing, he figured his odds of getting chosen as one of the crew were good. With Tim Reed getting assigned as the deck crew chief, he was almost certain that he'd be brought along. For Charlie, it didn't matter how he got chosen, just as long as he was chosen.

And then he learned that Lauren had applied for, and won, the opportunity to run the ship's fitness center. Charlie felt strongly that the mission would be dangerous, so he was less than thrilled when he discovered his sister would be joining him on the interstellar voyage.

"It's amazing isn't it."

Charlie immediately recognized the voice talking to him. He spun on his heel to face Sabre.

"Yeah, it is," he said.

Sabre casually drew near him, finally stopping beside him. "What an amazing moment in human history that we're getting to experience," he said, crossing his arms. He took a deep breath as if he were testing the air.

"Can I help you with anything?" Charlie asked, purposely looking away from him.

Sabre looked over at him. He was practically staring at the back of his head. "Yeah, actually you can."

Charlie closed his eyes as he immediately realized what Sabre was going to say next. "You're not good enough for Lauren," he quipped. "I'm sorry, but if you think you're going to change my mind you're mistaken."

Sabre sighed and rocked on his heels. "Charlie, why aren't you willing to give me a chance?"

There was a sadness in his voice and Charlie noticed it. "My sister is a grown woman and if she chooses to date you then there's nothing I can do about it," he replied. "But, she doesn't know you the way that I do. I've heard your frequent proclamations of one-night stands and sexual conquests and forgive me for doing everything in my power to spare my sister from a little heartache."

Sabre looked down at his crossed arms and shook his head slowly. "I told you that it's different with Lauren," he said, almost pleadingly. He looked over to find that Charlie was still looking away from him. Sabre walked around in front of him, so he had no choice but to see him. "I love her, Charlie," he said, locking eyes with him.

"I'm not her father," Charlie groaned. "You don't have to tell me or ask for my permission."

Sabre laughed, clearly out of frustration. "You keep insinuating that Lauren can make her own decision where it concerns me, but you know damn well that's not the case. She wants you to be on board with her decision."

For the first time Charlie finally looked at him. "And I told you I can't give you the answer that you want."

Sabre could feel his blood pressure rising and he resisted the urge to say something he knew he'd regret. Instead he closed his eyes and slowly counted to five. It was an old trick he'd been taught during his pilot training. As he did so, he could feel himself calming down. "What can I do to change your mind?"

It was Charlie's turn to sigh. He rubbed at his temples to fend off an oncoming headache. "Look," he said, sounding almost apologetic. "I'll stop short of saying that swaying my opinion is impossible."

Sabre stared at him, his blue eyes brightening a bit. "Just tell me what I need to do," he said with renewed vigor.

Charlie shrugged. "I don't know yet," he said. "You'll have to earn my trust and that takes time. If it happens, I'll let you know. In the meantime, you and I both have a job to do up here."

Sabre looked away, not exactly pleased with Charlie's answer, but also cognizant of the fact that it appeared he'd made a slight amount of progress. "I'll prove it to you," he said.

"I hope so," Charlie replied. "Whatever happens, you always keep in mind that I'm the guy turning the wrenches on your Comet."

CHAPTER 14

Commander Roger Stellick was known for his cool and calm demeanor. No matter how bad things got, or how much pressure he was under, Stellick always found a way to stay calm. Although it seemed like ages ago now, Stellick could remember the instructors from his pilot training days commenting that he must have ice water in his veins because nothing rattled him. It eventually led to him getting the call sign "Ice" and anyone that served under him knew the meaning.

As Roger stood just behind Captain Hightower and Colonel Madigan on the bridge of the SC Titan, for the first time in as long as he could remember, he didn't feel calm. His pulse raced, though he could not figure out why. His palms were sweating, and he fought off a tremble.

Am I getting sick?

As he contemplated that possibility, he shook the thoughts from his head.

No, you're not getting sick, he told himself. *You don't have time to get sick...*

"Are you alright?" Lieutenant Hayden Carter said as he walked up beside him.

Roger smiled and shook his head. "Yeah, I'm good," he said with a look of assurance. "Is it warm in here to you?"

Lieutenant Carter cocked his head slightly and looked up as if he were trying to visualize the air around them. "No, it's comfortable to me," he replied.

Roger nodded, but said nothing. He silently cursed himself for showing weakness at such an inopportune time.

Captain Harry Hightower strolled over to the communications section of the bridge and placed a firm grip on Jake Crosby's shoulder. The young man had headphones over his ears and appeared to be reading a manual explaining the communications system on board the Titan. When he felt Hightower's grip, he pulled one side of the headphones away from his right ear.

"Are you alright, Private?" the captain asked.

Crosby glanced over his shoulder and smiled. "Yessir," he said, sweat glistening on his forehead.

Roger was pleased to see he wasn't the only person sweating.

"I want you to know I appreciate your adaptability and willingness to serve on such short notice," Hightower told him.

"It's my honor, sir," Jake replied.

"Very good," Hightower said with a slight nod, then he turned all business. "Contact Captain Steiger at once."

Jake replied, returned the headphones over both ears, and immediately pulled a microphone close to his mouth and pushed a button. Seconds later, he turned to Hightower and said, "I have Captain Steiger on the comm," he said.

"Put him through on the bridge speaker," Hightower commanded.

Jake turned a knob and then nodded at the commander.

"Captain Steiger," Hightower called out. "We're ready to enter the gate when you tell us it's safe to do so."

"Very good news," Malcolm replied, his voice boomed through the bridge speaker with a cheerful tone. "The Pinnacle will commence entry in approximately five minutes. If you find reason for us to delay entry, please let me know immediately. Otherwise, wait for the Pinnacle to completely enter the gate. After five minutes, the SC Titan may follow, but make sure you give us at least five minutes to get clear of the gate. We don't want to have a collision on the other side."

"Understood," Hightower replied. "Once you determine our position on the other side of the gate, we'll reconvene and discuss our next course."

"Very well, Commander," Malcolm replied. "We're about to activate the gate and prepare our entry. See you all on the other side."

Roger watched as a rare smile formed on Colonel Madigan's face. Lieutenant Hayden Carter also appeared to be slightly excited.

"See you on the other side," Hightower replied. "SC Titan, out."

The captain immediately turned to his officers. "I want every person on this ship at their stations. We must be prepared for every scenario," he barked.

Madigan nodded. "We will be ready," he said.

Captain Hightower then turned his attention directly to Roger. "I want every pilot in their flight gear and ready to go up at a moment's notice. Make sure you communicate with the Deck Chief as well."

"I'll get them ready," Roger replied with a quick salute. "Sir, is there anything we should know about?"

Hightower glared at him with annoyance. "If there is a problem, you'll know about it when I tell you, commander," he snapped. "Get your people ready...you only have ten minutes."

Roger nodded and made his way to Jake Crosby, so he could make a quick call to Tim Reed.

As the crew of the SC Titan scrambled to their stations, Captain Malcolm Steiger gave the order to initiate the power up of the

Hyperspace Teleportation Gate. In mere seconds after the commands were sent over remotely, the vast circular structure began to slowly move around like a giant Ferris wheel.

Captain Hightower watched in awe as the strange symbols and engravings on the structure began to light up a brilliant white. The spinning motion of the gate became faster and faster until finally the symbols showed so brightly they were impossible to stare at. Hightower and the other officers on the bridge instead turned their attention toward the interior of the gate. They watched as the distant stars on the other side of the gate became distorted and they were soon turning in a circular motion in the same direction as the gate itself. As the gate continued to gather even more speed, the framed area within the gate spun so fast that it resembled a whirlpool.

"This is amazing," Lieutenant Carter muttered softly. "I can't believe this is actually happening."

Captain Hightower looked over at his young lieutenant and watched him for a moment as the bright white lights danced over his face like flashbulbs from a hundred cameras. By the time he looked back toward the gate, the whirlpool motion within it had begun to funnel inward.

"Captain Hightower," Jake Crosby called out. "Captain Steiger just informed us that they are proceeding into the gate."

Hightower nodded and watched anxiously as the Pinnacle began to slowly drift toward the gate. As the massive ship drew closer and closer, it soon became apparent that the gate was actually pulling the Pinnacle toward it. Though the ship remained steady and true to her course, the motion of the gate coupled with the Pinnacle's lazy drift toward its interior, reminded the captain of a tiny boat being pulled into a bathtub drain.

The nose of the large ship entered the gate and suddenly the pace of its entry picked up significantly. Captain Hightower continued to look on as long as he could but was soon forced to shield his eyes with his hand. As the ship continued into the "funnel", the surrounding space around it began to light up a brilliant white just as the symbols and engravings on the gate had. Everyone on the bridge of the Titan looked away as the light intensified, and then suddenly…it was over. The Pinnacle was gone.

For a long moment, there was silence. Everyone on the bridge looked at each other as if they needed confirmation from their counterparts that what they'd just seen had indeed occurred.

"Did they make it?" Lieutenant Carter asked, breaking the silence.

Captain Hightower narrowed his eyes and his mouth became a straight line. He appeared to be deep in thought.

"Of course they made it," Colonel Madigan said gruffly. He looked around at the rest of the surrounding crew members. "What were you all expecting?" he asked, raising his eyebrows.

Hightower stared at Madigan a moment and then walked over to Jake Crosby. He reached for a phone on the wall and said, "Patch me through to Commander Stellick."

Jake nodded and punched a couple of buttons.

"Is your team all set?" Hightower asked. There was a brief pause, and then, "Very good. Stay near the horn in case I need you again."

Hightower then handed the phone back to Jake and then casually strolled over to the helm where a short-haired woman wearing dark rimmed glasses was seated at the controls. The woman was Rowena Walker, and she'd been hand-picked by East President Akagi Hiro three years earlier to be the eventual helmsman of the SC Titan. Rowena was a technology genius and had ultimately been the winner of a vigorous search involving hundreds of candidates to find a suitable person to pilot the Star Cruiser. Once Rowena was chosen, she'd spent the past two and a half years training to take on a job no one had ever done before. The SC Titan was a one of a kind ship and her successes and failures would be used to train future Star Cruiser pilots. She'd spent countless hours in a simulator to make sure that the failures were kept to a minimum.

"Walker, commence to enter the gate in three more minutes," Hightower commanded.

"Yes, commander," Rowena replied in monotone. She placed her hands on both levers in front of her and slowly maneuvered the ship in position to enter the gate cleanly.

Captain Hightower glanced at the large digital clock on the wall over the elevator entrance and then back to the crew that surrounded him. "I want everyone seated when we enter the gate. We don't know if the ride will be smooth or turbulent and we cannot afford for anyone to get injured in such a careless manner." He paused and looked over at Jake Crosby. "Private, I want you to tell the entire crew of this ship that they are to be seated until I tell them otherwise and that it's a direct order."

Jake nodded and turned back to his station. He pulled the microphone close to his mouth and after turning a knob he began to relay the commander's orders. Hightower again glanced at the clock. "Okay, we've got ninety seconds. Ms. Walker, take us toward the gate," he told her with a nod.

Rowena responded by slowly pushing both levers on the console forward as every member of the crew took a seat at once. The Star

Cruiser was so large that the sensation of movement was very slight, yet it was still noticeable.

Captain Hightower kept his eyes focused intently on the spinning gate ahead of them and the strange funnel-like tunnel that beckoned them inside it. He felt his heart rate increasing as the Star Cruiser drew closer, but his face remained emotionless. The ship began to pick up speed as Hightower looked at the array of gauges on the monitor beside him, he was very much aware that Rowena Walker had done nothing to increase the Titan's pace. It was the gate…it was pulling them toward it like some sort of giant tractor beam Hightower remembered seeing in science fiction movies as a child.

Rowena looked nervous and peered back at the captain over her shoulder. "Speed is increasing but I'm—"

"I know, Ms. Walker," Hightower replied, cutting her off. "Just hold the ship steady and everything will be fine." He smiled at her, but it was forced. The captain then looked to his right to find Colonel Madigan staring at him. He could see the concern on his executive officer's face, and as much as he wanted to reassure his old friend, he did not dare say a word. It was important that everyone on the bridge remained calm, and if he and Madigan at least *appeared* that way, all would be well.

The captain turned his head to look forward out of the large curved viewport that encompassed the entire front wall of the bridge. The nose of the Titan had now penetrated the gate and continued to pick up speed. Suddenly, the exterior of the ship became enveloped in bright light. It was as if a million flashbulbs had gone off at once in all directions. Every crew member on the bridge immediately had to close their eyes for fear of going blind. There was a loud humming noise that seemed to drown out every other sound on board the Titan. The piercing hum, coupled with the blinding light, made everyone on the bridge feel eerily alone. The strange sensation did nothing to calm the commander's heart rate and he felt himself becoming lightheaded. Just as he felt that he was about to faint, suddenly, the white light vanished, and the humming ceased.

For a long moment, everyone on the bridge was almost completely silent. Captain Hightower rubbed at his eyes, desperately trying to regain his vision. Everywhere he looked, all he seemed to be able to see was giant white splotches that hindered his eye sight. For a panicked moment, he wondered if he'd in fact gone blind. The irony of the situation wasn't lost on him as he considered the possibility that the cybernetic implants he'd just adjusted to may now be useless.

"Is everyone alright?" he heard a voice call out.

It was Colonel Madigan.

"I—I think so," Hayden Carter replied.

Hightower heard someone groaning. It sounded like Rowena Walker.

"Private Crosby, I want you to check in with every station of the ship…make sure everyone is alright," Hightower commanded.

Jake nodded as he too rubbed at his eyes. Hightower looked in his direction and was pleased to find that his vision was slowly returning. He could see Jake reaching for the switches in front of him, headphones already planted firmly over his ears. Suddenly, the young man paused and slowly turned toward the commander.

"What's wrong?" Hightower asked, seeing unmistakable concern etched on Jake's face.

Jake squinted as he looked at the commander. He was obviously still trying to regain his eye sight. "It's Captain Steiger, sir," Jake replied.

"He wants to speak to me?" Hightower asked.

Jake shook his head. "No sir. He uh—he wants you to look out the window ahead of us."

Hightower swallowed as his mouth suddenly felt dry. He turned back toward the massive viewport and again rubbed his eyes to make sure he'd be able to see.

"Oh my god," Madigan said softly. He sounded nervous.

Captain Hightower removed his hands from over his eyes and was pleased to find that the white splotches he'd been seeing had finally disappeared. As he blinked his eyes, an unexpected sight came into focus in front of him.

CHAPTER 15

The familiar Kaloian ship, the Pinnacle, was the first object that Captain Hightower's eyes seemed to focus on. A mere second later, the ominous shapes of the other four ships then began to materialize and Hightower heard an unmistakable gasp in the room.

"What's this about?" Madigan asked in a voice just above a whisper.

The Pinnacle was flanked by two ships on either side. The other four ships had the similar almond shape as the Pinnacle, but were half its size. There appeared to be a large asteroid field spread across the empty space behind the Kaloian ships, serving as a fitting backdrop for such an unsettling moment. All five ships were facing toward the Titan and each of them had some sort of port holes that had opened on the front of each. There was a sinister blue light flickering beyond the open ports, and it reminded Hightower of a propane flame. In his mind there was only one thing those holes could be, and it now seemed that each one of them was on the verge of spewing some sort of hellacious death upon them.

"Get Steiger on the comm," Hightower said through clenched teeth, his eyes fixated on the sinister ships in front of him.

Jake Crosby immediately went to work and within seconds the familiar voice of Captain Steiger boomed loudly through the bridge again. Only this time, the kindness seemed to have left his voice.

"Captain Harry Hightower, this is Captain Malcolm Steiger of the Supreme Regency's Galactic Navy, you are ordered to surrender at once or risk being destroyed in a matter of seconds," he said. His tone was not exactly evil, but very matter-of-fact and business like.

Hightower's jaw tightened even more, and he turned his head slightly, his neck popping as he did so. Colonel Madigan and other officers on the bridge slowly turned to look at him. There was a long and awkward silence. Finally, he said through clenched teeth, "Steiger, what is the meaning of this?"

"Commander, I think that it's quite obvious," Malcolm replied smugly. "You surrender right this minute, or you all die. It's your choice."

Hightower sighed and shook his head. "You tell me why," he demanded.

There was a moment of silence, and then, "Commander, I do not owe you an explanation, please understand that. Having said that, I do want you to know that as I've gotten to know you these previous weeks,

I've discovered a genuine fondness for you and some of the other humans…especially Commander Stellick," he said. "In case you haven't figured it out yet, everything you've been told has been a ruse. The arm of the Supreme Regency reaches far and wide to every corner of the galaxy, and no planet is exempt from the rule of Potentate Romulus Shade."

"Romulus Shade?" Hightower spat, disgusted. "I don't know who Romulus Shade is, but I know who Malcolm Steiger is—or at least I thought I did! How dare you betray us?"

"This is not a betrayal," Steiger quipped, and his tone for the first time flirted with anger. "This is an opportunity that I'm giving you for survival. We will take Earth with or without your help. The gateway to do so is now in place, and our ship's cannons have currently taken aim at Earth's mightiest vessel…the SC Titan."

Suddenly, it began to make sense to the Commander. His shoulders slumped as he forced himself to relax into his chair. It was now quite clear that there were no alien creatures threatening the extinction of the Kaloian race. Instead, it now seemed that the threat to the entire galaxy was at the hands of the Kaloians. The entire story was a clever trick to not only earn Earth's trust, but to also lure its most powerful spacecraft into a trap. With the Titan out of the way, and a gateway providing easy access, there would be little to stop the invasion and eventual takeover of Earth.

"I'm growing impatient, Captain Hightower," Steiger said. "I need an answer."

Hightower suddenly rose from his chair and marched over to Jake Crosby. He leaned over and whispered into the young man's ear. Jake nodded and immediately flipped a switch in front of him.

"Okay, we can hear him, but he can't hear us," Jake said confidently.

Hightower nodded, and turned to Colonel Madigan. "Alright, we have to move fast, and we only have one chance at this. Merrill, I want you to command Stellick to get himself and every one of our pilots in the Comet fighters. They need to be ready to launch in a matter of minutes." The colonel saluted and immediately snatched up the receiver that would provide a direct line to the launch bay. He then barked the orders to Commander Stellick.

Next, Hightower looked to Rowena Walker. "Ms. Walker, on my command I want you to head straight for that asteroid field behind those ships," he said, pointing.

"You want me to fly straight toward the Kaloian ships sir?" she asked, unable to contain her worry.

"Yes, and make sure you fly over them. Their cannons look like they'll have a harder time reaching us if we fly above, than they would if we flew under them—and you'll have to move fast!"

"Yes sir," she replied, and Rowena moved her hands over the controls in front of her.

"Commander, I want an answer!" Malcolm's voice boomed suddenly.

Hightower made a gesture toward Jake and he in turn opened the microphone again. "Alright, Steiger," the captain said, doing his best to sound defeated. "We will surrender, but I beg of you to give me a few minutes to alert my crew. I don't want anything to happen that would endanger them...I need them to know what is happening."

He could hear Malcolm take a deep breath as he pondered the request. "How long do you need?" he asked.

"Ten minutes," Hightower replied.

There was a momentary pause, and then Malcom said, "I'll give you seven minutes."

"Thank you," the captain answered, and he then looked to Jake, raking a finger across his throat so he'd kill the microphone again. Jake complied, and Hightower immediately began shouting orders.

"Ms. Walker, use the forward scanning sensors to plot the best possible course through that asteroid field, and as soon as we're through keep it steady until every one of our fighters are back on board. Then, we switch to light speed. Is that understood?"

"Yes sir," she replied, her hands still firmly on the controls.

"When I give the command, there can be no hesitation," he said.

She waved a hand at him, but kept her eyes focused on the monitor in front of her as it plotted a course.

"Merrill, are we ready to go?" he asked, turning toward the Colonel.

Madigan gave a thumbs up as he held the receiver to his chest. "Every Comet is ready to go. Awaiting your order."

"Good," Hightower replied, and he stepped toward his old friend. "Tell them that as soon as I give the order, I want them to go destroy the gate."

Madigan stared at him wide-eyed, his mouth falling open. Hightower stared right back at him, stone-faced. Every crew member on the bridge had a look of surprise on their faces and there was an eerie silence. The colonel suddenly regained his composure and then returned the phone to his ear, so he could relay the instructions to Roger.

"But, how will we get back?" a voice called out. It was Jake Crosby.

"We'll worry about that later, do not question the captain's authority," Madigan snapped.

Captain Hightower glanced at his watch. Only two and a half minutes had gone by. He then looked around at Lieutenant Hayden Carter.

"Carter, get to the weapons console and ready the laser turrets. When we move toward the asteroid field, I want both cannons unleashing a firestorm on those alien bastards. Our fighters will need plenty of cover if they're going to get back."

Lieutenant Carter moved to the controls for the left turret and instructed the other assigned crew member to man the right one. "We will give them all we've got, sir," Carter replied with determination.

Hightower again peeked at his watch. He had another two minutes before he would be forced to show his hand. "Merrill, you're sure we're ready in the launch bay?"

Madigan nodded at him. "All forty fighters are ready. Stellick is awaiting orders in the cockpit as we speak."

The captain nodded. "Tell him to be ready in another sixty seconds. I want them off the ship about thirty seconds before the seven minutes are up."

Madigan nodded again and relayed the message to Roger.

Hightower again glanced at his watch, anxiety welling up in him. The seconds ticked by when finally...

"Launch the fighters!" he roared furiously.

***

Commander Roger Stellick heard the command in his ear at the very moment the light on his console illuminated green. He immediately throttled up the engine of his fighter and zipped out of the starboard launch bay as if he'd been fired from a cannon. Once in space and clear of the Titan, he glanced at the radar screen in front of him to see that the other four members of his squad were tight on his tail, just as they'd been trained.

The 40 Comet fighters made up eight squads that comprised of five ships per squad. Each squad was assigned a code name along with an experienced squad leader. Once out of the Titan, the squad leader had complete control over his or her squad until they all returned to the ship. Stellick was in command of Alpha squad and their sole objective was to destroy the H.T.G. before the Kaloians would be able to use it to return to Earth. The remaining squads were instructed to scatter high and low and inflict as much damage as possible to the four ships that flanked either side of the Pinnacle. Captain Steiger's ship would receive its due attack courtesy of the SC Titan.

"Alright Alpha squad," Roger said, addressing his team for the first time since they'd left the safety of the Titan. "Our objective is very simple. We lock onto the gate and destroy it. Once that is done, we make a mad dash back to the Titan…is that understood?"

There were multiple responses, all indicating that they did indeed understand. "Cowboy, I want you watching our six while we get this done. Let us know if any enemy aircraft begin an approach."

"Roger that," Gentry "Cowboy" McNevin replied confidently.

While Cowboy slowed his Comet significantly, Roger and the other three fighters continued onward and reached the gate within mere seconds. He took aim on the right side of the gate, along with Blackout while Subzero and Wrench opened fire on the left side. As he squeezed the trigger, Roger found himself wondering if he'd ever see Earth again. As far as he and anyone else knew, this was their only way back home. As soon as the missiles made contact, the gate exploded in a brilliant burst of white light. Pieces of shattered metal jettisoned in all directions and resembled a glass plate breaking.

"That was easy enough," Roger said, sounding somewhat relieved. "Cowboy, how are we looking back there?"

"Nothing yet, sir," he replied. "The other squads are on the attack but—wait, enemy ships are launching fighters!"

"This changes nothing," Roger replied. "I want this entire squad back on the Titan right now!"

"They've launched just as many fighters as we've got sir," Cowboy added. "Maybe even more."

"Again, this changes nothing," Roger snapped. "That's thirty-five of our best pilots and they can handle it…we can't afford an unnecessary risk that would jeopardize losing all of our fighters. Get back on the ship immediately."

Roger's squad all replied with compliance, though he could clearly hear the disappointment in their voices. As much as he too wanted to join the fight, he'd been given very strict instruction by Colonel Madigan to destroy the gate and return immediately. As he led Alpha Squad back toward the starboard launch bay, he looked on as the enemy fighters began to engage the incoming Comets. The tiny spacecrafts were shaped like diamonds, but the points on either side of the "diamond" jutted sharply outward to form wings. Just as he re-entered the Titan, he began to see streaks of purple emitting from the enemy fighters. They were obviously equipped with laser weapons. Roger thought of the limited supply of missiles and cannon ammunition on board the Comet fighters.

He felt his heart sink as he realized that the odds were overwhelmingly not in their favor.

***

"Fighters have been launched, sir," Tago Mari barked proudly over the intercom.

Captain Malcolm Steiger made a tight fist and pounded the arm of his chair hard. He'd looked on in genuine shock as five of the Titan's fighters promptly destroyed the H.T.G. Potentate Shade would be furious when he learned of this failure and he knew there would be terrible consequences that he would have to face. The only thing he could do now was destroy the SC Titan along with every one of the Comet fighters. If he did so, hopefully it would soften the blow he'd sustain from Shade.

"I want every one of those fighters destroyed," Malcolm said through clenched teeth. "I want the Pinnacle's plasma cannons unleashed on the Titan at once."

"Sir, it appears that the Titan is moving toward us at a high rate of speed!" Tago Mari announced suddenly.

"Well what are we waiting for?" Malcolm growled. "FIRE!"

***

Merissa "Banshee" Voight had been named leader of Echo squad soon after she'd boarded the SC Titan. The assignment was a mixture of surprise and pride as it was the first time she'd been assigned a leadership role. The decision had been made quickly and she wondered if General Porter Buchanon had been involved in the decision. He'd taken a liking to her, and she didn't understand why. Although she herself felt inadequate for such a role, she accepted it proudly. Truthfully, she never dreamed that she'd be entering a combat scenario so soon. If she had, she'd have probably protested it. No sooner had the Titan entered the Ara Constellation, she and all the other pilots had been ordered to their respective fighters. Banshee embraced the moment as she never felt more at home than she did in the cockpit of a Comet. What did trouble her, however, was that now she felt very responsible for four other pilots in her squad—men that she had not even had an opportunity to get acquainted with.

The orders Echo squad were given were simple and to the point. She, along with Franklin "Bull" Fuller, Simon "Shadow" Richardson, August "Waldo" Johnson, and Steven "Hogie" Hunt, were directed to head straight for the two sinister looking port holes on the front of the Pinnacle and destroy them at all costs. As they made a beeline for the port holes that they believed to be cannons, Banshee noticed that Kaloian fighters swarmed out of the other ships flanking the Pinnacle. Without even counting, their numbers appeared to be greater than those of the Comets.

"What about those fighters?" Hogie shouted over the radio, a little more panicked sounding than he intended.

"Forget about them," Banshee replied. "The other squads will deal with them. We must take out those cannons or we will not have a ship to go back to."

"Roger that," Hogie replied, this time sounding composed.

"What about the cannons on those other ships?" Waldo asked.

Banshee had to force herself not to scream over the radio. She reminded herself that things had happened extremely fast and that only the squad leaders were given specific instructions on what was to be done. The other 32 pilots were left in the dark and would be understandably curious as to what the plan would be to ensure the safety of the Titan.

"The other squads have assignments regarding the other ship cannons," she answered firmly. "Our focus right now is to destroy the cannons on the Pinnacle. After we've done that, we'll join the fight until we receive orders to return to the Titan."

"Roger," Waldo replied. "We'll follow your lead sir."

Banshee swallowed and allowed herself a slight smile. "Bull and Simon, take the portside cannon. Waldo and Hogie, you guys take out the starboard. Use your missiles and then fill them full of lead just to be sure. Fire at will."

Echo squad launched their missiles in unison and they all reached their targets with precision. As the four fighters that flanked her on both sides unleashed a barrage of cannon fire to follow up the direct hits by the missiles, Banshee pulled back on the stick which in turn sent her Comet streaking in a slight upward trajectory. She had not used her missiles on the Pinnacle cannons, instead opting to save them for what she hoped would be the bridge of the ship. Banshee could not be sure since the Pinnacle was covered in a sleek metal skin that did an incredibly good job of camouflaging any viewport that would give an indication of the location of the ship's bridge. Instead, she was forced to take a guess—something she was almost certain she'd be reprimanded for later.

As her Comet skimmed close to the front of the Pinnacle's hull, Banshee released her missiles and they made direct contact, evidenced by the bright explosion and concussive vibration that reverberated through her cockpit. As she continued to climb, she keyed her mic and said, "Echo squad, I need you on my six at once."

She glanced down at her radar screen and could see the blue dots that represented her team chasing after her as instructed. "Did we take out the cannons?" she asked.

"Starboard cannons took a direct hit," Hogie called out in response.

"Same for the port side," Bull said.

"Alright," Banshee said, pleased. "Now we focus our attention on the fighters. We stay together, and we fight together. I want each of you to follow my lead—and communicate, but let's keep the chatter to a minimum. Understood?"

As Echo squad radioed their affirmations, Banshee again pulled the stick toward her. The stars against the backdrop of the vast blackness of space streaked by outside her canopy. Her Comet fighter did an inverted loop and then began a sharp dive straight toward the ensuing dogfight below. She saw streaks of purple bursts, along with streaks of orange cannon fire directly below. It quickly became apparent how advanced the weaponry was on the diamond-shaped Kaloian fighters.

Banshee smiled as she continued her dive toward the chaos, and Echo squad remained tight on her six. She'd been waiting her whole life for a moment like this.

CHAPTER 16

Captain Malcolm Steiger's order had come just seconds too late. The gunner for the Pinnacle responded to his captain's order to fire the cannons as soon as he'd heard the word pass Steiger's lips. Unfortunately, the plasma cannons did not respond.

"Something's wrong, sir," Tago Mari said with disgust.

He turned to Malcolm. His mouth had become a straight line, his brow furrowed. "Some of their fighters seem to have disabled our cannons," he added.

Malcolm glared at him with an icy stare. "Disabled or *destroyed*?" he snapped.

Tago Mari picked up a small microphone in front of him and barked instructions to the engineering department. As he did so, Malcolm stood and looked on through the viewport as the SC Titan continued streaking toward them in a downward trajectory.

"Lieutenant Eskar," Malcolm said, turning to his helmsman. "Prepare to pursue the Titan. We'll pursue them until we can either blast them out of the sky, or reinforcements arrive."

"Very well Captain," Makot Eskar replied.

Suddenly, there was a thunderous sound above them and the entire bridge rocked so hard that Malcolm fell hard to the ground. Tago Mari quickly appeared at his side and helped him to his feet as an alarm wailed loudly around them.

"What happened?" Malcolm asked. His forehead was bleeding and he had to close his right eye to keep the blood out of it.

"It seems one of their fighters just attacked the top of our ship," Tago replied. "We were lucky…it just missed the bridge."

"The enemy ship is firing on us!" Makot Eskar yelled. "It's going to—"

Eskar's words were cut off as the Pinnacle once again took a direct hit. This time, the blast seemed to have originated from the bottom of the ship and Malcolm knew immediately that it had come from the Titan's laser cannons.

So much for repairing our plasma cannons, he thought with disgust.

***

Christian "Sabre" Smith and Bravo squad made quick work of the cannons on their respective target, but not before the smaller Kaloian ship managed to get off a shot. Sabre rolled his Comet fighter and managed to avoid the glowing ball of blue plasma as it darted by. He immediately checked on the rest of his squad and was pleased to see that they too had managed to avoid disaster.

"Can anyone see if that shot hit anything friendly?" Sabre asked, as he instinctively looked over his shoulder in desperation to see for himself.

"It looks like it cleared all the other Comets and the Titan too," a female voice called out. It was Charity Price, call-sign Covergirl.

"Great!" Sabre replied. "Now let's go to work on these enemy fighters."

Due to the fact that, aside from Alpha squad, Hotel squad had no ship to target, they were immediately under serious duress from the attacking Kaloian fighters. Sabre noticed their squad leader, a nine-year S.A.M.A. veteran named Harlan "Howler" Wolfe, taking fire from a pursuing diamond fighter. His squad members were unable to assist him since they too were under fire.

"Hotel squad needs help," Sabre said. "Break off and let's get our guys out of trouble!"

No sooner had the words passed his lips, a bright flash of light illuminated Sabre's cockpit. The unfortunate source of the bright light came from an exploding Comet fighter. It was one of Hotel squad's, and it seemed that the Titan had suffered its first casualty.

"Oh my god," Morgan "Moose" Cross said with an unmistakable sadness.

"Who was it?" Covergirl shouted.

"Doesn't matter now!" Sabre quipped. "Let's make sure they don't get another one from Hotel squad...now shut up and fight!"

He guided his own fighter toward the relentless pursuing diamond fighter behind Howler. Sabre used his target guidance system to engage the pursing Kaloian fighter with ease. He squeezed the trigger on the stick in front of him and quickly disposed of the enemy ship. "Hell yeah!" he shouted, victoriously.

"I owe you one!" Howler said, after flipping over to Bravo squad's frequency.

"Did you take any hits?" Sabre asked.

"Yes, they've got plasma cannons," Howler replied. "One of their bolts glanced off my right wing...it's making my bird pull hard to the right...I've gotta constantly pull the stick toward the left to keep her straight."

"You should get back to the Titan," Sabre urged.

"No," Howler replied immediately, and there was a hint of anger in his tone. "They just took out Cyclops...and now we've got to make them pay."

The revelation that the doomed Comet pilot was Cooper Jenkins was a hard pill to swallow. Sabre was very much aware that Covergirl knew him well and had received her pilot training alongside him. He knew the news must have been tough for her to hear, but she somehow remained silent.

"I can't order you to do anything," Sabre said. "But I think you should head back," he urged.

"I'm going to switch back to my squad's frequency now...but I'm not heading back until I take one of these bastards out," he said with determination.

Sabre shook his head and considered switching over to Hotel squad's frequency to argue the matter further, but thought better of it. He had no right or authority to tell Howler what to do. The best he could do was stay with him and do what he could to keep him alive.

"Bravo squad," he said, addressing his team. "We are going to stick with the remaining members of Hotel squad until this is over."

"Roger that," Covergirl said, seemingly pleased with the orders.

She then applied a burst of thrust and pulled alongside another female pilot, Georgia Clarke. "I'm going to cover Peach," she said.

"I'm going to switch our frequency over to Hotel squad," Sabre said. "Let's communicate and make sure the rest of them get back to Titan alive."

He flipped a switch and proceeded to explain Bravo squad's intentions. Howler then extended his thanks and took off in pursuit of a nearby diamond fighter. Sabre was tight on his tail and looked on as his fellow squad leader fired his cannons and took out the enemy space craft with ease.

"That was too easy," Sabre said with amazement.

As soon as the words left his lips, a pair of purple plasma bolts flashed by his cockpit, narrowly missing the right wing. Unfortunately, Howler wasn't as lucky. Though the shot struck the rear of his Comet, the impact wasn't clean. It seemed to be another glancing blow much like the one that had damaged his wing. Sabre could only look on as the ion afterburner on Howler's engine began to flicker.

"I'm hit," he said, sounding remarkably calm.

"Yeah...get back to the Titan right now!" Sabre replied, unable to match his calmness.

"Alright," he said, defeated. "I'll limp back...look after my squad."

"I'm looking after you, first," Sabre protested. "Once you're safely on board, I'll get back in the fight."

"No!" Howler said, a little louder than he expected. "I'll make it back. Stay with the squads."

"This isn't up for debate," Sabre continued to argue.

Howler pounded his fist on the control panel next to him in frustration. He wanted to continue arguing, but he was fully aware that no one had ever won an argument with Christian Smith. He returned his attention back to the control stick and steered the injured craft toward the launch bay of the fleeing Titan. The large ship had swooped in low under the badly damaged Pinnacle and was making its way toward the asteroid field for cover.

Howler attempted to give his Comet more throttle since at his current pace, he'd never catch the ship. He felt the engine lurch and cough as it struggled to comply. It made a sickening grinding noise and seemed unable to accelerate.

"What's the problem?" Sabre asked as he noticed the damaged craft struggle to keep up.

"The engine...it's gone," Howler grumbled. "I told you, get back to the squad. I'll keep trying to catch up."

"Cut the engine," Sabre said, ignoring his plea.

"What? Why?" Howler asked.

"Just do it!"

As Howler flipped the switch that cut the power to his ion engine, he glanced upward and noticed one of the diamond-shaped Kaloian fighters bearing down over him.

"Sabre!" Howler shouted.

"I see it!"

Without another word, Sabre moved in on the rear of Howler's Comet. He pushed the blunt nose of his own craft hard into the exhaust cone of Howler's. Though the contact was much harder than he'd wanted it to be, once he'd planted the nose, Sabre then throttled up his own engine. The two Comets darted forward just as the diving diamond fighter fired off a couple of plasma bolts.

Howler was relieved, but didn't have an opportunity to reflect. He had no idea that Sabre was planning such a bold maneuver to get him caught up with the Titan and it took all the skill he could muster to keep his own ship steady and pointed the right direction.

"Just keep her straight," Sabre said as they closed in on the Titan. "When I get you close I'm going to pull back...you fire your engine and apply full thrust to get in that bay."

"Alright, just get back to the squads," Howler snapped back. "This was foolish, Christian."

Sabre smirked as he became satisfied that he'd gotten Howler close enough. "No need to thank me, Harlan," he said as he pulled away and then sped back toward the fight.

***

When Banshee entered the chaotic dogfight, she immediately engaged a diamond fighter she spotted pursuing a Foxtrot squad pilot, evidenced by the gold stripes on the crafts wings. She was unable to tell exactly who the pilot was, but whomever they were, their skill level was one of the best she'd ever seen. The pursuing Kaloian repeatedly fired plasma bolts at the Foxtrot Comet, and the skilled pilot continuously responded with numerous barrel rolls before finally making a Split S maneuver.

Banshee took this to mean that the Comet pilot noticed her approach and he or she was seemingly baiting the pursuing Kaloian into a trap by abruptly turning back into her direction. The Comet streaked by her and as the unsuspecting diamond fighter approached, Banshee pulled the trigger on the stick and unleashed a barrage of lead into the enemy craft. Both wings tore off the Kaloian ship at almost the same time and the disabled vehicle spiraled wildly downward toward the infinite blackness below it.

"Thanks!" the Foxtrot pilot said—he'd apparently flipped over to Echo frequency. "Who just saved my ass?"

"Merissa Voight," she answered.

"Banshee!" the pilot replied, obviously familiar with her. "I know all about you! I'm Nathan Carmichael."

"Moon Dog," Banshee replied as she pulled on the stick to re-enter the battle. "I've heard of you too," she quipped. "Let's kiss each other's ass later, right now we need to get back in the fight!"

"Roger that," Moon Dog replied, and rolled over to chase after her.

***

"I need a report!" Captain Hightower's voice thundered across the bridge.

"The Pinnacle seems incapacitated for the moment," Colonel Madigan replied. "It seems the two of the smaller ships are badly damaged, though the other two are still in reasonably good shape. All of them are currently unable to fire their weapons. It looks like your plan worked Harry," he added thoughtfully.

"Yeah, but I never dreamed they'd have this many fighters tucked away," the Captain replied somberly. "How many of ours have we lost?"

"Two," Madigan replied with a regretful sigh.

Hightower closed his eyes and nodded slowly. "Call our birds back...let's not add to that number." He then glanced over at Rowena Walker. Her forehead glistened from the illumination the numerous monitors and controls in front of her produced. She'd apparently been sweating profusely. "Are you alright, Rowena?"

She looked over at him, her mouth was a straight line and her brown eyes seemed darker than usual behind her glasses. "Yessir," she said nervously.

"Do you have a safe course charted through this asteroid field yet?" Hightower asked.

She nodded. "Awaiting your command sir," she said as she moved her hand toward the lightspeed control.

"Merrill, as soon as the last Comet is back on board, give the order directly to Rowena to engage lightspeed."

Madigan nodded and pulled the phone to his ear to call the launch bay.

***

Commander Roger Stellick and Alpha squad had been in the launch bay for a mere five minutes when he received the command to call the Comets back. He'd been given stern instructions to make sure every surviving fighter returned to the Titan before he reported to the bridge that all had been accounted for. As the fighters returned one by one, he checked the pilot names off on a checklist. He instructed Cowboy (Gentry McNevin) to do the same on another checklist to ensure that no one was missed. Regretfully, before the first fighter returned, he had already checked two names off in addition to those of his own squad when he became aware of the deaths of Cyclops (Cooper Jenkins) and Ruffles (Peyton Kelly).

Howler had somehow made it back onto the Titan, though Roger had a hard time understanding how he'd managed to do it. The right wing was almost completely torn loose, and the engine was barely sputtering when he came hard onto the metal landing deck. Shortly after he'd exited his Comet, the others began pouring in, many with significant damage. As Roger and Cowboy continued to check off names, Howler and Peach (Georgia Clarke) ran up to him. They both looked distraught. When Roger locked eyes with Howler's, the Hotel squad leader's eyes began to well up.

"Ben Foster won't be returning either," he muttered. "Peach just told me he was shot down too."

Roger put a firm hand on Howler's shoulder. "Get to the infirmary and let them look you over," he said.

"I'm fine," Howler grumbled, fighting back tears.

"Well that Comet you rode in on looks like hell," Roger countered. "And that was a hard landing you made...go get checked out. That's an order."

Howler appeared to clench his jaw, but he stood straight and offered a salute before heading for the infirmary. Sadly, Roger checked the box next to Ben "Bones" Foster's name.

***

Colonel Madigan slammed the phone down and turned toward Rowena Walker. "Engage lightspeed!" In mere seconds, the SC Titan zipped way and seemed to simply vanish. Almost immediately after it was gone, a small shuttle launched off the surface of one of the nearby asteroids. The space craft was boxy in shape with a slanted nose. It was gray in color and blended in nicely with the hue of the asteroid on which it had been parked. The occupant of the mysterious shuttle watched in awe as a foreign ship had somehow engaged in battle with four Supreme Regency Vindicator ships and one Star Voyager battleship—and then miraculously beaten them! Without hesitation, the small shuttle darted away at lightspeed in chase of the foreign ship.

CHAPTER 17

Captain Malcolm Steiger did not like to refer to what had happened to his ship, the Pinnacle, as a defeat. In his mind, a defeat meant that one must surrender or be destroyed. He had done neither. Alas, he was also very cognizant of the fact that Potentate Romulus Shade would have a very different take on the events that unfolded soon after he'd led the Earthlings through the H.T.G. and into the Vega solar system.

The Pinnacle was towed into the Kalo orbit where it would spend the next week obtaining the necessary repairs to make it worthy of space flight and battle once again. During that time, Malcolm knew he'd have to spend almost all of it convincing the potentate that what had happened was a terrible mistake that he'd make sure would never happen again. He'd hitched a ride on a shuttle down to the Kaloian capital city of Clona and now found himself gazing upward at the tall gemstone encrusted steps that led to the entry of Potentate Shade's palace.

The palace was a marvel, not just on Kalo, but throughout the entire galaxy. It was rectangular, with large turrets on each corner. Atop each turret, tall cone-shaped roofs extended upward to a point and beyond that, a steeple with the Kaloian symbol—a diamond with an 'X' in the center—reached ever higher toward the sky. The four-story structure was built with bricks of pure silver, all of which had been mined from the Kalo moon, Japra. The light that shone brightly from the sun, Vega, gleamed a piercing reflection of blinding light off the metallic bricks. In the middle of the day, it was nearly impossible to approach the palace without some sort of protection for one's eyes. Malcolm was forced to squint as he moved closer and as he did so, he felt the nagging pain behind his bandaged forehead. The injury he'd received when the Pinnacle's bridge narrowly escaped disaster was minor, but still required stitches.

Each story of the palace was well equipped with a generous and beautiful array of windows. Every other window contained a stained-glass painting that depicted major events throughout the history of the planet. Most of the events illustrated were of conquered planets and enslaved peoples throughout the galaxy. Due to the reflective nature of the palace's bricks, the interior of the structure was naturally cool, so much so that the potentate and all of his security and staff could always be found adorned in heavy robes of various colors. Each color depicted the individual's role in the palace. For instance, black was reserved for the palace guards. White was for the various politicians and advisors to the potentate, and red was reserved only for Romulus Shade himself.

As Malcolm walked into the foyer, he was met by the chief guard, Hugo Horne. Horne was an enormous man with broad shoulders and arms like tree trunks. On one hip, there was a holstered red plasma pistol. On the other hip, there was a sheathed battle axe. His black robe—one of the largest Malcolm had ever seen—fit him tightly due to his size. There was a hood over his head which just made his appearance even more sinister. His black mustache was so thick, it almost completely covered his mouth.

"Captain Steiger," Hugo's deep voice murmured. "Potentate Shade is expecting you."

"Yes, I'm aware," Malcolm said, doing his best to keep his tone all business. "Will you escort me to him at once?"

Hugo's bushy eyebrows bristled, and he cocked his head to the side. "Follow me," he grumbled deeply.

The throne room was located just beyond two large metal doors. As Hugo approached, the doors slid open and disappeared through a slot in the edge of the adjoining walls. Suddenly, Malcolm was peering into the vast room. There were various golden columns throughout and the ceiling was vaulted through the second and third floors above. Only the fourth floor was hidden away. The floor under Malcolm's boots was made of stone tiles that were polished so well he could see his reflection in them. The surrounding walls were adorned with massive tapestries that hung from the top of the ceiling all the way down to the floor. Each tapestry represented a planet that had been conquered by the Supreme Regency. Potentate Romulus Shade was seated on the massive throne at the back wall of the room. His wooden seat had an enormous back covered with intricate carvings of Kaloian symbols. Shade shifted in his seat and his red robe ruffled as he did so.

Malcolm stopped in front of the first step that led up to the potentate's elevated position and kneeled on one knee. "Your excellency," he said, his head bowed.

"Get up Captain," Potentate Shade said, his voice gravelly. "I want to see your face."

Malcolm sighed and slowly stood. He then looked up at the potentate's face. Romulus Shade had gray, watery eyes. His skin was pale and appeared sickly, but his muscular frame suggested quite the opposite. When standing, Shade towered at seven feet in height—even taller than Hugo Horne. His hand moved slowly toward the small table next to his throne. On top of the table was a coiled whip. The sight of the whip made Malcolm tremble.

"I want to beg for your mercy, sir," Malcolm said, just as he'd rehearsed. "I've failed you, but I'd like to make amends."

Shade turned his head and his neck cracked in protest. "Captain Steiger, I contemplated killing you right here in this very throne room," he said very matter-of-factly.

Malcolm swallowed hard.

"However," Shade continued. "I believed that perhaps you'd give me a good reason to spare your life."

Malcolm felt his pulse quicken and struggled to control his breathing. The pain in his forehead intensified. "Allow me to prove my worth, sir," he said, a hint of desperation in his voice. "When the Pinnacle is repaired, I will hunt down the Earthlings and I will kill them with ease."

The potentate frowned and shook his head. "And how do I know that you will succeed this time?" he asked with an icy tone.

"The only reason they managed to escape is because they used the element of surprise," Malcolm said, trying not to stammer. "That advantage exists no longer. I tried to show them mercy, but next time there will not be any."

Romulus Shade again shifted in his chair and appeared agitated. He sighed deeply and again shook his head. "Captain Malcolm Steiger, your incompetence has cost the Supreme Regency two Vindicator ships and sixty-two lives. I read the report of your second in command, Tago Mari. Though he is obviously loyal to you, he is also quite honest. He stated that you negotiated with the Earthlings…that you gave the captain extra time to alert the entire ship of a supposed surrender."

Malcolm closed his eyes. As much as he wanted to be mad at Mari for adding that tidbit to the report, he could not. It was the truth, and he himself would have done no different had he been in the same position.

"It's true," he said. "The odds were significantly in our favor and I genuinely believed they were going to surrender. In hindsight, it was a terrible mistake and I assure you it will not happen again."

Shade clacked his teeth together, a quirk he was well-known for when he became angry. It was not a good sign for Malcolm. "Captain, it was an obvious sign of weakness and it is unacceptable." He then glanced at Hugo Horne. "Kill him."

Malcolm looked around as Hugo Horne moved toward him while simultaneously reaching for his axe. "What? No!" he screamed. "Wait, I beg of you."

"Wait for what?" Shade snapped. "You know what's at stake! Your actions are intolerable."

Hugo now had his axe in both hands and was drawing back to take a swing.

"Jado Baylor has it sir!" he shouted in sheer terror.

Shade held up a hand at Hugo. "Stop!"

Hugo Horne stopped his axe mid-swing, a mere foot away from Malcolm's neck.

"Jado Baylor has *what*?" he asked, already thinking he knew the answer.

Malcolm breathed deeply, and his forehead became a mixture of sweat and blood as his wound began to bleed. "The ability," he answered quickly. "He used it while we were helping the Earthlings prepare their ship for the journey. He managed to injure one of them without even physically touching him."

Potentate Romulus Shade stood from his throne and made his way down the steps to where Malcolm was standing. "Are you certain of this?" he asked as he drew near.

Malcolm nodded. "Yes," he replied. "Tago Mari witnessed the event. I was going to tell you, but I felt it was something we needed to discuss in person."

Shade's gray eyes brightened a bit. "How is it possible?" he asked. "Did he have any of the elixir?"

Malcolm shook his head. "No," he answered. "We checked his quarters and found evidence of nothing. We even administered a blood test and still found nothing to suggest he'd taken anything that would give him the ability."

The potentate rubbed at the stubble on his chin as he pondered what he'd just learned. "Was he able to demonstrate the ability to you?"

Malcolm frowned. "No, I'm afraid not. I asked him to, and he did try. It seemed that his emotions triggered it. He was angry with one of the Earthlings when it happened."

"I see," Shade replied, deep in thought. After another moment, he said, "Captain Steiger, bring this Jado Baylor to me at once."

Malcolm suddenly felt a tremendous wave of relief wash over him. "Of course, your excellency," he said gratefully. He turned to walk away, then paused briefly.

"Is there something else?" Shade asked as he turned to make his way back to the throne.

"Yes," Malcolm said. "Our scanners found an abundance of the seed you've been seeking on planet Earth."

"I'm aware," Shade replied as he sat back down. "And now our opportunity to harness it is delayed due to the unfortunate fact that the gateway was destroyed."

"There is another way," Malcolm said. "The gate we constructed in their solar system is still there."

"Do you take me for a fool?" Shade hissed. "I know what needs to be done, but I also know that the situation would not be so dire if you had not failed." His voice began to rise. "Captain Steiger, I strongly suggest you get out of my sight before I change my mind about your fate. Do not show your face here again unless Jado Baylor is by your side."

"Yes, your excellency," Malcolm replied, and he glanced over at Hugo Horne. The large guard's eyes narrowed, and he tightened his grip on the axe he held. He appeared to be disappointed that he was unable to use it.

Malcom decided he'd tempted his fate enough and then proceeded to stroll out of the palace without saying another word.

***

Somewhere on the outskirts of the Ara Constellation, the SC Titan blazed across the cosmos at lightspeed. As soon as Captain Harry Hightower felt it was safe to do so, he immediately ordered all officers and squad leaders to the conference room so that they could debrief. After Dr. Phoebe Holtz, Lieutenant Hayden Carter, and Roger Stellick, the squad leaders filed into the room, all of them still adorning their gray flight suits. As everyone took their respective seats, Captain Hightower moved to the front of the room with Colonel Madigan at his side.

"Good work everyone," Hightower said as he rubbed at his eyes. "Without your bravery, we would not have gotten away."

"I second that," Roger Stellick said. "Each of you did a damn fine job and you should be proud. You just proved why you were chosen for this mission."

"Excuse me," Howler said bitterly. "But everyone didn't come back."

Colonel Madigan stepped forward. "Lieutenant Wolfe, you're flirting with insubordination," he growled.

Captain Hightower held a calming hand up toward Madigan. "It's alright, Merrill," he said softly. He then looked to Howler. "I'm aware of the losses, Harlan, and I assure you that it's weighing heavily on everyone in this room right now."

"I lost two pilots," Howler replied, his voice quaking. "Two pilots that I'd barely even met."

"They died so that we could live," Hightower said. "Don't ever forget that."

Howler looked away toward a nearby view port and stared at the blackness beyond it. "My men did not have to die," he said, sounding almost as if he were in a trance.

Sabre shifted uncomfortably in his seat.

Hightower stepped around the table to get a better view of Howler. "Don't do this, son," he said, almost pleading. "I've lost way too many men in my career and I will tell you from experience that blaming yourself is not going to accomplish anything good."

Howler chuckled. "I'm not blaming myself sir," he said, and then he glanced over at Sabre. "I blame him."

Hightower looked at Sabre curiously and then back to Howler. "I don't have any idea what this is about," he said. "But now is not the time," he added through clenched teeth.

Sabre looked away and down at the table in front of him while Howler continued to stare out the viewport. Captain Hightower shook his head and returned to his original position alongside Colonel Madigan. "Chief Reed, how are our fighters?" he asked.

The deck chief, Tim Reed, crossed his large arms and his dark skin rippled as his muscles flexed. "I've got my crew looking them over now," he said. "We've got one from Hotel squad that is in very bad condition...I don't know if it's salvageable yet. A couple of others that have some serious wing damage and then another dozen at least with minor issues. All in all, we may be down one..." he paused as he considered his next words. "And obviously the others that never came back...so four total."

"Alright, when you have an accurate number, I want to know immediately," Hightower replied. "If you can't get them back perfect, then they don't fly...understood?"

"Yes sir," Tim replied.

"Dr. Holtz," Hightower said, turning to Phoebe. "Any injuries I need to know about?"

Phoebe ran a hand over her curly black hair. "I'm sorry Commander, but I'm in the same boat as Tim...it's too early for me to give you an accurate assessment. I know of a few minor burns from some of the more seriously damaged Comets, but overall I think everyone that made it back is in fairly good shape." She paused and glanced over at Howler. "I do want to see Lieutenant Wolfe as soon as possible," she said. "After seeing his fighter, I'm amazed that he's sitting here talking to us right now."

"Thank you, doctor," Hightower said. "Harlan, you go to the infirmary as soon as you leave this room, is that understood?"

Howler sighed deeply through his nose. He still refused to look at anyone in the room and kept his attention squarely on the same viewport he'd been staring at. "Understood sir, Commander Stellick had already ordered me to go," he said, monotone.

Hightower looked at Roger. "And you will see to it that every pilot gets looked over, per S.A.M.A. regulations?"

"Yes sir," Roger replied. "I'll make it a priority."

"Very good," Hightower said, and finally he himself took a seat at the head of the table. He again rubbed his eyes, evidence that he was clearly exhausted. "I know you're all wondering what the plan is from here...or more specifically, how we're going to get home," he said. "And to be completely honest, I don't have an adequate answer for you right now."

Roger expected this, and he didn't see how anyone else in the room could've expected anything different. He glanced over at Phoebe and could see she was visibly shaken. He figured she too already knew it to be true, but hearing the captain vocalize it was a shock.

"One thing that we do have going for us," Hightower continued, "is that we've got a ship full of highly skilled and smart folks. The best of the best was chosen for this mission. If anyone in this room—or if any of you know of anyone else on the ship that may have a good idea—then by all means let's get it out on the table. No matter how radical or how crazy it may seem...I want to hear it."

"Sir, if I may," one of the pilots said. It was Robert Drake, call-sign Tombstone. He was the squad leader for Foxtrot. "Although we destroyed the gateway that we exited through, obviously the gate near Titan still exists. There has to be more of these gates throughout this galaxy and one has to assume that at least one of them could be a connecting portal back to Titan."

Hightower nodded. "I agree," he said. "I've been giving it a lot of thought and if we're going to find another one of these gates, I feel strongly we'll have to have assistance in doing so. Otherwise it's going to be like looking for a needle in a haystack."

"I say we kidnap one of the Kaloians—a high-ranking one," Banshee said suddenly. "We force them to tell us where the other gates are."

Hightower smiled. "Ms. Voight, I admire your spirit," he said. "And if we get an opportunity to do that, then I assure you we'll entertain the idea."

"If you need a volunteer, I'm up for the job," she replied. Her face was expressionless, but she sat up straight and seemed to have the most energy of everyone in the room.

"I'll keep that in mind," Hightower said.

"Commander, how long will we be at lightspeed?" Lieutenant Carter asked.

"Not too much longer," he answered. "As a matter of fact, as soon as this meeting is adjourned, I want you to order Rowena to bring us out of it—obviously we need to conserve fuel. I just wanted to make sure we get far away from those Kaloian ships before we slow down. And when that happens, you need to be on the cannons and ready for anything."

"Any particular planetary destination?" Carter asked.

"Not at this time," Colonel Madigan answered. "Sooner or later, it'll probably become a necessity, but we're not at that point yet."

"Until we get more answers, or at least some sort of direction, there is going to be a lot of tension on the ship," the Captain said. "Everyone in this room is a leader on this ship, and I'm relying on all of you to keep morale up until we discover what our next move will be."

"Can we count on each of you to do that?" Madigan asked, raising his eyebrows.

Everyone in the room nodded and vocalized their assurances.

"Unless anyone has anything else, you're all dismissed," Hightower said, rising from the table. As the room disbanded, he said, "Stellick and Banshee, you two stay here a moment longer."

Roger and Merissa looked at each other simultaneously as if they were looking to the other for some sort of explanation. When everyone was gone, and the mechanical doors swept closed, the Captain sat down across from the two pilots.

"Roger, you need to speak to Howler, and see what you can do to settle whatever issues he has with Sabre," he said.

Roger nodded. "I'll talk to them, but I think Harlan will settle down once he's had a little time to grieve."

Captain Hightower chewed his lip a moment, then said, "He doesn't go back up until his head is right."

"Of course," Roger agreed. "I'll do what I can to diffuse the situation."

"Very well," the Captain replied. He then turned to Banshee.

"Merissa," he said, allowing a slight smile. "I hear you put on quite a show out there," he said.

She smiled back at him, but it was clearly forced. "I was just trying to do my job," she said, uneasily.

Hightower nodded. "Would you care to explain what you were thinking when you broke off from your squad to attack the bridge of the Pinnacle?"

Roger glanced over at Banshee and found that she suddenly became very calm.

"The other four pilots had the cannons covered," she answered. "I wanted to make sure my missiles did not go to waste...I thought I could—"

"Stop," Hightower interrupted. "You not only broke away from your squad, but you also disobeyed orders when you decided to go rogue."

Roger kept watching her and suddenly Banshee's expression turned to one of genuine confusion. Her nose wrinkled, and her mouth dropped open. She remained in that expression for a few moments and took turns glancing at each man in the room.

"Sir, I—"

"Save it," he snapped. "Everything worked out and every member of your team came back unscathed. It's also important to mention that you *did* complete your assignment and essentially cleared the way for the Titan to make a quick escape," he added.

She sighed. "Yes sir."

Hightower smirked. "And I'm sure your little stunt scared the hell out of Steiger."

Roger and Colonel Madigan suddenly found that they were smiling as well.

"With all that in mind, all I'm going to say to you is that next time you're given an objective, you stick to that objective and more importantly, you stick with your squad. Is that understood?"

For a moment, Roger thought that Banshee was going to argue the matter further.

Let it go, Voight, he thought to himself.

Finally, she said, "Understood sir."

"Very well," the Captain said. "You're dismissed."

Once she was gone from the room, Roger said, "Technically, Christian Smith left his squad too sir."

Hightower huffed and shook his head. "Not the same thing, Stellick. Sabre was put into a precarious position and made a decision to save the life of another squad leader."

"True, but another life was lost in the process," Roger countered.

Colonel Madigan looked over at him, frustrated. "It was a horrible thing that happened, Stellick," he said. "Playing the blame game isn't doing anyone any good. Are you going to be able to mediate the conflict between Howler and Sabre or do I need to?"

Roger felt his jaw tighten but resisted the urge to say what he was thinking. "I can handle it, Colonel," he muttered.

Madigan nodded and let out an exasperated breath before looking back to Hightower. "So, unless there is some new Kaloian technology the ship has been outfitted with that you haven't told me about, I assume any chance of getting a message back home in a reasonable time is out of the question?"

Hightower rubbed at the back of his neck and suddenly all three men felt a subtle lurch under their chairs as the SC Titan came out of lightspeed. "It would take years to get a message back home," he said begrudgingly. "Our focus right now needs to be on maintaining a decent level of morale with the crew while we try and find another gate."

"What do you mean by that?" the Colonel asked curiously.

"I mean we relax some rules," the Captain replied. "Little things...like allowing more time in the recreational areas of the ship. Forget the rules regarding wearing the uniform outside the cabins while off-duty on the third and fourth decks. Anything we can do to make these people more comfortable and relaxed will be paramount to our long-term survival."

"Alright," Madigan said while he nodded. "Agreed. So, what do we do when...*if* we find another gate? We don't know exactly how to operate it."

"Yes, I know it's a concern," Captain Hightower said as he leaned back in his chair. "Personally, I liked Merissa Voight's idea."

Roger's eyes widened. "Captain, are you saying you'd be open to kidnapping one of the Kaloians?"

Hightower screwed his face up and shook his head. "Do you have a better idea, commander?"

Roger took a deep breath through his nose as he too leaned back in his chair. "No sir, I do not," he admitted.

"So how would we go about getting a Kaloian?" Madigan asked, skepticism in his tone.

"The only thing I know to do at this point in time would be to return to where we last saw them, but this time we'll be more prepared," Hightower answered.

"I doubt they'd still be there, but it's a start," Roger said. "However, before we make plans to head back, I would request that we wait until I get a full report from Tim Reed on the status of our Comets."

"Very well," the Captain replied with a nod. "I want a full report on my desk in eight hours. That also gives the crew—and us—time to rest and decompress."

"I'll make sure you have the report, sir," Roger said assuredly.

"Let's meet back here in at least eight hours," Hightower said, and he paused to look at the colonel. "Merrill, you and I will obviously need to take shifts on the bridge. I'll take the first one, so you go and get some rest. You too Roger…that's an order."

Madigan and Roger nodded and stood from their chairs. As soon as they did the door to the conference room burst open. It was Tobias "Shephard" Bancroft, Charlie squad leader.

"Sirs, I'm very sorry to interrupt, but you're needed on the bridge at once," he stated, very quickly. "Another ship just appeared on our tail, and it's hailing us."

CHAPTER 19

"Stop blaming yourself," Lauren said. She sat down beside Sabre and put an arm around him, squeezing slightly.

Sabre was seated on the bed in his cabin leaning forward with his face resting in the palms of his hands. He was glad Lauren was there, although he couldn't figure out why. She'd clearly been angry with him the last time he'd spoken with her about her brother, Charlie.

"It is not your fault," she added, as he continued to sit in silence.

"I know," he finally answered. He then pulled his hands away from his face and sat up straight, looking over at her. Her blue eyes were bright and seemingly the brightest thing in the room. As usual her hair was pulled into a pony tail. She was a natural beauty—no makeup necessary.

"If you know, then why are you beating yourself up about this?" she asked.

Sabre sighed. "I mean...logically, I know it's not my fault. But there is still a pang of guilt in my gut I can't seem to shake...I keep running all the *what if* scenarios through my head."

"You said yourself that the captain supported your decision...is that not enough?"

He smiled weakly. "No, it's not," he answered. "I've got another squad leader that absolutely believes it's my fault, and who knows how many pilots that feel the same way."

Lauren frowned and turned away from him but kept her arm still around his shoulders. "It's not your fault, Christian," she said sternly. "You did what you thought was right and it saved Howler's life."

Sabre smiled and looked down. "Thanks," he said. "Thank you for being here."

"As soon as I heard what happened, I knew I needed to come see you," she said.

"Yeah, but last time I saw you, you were pissed at me," Sabre replied.

"It doesn't matter now," Lauren said. "I think right now we've got bigger issues than you and Charlie not getting along. What can you tell me? Is there a plan to get back home?"

Sabre continued to stare at the floor. "They're not telling me much...I'm sure I don't know much more than you already do," he said. "But I can tell you that right now, there is no plan. They're working on that right now."

Lauren raised her chin slightly and said, "Oh…okay."

Sabre could see the disappointment and fear in her expression. He gently removed her arm from his shoulders and then put his own arm around her. "Don't worry," he whispered. "The captain will figure this out and we will all get home…you'll see."

She sighed and then fell over onto the bed. "I hope you're right," she said.

Sabre dropped beside her and gently caressed her face. "I'm always right," he said.

Lauren rolled her eyes. "So, what do we do until this is all figured out?" she asked.

Sabre leaned close and kissed her on the lips. "I can think of a few things to pass the time," he whispered.

Lauren kissed him back and pulled a blanket over the both of them.

***

Jado Baylor appeared both honored and scared all at once. It wasn't every day that the Potentate Romulus Shade requested to see an ordinary Galactic Navy crewman. That was the part that scared him.

"I don't know how I did it, Captain," Jado said. "I told you…it just happened."

Malcolm smiled. "I remember what you said," he replied, "and I believe you. I'm sure the potentate will believe you also. However, you must understand that for you to be able to do it without the aid of the elixir—well, it raises questions."

"Yes sir, I suppose it does," Jado replied meekly. "I just don't know what else I can tell the potentate that you haven't already said."

"Me either," Malcolm said. "But he still requests to see you all the same. It's a rare opportunity and you should embrace it."

Jado fidgeted in his chair. They were sitting on a bench along a busy street in downtown Clona, watching as the hover cars sped back and forth mere feet off the ground. It was a beautiful day and the rays from the setting sun, Vega, bathed them in warmth.

"Do I have reason to be afraid?" Jado asked.

Malcolm shook his head. "No, I do not believe so. Just meet with him and answer his questions honestly."

"Alright," Jado replied, and he stood. "I trust you Captain. I think I'm ready to go see the potentate now."

Malcolm looked up at him and smiled. "Very well," he replied, standing.

Upon his return to the palace, Malcolm was again met by Chief of Security, Hugo Horne. When Hugo noticed him, the mammoth man shook his head and smiled, and the corners of his bushy mustache moved upwards as he did.

"I sure hope you were telling the truth," he said with his deep baritone voice.

"Please take us to see Potentate Shade at once," Malcolm said sternly. He still outranked Hugo Horne and he did not want the big man to forget it.

Hugo snorted, and his mustache bristled. "Follow me," he snapped.

Jado Baylor looked to his captain for some sort of reassurance, but got none. Captain Steiger kept his eyes directed ahead of him and seemed to be deep in thought. When Hugo Horne approached the metallic doors that led into the throne room, they hissed and slid open. Jado had never even seen a picture of the throne room, but it was exactly what he imagined. The ceilings were massive and the massive tapestries that hung from them were as wide as the street he and Malcolm had just been watching.

"Come forward, Captain Steiger," a gravelly voice called out from the opposite end of the room.

Jado then noticed a massive throne on which a very tall man sat. It was no doubt the potentate.

"Thank you for returning promptly, Captain," Shade hissed as he craned his neck to get a better look at Jado Baylor.

Malcolm knelt to one knee and nodded as he did so. "I live to serve you, sir," he said.

Jado quickly dropped to his own knee when he noticed his captain do so and he instinctively dropped his head as well. He wasn't sure why, but suddenly he became fearful of even looking at the potentate.

"And thank you Jado Baylor," Shade said very politely. "Rise to your feet, young man. It should probably be me kneeling to you."

Jado quickly rose to his feet and looked at the potentate, confused. "I live to serve you, sir," he said. He realized he'd just repeated exactly what Malcolm had said, but truthfully could not think of anything better.

Potentate Shade laughed. "Enough of that," he said as he ran a long-fingered hand over his white hair. "Did you not hear what I just said? I should be kneeling before you."

Jado looked to his captain for some sort of guidance, but again there was no response. Malcolm remained on his knee and kept his gaze forward.

"I don't understand," Jado said, confused.

Shade clacked his teeth. "I understand that you have the ability," he hissed.

Jado shook his head. "No sir, I don't know what happened—I mean, it just happened," he stammered.

"*What* just happened?" Shade asked, his gray eyes narrowing.

Jado cleared his throat. "Umm...the incident I believe you're referring to sir...I moved one of the Earthlings without touching him. I do not know how."

The potentate gathered his robes tight around him and stood from the throne. He then walked down the steps and placed a hand on the younger man's shoulder.

"Have you taken the elixir?" Shade asked, staring intently into Jado's eyes.

"No, your excellency, I have not," he replied.

"Then how is it possible?"

Jado looked over at Malcolm again looking for some sort of guidance. Once again, he was disappointed. "I don't know, your excellency," he muttered nervously. "It just happened. The Earthling man was trying to intimidate a friend of mine. It angered me."

Romulus Shade's eyes widened at the revelation. "So, an emotion of anger seemed to spark it?" he asked anxiously.

Jado nodded slowly.

The potentate momentarily moved away from Jado and approached a basket of fruit that was seated on a table against a nearby wall. He placed his long fingers around a large melon and carried it back to the steps directly in front of Jado. After carefully placing it on the highest step, he turned back to face the young man.

"I want you to attempt to move this melon," he said very matter-of-factly.

Jado looked to the melon and then back to the potentate. He then laughed nervously.

"Is this amusing to you, boy?" Shade asked coldly.

Jado immediately closed his mouth and returned his gaze to the melon. "Sir, I told you. I don't know how."

"Did you eat any Earthling food?" the potentate asked suddenly.

"Y-yes," Jado replied.

"Did you eat anything that came from Earth's oceans?" he asked.

Jado stared at him with a mixture of curiosity and confusion. "I don't know, sir."

Potentate Shade snapped his head toward Malcolm, still kneeling on the floor.

"Did he?" he asked.

"It is possible," Malcolm replied. "I did not think it was important to question them on the origins of their food your excellency, but to my knowledge he did not consume any of the substance you're inquiring about."

The potentate again turned his attention to Jado. "Young man, I need you to imagine something in your life that has made you angry. I need you to find something that would stoke similar emotions you experienced that day you attacked the Earthling. Find it and use it to move this melon," he commanded.

Jado looked at him with an expression of helplessness but it had become quite obvious that arguing or trying to explain the matter further was a useless endeavor. Reluctantly, he turned his eyes toward the melon and began to concentrate as hard as he could. He used every fiber in his being to concentrate on something that made him angry in his past. Immediately, his mind's eye returned him to a terrible period in his grade school years in which he was bullied relentlessly by his teacher's son. His teacher was very much aware of what was happening, but since the boy was her son, she refused to intervene. The end result was Jado receiving numerous bruises and a couple of black eyes. He'd told every adult that he trusted what was going on, but instead of one of them intervening, he was often instructed to either fight back, or avoid the boy altogether. The more he replayed the memories through his mind, the madder he became. He kept his gaze firmly on the melon but there was no movement.

"Are you thinking of something that angered you?" Shade asked impatiently.

"I am," Jado said, closing his eyes. "I'm trying very hard your excellency, but it's not working."

"Keep trying," the potentate hissed.

Jado squeezed his eyes tighter and again replayed humiliating and frightening images from his childhood. No matter how hard he tried, the melon did not move.

"Enough," Shade barked finally. "He then turned to Chief Hugo Horne. "Give me your axe."

Without hesitation, the chief guard handed it over. The potentate looked at the blade for a long moment and then looked down at Captain Steiger. He was still on his knee, but his eyes were closed. He seemed to be concentrating and doing his best to remain quiet.

"Are you certain that you can't do it?" Shade said as he glared at Jado, his eyes just above the blade.

Jado felt his pulse quicken and he swallowed involuntarily. "Yes, your excellency," he answered quickly. "I'm very sorry...I tried very hard."

The potentate pulled the blade away from his face and let it drop down beside him. "Relax, young man," he urged. "It's not your fault."

Jado felt slightly better when he noticed Shade's polite tone, but still the axe remained in his grasp. "Thank you, sir," he said, sounding somewhat hopeful that the potentate was finally believing him.

"You just need the proper spark to awaken the appropriate emotion," Shade said. At that moment, he quickly lifted the axe and then thrust it downward. The blade chopped straight through the back of Captain Steiger's outstretched legs, immediately severing both just below the knees.

Malcolm howled. He was clearly in excruciating pain. The captain fell on his side and reached for what remained of his legs. Instinctively, he placed a hand over the bloody stumps, but it continued to pump red liquid all over the tiled floor.

"Why did you do that?" Jado shouted, much more out of fear than rage.

"Move the melon!" Potentate Shade screamed.

Jado turned his eyes to the melon, concentrated, and much to his surprise the melon shot through the air as fast as a rocket. Hugo Horne almost fell backward as he watched it fly through the air. The melon didn't stop until it reached the ceiling where it then burst. Pieces of blue, wet fruit rained down over them, most of which ended up on the potentate. However, Shade did not care. He immediately turned to Hugo Horne.

"Take Captain Malcolm Steiger to the infirmary," he commanded as he made his way back to his throne. As he sat, he added, "And have your men escort Jado Baylor to a holding cell."

"What?" Jado said. "I haven't done anything your excellency!"

"You're not being punished, boy," Shade spat. "But I must have my personal physician examine you. Don't you understand? You are the key. The key to opening the path that will lead us to the galactic domination all Kaloians desire. If we can find out how you are able to harness your ability without the aid of the elixir...well, nothing will be able to stop us!"

CHAPTER 20

"Stellick, which squads came out of the battle in the best shape?" Captain Hightower asked as he, Madigan, and Roger marched toward the bridge.

"In terms of damage?" Roger asked, trying to keep up.

Hightower nodded.

Roger thought a moment, then answered. "Alpha, Bravo, Delta and Foxtrot."

"Good, get Delta and Foxtrot ready to go up immediately," the Captain replied as the metal doors in front of them slid open to reveal the bridge.

"You think it's the Kaloians?" Madigan asked.

Captain Hightower nodded, but said nothing. He made his way straight to Jake Crosby.

"Who is hailing us?" he asked, very matter-of-factly.

Jake pulled a hand over the microphone and leaned back. "He says he means us no harm, but he only wants to talk to the captain."

"Is he a Kaloian?"

Jake shrugged. "I don't know sir."

Hightower gestured for him to put him through. Jake nodded and flipped a switch.

"Identify yourself," Hightower said.

"My name is Amus," a deep voice answered. "I mean you and your ship no harm, but I wish to speak to the captain."

"My name is Harry Hightower. I am the captain of this ship," he replied. "Are you a Kaloian?"

There was a chuckle. "No, I am not," he answered. "I am from the planet Avax."

Hightower tightened his jaw and glanced over at Madigan. The colonel's lips were a straight line and he shrugged.

"Okay, Amus," Hightower said. "Forgive me if I'm a little skeptical but I'd be remiss if I didn't inform you that we're prepared to destroy your ship if we feel threatened."

There was a long pause. "Captain Hightower, as I said, I mean you no harm. You appear to be a foe of Supreme Regency and in my view, that makes you an ally to the Avaxians."

Hightower rushed over to the switch in front of Jake Crosby and turned the speaker comm off. "*Another* race of aliens?" he asked, directing the question at Colonel Madigan.

"Harry, if he is what he says he is, this is the break we're looking for," Madigan said.

"And if he's not?" Hightower asked.

"Then we do exactly what you said," Madigan replied. "We destroy him and his ship."

Hightower flipped the switch again. "Amus, how do I know I can trust you?"

"I suppose you don't," Amus responded. "But if you'd have me, I'll come on board so that we can discuss the matter in person if that would make you more comfortable."

Roger looked on as the captain crossed his arms and sighed deeply. He could see that the decision he was about to make was a big one and it weighed heavily on him.

"Sir, if I may," he said suddenly.

Hightower reached over and flipped the switch again so that Amus would be unable to hear. "Go ahead Stellick," he said.

"Sir, I'd suggest we sent up a squad to patrol the space around us if we allow this person on board," Roger replied.

The captain nodded. "Good idea, do it," he said quickly as he flipped the switch again. "Amus, you are to bring your shuttle in through the starboard launch bay. I am warning you that you will be met with armed guards. They will not harm you unless you give them a reason to."

"Very well," Amus replied. "You have my word that I will cause no trouble or harm to anyone on your vessel."

"And you have my word that you'll be treated fairly as long as you stand by that," the Captain said. "I'm ending this transmission and will see you shortly." He flipped the switch for the final time and looked to Madigan.

"Merrill, I want twenty armed men there to meet this...alien," he said anxiously.

"I'm on it," Madigan replied as he turned away to see that it would be done.

"I'm sending up Foxtrot to watch the sky," Roger said as Madigan shuffled past him.

Captain Hightower moved toward him and leaned forward so only Roger could hear. "Should I trust him?" he asked, obviously still torn on the decision.

Roger was taken aback by the question as it was highly unusual for Captain Hightower to second-guess any decision he made.

"Yes sir," he whispered. "I don't see that we have any other choice here. As the colonel alluded to, this may be the break we need."

Deck Chief Tim Reed and Charlie West were among the twenty men armed with assault rifles that awaited the mysterious shuttle's arrival. They looked on through the bay windows as a small, oval-shaped vessel glided into the bay. The shuttle came to a lazy stop, hovered a moment, and then slowly lowered until its landing skids contacted the metal runway.

"If your safety is on, now's the time to take it off," Tim said as he readied his weapon. "No one fires unless I give the command."

The other men nodded, some rather nervously, but all were focused on the task at hand. After the launch bay pressurized, the shuttle was motionless for almost a full minute before a door on the rear of the vehicle finally hissed open and lowered downward to form a ramp. A strange being exited the shuttle and Tim Reed felt his heart race.

The alien was humanoid and of average height, no more than six feet in height. Its skin was as blue as a midday Earth sky.

"What the hell is that?" Charlie asked, his mouth agape.

Tim squinted as he tried to make out the approaching alien's facial features. It seemed to have eyes as dark as midnight and no nose to speak of. The mouth was similar to that of a human's, though the lips were a darker shade of blue. There was no hair atop its head. The clothes the alien wore were surprisingly similar to those of Earth, and they resembled military attire. A case of some sort dangled from his right hand.

"Welcome to the SC Titan," Tim said, keeping his rifle pointed at Amus' midsection.

"Thank you," the alien said politely. He took note of the numerous guns pointed at him and slowly raised his hands. The case rose too.

"What's that?" Tim asked, nodding toward the case.

Amus smiled, revealing two rows of pointed teeth. "This is the proof I need to show your captain so that he will trust me when I say I am his ally," he said.

"Place it on the ground beside you," Tim commanded.

The alien complied, then quickly returned both his hands above his head.

"Charlie pat him down and grab the case," Tim said.

Charlie moved cautiously toward the mysterious alien and kept his gun pointed directly at him until the toe of his boot tapped the case. He gently kicked it aside and then proceeded to pat over Amus' clothes, top to bottom.

"He's clean," he said, taking a step back and reaching for the case.

"Alright," Tim said, taking a deep breath. "Amus, we're going to escort you to a room where you can speak with Captain Hightower. We're going to check inside your case before we take it up."

Amus' smile disappeared and though he did his best to hide it, there was evident uneasiness on his blue face. "Very well," he said. "Please just make sure it gets back to me as soon as possible. Much of the documents in that case are written in a language I'm certain you will not be able to decipher."

"We'll take good care of it," Tim assured him, and he then gestured for Charlie and a couple of the other armed men beside him to take the lead on escorting Amus to the elevator. "Take him straight to the conference room. I want two of you with a hand on him at all times and two of you to keep guns pointed on him. The rest of us will take the other elevator and meet you up there."

Charlie nodded, and immediately grabbed Amus under his left arm. "Let's go," he said, and pulled him rather forcefully.

"Again, you have nothing to fear from me," Amus said, pleading.

"We've heard that one before," Charlie quipped.

Once Amus was safely on the elevator, Tim raced over to the other one and quickly made his way to the top deck. There, all of the armed men escorted the alien into the conference room and forced him to have a seat. Only then did Captain Harry Hightower enter the room, followed by Colonel Merrill Madigan.

"Captain Hightower, I presume?" Amus said cheerfully.

Hightower raised an eyebrow as he noticed the Avaxian's blue skin. Though the Kaloians were aliens, at least they *looked* the same as Earthlings. Seeing a humanoid being that truly appeared alien was a bit of a surprise.

"And you are Amus," Hightower replied, his tone flat. "Do you have a last name?"

Amus looked at him curiously, then smiled slightly, revealing his pointy teeth. "No, on Avax everyone has a different name so there is no need for a last name."

Colonel Madigan chuckled and looked over at the captain. "*Every single being on his planet has a different name?*" he asked, as if Amus were no longer in the room.

Hightower cleared his throat and shook his head ever so slightly as if to say, *Don't be rude...*

"It's alright, Captain," Amus said, noticing the interaction. "I know it may be hard to believe, but it is true. No living Avaxian is allowed to have the same name."

"How many people are on your planet?" Hightower asked.

Amus looked down at the table in front of him glumly. "I'm afraid our numbers are dwindling significantly," he stated sadly. "There are less than eighty thousand of us now."

Captain Hightower moved to the chair nearest him and sat down. "What is happening to your people?"

Amus looked up and showed his teeth again. "The Kaloians," he said bitterly. "They believe they are the supreme race. It's why they refer to their own government as the Supreme Regency. The Kaloians have one desire...one goal."

"To eliminate every other race in the galaxy," Hightower said.

Amus nodded. "I suppose you've gotten a taste of what I'm talking about."

Suddenly, Roger Stellick appeared at the door with the case in his hand. "Captain, we've looked it over and there is nothing dangerous in this," he said, holding the black object up.

"Give it back to him," Hightower said, glancing back at Amus. "I hope you understand why we're being so cautious."

Amus held a hand up and Hightower noticed that he only had three fingers and a thumb. Each digit was adorned with a small black claw. "You don't need to explain, Captain," he said as he eyed Tim Reed and the other armed men around him.

"How did you find us?"

"I'm a scout for Bothian and Avaxian Federation military alliance," he answered. "I was on a reconnaissance mission. Our satellite radars picked up four fully loaded Vindicator ships moving near the Katoo Asteroid Belt two days ago. Our spies had recently alerted the Federation about the new construction of a Hyperspace Teleportation Gate near that very sector. We had to find out what was going on, so I was sent to check it out."

"They sent you alone?" Hightower asked, surprised.

Amus nodded. "I'm the most experienced spy the Federation has— and I prefer to work alone."

"So, you were there when we came through the gate behind the Pinnacle?"

"I was," Amus confirmed. "I was hiding on an asteroid monitoring everything with my ship's sensors. At first, when I saw the size of this ship, I figured it must've been a newly developed Kaloian vessel that we were unaware of, but then the battle ensued...and I knew."

"You knew what?" Hightower asked, leaning forward.

"I knew you were from Earth," Amus answered. "The Kaloians have aspired of visiting Earth for quite a while. So much so that they sent one of their most decorated captains, Malcolm Steiger, on a decade-long voyage to enter your solar system so that he and his crew could construct a gateway that would allow a fleet of Kaloian ships to return and overtake Earth."

"Your people have known of this plan?"

"We've known about it for years, but considering the distance between our solar systems, we didn't know if they'd ever get desperate enough to make the voyage to Earth. It seems that they did."

Madigan stepped forward. "Desperate? Why were they desperate?"

Amus shrugged and then frowned as he returned his gaze to the wooden table top in front of him. "We think that you may have a resource that they deeply desire."

"What resource?" Hightower asked, intrigued.

Amus shrugged again. "We don't know what it's called but..." he paused as if he were trying to consider the right words. "It gives them...an ability."

"What ability?" Roger asked as he too took a seat near the alien.

"I think you Earthlings refer to it as telekinesis," he answered.

There was an awkward silence in the room. Captain Hightower crossed his arms and leaned back in his chair. He looked over at Madigan.

"You mean they can move things with their minds?" the Captain finally asked.

Amus nodded. "Yes. They can move an individual with ease. They could pick up any of your men and throw them high enough in the air to kill them once they're dropped. They can move extremely heavy objects and crush you. We've even heard of rare instances where one of them was able to affect the trajectory of a star ship."

"This sounds like a science fiction movie," Roger said, awestruck. He then looked to Hightower. "Sir this would definitely explain the incident that occurred on board the Titan between one of our men and the Kaloian."

"That's exactly what I was thinking, Harry," Madigan chimed in.

"How?" Hightower asked. "How can they do this? What resource would give them this ability?"

Amus sighed. "Again, we are not aware of exactly what the resource is," he said. "What we did know was that they were getting a lot of it off the Kalo moon, Jara. We think they discovered it about twenty-five Earth years ago. They would gather the resource and process it into some sort of liquid that they drink. They refer to it simply as the *elixir*."

"Wait," Roger said suddenly. "Captain Malcolm Steiger told me that Jara had become overrun with some sort of creature—he said it was similar to insects on Earth. He said that creature eventually made its way to Kalo and had forced his people to leave their planet."

"Ha!" Amus said, slapping the table in front of him. "About 95% of what you were told about Jara is a lie."

"Well please enlighten us," Madigan urged.

"There is an insect-like creature on Jara. It's called a Jutrian crab, and the Federation put them there for the sole purpose of overtaking the entire moon and making it nearly impossible for the Supreme Regency to harvest their precious resource. The Jutrian crab is a nasty creature with large mandibles capable of severing an individual in half. It also is known to devour almost anything in its path and turn entire planets into vast wasteland. Whatever the Kaloians were after, it was the Federation's hope that the Jutrian crabs would snuff it out—and it appears that they did."

"But this forced them to look for their resource elsewhere," Hightower said.

"I'm afraid it expedited their voyage to Earth," Amus admitted. "For the Federations role in that, I am truly sorry."

Roger looked to Captain Hightower. "It was only a matter of time," he said.

Amus continued. "I'm afraid that one of the Supreme Regency's most well-known strategies is that they will trick and lie their way to get an adversary to trust them—then they crush them. It's what happened to Avax and it is what happened to the planet Botha. The betrayals resulted in many deaths and enslavement of many of our peoples. Botha and Avax were once enemies. If anything good came out of what the Kaloians did to our races, it's that we are now fierce allies."

Hightower drummed the fingers on his right hand across the table as he thought. "Amus, we need to get our ship back home. We're aware that there are other gates throughout the galaxy. Can you—or the Federation—help us not only find one, but also operate it so we may return to our solar system?"

The Avaxian alien frowned and shook his head somberly. "We'd need a Kaloian star chart to find all of the gates," he answered. "Most of their starships have at least one. It will be a difficult object to acquire."

"Would the Federation consider helping us?" Hightower asked, a hint of desperation in his voice.

"That depends," Amus answered.

"On what?" Madigan asked.

Amus looked over at the colonel and again showed his pointy teeth. "On whether or not you are willing to help us."

CHAPTER 21

"Physically, you're fine," Dr. Phoebe Holtz said.

She was seated on a small black-padded stool with wheels, her legs crossed and a clipboard resting across her lap.

Harlan Wolfe was resting on the edge of the examination table in front of her, his feet dangling inches above the floor.

"Of course, I'm fine," he said. "I've been telling all of you that."

She scribbled something on the clipboard and then looked up at him, her green eyes sparkling just above the rims of her reading glasses. "Yeah, well you guys and gals tend to fib a little when it comes to your health if it means keeping you in the cockpit."

Howler rolled his eyes. "If I say I'm good to go, then I'm good to go. The sooner I can get back in the saddle and take out some of the Kaloian bastards, the better," he grumbled.

"Just because you're okay physically, doesn't mean you're okay mentally," Dr. Holtz quickly reminded him. "It's my job to give you clearance in both areas."

Suddenly, Howler appeared somewhat worried. "Mentally, I am okay," he said, a bit of annoyance in his tone.

"No, I don't think you are," Dr. Holtz replied, staring directly at him. "You blame yourself for the loss of Cooper and Ben."

"No," he snapped, and his face flushed red with obvious anger. "I blame Christian Smith for what happened to Cooper and Ben. They didn't have to die. I was supposed to be the one to die."

Dr. Holtz pushed back with her feet so that the stool would roll back toward the wall behind her. When she found it, she leaned against the wall and tossed the clipboard onto the counter beside her. "Harlan, are you *really* going to blame Sabre for saving your life?"

"I don't expect you to understand," he answered, crossing his arms, and looking away from her.

She stared at him a few seconds. "I should have you grounded," she said.

The worried expression returned to Howler's face. "Please, don't do that," he said, almost pleading.

"Why shouldn't I? If your mind isn't clear, how can you perform your job safely and effectively?"

"When I'm in that cockpit, my mind is on nothing but completing my duties," Howler replied.

She pulled her reading glasses from her face and tossed them onto the nearby clipboard. "I don't believe you," she said flatly.

Howler raked his fingers through his brown curly hair. "Doc, please," he said. "It's my job. I'm a squad leader."

Dr. Holtz shook her head. "Harlan, Hotel Squad is being disbanded. Georgia and Garrett are being reassigned, as will you."

He looked at her, surprised. "I guess I should've known that would happen," he said begrudgingly.

"Tell you what," Dr. Holtz said as she reached for her glasses and clipboard. She flipped to the second page and scribbled a note. "I'm going to give you something to help you sleep. I want you to take it, get plenty of rest, and come back and see me in forty-eight hours."

"Oh, come on," Howler grumbled. "Doc, I don't have time for that. Some bad stuff could break out at any moment and I need to be available."

"I'll make the decision on that in 48 hours," she answered. Dr. Holtz walked to the opposite side of the exam room where large cabinets adorned the wall. She opened the middle door and retrieved an amber colored pill bottle. When she turned back to him, she said, "The unfortunate reality is that right now we have more pilots than we do Comets. I think forty-eight hours is not a long time for you to rest and let me reevaluate you before I make a final decision." She tossed him the bottle and he caught it.

"So, there is no talking you out of letting me take the pills *and* giving me clearance?" Howler asked.

She glared at him. "Absolutely not."

***

"How are we looking out there?" Roger asked, radioing Robert Drake, call-sign Tombstone.

"Nothing out here but us and a bunch of stars," Tombstone replied.

He and Foxtrot squad had been patrolling the perimeter around the Titan for almost an hour and their fuel was beginning to expire.

"Alright, it seems that our visitor is indeed a friendly and we think he's definitely out here alone," Roger answered. "Bring the squad in, I know you guys are about on fumes."

"Roger that," Tombstone replied. "Headed in."

Commander Roger Stellick was seated in his office and since Captain Hightower had ordered him to call the fighters back in, he decided to take a moment for himself. He knew that when he returned to the conference room he'd be in there a while. The alien, Amus, seemed trustworthy but it troubled him deeply that he'd been so wrong about Captain Malcolm Steiger. Roger had always felt that he was a decent judge of character, but now he wasn't so sure. Ironically, it seemed that Captain Hightower gave his trust to Amus with relative ease, and though there appeared to be no reason to doubt him, the recent betrayal of Steiger weighed heavily on Roger's mind. The last thing he wanted was for them to make the same mistake twice.

Colonel Madigan, for his part, appeared to be somewhere in between. He didn't seem to trust, nor distrust, the blue alien. However, Roger knew that when the chips were down, he'd always side with Hightower—as he should. Harry Hightower was captain, and everyone on the ship depended on him to make sound decisions. If he did not, they would most likely never see Earth again. Hightower seemed to be ready to arrange a meeting between he, Madigan, Roger, and the leaders of the Federation.

Amus made it clear that he felt the possibility of finding another gate and getting the Titan and its crew home was a strong possibility, but also the Federation had its own problems that needed to be addressed. With all that in mind, Roger was also cognizant that Earth was on borrowed time. Sooner or later the Supreme Regency would invade. If there was anything that could be done to snuff out that possibility now, it was a worthwhile endeavor. Ultimately, Hightower was going to agree to help them, at least until he received the help he needed. As conflicted as he was, Roger didn't see any other option.

There was suddenly a knock on the door.

"Come in," Roger said.

The metal door retracted into the wall and Dr. Holtz stepped in with a file folder in her hand.

"I spoke with Howler," she said, casually placing the file folder on the desk in front of him.

"And?" he asked, opening the folder to review the enclosed document.

"Physically, he's fine...no surprise there," she said. "However, he's very angry and he's hurt. He's grieving and in my opinion, he's doing it in an unhealthy way. He feels tremendous guilt as he believes he should've been the one that died out there." She glanced down at the document. "I was going to see if you could give this to the captain...he wanted a report as soon as possible."

Roger looked up at her and nodded. "Of course," he said. "So, you're going to make a final determination in forty-eight hours?"

"Yes," she said. "I'm hoping a little rest and decompression time will clear his head, so he can think straight."

"Alright, but if he's not good, don't let him talk you into giving him clearance," Roger said. "He can be persuasive."

"Yeah, he's already trying," Phoebe replied, she paused and looked back to the door to make sure no one was in earshot. "What's the scoop on our mysterious visitor?"

Roger looked at her with a disapproving look. "Phoebe, you know I'm not at liberty to say."

She glared at him and rolled her eyes. "Don't give me that crap...tell me what's going on."

Roger sighed and pressed a button under his desk to close and lock the door.

He pointed at her and said, "You tell anyone what I'm about to tell you and—"

"Oh hush," she quipped. "I'm not going to tell anyone, and you know it." She smiled, revealing her perfectly white teeth.

Roger admired her a moment and then tried to regain his train of thought. "His name is Amus. He says he's from some planet called Avax. He's blue."

Phoebe's dark eyebrows arched higher. "Oh really?" she said, her jaw dropping a bit. "He's *blue*?"

"Yeah...we're in deep space, don't act so surprised," he replied. "He says his people on Avax, and another race from another planet called Botha, form a group they call the Federation. They've been in battle with the Kaloians and he basically says the Federation would consider helping us get back to Earth if we'll help them with the Kaloians."

Phoebe huffed, her shoulders rising as she breathed in. "Of course," she said, disappointed. "Just helping us get home would be too simple."

"This is our shot at getting out of here," he said. "Be a little more optimistic."

She pursed her lips and stared out the round window to her left. "This is just so surreal," she said wistfully. "I'd always dreamed of travelling into deep space, but not like this."

Roger could see a sadness in her emerald eyes. "Something you want to talk about?" he asked.

She whipped her head around to look at him and smiled. "No, why do you ask?"

"We've never talked much about your family," he said. "You got someone back home you're thinking about?"

She stared at him and licked her lips. "I have a daughter," she said.

Roger's eyes lit up. "Wow...really?"

She nodded, but the sadness remained. "Yes, she's eight now," she said.

"Well that's great," Roger said, leaning forward. "Tell me about her."

"Well, she's got curly dark hair," she began as she grabbed one of her own curly dark locks. "Her favorite color is pink. She loves pizza and ponies—she's just your typical American little girl."

Roger smiled. "That's great Phoebe," he said. "Maybe one day I can meet her."

She smiled nervously and looked away. "Well, that'd be great...hopefully I'll get to see her again too."

"Phoebe, we're going to get back, don't you—"

She held up her hand to stop him. "That's not what I meant," she said. "I haven't seen her in person since she was two."

Roger frowned and sat up straight. "I don't understand."

"She's with her father," she whispered. "He sends me pictures frequently, and I send him money, toys, clothes..."

"And why don't you get to see her?" he asked, obviously confused.

She suddenly stood, and Roger could see moisture welling up in her eyes. "Long story...sometime I'll share it with you," she said, straightening the front of her navy blue uniform jacket. "I've got to get back to work."

As she headed toward the door, Roger hit the button under his desk to unlock and open it. "Phoebe," he called after her.

She paused and looked back at him.

"If you ever need to talk to someone, I'm always here," he said as he thought of his own estranged daughter.

"I know," she replied. "Please don't forget to get that report to the captain...and don't worry, nothing you told me will leave these lips," she added, and she mimicked zipping her mouth shut.

Phoebe then disappeared into the hallway.

CHAPTER 22

The case that Amus had been carrying contained a wealth of information on the Kaloians. There were photographs of their planet and Hightower was surprised to see that it resembled Earth. It seemed to be covered in dense forest. Near the city of Clona, the most striking picture of all was of an enormous palace, seemingly constructed with blocks of pure silver.

"Who is this?" the Captain asked, sliding a photo over to Amus.

The Avaxian's dark eyes narrowed. "That's Potentate Romulus Shade," he said. "That is the only photograph that we have of him. He is the head of the Supreme Regency."

Colonel Madigan leaned over so that he could get a good look. The man in the photo had long hair the color of snow and eyes that were only slightly darker. His skin was pale, but the man looked very healthy. He appeared strong.

"He's an albino," Madigan said gruffly.

"So, he's the one driving all of this?" Hightower asked.

"Yes," Amus replied. "Many Federation assassins have perished trying to murder him."

"I assume you know how to find this palace?" the Captain asked, sliding over the photo of the silver structure.

"Yes," he answered. "The potentate rarely leaves the palace. That's why it's so hard to get to him. It's heavily guarded by his personal security force headed by the brute Chief Hugo Horne. He's been known to crush a Bothian skull with his bare hands."

"How would the Federation feel about you sharing all of this with us?" Colonel Madigan asked.

Amus' eyes widened and he shifted in his chair. "They would not be happy," he admitted. "However, if you agree to assist us, I think all would be forgiven."

Hightower crossed his arms and stared up at the ceiling. "All this sounds so familiar," he muttered. "An alien race asking Earth for help."

"We need each other's help, Captain," Amus responded. "Allow me to set up a meeting with the leaders of the Federation. Please do not hold us accountable for a betrayal we did not commit."

"I don't have any other choice," Hightower said. "Give me the coordinates where we can meet."

"Allow me access to my shuttle. I need to explain the situation. They will be unwilling to grant you access to one of their bases at this time, but a meeting in space would not be out of the question."

"Very well," the Captain said. "But I would appreciate it if you would allow Colonel Madigan to accompany you to the shuttle."

Amus smiled a toothy grin and nodded his agreement.

***

"You girls have a rough day at work?" Ray Compton asked with his southern states drawl.

"Something like that," Covergirl answered, recognizing his attempt at humor.

"Yeah, at least you were called to the principal's office," Banshee said as she picked up the small glass and took a shot of whiskey.

Ray was polishing the glasses behind the bar but stayed within arm's length of the two pilots in case they needed anything. The arrival into the Ara Constellation had been very eventful and he imagined there would be more pilots filing in soon to have a drink and unwind too.

"You know, I thought it was odd when I was approached to be a bartender on this ship," Ray said as he put the glasses aside to wipe down the counter. "But after what we just went through, I now understand the need for a bar."

Banshee smiled and slid her shot glass over to him. "I'll drink to that," she said.

He poured the drink and noticed a man enter through the door behind them. He was tall, and his head was shaved slick. "One of your colleagues?" Ray asked, nodding toward the approaching man.

Banshee eyed him as she quickly noticed he was coming directly toward her.

"They told me you wouldn't be hard to find," he said as he rubbed the stubble on top of her head. "Do you mind if I ask why you shave your head?"

Banshee thought she recognized his voice.

"Yes," she replied. "Do you mind if I ask why you shave yours?"

"Not at all," he answered. "It started turning loose and finally I decided to help it along."

She nodded and then turned back to her drink.

"So?" he said.

"So, what?" she replied.

"Why do you shave yours?"

She swallowed another shot and slammed the glass down. "You asked if I minded you asking and I said yes."

"Alright," he said defensively, and he glanced at Ray Compton.

The bartender shrugged and went back to polishing glasses.

The man placed each of his hands on both women's shoulders. "I'm buying the drinks," he told Ray.

"What?" Covergirl said, turning to look at him. "Wow, thanks!"

"It's the least I could do since Banshee here saved my life," he said.

Suddenly she realized who he was and turned to look at him again.

"You're Moon Dog?" she asked.

He nodded. "That's me. Nathan Carmichael," he said offering his hand.

They shook.

"It was nothing," Banshee said. "I'm sure you'd have done the same for me."

"Oh, it was *something*," Moon Dog answered. "You are one hell of a pilot."

He moved to the stool next to her and took a seat. "They also say you're smart as a genius," he said.

Banshee glanced over at Covergirl and her counterpart grinned. "You know, I think I'm gonna go get some rest," she said, rising from the bar.

"What?" Banshee said, wide-eyed. "We've only been here a few minutes."

"Yeah, but I'm *really* tired," Covergirl lied while faking a yawn.

Banshee pleaded with her to stay with the use of her eyes, but Covergirl only winked and walked away. "Thanks for buying my drink," she said to Nathan as she left.

"So, who are 'they'?" Banshee asked.

Moon Dog looked at her, confused. "Pardon me?"

"You keep saying 'they' told you where to find me, and 'they' told you I'm smart," she replied. "So...who is 'they'?"

"Oh," he said, slightly embarrassed. "Umm, I'm good friends with Franklin Fuller."

Banshee gestured to Ray for another shot. "Oh yeah?" she asked. "You're good friends with Bull?"

"Yeah, we were cadets together once upon a time."

"He's good," she said. "Good enough to be a squad leader in my opinion."

"All of us are good," Moon Dog said. "But you're exceptional," he added. "I'm not kidding, you're the best I've ever seen."

She downed another drink and then turned to look at him. "Nathan, is there some particular reason you're kissing my ass? Because if you're wanting to sleep with me, all you need to do is ask."

Moon Dog felt his jaw drop. "Wh-what?" he stammered.

She leaned over and kissed him hard on the lips. He could taste the whiskey.

"If you're wanting to sleep with me, all you have to do is ask," she repeated.

"Umm," he said, obviously confused. "No, that's not what I was trying to do at all."

"Alright, good," she quipped as she slid off her stool. "Ray, you have a good one, okay?"

"You too Merissa," Ray said, as she walked away.

Moon Dog watched her disappear from the bar and then glanced over at the bartender. "What the hell just happened?" he asked.

"I think she likes you," Ray said with a mischievous grin.

***

Once things calmed down after Amus' arrival, Tim Reed led his men back to the hangar to continue prepping the Comets for their next flight. The ships with no visible damage were inspected and serviced first. Fortunately, most of the fleet fell under this category. Charlie West was assigned the first Comet to repair and it just happened to be Sabre's.

"What happened to the nose?" he asked as he looked over the severely bent and twisted cone. The fighter's radar antennae was barely hanging on and would have to be entirely replaced. This was usually a tedious and frustrating job that would probably take more time than actually replacing the cone. There were burn marks on the port side wing, probably a near miss from a plasma bolt. Otherwise, the Comet appeared to be fine.

"That happened when Sabre pushed Howler's ship back to the launch bay," Tim Reed said, as he crossed his arms. His muscles bulged under his tight short-sleeved shirt.

"How is that even possible?" Charlie asked as he kneeled, so he could get a look under the belly of the ship.

"We've got the world's best pilots on this ship, is it really that surprising?" Tim asked.

"It's not just that," Charlie said, standing up. "I didn't know Sabre was capable of being so unselfish."

Tim eyed him curiously and adjusted his cap. "Charlie, I know you got a little tiff going with Sabre, but that better not have any effect on how you do your job."

Charlie looked at his boss and scowled. "Chief, come on," he said. "I don't like the guy and I want him to stay away from my sister, but I'm also a professional."

"So, what's your deal with him then?"

"I just told you, he's dating Lauren," he replied.

Tim chuckled. "Ain't your sister a grown woman?"

"Yes, of course," Charlie answered as he grabbed a wrench from his tool box and began working to get the nose cone loose.

"So why can't she decide who she dates?" Tim asked. He pulled the dangling radar antennae out of the way, so Charlie could seat his wrench.

"Because," he grunted as he jerked the bolt free. "You know, and I know, that Christian Smith has a reputation of being a bit of a heart-breaker."

"Have you talked to him about it?"

"Of course, I have," Charlie replied. "I told him I'm not completely opposed to it, but he needed to prove to me that he can be trusted if he wanted my blessing."

The nose cone broke free and Charlie was relieved to see that the radar antennae was one of the newer styled ones and it had a plug so that it could be easily replaced. He unplugged the damaged one and tossed it aside.

"I know he's a little rough around the edges, but I don't think he's all bad," Tim said. "If it weren't for him, Howler would be dead. And the bad thing is that Howler is pissed at him about saving his life."

Charlie paused and grabbed a rag out of his pocket to wipe his hands. "What? Why would he be mad about that?"

"Something about deserting the rest of the squad," Tim answered with a shrug. "Howler lost Cyclops and Romeo. I guess he thinks if Sabre had been back there to lead them, maybe it wouldn't have happened."

"That's ridiculous," Charlie said.

"Yeah, I think so too, but the man just lost two pilots. He's not thinking straight," Tim said and then he too wiped his hands. "You got this now?"

"Yeah, I'm good," he said. "Thanks."

Tim nodded and moved on to help another mechanic on another Comet. Once Charlie was alone, he grabbed a roll of tape and climbed the ladder to get into the cockpit. Once he sat down at the controls, he pulled a strip of tape loose and stuck it across the top of the console. Then he pulled a permanent marker from his pocket and began to write on it.

CHAPTER 23

Amus had no trouble setting up a meeting in space with the leaders of the Federation. He was enthusiastic when he shared the news with Captain Hightower.

"President Dala is excited about meeting a new ally," Amus said excitedly.

"Does he know of our predicament?" Hightower asked.

Amus chuckled. "President Dala is female," he said. "And yes, I told her that you are trying to return to Earth. They are ready to rendezvous with you immediately at the coordinates I provided."

"Rowena Walker is turning our ship in their direction as we speak," Hightower replied. "Did your president give any indication of what she expects from me and my ship?"

Amus shook his head. "No, she did not," he answered. "But knowing her and the other Federation advisors, I'm sure they are already developing a plan. They waste little time."

It took only two hours for the SC Titan to catch up with the similarly sized Federation starship. Jake Crosby wasted no time hailing the blimp-shaped ship and soon got the friendly response he expected.

"They are inviting you aboard, sir," Jake said, glancing at the captain over his shoulder.

Colonel Madigan looked at him uneasily. "You sure about this Harry?"

Hightower half-smiled and patted the executive officer on the shoulder. "Of course, I'm not," he said with a chuckle. "But I have to go."

He grabbed a radio communicator and clipped it onto his belt. "If something goes wrong, I'll let you know."

"Take this too," Madigan said, handing him a handgun.

The captain shook his head and gently pushed the weapon away. "No, I need them to trust me and they need to know that I trust them."

Colonel Madigan reluctantly replaced the sidearm into the holster on his side. "Our cannons will be pointed on that ship until you return," he said.

Hightower nodded. "The bridge is yours, Merrill," he said, stepping away.

When he reached the launch bay, Amus was waiting for him and he still seemed very excited. The captain was unsure whether to consider his demeanor to be a good or bad sign. Amus sensed his uneasiness.

"Do not worry, Captain," he said. "Your willingness to come aboard our vessel and speak with our president speaks volumes. I assure you that this will be a friendly and cordial exchange. We aren't used to encountering humans as friendly as you Earthlings."

"I trust you," Hightower said, and he looked past Amus to the shuttle. "Shall we?"

Amus nodded and then gestured for him to board ahead of him. Once on the shuttle, Hightower glanced around the cabin and was surprised to find that it wasn't much different than their own shuttle on board the Titan. There were signs on the wall with strange symbols that he didn't recognize, and the controls appeared different, but otherwise the Avaxian shuttle was very similar.

The captain found that all the seats were against the wall. He found one and quickly fastened the seat belt. Meanwhile Amus took his place in the cockpit and quickly began flipping switches and turning knobs. Within seconds Hightower heard the vehicle hum to life and then felt it rise. It was remarkably quiet. Once outside the ship, he peered back toward the SC Titan. He longed to be back onboard within its relative safety but tried to push the thought aside so he could focus on the job at hand. He was unsure at present exactly how much help he could agree to give, but anything that could be done to accelerate their return home, he was prepared to do.

As the small shuttle drew near the large Avaxian vessel, Hightower noticed viewports sprinkled across the side and a large slim, rectangular window across the front. He could easily see movement beyond the window and the blue beings, the Avaxians, going about their usual jobs and routines.

"How many of your people are on board?" he asked.

"Around two hundred...and then another hundred Bothians," he replied.

Hightower found himself wondering what a Bothian would look like. He wanted to ask Amus but did not want to seem rude.

"So, you said that Bothians and Avaxians used to dislike each other?" he asked, trying to make conversation.

"Yes," Amus answered. "If we had been able to put aside our differences sooner, it's widely believed that Romulus Shade would not have been able to overtake our races as easily. Unfortunately, he used the hatred we had toward each other as an avenue of plotting our defeat."

Amus glided the shuttle through a circular tube on the front of the ship that Hightower initially thought was an opening for some sort of cannon. The tube was short in length and before long, the shuttle emerged inside a vast opening in the center of the ship. It was bright white in color and there were blue Avaxians strolling about in all directions. The shuttle landed gently and Amus quickly opened the door on the back of the vehicle.

"Come, meet my people," he said, his pointy teeth gleaming.

Captain Hightower exited behind him and he immediately felt a pang of guilt. The Avaxian people surrounded him, but he didn't spot a single weapon being pointed at him. It was a far different reception than the one he'd ordered for Amus.

"Welcome to the Nebula," a female voice said.

It was the voice that immediately gave away her sex, but as Hightower studied the Avaxian female's features, he noticed other evidence. Her facial features were far softer, and her lips fuller. She had a noticeable bosom and the rest of the curves on her body were clearly feminine.

"Thank you," he said, offering his hand. "Are you President Dala?"

She laughed, and then stared at his hand. "No, I am not President Dala," she answered playfully. She continued to stare at his hand.

"Avaxians aren't familiar with that custom," Amus whispered, leaning toward him.

Hightower immediately retracted his hand, and was ushered quickly through the crowd until they reached a hallway that led directly to a set of double glass doors. The glass was distorted with some sort of coating that would not allow him to get a clear view of what was beyond them, but he could make out the familiar blue hue of Avaxian skin moving about. Amus pushed through the doors and the captain's eyes widened at the sight before him.

There were three large tables with what appeared to be Avaxian food on them. There were strange purple melons, what resembled pink apples and some sort of large roasted animal that reminded him of a pig. Beyond the tables of food there was another long table with another Avaxian female, though this one was significantly older than the one he'd met right off the shuttle. Beside her, sat a creature even more bizarre than the Avaxians. It was reptilian, and adorned in metallic armor. The head of the being reminded him of a dinosaur— tyrannosaurus rex specifically. Its skin was a deep gray in color. This, he assumed, was a Bothian.

"Welcome Captain Hightower," the female said, and she applauded lightly.

"President Dala, I presume," he answered, bowing his head.

She smiled and slightly nodded her head. "We are so grateful that you agreed to come and visit with us," she said. "Please partake in the feast before you, all that you see has been prepared specifically for you. We Avaxians love to eat while we discuss important matters."

Harry Hightower didn't anticipate having to eat a foreign food while in alien custody. However, as it seemed it was all for him, there was no way he'd be able to refuse it, even politely. Amus saw him eyeing the foods and then gestured for him to help himself.

"He doesn't want that garbage," the reptilian humanoid said suddenly. His voice was gravelly and exactly what Hightower was expecting.

President Dala looked over at the alien beside her incredulously. "Drago, do not be rude," she scolded, then looked back to Captain Hightower. "I'm sorry, Bothians have rather abrasive personalities."

Hightower held up a dismissive hand and smiled slightly. "It's fine."

The Bothian stepped forward, his armor clanged as he did so. "Tell the truth, Earthling, you have no desire to eat any of that fruit, but you feel as though you have to, so that you will not show disrespect."

"Oh no," the captain said quickly. "It all looks rather delicious."

Drago smiled, and his teeth were far more frightening than any Hightower had seen in the mouth of an Avaxian. "Suit yourself, liar," he said. "But I made sure that you had a boar from Katoo to ensure you're fed properly."

Captain Hightower couldn't help but smile. The Bothian was direct, unapologetic, and to the point, qualities he liked in any human. "Thank you, Mr. Drago," he said with a slight bow.

"Don't bow to me, human," Drago barked. "That's the very thing that Romulus Shade would have us do."

"My apologies," Hightower answered, and he quickly made his way toward the food to try and redirect the conversation. In an effort to be as diplomatic as possible, he gathered equal shares of the Avaxian fruit, as well as the boar from Katoo that Drago said he provided. He then hurried over to the table. Amus sat beside him while President Dala and Drago sat across from them. For a few minutes they all ate in silence. He did not know exactly what he was expecting from the Avaxian fruit, but Hightower found that he liked it. The purple melons were very sweet and reminded him of an orange, but much sweeter. It was so sweet in fact that he found he was unable to finish it. The pink fruit that resembled apples tasted unlike any fruit he'd ever had before, however he picked out a hint of coconut flavor. The boar from Katoo, as he expected, was his favorite part of the meal. The taste was almost identical to venison.

President Dala consumed only one pink apple before dabbing her mouth with a napkin and pushing her plate aside. "Amus has told us that you and your crew are trying to find a way back to Earth," she said, crossing her arms and leaning forward.

"Yes," Captain Hightower said, as he dabbed his own mouth. "We are hoping that the Federation could assist us in getting our hands on a Kaloian star chart. Amus tells me that if we had one, we could easily find a hyperspace gate."

"True, you could," Drago said. "But would you know how to operate it?"

Hightower looked at him and shook his head. "No, we honestly have no idea," he said. "Again, I'm hoping that the Federation could provide assistance."

The Bothian laughed and slapped the table. "So, you think that *we* know how to operate the gates?" he asked.

"I'm assuming that means you can't," Hightower replied as he stabbed another piece of boar with his knife.

President Dala was glaring at Drago. "Do you have to be so vile all of the time?" she grumbled.

"If we find a star chart, we should be able to find instructions for the gate as well," Amus offered, trying his best to diffuse the tension in the room.

"Right," President Dala agreed. "Thank you, Amus." She returned her attention to Hightower. "The point, Captain, is that we will find a way to help you get home. It's the least we can do since you're going to help us with our...problem."

Captain Hightower stopped chewing and slowly looked over at Amus. The blue alien smiled at him, again revealing his pointy teeth. "Amus, what exactly did you tell them?"

President Dala and Drago looked at each other, then back at Amus.

"You have a ship and you have some of the most skilled pilots I've ever seen in the entire galaxy," Amus said excitedly. "Captain Hightower your ship and your fleet of fighters can join us, and we can overtake the Kaloians in a matter of months."

"Months?" Hightower said, unable to hide his concern. "Amus, we don't have months. We'll need fuel and rations."

"That is not a problem," President Dala chimed in. "We have plenty of fuel reserves and I assure you we have plenty of food as well."

Though her offer was a relief to hear, Hightower suddenly realized he was being dragged further and further into the war with the Kaloians.

"He hasn't committed to anything," Drago said, eyeing him.

"Of course he has," President Dala said. "Amus said—"

"Right," Drago interrupted. "Amus said it. The captain here has not committed to anything. He has been taken by surprise by what Amus just said."

President Dala's eyes narrowed. "Is this true, Captain?"

Hightower sighed and again glanced over at Amus. "Well, not exactly," he said. "I told Amus that we'd help how we could. I think he may have exaggerated what I said just a bit."

President Dala looked over at Amus coldly. He in turn looked down and into his plate.

"I don't know how much help we can offer," Hightower added. "I'm not prepared to put my people in danger. This is not our war...we just want to get home."

"It's not your war...yet!" Drago snapped, and he slammed his fist onto the table. "I know that you Earthlings are a primitive race, but you can't really be this stupid. The Kaloians will find planet Earth and you will be enslaved just as many of our people have been."

Captain Hightower wiped his mouth again and shifted in his chair. "Yes, we realize that," he said, trying hard to keep his cool. "What we want to do is get back to our home world so that we can prepare for such an invasion."

Drago shook his head and rolled his reptilian eyes.

"In the meantime," Hightower continued. "If there is something we can do to help with your current efforts, we are willing to discuss it. Obviously, we know that we are burdening the Federation by asking for your help to get us to and through a hyperspace gate. That is why I'm open to discuss something we can do to assist you in the effort while we are here, but ultimately we can't commit to a long-term participation in this war."

President Dala frowned and sunk back into her chair. This was clearly not what she wanted to hear. Captain Hightower glanced over at Amus and saw that he too was disappointed. Only Drago's expression remained the same. He had his large arms crossed and he was smiling.

"Though I appreciate your honesty, I don't appreciate cowards," he quipped through his dagger-like teeth.

"Drago, stop," President Dala said. "Captain Hightower, we will help you and your ship get home, you have my word on that."

Hightower felt a rush of relief. "Thank you, president," he said gratefully.

"However," she continued. "You must use your own ship to acquire the star chart that you need. I will provide Amus to assist you. The charts and instructions you find will not be in a language you can read. I will also aid in deciphering all of that information."

"Thank you," Hightower said, though he was hoping for a little more assistance in gaining the objects needed. However, he also knew she was right; without her aid, they'd never be able to decipher any documents that they managed to obtain. "So how can I help you in return?"

"I don't need anything in return," President Dala said sadly.

"No," Drago said suddenly. "The Earthlings do not get our help unless they do something for us too."

President Dala waved him off. "There's no need, Drago. There is nothing they can do."

"Yes, there is," the Bothian argued, and he again pounded the table with his fist.

"What?" Hightower asked. "Please tell me."

"There is a Voyager starship called the Polaris," Drago began.

"No," President Dala interrupted suddenly. "It's much too dangerous."

"If they want our help, this is a task they can do," Drago snapped at her. "They can get the star chart and find him while they're on board."

"Find who?" Hightower asked.

"There is an Avaxian on board named Ralu," Drago answered. "He was captured almost a year ago and our spies recently discovered that he is being held captive on board the Polaris. Since a Kaloian ship is where you will easily find a star chart, you might as well board the Polaris—and while you're there, free Ralu."

"A Voyager is the largest class of starship in the Kaloian fleet," President Dala said. "The odds of you being able to get the star chart *and* free a prisoner are nearly—"

"We will do it," Captain Hightower said suddenly.

President Dala looked surprised, but not nearly as much as Drago.

"Are you sure?" Amus asked.

"Yes, we owe the Federation a debt and we will pay it," Hightower replied. "The Voyager starship is the same class that the Pinnacle was, correct?"

"That's right," Drago replied.

"Good, we've had a man on board the Pinnacle, so we are somewhat familiar with the ship's design," he said. "Of course, any intel you can provide would be greatly appreciated."

"That is why I'm allowing Amus to assist you," President Dala added. "He has gathered more intel on the Kaloians than any other spy in the Federation. He has a wealth of information on their daily operations, as well as the layout of their ships."

"Do you mind if I ask what is so important about Ralu?" the captain asked.

President Dala sighed deeply and shook her head. "Not at all. He is my husband."

"I see," Hightower said, surprised. "So, it's settled then." He offered his hand across the table.

President Dala looked at the gesture, confused.

"It's an Earthing way of sealing the agreement," he explained.

"Grab his hand," Amus urged.

She did so, and they shook.

"Are there other Avaxian prisoners on the ship?" he then asked.

"Possibly, and Bothians too," she answered. "However, for now Ralu is the only one you need to retrieve."

"Okay, do you have a picture of him, so I know what he looks like?"

"It won't be necessary," President Dala replied. "You have Amus and he looks almost exactly like Ralu."

Hightower looked over at Amus. "That true?"

"I would think so," Amus replied. "Ralu is my father."

CHAPTER 24

As Captain Hightower and Amus made their way back toward the shuttle, the sound of heavy footsteps made them stop abruptly. Hightower spun around to find Drago following them.

"Drago," Amus said, his blue forehead wrinkling. "Is something wrong?"

"Yes," the Bothian snapped sharply. "You're going to die."

Amus and Hightower looked at each other, perplexed.

"Going on board a Voyager starship is suicide and he knows it," Drago said, pointing at Hightower.

"I know that it's my only option if I'm going to get my crew back home," the captain argued.

"If there is any chance of success, you will require my assistance," Drago said, and his armor clanged slightly as he shifted his weight.

"You want to help us?" Hightower said.

"No, I do not," Drago answered dryly. "But, I owe President Dala something of a debt myself, and if helping you get Ralu back repays it, then so be it."

"I see," Hightower said as he turned and resumed his walk toward the shuttle. "You want to ride on our coat tails to repay your own debt."

The Bothian chased after him and when he caught up said, "Earthling, I'm not familiar with the strange expression you just used, but I assure you my desire to assist in getting Ralu back is pure. Bothians are known for our brute strength and I'm certain it'll come in handy onboard the Polaris."

"If you want to help, you'll get no resistance from me," Hightower said as he made his way up the ramp and into the rear of the shuttle.

"Does my mother know you're coming along?" Amus asked.

Drago shook his head. "No," he answered. "She'd never agree to it. She's begun to look upon me as another son."

Amus glared at him and Hightower noticed the slight hint of anger in the young Avaxian's dark eyes.

"Don't fret," Drago said, slapping Amus on the back. "I haven't taken the place as her favorite son—at least not yet."

The Bothian moved to the front of the shuttle and sat in the co-pilot seat. Hightower looked over at Amus. "Has he always been this charming?"

Amus frowned and shook his head. "It's a trait of his race," he said. "They are known as arrogant and see themselves as a superior race."

The captain chuckled. "Sounds a lot like the Kaloians."

"Yes," Amus agreed. "But when multiple races think that *they* are the superior race, it usually results in discord and conflict between them."

Hightower nodded and leaned in a little closer. "Is it to our benefit to have him with us?" he asked, whispering.

Amus nodded enthusiastically. "Yes, they are incredible warriors and what he said about his strength is true. Furthermore, he and the Bothians have become fiercely loyal to their alliance with the people of Avax. My only concern would be getting him on the Polaris undetected."

"If his being there will be to our advantage, we'll figure it out," Captain Hightower promised.

***

"You asked to see me, your Excellency?" Benedict Drayton asked, dropping to his knee.

"Rise," Potentate Shade commanded. He then stood from his throne and met his friend and physician at the base of the steps where they embraced.

"How is Captain Steiger?" he asked, grabbing the older man by both of his shoulders.

"He's now fitted with cybernetic legs and will be fine," Benedict reported.

"And Jado Baylor?" Shade asked anxiously. "Have you made any progress?"

Benedict sighed, his bony shoulders rising slightly under his green robe. "Young Jado is trying to be cooperative your Excellency, but I'm afraid his body is beginning to succumb to the strenuous testing."

"You've found nothing in his brain?" the potentate asked.

Benedict's eyes widened. "Oh, yes," he said, suddenly. "I've probed every region of his brain numerous times and I've noticed anomalies that I can only attribute to his natural abilities."

Shade was suddenly intrigued. "What anomalies?"

"There is substantial blood flow and enlargement within the corpus region. Though this was a breakthrough discovery, I've been unable to find a safe way to duplicate it in my other test subjects. All of them have died." Benedict paused, and his shoulders slumped. "Unfortunately, the immense probing I've performed on Jado has not left him unscathed either. He is now blind in one eye and has frequent seizures."

Shade frowned. "That is indeed unfortunate," he agreed. "If he dies, we'll lose this incredible opportunity to harness the ability without the use of the elixir."

Benedict shifted uneasily on his feet. "Your Excellency, it could be that his brain had a reaction to the elixir. A reaction that somehow became permanent and allowed him to use his ability without the aid of the elixir."

Romulus Shade sighed and waved his hand dismissively. "Thousands of cadets ingested the elixir," he said. "It was the way for us to figure out which ones had the ability. None of the others that had it have had these side effects."

"None that we know of," Benedict countered. "Jado was not aware of his ability either. Not until an emotional response triggered it."

The potentate pondered the thought, then asked, "Has he been able to move anything in your presence?"

"Yes," the physician answered. "At one point he fell under such duress that he managed to open the door. I think it was due to his deep desire to escape."

"I see," Shade said. "Interesting."

"As I said, I don't think he can take much more," Benedict said. "How would you like me to proceed?"

Again, the potentate pondered what he'd been told. Benedict sensed that Shade had an idea but was struggling on whether to follow through with it. Finally, he said, "Alright, if we're on the verge of losing him, we need to take drastic measures for the next test."

Benedict raised an eyebrow. "What do you suggest, sir?"

***

"Peyton Kelly, Cooper Jenkins, and Ben Foster. They were all brave men and each of them lit up with boyish excitement that I too felt when I learned of the SC Titan and the opportunity it brought us to travel across the galaxy," Commander Roger Stellick said somberly.

He was dressed in his officer uniform and standing on a small stage behind a podium overlooking hundreds of chairs that had been set up in the vastness of the starboard hangar. There were pictures of the deceased pilots displayed behind him and many of the faces of the living glistened from the tears that streamed across them.

"None of us had any idea that we were walking into a trap when we crossed through that gate a few days ago," Roger continued. "But I would venture to say that even if we *had* known it, the likes of Cooper, Peyton and Ben would've still signed up for this mission without an ounce of hesitation."

Harlan Wolfe, Georgia Clarke and Garret Butler—the remaining members of Hotel squad—sat on the front row in remembrance of

Cooper and Ben, two men that they'd only known a short time. Yet still, the pain of their loss was no less difficult than it would've been if they'd known them for ten years. It was the same for Tobias Bancroft, Calvin Reynolds, Moses Ward, and Parker Stevens of Charlie squad. The loss of Peyton Kelly had been a tremendous blow for each of them.

"It's unfortunate that we were unable to recover their remains," Roger said. "But a large part of me believes that those three guys would've been just fine with their final resting place being among the stars that they so desperately desired to be a part of."

Near the back of the hangar and in the shadows, Christian Smith leaned against the nose of a Comet fighter and watched the memorial service from a distance. Though he wanted to be among his fellow pilots, he'd been encouraged by Commander Stellick to consider watching from afar. The tension between he and Howler was still high and the last thing any of them wanted or needed was for a confrontation to break out during such a somber event.

Roger noticed him standing far away and secretly was relieved. "I'm certain that if those guys could talk to us, they'd tell us to move on and keep fighting," he continued, staring at Sabre. "They'd want us to get along and remember that the fight isn't—and should never be— among any crewmember on this ship. I can tell you that if Captain Hightower had been able to attend today, he'd tell you the same thing."

There were nods and quiet murmurs among the crowd, many of them obviously aware of the tension between Sabre and Howler. Each of the members of Hotel squad glanced over at Howler to see how their leader would react. He remained stone-faced, his eyes red and tired. Georgia reached over and grabbed his hand, but his expression remained unchanged and he barely acknowledged her.

Once he'd finished speaking, Roger stepped down from the stage and then he and Colonel Madigan shook the hands of all the pilots belonging to Charlie and Hotel squads. After nearly everyone had filed out of the hangar and back to their respective duties, Roger made his way toward Sabre.

"Thank you," he said, when he arrived near him.

"No need to thank me," Sabre replied with a humble smile. "This wasn't about me. It was about them," he said, nodding toward the three pictures on the stage. "I wasn't going to do anything to pull the spotlight away from where it belonged."

Roger stood next to him, staring at the pictures. He placed his hands in his pockets and rocked on his heels before saying, "I know you've probably heard it a hundred times, but I don't care what Howler or anyone else says... what happened to Cooper and Ben was not your fault."

Sabre smiled. "Yeah, deep down I know that," he said. "I just wish Harlan did."

"He's grieving," Roger replied. "I think ultimately he blames himself, but for some reason he seems hell bent on bringing you down with him."

"If that's what he needs to do to get past it, then so be it," Sabre muttered.

"I think I'm going to reassign Howler to Alpha squad leader," Roger said.

Sabre looked at him, surprised. "You're stepping aside?"

Roger chuckled. "Yeah, I'll be here when I'm needed but truthfully the captain wants me behind a desk anyway. And if you haven't noticed, we're short about three birds now."

"You think he's ready for that?" Sabre asked, referring to Howler's new assignment.

"Well he better be," Roger replied. "Technically the doc hasn't cleared him yet, but at some point, she will. When she does I think the best thing for him is to get back into the leadership position he earned and get his mind back on his job."

Sabre crossed his arms and thought of the other members of Hotel squad. "What about Peach and Romeo?"

"Hotel squad will be disbanded," Roger answered. "I'm gonna replace Peyton with Peach on Charlie squad. "Romeo—and his fighter—is going into reserves with me."

Sabre made a sour face. "Oh...I don't know if he'll like that."

Roger nodded and then looked over at Sabre sadly. "You're right, he probably won't," he said. "But the sad and realistic thing is that we will most likely lose another fighter before we get back home...and when that happens, I'll reactivate Romeo."

Sabre stared at the commander, his mouth opening slightly. He wasn't sure how to respond.

"Get your head right," Roger said as he began to walk away. "You don't want to be the one getting replaced."

CHAPTER 25

"They obviously fear me," Drago said with pride.

"They've never seen anything like you," Captain Hightower whispered to the Bothian.

Sensing the awkwardness, Amus felt the need to intervene. He stepped up to Chief Tim Reed, Charlie West, and the other crewmembers that were there to greet them all when they stepped off the shuttle. "This is Drago Rexpian," he said, waving a hand toward the large reptilian alien.

Drago stepped down the ramp and moved in front of Captain Hightower. His armor clanged as his heavy feet propelled him forward. "Greetings Earthlings," he said, his voice deep and gravelly. "I'm here to help..." he paused, then added, "you're welcome."

Tim Reed adjusted his cap. His jaws moved rapidly as he chewed a large glob of bubblegum. "Welcome to the SC Titan Mr. Drago," he said, then blew a large pink bubble that popped loudly.

Captain Hightower smiled and put a firm hand on the large Bothian's shoulder. "He's right," he said. "Drago is here to help us. His race is also being tormented by the Kaloians. His enemy is our enemy so that makes us allies."

Suddenly Colonel Madigan stepped off the elevator and marched through the crowd to get to the captain. When he noticed the Bothian, his eyes widened.

"Good to have you back, Harry," he said, still staring at the large alien.

"Good to see you Merrill," Hightower said. "Let's all go to the conference room to debrief."

"Great idea," Madigan said, finally pulling his attention from Drago. "Are you hungry?"

"I could eat, yes," he answered.

"I'll have some food brought down," Madigan said, and he then led them away.

They'd been in the conference room for only a few seconds when the colonel finally mustered up the courage to hold out his hand and introduce himself to Drago.

"Merrill Madigan. I'm the executive officer on this ship," he said.

Drago stared at the human's hand, and then took it cautiously. "Your hands are quite soft," he said with a chuckle.

Madigan smiled nervously and resisted the urge to jerk his hand away. "And you are?"

"Drago Rexpian," he replied.

"Well by all means," Madigan said. "Please have a seat. We'll have food up here in a few minutes."

Drago looked around the room at the padded chairs surrounding the table. "These chairs will not hold my weight," he snapped.

Madigan's jaw dropped, and he glanced at the chair in front of him. He then looked over to the captain.

"Call for one of those metal stools from the kitchen," he said calmly. "That should be sufficient."

Several minutes later the food and a stool for Drago arrived. In addition to the presence of Hightower, Madigan, and Amus, Roger Stellick also arrived. After more formal introductions, they all sat and began to eat. In contrast to the feast that Hightower had partaken in on the Federation ship, Nebula, the food now before them was much smaller in scale. It was a combination of pasta and chicken. Drago seemed to love it.

"This is far better than the garbage you Avaxians eat," he told Amus with a mouth full of food.

The blue alien glared at him.

"I'm glad you like it," Hightower said.

"There is nothing better than meat," he replied. "That's why I made sure you had your fill of it on the Nebula." He paused and plunged his fork into a large hunk of chicken. "Thank you for returning the favor."

"So, don't hold us in suspense," Roger said as he reached for a pitcher of water. "Do we have a plan?"

The captain smiled and nodded. "We indeed have a plan," he said.

Hightower proceeded to catch Madigan and Roger up on the conversation he'd had with Drago and President Dala regarding the star chart and imprisoned Ralu. When he explained that the plan involved sneaking aboard the Polaris starship and stealing a star chart, while also freeing Ralu, the reaction was what he expected.

"Harry, lives will be lost," Colonel Madigan said. He sounded shocked that such a plan was even considered.

Hightower nodded. "There is a very good possibility of that, yes," he admitted. "But if we are going to get home, this is what will have to happen."

Roger bit his lip and leaned back in his chair. "Captain, I don't understand why we need to get involved with freeing a prisoner. Why can't we just acquire the star chart and get out of there?"

"Because your captain made a promise," Drago growled.

Roger stared at the Bothian and did his best to give him the impression that he was unfazed by the alien's overbearing demeanor. "I understand that," he snapped. "But why?"

"Because acquiring the star chart is not enough," Hightower said. "Once we get it we will have no idea how to read it and we will also be unable to understand any instructions we find on how to operate the hyperspace gate. We return Ralu to President Dala, she will be more than willing to assist us with whatever we need."

Drago eyed the captain suspiciously but said nothing.

"Okay," Madigan said, seemingly ready to accept the difficult situation and move forward. "How do we find the Polaris starship?"

"Amus is in contact with the Federation and they've got all of their operatives looking for it," Hightower explained. "When they find it, they will radio his shuttle and let him know. At that point, we will need to strike fast before we lose it again."

"Alright, so we find it," Roger said. "Then what? How do we get on it?"

"Amus is a spy for the Federation. He's got several different Supreme Regency uniforms to choose from—although they're only in his size. This will mean the men that go on board will have to be his same build." The captain paused and glanced at Roger.

The commander sighed. "I guess that means me," he said, realizing he and Amus were the same height.

Hightower nodded. "Yes, and the Polaris starship is the same class as the Pinnacle...the very ship you boarded. No one else here is as familiar with the inside of that ship as you," he explained, then paused. "And I'm roughly the same build as Amus too," he said after a moment.

Colonel Madigan slapped the table and turned toward his friend and captain. "Harry, absolutely not. Now I went along with your ploy to go and meet with the Federation president...but that was only because I'd put my faith and trust in Amus. This is far different. There is no doubt that you're stepping into the lion's den and as executive officer I have to insist that—"

"That's enough Merrill," Hightower said. He reached over and patted his old friend on the back. "I'm the captain and it's ultimately my responsibility to get everyone home. I'm going to do what is required to make that happen, no matter the risk."

Madigan stared into the captain's eyes and shook his head. It was blatantly obvious that he was holding back and wanted to say much more. Hightower could see it too but chose not to acknowledge it.

"I'll be boarding the ship too," Drago said suddenly.

Everyone in the room looked over at him.

"How?" Roger asked. "You're much too large to fit into anything that Amus could wear."

"True," the Bothian agreed. "I'll have to kill a fat Kaloian once we get on board the Polaris. Many of their guards wear helmets. I'd have to kill one of them, so I may conceal my face."

Roger exhaled deeply through his nose and laughed. "Though it's true about the guards and their helmets," he began. "Drago, no offense but I don't see your head fitting into any of those helmets no matter how fat the guard may be."

Drago bared his teeth and pounded his fist on the table. "That will be my problem to overcome," he growled. "You will need me as you Earthlings are much too puny and weak to fight off the Kaloians."

Roger glanced over at the captain and scratched at the side of his head.

"Drago is very…opinionated," Hightower said with a smirk. "His being involved in this operation is non-negotiable."

Roger rolled his eyes. "Okay, so how do we get on board undetected?"

The captain sighed. "I'm still trying to figure that part out," he admitted.

"I have an idea," Drago said with a sneer.

There were more sighs.

"Let's hear it," Colonel Madigan urged.

Drago stood from his stool. "You need to send some of those fighters of yours to attack the ship…it'll create a diversion."

Hightower cleared his throat and ran a hand over his head. "Please elaborate," he said.

"The Voyager star ship has a lot of scanning equipment outside its hull, however almost none of it is used or paid attention to when under attack," he explained.

"That's true," Roger chimed in. "Captain Steiger told me that Kaloians don't take chances and are more dependent on their crewmembers monitoring the surroundings of the ship from the observatories located on the bottom and top of the ship."

"Exactly," Drago said. "But don't interrupt me again."

Roger's jaw dropped open and as he prepared to express his displeasure, Hightower gestured for him to remain silent.

"As I was saying," Drago continued. "During a combat scenario, all the attention—both from the ship scanners, and the observing crew members—is fully directed on whatever is attacking them. If some of your fighters make a surprise attack, it should give us a window of opportunity to sneak aboard in a small shuttle."

Hightower looked around the room. "Thoughts?" he asked no one in particular.

"I have to admit," Madigan said, "it sounds like a legitimate plan."

Drago's eyes narrowed. "Of course, it's legitimate," he quipped. "Once on board, we find a large, plump Kaloian, and then I get in disguise."

Roger again rolled his eyes. "Captain, it all sounds feasible. It's true that I've been on board a Voyager starship, but that doesn't mean I have any idea where to find one of these star charts."

"That's where I come in," Amus said. "I've got plenty of intel to guide us."

"And I assume you know where to find this Ralu character?"

"I do, Commander Stellick," Amus replied. "If it's intel you need, I have it—and what I don't have, I can get."

"So, it's settled," Drago said, happily. He glanced around the room looking for support. "Is it settled?"

"As far as I'm concerned, it is," Hightower said. He turned to Roger. "Stellick, I want the five best pilots out of all the squads assembled and briefed on what we're planning. Do what you must to prepare them, but when the moment arrives, I need them sharp and ready to fight."

Roger nodded. "I'll handle it," he said.

"Amus, gather all the intel you can on the Voyager starship—specifically the Polaris if you can get it," Hightower said as he rose from his chair. "Obviously we are pressed for time and our moment to strike will be unpredictable. Let's use the time we have wisely and prepare."

"Agreed," Drago said. "Now can someone tell me where the drinking establishment is?"

Hightower shook his head and looked to Madigan. "Show him," he said.

***

"So, did you get plenty of rest like I prescribed?" Dr. Phoebe Holtz asked.

She could tell by looking at him that he probably did not take the medication she'd given him to help him sleep. His eyes were red and outlined with dark circles.

"Some," Howler replied dryly.

"How much is some?" she asked as she scribbled something onto the pad in her lap.

Howler shrugged. "I don't know...maybe a couple of four—no five-hour stints."

Phoebe pulled her glasses off and tossed them onto the counter beside her. "Oh Harlan," she groaned.

"I know, I know," he said apologetically. "Doc I want you to know I feel a lot better though."

"Well feeling better isn't quite enough," she replied. "I specifically told you to take the pills and get some rest. All I wanted was forty-eight hours, Harlan."

"I had to go to the memorial service," he countered.

"So, did I. And that lasted a grand total of twenty-five minutes," Phoebe snapped at him.

Howler leaned forward and rested his face into the palms of his hands. "I'm sorry, doc," he said.

"Well I am too," she replied. "I'm sorry because I cannot clear you to return to duty. At least not yet."

"What?" he asked, his voice rising. "Because I didn't sleep as much as you wanted me to?"

"Your life is not worth the gamble, and quite frankly losing another Comet is not worth it either," she said firmly.

"Doc...I'm fine, really," he said, and his eyes pleaded with her to clear him.

"I've made my decision," she said. "Emotionally, you're not where you need to be, and I will not endanger your life and the lives of your fellow pilots. We'll meet back here again in another forty-eight hours. This time try taking the pills and getting some rest."

Howler stared at her and considered begging. Ultimately, he stood up, glaring at her before storming out.

***

When Roger returned to his office, he spent a great deal of time looking down his roster of pilots. Captain Hightower demanded the best he had to offer, and he whole-heartedly felt the same way. If they were going to successfully complete the mission, everyone involved would have to be on the top of their game. The five pilots would come under serious duress from not only the Polaris' cannons, but possibly from a barrage of diamond fighters as well. There was one name on the list that was a no-brainer. Merissa Voight showed incredible skill and bravery during battle. However, she was brash, and he'd seen that before in other pilots that had ended up dead. If he could somehow get her to reign that in, she'd be nearly unbeatable.

Christian Smith would be another easy choice. In his opinion, Sabre was second only to Banshee in sheer talent. One thing that he had that she didn't, was experience. Unfortunately, recent events between he and Harlan Wolfe seemed to have affected his confidence. Nevertheless, Roger felt certain that Sabre would be able to rise to the occasion. The third choice would have to be Gentry McNevin, a member of his own Alpha squad. Gentry, call-sign Cowboy, reminded Roger a lot of himself when he was younger. The pilot was smart and calculated with every decision he made while in the cockpit.

With three relatively easy choices made, Roger still had two more pilots to assign and the decisions got far harder. In his mind, the rest of the pilots were for the most part mirror images of each other—at least in regard to talent. One pilot that did slightly outshine the others was Harlan Wolfe. Howler, much like Sabre, had a wealth of experience that would serve him well in just this sort of mission. Roger knew there was a conflict going on between the two men but believed when it came to the mission, and their execution of it, it would be a non-issue. There was also the matter of Howler's medical clearance. That would depend on Dr. Phoebe Holtz.

He snatched up the phone and pressed a button to contact the infirmary in hopes she would be there. She picked up almost immediately.

"Wow, that was quick," he said. "Do you have a minute?"

"Yes," she replied. "As a matter of fact, I was just getting ready to call you."

"Alright, what's up?"

"It's about Harlan," she said.

Roger chuckled. "That's amazing…I was calling you about him. Is he clear?"

There was a pause and then she said, "I'm afraid not."

Roger was taken aback. It was not the answer he expected. "Oh," he said. "Why not?"

"I think he's still struggling…emotionally," she answered.

"Okay…what's he saying?"

"Oh, he's saying he's just fine," she replied with a chuckle. "But it's clear to me that he's not. He seems distant and emotionally drained."

Roger leaned forward and again looked down his list. "How is he physically?"

"Fine," she answered. "But he's exhausted. He needs rest."

"So, if he was rested up, you'd clear him?" he asked hopefully.

Phoebe sighed. "Roger, don't do this. You're the one that told me not to clear him if he wasn't ready."

Roger smiled, despite himself. "I'm not doing anything," he said. "I just asked a question."

"Then the answer is no, I would not," she replied. "Not until his emotional state is in a better place."

"Phoebe, I think that the best way to get him out of this dark place he's in is to get him back in a Comet," Roger said, pleading his case. "Pilots are like that. Moping around this ship isn't doing him any good, but you get him back in the air...I'm telling you, he'll be back to his old self in no time."

"You're making a lot of assumptions," she quipped.

"Yes, based off my experience as a pilot myself," he countered. "If he wasn't ready physically...or if there was something neurological going on...that would be different."

There was a long awkward pause before she finally replied.

"If you want to send him up and endanger the lives of your other pilots, then that's your call," she huffed.

"You know I can't send him up unless you sign off on it," Roger countered.

"So then if he kills himself or something else, it'll be pinned on me. Is that what you want?"

"No, we'll make it formal. I'll type up a letter encouraging you to clear him. It'll have my signature on it and you hang on to it in case something happens—but nothing will."

Phoebe wanted to argue the matter further but knew ultimately it would do no good. Roger Stellick could be very persuasive and had a knack for being stubborn.

"Fine," she said finally. "But I'm not clearing him until I get your letter."

"You'll have it in a couple of hours," Roger replied.

Phoebe sighed again and disconnected. Roger smiled, knowing full well that he hadn't heard the end of this. Phoebe didn't like being told what to do and he wondered if anyone else on the ship would've been able to persuade her to change her mind. With four pilots chosen, he needed one more.

Again, he looked carefully at each name on the list. Finally, he settled on Arthur Law, call-sign Lawyer. Law was from Delta squad and had the dubious record of being the only pilot to not use a single missile during the battle with the Kaloian starships and fighters. Every one of his kills had been performed using his fighter's cannons only. It was a testament to the pilot's accuracy and could make him an important factor in making sure they all got back to the SC Titan in one piece.

With the last name written down, he grabbed the phone again. This time it would be Chief Tim Reed he would be calling. All five Comets would need to be fully loaded and ready to fly at a moment's notice.

CHAPTER 26

"So, we're bait?" Banshee asked with a raised eyebrow.

"Essentially, yes," Lawyer replied with a chuckle.

They, along with the other three pilots, had just been briefed on the complicated plan to retrieve the star chart off a Supreme Regency star ship.

"Sounds like a suicide mission to me," Gentry McNevin, call-sign Cowboy, said.

"I have no intentions on dying," Lawyer snapped back at him. "If you plan on getting shot down then you just go ahead and keeping calling it that."

Sabre listened to the three pilots bicker, but he kept his eyes on Howler. Harlan Wolfe remained very quiet while Commander Stellick laid out the plan, and once he finished, the pilot immediately made a beeline for the exit without saying a word to anyone. As Sabre watched him disappear around the curvature of the hallway, he felt a gentle squeeze on his shoulder.

"How do you feel about him being a part of the mission?"

It was Commander Stellick.

Sabre turned to face him and shrugged. "Not my decision, sir," he answered. "I trust your judgement."

"I think it'll do him good to get back in the saddle again," Roger replied. "But if you've got some reservations about it, I'm willing to listen."

Sabre shook his head. "No sir, I trust your judgement." He opened his mouth to say more but then thought better of it.

Roger pretended not to notice and instead asked, "Have you and Howler spoken yet?"

Sabre shook his head. "Haven't really had a chance to," he replied. "Ever since we passed through that gate, things have happened so fast."

Roger nodded in agreement. "I understand that, but I'd like for you to try and talk to him before we get the go-ahead on this mission. The sooner the better."

Sabre put his hands in his pockets and considered what Roger had said. "Is that an order, sir?"

Roger smiled. "No," he answered. "It's not."

There was a moment of awkward silence before Roger finally walked away without another word. As Sabre stood there, still pondering what the commander had suggested, a feminine voice spoke up suddenly behind him.

"You should've told him the truth," Banshee said. She stepped around him, so he could see her.

He shot her a confused look. "And what exactly is the truth you're referring to?" he asked.

She crossed her arms and leaned her back against the wall. Sabre looked her over. She was roughly six inches shorter than him, but very fit. Her flight suit looked good on her and he considered her very attractive, despite being completely bald. She pursed her plump red lips before she spoke as it seemed she too was looking him over.

"You don't want Howler flying with us," she said. "Why didn't you just tell him that...you're one of the best pilots on this ship. Stellick would've listened to you."

Sabre chuckled and crossed his own arms. "Sounds like *you're* the one that doesn't want him up there."

Her eyes widened, and she took in a deep breath. "I don't," she admitted matter-of-factly.

"Then why don't you be the one to say something?" Sabre asked, pointing a finger toward her chest.

Banshee glanced at his finger and casually pushed his hand aside. "Because I'm not the one he asked," she grumbled. "However, if Stellick *had* asked me, I'd have the balls to tell him the truth. His head isn't right and he's going to get himself—or one of us—killed. It's going to be dicey enough trying get us all back alive as it is."

Sabre glared at her and held his hands out. "Alright, so get to the point. What is it you want me to do?"

Again, she pursed her lips as she considered the question. "At this point, you go, and you talk to Howler. You tell him whatever you've got to tell him to get his head right."

"And if he shuts me down?"

"Then you go back to Stellick and you tell him how you really feel."

Sabre laughed.

"What's so funny?" Banshee asked, clearly unamused.

"Oh nothing," he quipped. "It's just that you make it all sound so easy. You're not the one Howler is going to punch in the face...I am."

She squinted at him and snorted. "I've been punched by plenty of men and women too. I'll have you know that the women hit harder. Be a man and handle this."

Banshee spun on her heel and strutted away leaving him there dumbfounded.

***

"I've got everything you need," Amus said as he spread multiple documents all over the table. "Brave Avaxians died to get this sort of intel."

Captain Hightower looked over the various photographs and blueprints. He was pleasantly surprised to see that the intel he'd been provided far exceeded what he'd expected to actually get. Before him, it seemed there was a wealth of information on the Voyager class starship—and specifically the Polaris.

"The captain of the ship is a Kaloian named Stuart Lord," Amus said, sliding a picture of the man across the table.

Hightower was surprised to see that the Kaloian appeared very young...much too young to be given captaincy over such an important starship as the Polaris. It was clearly a testament to his intellect and Hightower made a mental note to not underestimate him.

"It's going to be challenging enough to get the star chart *and* freeing my father," Amus said. "But to make matters worse, the brig is located on the bottom deck while the chart is most likely going to be kept on the top deck near the bridge."

Drago licked his lips with his pointed tongue and let out a low growl. "Stop trying to find reasons for us to fail," he said.

Amus glared at him. "I'm just stating facts," he snapped back.

The Bothian rolled his eyes and drummed a claw on the table.

"This is going to be extremely helpful," Hightower said as he glanced over the blueprints to the Polaris. He then looked to Commander Stellick, who was seated at the opposite side of the table. "Stellick, you need to study every document in here backwards and forwards until you know it by heart."

Roger nodded. "With all due respect, I think we both should," he shot back.

"Don't worry about me, I'll know it," he assured him, and then he glanced to Drago. He was still tapping a claw on the table. "You should study it as well."

Drago snorted and waved him off. "Captain, I will follow you and I'll be there to clear a path when needed. There is no need for me to memorize all of this."

Hightower glanced over at Roger. He shrugged and answered with a smirk.

Fully aware that there was no point in arguing the matter further, Captain Hightower returned his attention to Amus. "Do we know when and where we will be able to board?"

The alien's dark blue lips curved upward, and he showed his pointy teeth. "In two days Polaris will be in deep space and at its furthest point from any other Supreme Regency starship. We've discovered that its mission is to send down multiple scanning probes in a grid pattern around the entire planet."

"What are they looking for?" Roger asked.

Amus shrugged. "My guess would be the resource they're missing for their precious elixir. I doubt they'll find it on Pana. It's a planet covered in jungle and considered extremely dangerous."

Hightower raised an eyebrow. "Dangerous how?"

Amus narrowed his eyes. "It's said that it's inhabited by savages—or, well, cannibals."

Roger shuddered. "So, I guess that's why they'll be sending down probes instead of putting boots on the ground."

"Well, yes and no," Amus answered. "The probes obviously cover much more ground in a shorter amount of time and they've been proven to be extremely accurate. However, there is no doubt that the savage tribes that inhabit Pana made it an easy decision."

"So, when is the best time for us to strike?" Roger asked as he leaned back in his chair.

"We wait until they send down their probes," Amus answered. "The ship has to remain stationary for the data that is collected to be as accurate as possible. Sending out multiple probes to monitor an entire planet takes a great deal of planning and time. The crew of the Polaris will be very focused on getting it right the first time. When your fighters attack, trust me, they will be caught completely off guard."

Captain Hightower sat motionless but continued to study all the intel displayed before him. Roger could see the wheels turning in his head.

"Captain, what are you thinking?" he asked.

Hightower looked up at him abruptly. He smiled slightly and rubbed at the back of his neck. "I think we've got a good plan—until we get to the part where we have to leave. We haven't discussed that part very much."

Amus looked at him, confused. "Captain Hightower, it's quite simple in theory. We split into two parties. One party goes to get the star chart. The others then go down to the brig, incapacitate the guards, get Ralu into one of their uniforms, and then we all regroup and sneak out the same way we came in. All we need is for your fighters to keep all of the attention on them while we complete these tasks, and everything will fall into place."

The captain glanced over at Roger and laughed. "You hear that Roger?" he asked skeptically. "Everything will just fall into place...we have nothing to worry about."

The large Bothian watched the exchange with great interest and suddenly began laughing too. "You humans worry too much," he barked. "As I said before, I will follow you and I will clear the path when needed. You have nothing to fear."

Hightower sighed and began to gather up all the documents spread across the table. He glanced up at Roger and said, "I mean it, Stellick. I want all this memorized."

Roger nodded. "I'll begin tonight," he said.

"And your team is ready?" the captain asked, almost as an afterthought.

"They are," Roger answered. "Tim's got our birds fully loaded and I've got what I believe to be the best five pilots on the ship. If there is time to be bought, they'll give us plenty to complete this mission."

Captain Hightower stood from the table and tossed the compiled file across to Roger. "You know the odds are great that we could lose one or more of them," he said, sadly. "Are you certain you've got the best five?"

Roger stared him in the eye and briefly considered each of his choices. The only one that seemed to worry him was Howler. "I'm certain, sir," he answered confidently. "My pilots will be ready, and I think you underestimate them," he added.

The captain raised an eyebrow at him. "How so?"

"I think the odds are greater that all five of them will return back to the Titan," Roger replied.

Captain Hightower kept his eyes focused right on Roger's. "Very good," he said. "I expect nothing less."

CHAPTER 27

Benedict Drayton held up the tiny vial of white liquid and then withdrew the appropriate dosage into the syringe. He then looked down on the unconscious body of Jado Baylor. The young Kaloian was lying on a metal table with a portion of his brain exposed. Benedict glanced at the syringe and then back to Jado. The physician was very cognizant of the fact that what he was about to do would probably kill his unwilling subject, but the decision had not been his own. Romulus Shade was desperate for answers and was willing to get them by whatever means necessary. It surprised him that the Potentate was willing to give up some of the remaining stock of elixir to see what effect it would have on Jado's brain. Injecting the elixir directly into the brain of a subject had never been tried before, but since it seemed Jado had nearly fulfilled his usefulness, Romulus felt it was a worthy endeavor.

Without contemplating the matter further, Benedict suddenly thrust the needle into the exposed portion of Jado's brain. He began pushing the plunger in at a gradual pace and knew it would not take long before he knew if Jado survived the ordeal or not. At first, there was no response at all and in fact, a lot of the elixir seemed to ooze right back out of the tiny hole in which it was injected. Benedict used gauze to dab the excess fluid away and then proceeded to replace the portion of Jado's missing skull. Within a matter of seconds, the physician managed to weld the flesh and bone back together with a laser. Once finished, he placed his surgical tools neatly onto a nearby metal tray and then removed his gloves. Jado still remained motionless and it seemed all life had left him.

"Thank you for your sacrifice," Benedict said, lowering his head.

He then turned away and headed for the exit. The potentate would not be happy to hear of Jado's passing but Benedict hoped he'd be able to show him that it wasn't a complete loss. Though he was dead, Benedict would still be able to conduct more studies on Jado's body. The key to how he was able to unlock the ability without the aid of the elixir was still there, he just had to find it. As the door in front of him slid open, Benedict heard a shuffling sound behind him. He paused and turned to look over his shoulder. Jado's body was shaking slightly.

Dying tissues contracting...nothing more, he thought as he again turned away.

"He-Help m-me," Jado called out suddenly in a sickening groan.

Surprised, Benedict dashed back to the table. "Jado, do you hear me?" he asked.

"Wh-what have you d-done to me?" Jado asked. His tone was a mixture of fear and anger.

"I injected some of the elixir into your brain," Benedict replied. "Are you able to use your ability?"

Jado suddenly opened his eyes and glared at the physician. His right eye was grayed and blind but still, it glared at him. "Why?" he asked, now clearly angered.

Benedict was taken aback by the question. "Why?" he asked in return. "Because we are trying to help you harness your power. If we can help you do that, we'll be able to help others do it as well. It's for the betterment of all Kaloians."

Jado sat up straight on the table and reached out, wrapping his fingers around the throat of Benedict.

"What are you doing?" Benedict rasped as he tried to pry the fingers away.

Jado kept his hand firmly around his captor's neck as he swung his legs off the table and stood.

"Let me go," Benedict said, still struggling to get the words out.

Jado cocked his head to the side, took a deep breath and released his grip. Benedict fell backward and gasped for air. He clutched at his now sore throat and glanced up at Jado. "The potentate will not be happy when he learns of this...this assault!" he spat with fury.

Jado stared at him. "You wanted to unlock the secret of how I used my ability? Well, I think you succeeded."

Benedict stared back at him, bewildered. Suddenly, he felt his body begin to float off the floor.

"W-what are you doing?" he asked, now panicked.

Jado's good eye watched him intensely but he said nothing. Benedict continued to float until he reached the ceiling.

"Release me!"

It came out more like a plea than a demand. Benedict then began to feel pressure around his skull.

"Please...no," he said, unable to conceal the pain.

Jado looked on as the physician opened his mouth to say more, but before he could, his head imploded.

***

Malcolm Steiger was impressed with how quickly he'd adapted to his new legs. In only a weeks' time he'd figured out how to walk briskly and was ready for the next challenge: climbing stairs. Benedict Drayton was a very gifted physician and it was easy to see why the potentate had employed him to be his own personal doctor. Though he was grateful for the new legs, he was now full of newfound hatred for the man responsible for putting him in that condition. He felt as if he were a prisoner in the palace and wondered what his future may be. Malcolm vowed that the first opportunity he found to escape, he would take full advantage of it.

The room in which he now found himself, was windowless but furnished with all the luxuries necessary to make him comfortable. His best guess was that he was being held on the upper level of the palace which would only compound the complications he would face if there was any chance of escape. Once a day, Benedict Drayton would visit, supply him medicine, and coach him on the use of his new cybernetic legs. Afterwards, he'd leave him instructions on a particular exercise he wanted him to practice until their next meeting. As much as Malcolm wanted to do anything but cooperate, he also knew that if he was going to get away, he'd need his legs to do so. So, rather reluctantly, he followed every instruction he was given. His time would come and when it did, he would be ready.

Suddenly he heard screaming. Malcolm made his way to the door, his new metallic feet clanging with each step. He then put his ear against the door and listened. He heard more screaming, and then a sickening *thud* that sounded like flesh being pummeled. Now there were footsteps (it sounded like bare feet) and they were approaching his door. Malcolm instinctively stepped back and looked around the room for something that would serve as a weapon. Within seconds he settled on a metal stool. As soon as the footsteps reached the other side of the door, they ceased, and it was clear that whomever was there was interested in the contents of his room. Malcom gritted his teeth and gripped the stool tightly. Something told him that he was going to have to use it.

As he watched, unblinking, the metal door began to creak and vibrate. Without further warning, it suddenly tore loose from its frame and rocketed across the room, narrowly missing Malcolm in its trajectory. Without thinking, Malcolm threw the stool in the direction of his unknown visitor. He then watched in utter amazement as the stool stopped in mid-air.

"Jado?" Malcolm asked, looking past the floating stool.

His former crewman stood in the mangled doorway and stared at him. One of his eyes was grayed and dead. His head was hairless and now melded together in a bloody pulp. The only clothing he wore was the underwear around his waist.

"Captain Steiger," Jado replied. "I've come to free you from this place."

"What have they done to you?" Malcolm asked. "Did the potentate do this to you?"

Jado cocked his head to the side and stared at him, expressionless. "His physician did this to me."

Malcolm's brow tightened. "At Romulus Shade's command I'm sure," he replied. He then glanced over at the stool, still floating in the air. "Jado, how are you...?"

Jado, suddenly remembering the stool, turned his attention to it and allowed it to float slowly to the ground. "Come, let's leave this place," he said.

Without saying another word, Jado turned away and Malcolm chased after him. Once in the hallway, he discovered that he'd been correct in assuming he was being held captive on the upper floor of the palace. As they approached the spiraled staircase that led downward, they were met by four armed palace guards. Jado slowed his pace but did not stop moving forward. The guards shouted a command for him to stop and lifted their plasma rifles as they did so. Malcolm expected that this would be where he'd surely meet his demise but was shocked and amazed to see that instead the guns held by each guard suddenly twisted violently as an unseen force ripped the weapons from each man's grasp. As Jado continued to move forward, all four men—two on the left and two on the right—were suddenly thrust hard against the walls next to them.

As Jado began his descent down the stairwell, Malcolm quickly retrieved one of the discarded plasma rifles before continuing after him. Miraculously, they met no new opposition until they reached the bottom floor of the palace. It was there that Hugo Horne and at least twenty more armed guards were waiting.

"Stop right there!" Horne commanded with authority.

Malcolm was shocked to see that Jado complied. He held up his rifle, ready to fire when necessary.

"I have no desire to hurt any of you," Jado said, seemingly taking a moment to look each guard in the eyes. "None of you have caused me or the captain any harm. Allow us passage so that we may see the potentate."

Hugo Horne raised one of his bushy eyebrows and stared at Jado incredulously. He then looked to the soldiers on either side of him. Slowly and softly, they began to chuckle. The chuckles soon evolved into roaring laughter. "Do you *really* think we're going to allow you to see the potentate?" he asked, breathless.

Malcolm kept his head pointed straight at the guards, but he allowed his eyes to drift over at Jado. As he expected, the young Kaloian was not amused. His brow tightened, and his mouth became a straight line.

"So be it," he whispered.

At that moment, Hugo Horne's rifle was torn from his grasp in the same fashion that Malcolm had witnessed with the guards at the top of the stairwell. Malcolm watched the weapon whirl through the air until it crashed into the wall near him, seemingly rendering it useless. At that exact same moment, the other twenty guards turned their own weapons onto each other. Malcolm could see by the expressions on their faces that they had absolutely no control over their actions. He wanted to close his eyes because he knew what was coming, but somehow, he forced his eye lids to remain opened. The next few seconds became a horrifying spectacle of terrified men falling to the ground in expanding pools of blood, plasma rifles still smoking in their grasps.

The display startled Hugo Horne severely, and he literally ran toward where Jado and Malcolm stood to get away from the carnage. Once it was over, he looked over at Jado, his bottom jaw drooping.

"How?" he asked, dumbfounded.

Jado took a step toward him. A trickle of blood originated from the surgical wound on his head and eventually slid down the front of his face, its path going right over the blind eye.

"Allow me passage to see the potentate," he said in a voice just above a whisper.

Hugo continued to stare at Jado, but his mouth closed as he seemed to regain his composure. Without speaking, he reached for his axe.

"Don't do it," Malcolm cautioned.

Hugo momentarily looked over at him, but he ignored the warning. In a spilt second the axe was streaking through the air in an arc directly toward Jado's head. It came within a fraction of an inch of Hugo's skull before stopping abruptly. The large security chief's eyes widened with disbelief. The muscles in his arms tightened as he tried to force the axe onward into its intended target, but to no avail. The disbelief quickly turned to panic and before long, Hugo had completely released the axe and ran away.

"Should we kill him?" Jado asked, still seemingly willing to take orders from his captain.

"No," Malcolm replied, lowering his gun. "Let him go."

They watched as the large Kaloian man retreated from the palace, his black robe billowing in the wind behind him as he fled. Once he was gone, Jado marched toward the throne room and barged through the metal doors. At the opposite end of the room, Potentate Romulus Shade was seated upon his throne. There was a small table next to him with the coiled whip resting upon it.

"Good to see the two of you are back on your feet," he said, his teeth clacking. He paused and glanced at Malcolm's new legs. "That is a definite improvement," he said, with a smirk.

Malcolm raised the plasma rifle and pointed it at the potentate's chest. "I should kill you right now," he grumbled through clenched teeth.

"I don't think I'm going to allow that today," Romulus countered, and with a dazzling display of speed and agility, he reached for, and uncoiled the whip.

Malcolm fired the plasma rifle but missed as the potentate ducked and then rolled behind the throne. With more quickness, he emerged from the other side but now the whip was illuminated with blue light— electricity. In a fluid motion, the potentate flicked the whip at Malcolm. The end of it wrapped around his throat and jerked him forward, toward Romulus. Suddenly, with no control of his basic motor functions, Malcolm was unable to move, and the gun fell from his grasp. He was having trouble breathing as the electrical current ripped through his throat and then blossomed throughout the rest of his body.

"Stop!" Jado shouted. He attempted to use his ability but found he had trouble using it on the potentate.

"It won't work," Romulus said with a sneer. He then waved his free arm, and the throne behind him suddenly hurtled through the air at Jado. After narrowly missing the flying chair, with seemingly no other option, Jado began to plea for the captain's life. "Let him go, please!" he shouted.

The potentate laughed and flicked his wrist in a motion that released the whip from Malcolm's neck. The electrical current then ceased and the whip became ordinary again. Malcolm immediately wrapped his hands around his neck and began to rub away the pain as he coughed and gasped for air.

"Only temporarily," Romulus said as he pulled a small glass vial from the pocket of his robe. Jado could see it was empty, with only a small trace of a white substance remaining inside it. He held the glass container up to the light that shone through the large stained-glass window behind him. "This was one of the last ten vials left in my personal stock of the elixir," he explained. "I'm now down to eight," he added as he slid the vial back into his pocket.

"I suppose the other missing one was injected into my brain this morning," Jado snapped.

The potentate nodded and casually walked down the steps toward Jado. He recoiled the whip he'd used as he did so. "That's correct," he admitted. "Somehow the ability exists in you without the aid of the elixir. We were trying to figure out which portion of your brain was responsible for that. Benedict was going to try whatever means necessary to figure that out. He was obviously working under my orders." The potentate paused a moment and stared at his coiled whip. "Did you kill him?" he asked.

Jado sighed, and then nodded. "Yes, I did." There was no remorse in his tone.

For a split second, a sadness came over Romulus, and his gray eyes seemed to glisten with moisture. He frowned and clenched his fists. After looking away for a moment, he suddenly returned his gaze upon Jado. "I am not your enemy," he said, doing his best to sound genuine.

"You *are* very much his enemy," Malcolm rasped. He was still clutching at his throat while lying on his back.

"Your ability," Romulus continued as he ignored Malcolm. "I can help you control it."

"Do not listen to him," Malcolm said. Now he was struggling to get onto his hands and knees.

Jado regarded him skeptically. "Why should I believe you?"

"You shouldn't," Malcolm said. He was now standing and had grabbed Jado by the arm. "In case you've forgotten, he's responsible for this," he added, pointing to his cybernetic legs. "And he's responsible for the condition you're in now."

The potentate smiled smugly and placed the coiled whip over his shoulder. He then crossed his arms and glared at Jado. "Young man, you're now the most powerful Kaloian I've ever seen," Romulus said. "Captain Steiger is correct...I'm responsible for that. If there is a price to be paid, then I'll gladly pay it, but I challenge you to consider your worth now. All I have ever wanted is for our people to be safe and in control of this galaxy—with you by my side, we can easily make that a reality."

"Control the galaxy?" Jado asked, taken aback. "Why is that so important to you?"

Romulus sighed and then glumly walked over to where his throne rested on the stone floor in front of him. He turned it upright and took a seat. "Our control of the galaxy is the only way to guarantee our complete safety. There are many other races in the universe that could potentially threaten our existence. Those races must be wiped out. Kaloians must take a proactive approach." He paused and then pointed toward Captain Steiger. "He is very much aware of what our agenda is."

Jado listened intently to what the potentate had said, and then he turned to look at his captain. "Is what he says true?" he asked. "Are there races in the universe that want to destroy us?"

Malcolm clenched his jaw and closed his eyes. "Yes, it's true," he said finally. "It's been the goal of the Supreme Regency since its inception...to be the supreme race in all the galaxy."

"And it's been my job to lead us there at all costs," the potentate said, glancing down at Malcolm's legs.

"How long does the elixir last?" Jado asked, his eyes focused on the empty vial in Romulus' hand.

"A dose this size will last me a few hours," he replied. He tossed the vial aside. It shattered when it hit the stone floor. "You're at a crossroads now," Romulus continued, staring at Jado. "You can try and defeat me, or you can get on board and join me in my efforts. With my experience and your power, no one will be able to stop us."

Jado looked away from the potentate and over at his captain. "What about Captain Steiger?"

Romulus looked at Malcolm with indifference. "Captain Steiger's expertise is still valuable to us," he said. "In fact, I have an important task for him if he is interested."

Malcolm's interest *did* pique but he did his best not to show it. "What would you like for me to do?" he asked flatly.

"Are you familiar with the Polaris starship?" Romulus asked.

Malcolm considered the question and then nodded. "Yes," he replied. "Captain Stuart Lord's ship."

The potentate nodded in reply and seemed pleased that Malcolm was familiar with him. "Yes, the youngest captain in the entire Supreme Regency's fleet," he said. "Are you familiar with the cargo that he is carrying?"

Malcolm and Jado looked at each other, and Malcolm shrugged. "I assume he has the same cargo as almost any other Supreme Regency ship," he answered. "I think I heard they're primarily a research ship."

"President Dala's husband is in their brig," Romulus said, very matter-of-factly. "He was captured almost a year ago and has been on board the Polaris ever since."

Jado looked at the potentate curiously. "You've kept one of the most powerful Avaxians on board a research vessel for almost a year? Why?" he asked.

"Because I've been using him as bait," Romulus replied sharply. "I've believed for a long time that sooner or later, the Federation would come for him. But it has not happened, and I've grown tired of waiting. I think the time has come to go and retrieve him."

"You want me to go and retrieve him for you?" Malcolm asked.

Potentate Romulus Shade smiled. "No, I'm afraid I don't trust you to handle a task as important as that on your own," he replied. "In fact, the only person I trust to perform such an important duty is myself. What I want is for you to pilot the shuttle that will take me to retrieve him."

"What are you going to do with him?" Jado asked.

Romulus seemed annoyed by the question. "He'll be brought back to stand trial and ultimately face execution," he replied. "It's my hope that if the news of his impending doom reaches President Dala, she'll do something rash. And when she does, our forces will be ready."

"If they haven't come for him on board the Polaris, what makes you think they'll come for him here?" Malcolm asked. "It stands to reason that an attempt to rescue him off that ship would probably be easier than getting him here."

"I can't answer that question," Romulus admitted. "It's obvious that they're cowards, but I just didn't know how badly. I would guess that if the stakes were higher and the president's husband was facing death, maybe they'd finally get the courage to come and fight."

"What about the Bothians?" Malcolm asked.

"What about them?"

"They're aligned with the Federation as well," Malcolm answered. "If you don't fear the Avaxians, surely you respect the fighting spirit of the Bothians."

"Of course, I do," Romulus answered. "Why do you think I've gone to great lengths to find the resource needed to produce more of the elixir for our armies? It's the only way to gain us the advantage needed to overtake those barbaric lizards."

"Our armies outnumber theirs," Malcolm countered. "That's an important strategic advantage."

"Yes," the potentate agreed. "But it's not enough. Have you ever seen a Bothian warrior up close?"

Malcolm shook his head.

"If you had, you'd understand my cautious nature regarding them," Romulus answered. "But now we have him," he added, pointing at Jado.

Malcolm glanced at the young Kaloian and back to Romulus. "You expect him to take on an entire army?"

"Of course not," the potentate replied, with a dismissive hand. "But he and I together...we could be a force unlike anything they've ever seen."

Malcolm again looked at Jado. "Remember that any decision you make is your own," he said. "Do not let him persuade you to do anything you are not comfortable with."

"I want to help," Jado answered, but then he paused and reached for his blind eye. He then ran a finger across the bloodied meld of flesh on top of his skull. "But I've been made into a monster," he said, just above a whisper. He then turned toward the potentate and gave him a cold stare. "You're a cruel leader and I should murder you."

The potentate moved his hand over the handle of the coiled whip. "I do not regret my decision," he said. "Your abilities have been completely unlocked thanks to my decision. It's up to you what to do with them."

Malcolm took a step forward. "You chopped my legs off," he growled.

"And I gave you new ones—better ones," Romulus argued. "I've improved the both of you. You're both still here and you're both still alive. Now as I said, you are at a crossroads. Do you want to choose the path that will protect all Kaloians?"

Jado and Malcolm looked at each other but said nothing.

"If you decide the answer to that question is 'yes', then we do not have a moment to spare," the potentate said, rising from his throne. "If we leave now, we can reach the Polaris in less than two days' time."

"*We?*" Jado asked. "You want me to come along too?"

Romulus nodded. "I told you that I will teach you how to control your power. I can't exactly do that if you're not by my side."

If it had been up to Malcolm, he'd have killed Potentate Shade right where he stood. He did not trust him and wanted nothing more than to tell him. Jado, however, was younger and easier persuaded. Malcolm could see the light in the young Kaloian's eyes when Romulus spoke of protecting the entire Kaloian race. He made the cause sound extremely noble. It was all that Jado needed and Malcolm felt his heart sink as he came to the realization that he was on the verge of becoming Potentate Shade's personal shuttle pilot.

CHAPTER 28

When Sabre arrived at the door, he raised his hand to knock, but paused. He stood there for almost a solid minute before finally getting the courage to follow through and rasp his knuckles against the metallic surface. After a few seconds, the door slid open to reveal Harlan Wolfe. He looked exhausted, his eyes bloodshot. When he saw Sabre, he grunted and turned back toward the interior of his room.

"What do you want?" he grumbled.

Sabre marched forward. "You and I need to talk," he said.

Howler spun on his heel and then fell backward onto the faux leather couch behind him. There was a round window above his head and Sabre watched the stars move slowly past as he waited for some sort of response.

"There is nothing to talk about," Howler said finally, and he reached for a bottle on the small table next to him. He took a long pull from the beer, apparently finishing it off. He tossed it aside, and it clanged loudly on the metal floor. "Stellick put you up to this?"

Sabre sighed and put his hands in his pockets as he stood there. "No—well, yes," he admitted. "The truth is, he told me to come talk to you, but I wanted to do it myself anyway."

Howler stared at him for a long moment before finally rubbing at his eyes. "Okay, Smith, so talk," he said, sounding as if he just wanted it to be over with.

"Well, I was thinking that we could go somewhere else to talk," Sabre said.

Howler glanced around at his room. It was messy. There were clothes all over the floor and dirty dishes on the kitchen counter. Though he was probably nose-blind to it, he guessed it probably smelled quite bad in there too. "Go where?" he asked, sitting up straighter on the couch.

Sabre shifted on his feet. "I figured we'd go partake in one of your newest hobbies," he said with a smile. "Let's go to the bar for drinks."

Howler chewed on his lip as he considered the offer. Truthfully, he hadn't drank much in several hours. Before he even realized what he was doing, he felt himself rising from the couch. "Okay, but you're buying," he said, pointing at Sabre.

"I wouldn't have it any other way," Sabre replied, motioning for him to lead the way.

Howler glared at him as he moved past, but quickly made his way out of the room and into the hallway outside. Sabre walked alongside him, and they caught a glimpse of Moon Dog and Banshee retreating into her room. They were laughing and seemed to be drunk.

"How about that," Sabre said with a chuckle. "Never knew Moon Dog had a thing for bald chicks."

Howler smiled, though briefly. "She is one hell of a pilot," he said, referring to Banshee.

"Yeah," Sabre answered. "I've heard. I'm glad she's part of the team Stellick put together."

"And how do you feel about me being a part of that team?" Howler asked. He kept his eyes forward as they entered the bar.

Ray Compton, the bartender, was polishing off a section of the wooden bar top when he spotted the two men enter. He waved them over. "Got a spot just for you," he said.

Both men took their respective seats on a stool and Howler wasted no time ordering a shot of whiskey. Sabre looked at him, surprised.

"Is there a problem with that?" Howler asked.

Sabre held up both hands. "No sir," he said. "You're a big boy, drink what you want. Just keep in mind we could be called into duty at any moment. I'm not sure how the captain would feel—"

"You haven't answered my question," Howler interrupted.

Sabre ordered a beer and once Ray set about fulfilling their orders, he said, "I guess that depends."

"On what?" Howler said, turning to look at him.

"On whether you've still got some sort of grudge toward me," Sabre answered.

Ray returned quickly and slid a shot glass and a brown bottle in front of the two men. "Drink up fellas," he said cheerfully before retreating away yet again.

Howler downed the amber liquid in the glass immediately. "Did you ever meet Ben Foster?" he asked.

Sabre considered the question. Ben Foster, call-sign Bones, was one of the pilots lost from Hotel Squad. "Unfortunately, I never had the pleasure of meeting him," he replied softly.

"So, then I assume you're unaware that he was the youngest pilot on the ship."

Sabre swallowed hard. "No, I did not know that," he said.

Howler turned to look over at him. "I'd venture to guess you also were unaware of how terrified he was when we were called into action so quickly," he said.

Sabre stared back at him, wide-eyed and unblinking. He shook his head.

"It's true," Howler said. "He was young, and he was terrified. Mentally, he was not ready for this mission. The only way I was able to get him to calm down at all was to make him a promise before we went up. Do you know what I promised him?"

Sabre shifted uncomfortably. "No," he whispered before taking a pull from his bottle.

"I promised him that I'd see to it that he got back alive," Howler said, still staring over at him. "I made him believe that my leadership would be enough to get him through it."

Sabre sighed and shook his head. He began to feel anger welling up in him. "Well if you said that, you shouldn't have," he said, glaring at him. "You know, Cyclops died up there too. He died while you were still in the fight—but it seems as if you easily forget about him."

Howler's mouth dropped open slightly and his eyes narrowed. "What the hell did you just say to me?" he snapped.

"You heard exactly what I said," Sabre spat back. "Your leadership failed Cyclops and you seem to easily forgive yourself for that one."

"You don't have a clue about how I feel about Cyclops," Howler argued.

"Sure, I do," Sabre said. "You were about to give me a sob story about Bones and twist it to how I'm somehow to blame for his death, but you conveniently forget that you lost two pilots that day. You want someone else to blame and I'm the easy target."

Howler pushed back from the bar and stood up suddenly. "You need to quit while you're still ahead, Smith," he growled.

Sabre pushed back from the bar and stood too.

"You boys need to calm down," Ray Compton said nervously when he noticed the commotion.

Sabre ignored him. "What exactly are you going to do?" he asked Howler.

"Nothing...if you shut up now," he replied coldly.

Sabre shook his head and ran a hand through his hair. "Why don't you just get this over with?" he asked, wide-eyed.

"Get what over with?"

"Just hit me so we can move on," he snapped. "I'm sick of this and I won't have you endangering the other pilots because of some grudge you've got against me. So why don't you just go ahead and get it—"

Before he could finish the sentence, Howler connected with a right hook. As Sabre fell backward, the dim lights of the bar slowly faded to black.

***

When he awoke, Sabre immediately noticed that he was still in the bar, but he'd been moved to one of the tables in a darkened corner.

"Are you alright?" a voice asked. It took him a moment, but the face in front of him came into focus and he saw Arthur Law looking him over.

"L-lawyer?" he asked groggily.

"Yeah, it's me," Lawyer answered.

"You boys better be glad we showed up when we did," Cowboy said from the other side of the table.

Sabre looked over at him and noticed Howler was seated beside him. "You punched me," he said, glaring at him.

Howler smiled sheepishly. "You sorta provoked me," he said.

"And you both could be sitting in the brig if we hadn't showed up when we did," Cowboy said. "You're lucky Lawyer here is a smooth talker and kept Ray from reporting it."

"Whatever is going on between you two ends right here and now," Lawyer said, and his tone suggested there would be another fight if they argued with him.

"I'm done," Sabre said, holding up both hands. "I'm not the one that started any of this."

Howler cleared his throat and rubbed at the back of his neck. "I said what I needed to say," he muttered. "I'm done."

"Well I hope so," Cowboy replied. "Because we aren't too keen about flying with you boys on this mission if we gotta worry about the two of you killing each other when you're supposed to be watching each other's backs—and ours."

"No need to worry about that," Howler promised. "It's over." He then held a hand across the table. Sabre looked at it, and then back up to Howler. "I'm sorry," Howler added. "My anger was a bit…misguided."

Sabre sat up straight, rubbed his sore jaw but reached across the table. The two men shook hands.

"Aw, that's better," Cowboy said, sarcasm oozing off every syllable.

Lawyer took a deep breath and shook his head, but he smiled. "Alright, kids," he said as he began to get up. "If you'll excuse me and Cowboy, I think we're going to go have a drink and forget any of this ever happened."

"No," Howler said, and he motioned for him to sit back down. "I'll buy the drinks and I want you all to drink with me."

Cowboy and Lawyer looked at each other. After a moment, Lawyer shrugged and returned to his seat. "Well, I suppose it's not a bad idea since the gang's all here," he said. "Should someone go and retrieve Banshee?"

At that moment, it was Sabre and Howler's turn to exchange a glance. "Uh, I don't think so," Sabre said.

"Yeah," Howler added. "We saw her earlier...she's a little busy."

"Alright," Lawyer said with a questioning glance. "Well her loss I suppose."

The four men spent the next hour drinking and getting to know each other far better. Sabre, though his jaw was sore and one of his back teeth felt loose, believed all the strife he'd experienced that night turned out to be well worth it. For the first time, he truly felt he could trust *all* four of the men to watch his back during a dogfight.

CHAPTER 29

"Are we certain everything is in order?" Colonel Madigan asked.

His red hair was disheveled, and he seemed very concerned. In fact, Roger never remembered seeing him so worried before.

"Everything is in order, our time has come," Captain Hightower said. He grabbed his executive officer and friend by the neck and pulled him near. The two men hugged. It was an uncharacteristic gesture between the two senior officers and something about it made Roger feel a bit uneasy. Something in his gut made him wonder if the two men were seeing each other for the final time.

"I'll hold her down until you return, sir," Madigan said. "Good luck and God speed to you all," he added, glancing over at Roger, Amus, and Drago.

The large Bothian stepped forward. "Would you care to hug me as well, colonel?" He stretched out his large arms.

Madigan huffed and raised his chin defiantly. "Take care of the captain," he told Roger, ignoring the reptilian alien.

"When we return, just make sure the ship is ready for the voyage home," Hightower said in an effort to change the subject and ease the tension a bit.

"It will be," Madigan assured him with a salute.

Hightower nodded and followed Drago onto the small shuttle that Amus had arrived in days earlier. Amus explained that the shuttle had once belonged to the Supreme Regency. The shuttle was called a Sloop and was used primarily to transport senior officers to and from Supreme Regency star ships. The Federation managed to acquire the shuttle during a raid on a small Supreme Regency base on the planet Katoo. Though it was likely that the Supreme Regency was aware that the vehicle had been stolen, the Federation had gone to great lengths to change its identifying numbers and even disable the electronic beacon on board that would further identify the ship to any nearby Supreme Regency radar systems. It would not take long for the enemy to realize something was amiss about the shuttle once they discovered the beacon was nonfunctional, but the attacking Comet fighters would be able to provide enough of a diversion to hopefully give them the small window of time they needed to board the Polaris.

As Amus began to fire up the engines, Roger paused and took a moment to salute the five pilots he'd handpicked to pilot the Comet fighters. All of them appeared rested, and very focused on the job at hand. Roger was pleasantly surprised to see that Howler and Sabre had seemed to resolve the conflict between them. The two men stood beside each other, smiling and in great spirits. Roger was unable to shake the uneasy feeling he had when he looked at each of the pilots. It was similar to the feeling he had when he'd watched the captain and executive officer embrace just minutes earlier. There was a sense of dread that appeared to be intensifying and it was a very unsettling feeling. As bad as he was feeling, Roger did not dare show it or make it known to anyone else. Everyone needed to be focused. The mission was going to happen whether they would all survive it or not.

"Good luck, commander," Tim Reed said, offering a salute of his own to Roger.

Roger smiled and patted the big man on the shoulder. "Thanks Tim," he said. "Keep everyone in line until I return."

"You got it," he answered, and he made a gesture with his arm to indicate it was time for he too to board the shuttle.

Roger said nothing but nodded. He then trotted up the ramp as it began to rise behind him. Once the door was fully sealed, he made his way to a seat and buckled in. Hightower was seated beside him.

"Nervous?" the Captain asked as the men felt the shuttle begin to rise off the metal deck.

Roger cleared his throat and shook his head. He allowed himself to sink back into the white, cushioned seat. "No, not really," he said. "I think anxious is a better word to describe it."

"Good," Hightower said, and he turned to look out of the window. The shuttle had turned and began to pick up speed as it floated through the launch bay tube. Suddenly, they were in the expanse of space, stars littered their surroundings in all directions. He looked back to Roger. "A lot is riding on what your boys can do in those fighters," he said.

Roger wanted to roll his eyes and ask the captain how many times he was going to remind him of that, but he was disciplined. He instead said, "They're ready...and one of them is a girl."

Hightower smiled. "Oh yes, my mistake," he replied. "Merissa Voight...or Banshee."

"Yes sir," Roger said.

Suddenly there was a shrill sound outside the shuttle as the Comet fighters caught up to them. Roger watched them intently and soon realized the fighter nearest the window beside he and Hightower was piloted by Banshee.

"That's her there," he said, pointing.

Hightower stroked his chin and stared at the spacecraft a moment. "General Porter Buchanon was quite fond of her," he said.

Roger looked over at him, somewhat surprised. "Really?" he asked, intrigued. "What do you mean?"

"He said she reminds him a lot of his daughter," Hightower replied.

Roger's mouth opened slightly and transformed into a frown. "Didn't his daughter die?"

Hightower nodded. "Yes, but truthfully, he does favor her greatly. I can see why he took a liking to her. He said he believed she was destined for some sort of greatness."

Roger's frown suddenly disappeared and was replaced with a smirk. "Well she's certainly capable," he said. "But she is also very rough around the edges. She has a history of insubordination."

The captain bit his lower lip and nodded. "Yes, I'm aware," he said. "Has she shown you any of that?"

"Insubordination?" he asked, raising an eyebrow. "No, absolutely not."

"The Titan has now departed and is leaving this sector," Amus called out from the cockpit.

Hightower replied with a thumbs up. So far, everything was going according to plan. Within minutes, they'd be within sight of the Polaris, and then things would get serious. Each of them—with the exception of Drago—was already wearing black Supreme Regency armor. They each had a helmet as well that would easily hide their true identities. Once on board the Polaris, getting Drago a disguise would have to be a top priority if they were going to be able to move undetected.

"Let them know we're going to fall back and let them engage the ship," Hightower called out to Amus. "Remind them to stick to the plan and to disengage at the appropriate time they were given."

The blue alien nodded and pulled the mic close to his mouth to relay the message. Drago had been resting on a large bench seat near the back of the shuttle, but he suddenly rose to his feet and began pacing.

"You alright big fella?" Roger asked him.

The Bothian's lip curled slightly to reveal several dagger-like teeth. "I'm fine," Drago answered. "I'm eager to board the enemy vessel so I can begin killing."

The shuttle suddenly decelerated dramatically—to the point that Drago nearly stumbled over. The Comets streaked by on either side of them and all at once, they were all alone.

"The time is here," Amus said as he reached for the black helmet on the floor next to him. "I think we should all get ready."

Hightower and Roger quickly put on their helmets.

"Put the comm on speaker so we can hear what's going on," Hightower said, his voice muffled from under the helmet.

Amus flipped a switch and the static was immediately followed by the voice of Arthur Law.

"Polaris in sight," he said. "Engaging the enemy in 3...2...1..."

***

When Sabre climbed into the cockpit of his fighter, the last thing he expected to see was a note from Charlie West. But there it was, on a strip of tape applied horizontally across the very top of the instrument panel. The message was short and to the point.

Make sure you come back, Lauren needs you!

At first, the message confused him immensely. To the best of his recollection, the last time he'd spoken with Charlie, things had not gone well. But the more he thought about it, he began to wonder if perhaps it'd gone better than he'd initially thought. He remembered telling Charlie that he'd find a way to earn his trust, and apparently somehow, he'd managed to do just that. The note, as simple as it was, had given him a boost of confidence that seemed to increase his focus and vigor significantly. For the first time in a while, he felt unstoppable.

"Look alive guys and gal," Lawyer said, shattering Sabre's thoughts. "Our E.T.A. with the Polaris is three minutes. Check all your weapons and gauges...make sure you're all ready to go. Stay on top of your respective assignments and every one of us will be back on the Titan shortly. And when we are...drinks are on me."

"That sounds like a plan," Cowboy said.

"Everyone please confirm you've completed a final weapons check," Lawyer added.

"I'm good here," Cowboy replied.

"Weapons good," Howler said.

"Ready to go," Sabre confirmed.

"See if you boys can keep up," Banshee said. "If you get into trouble, just squeal."

"Thanks for the offer," Lawyer replied. "But how are those weapons?"

"The weapons are what they are...if there is an issue there isn't a damn thing any of us can do about it now," Banshee answered.

Lawyer sighed and rolled his eyes in his cockpit. "I think we'd still like to know," he said.

Banshee offered no response.

"Alright, time's up," Howler said suddenly. "I've got a visual on the Polaris."

"I see it," Lawyer replied. Behind the starship, looming large and covered in lush, green color, was the planet Pana. "Alright, let's do this! Keep radio silence while I alert the captain..." there was a pause, and then, "Polaris in sight. Engaging the enemy in 3...2...1..."

At that moment, he flipped the switch to reconnect with the rest of the squad and then immediately squeezed the trigger on the stick in front of him. The Comet cannons erupted in a thunderous roar of firepower. The barrage of large caliber bullets peppered the bow of the almond-shaped Kaloian spacecraft. Within three seconds, the Polaris responded by ejecting numerous balls of blue plasma from its cannons. All five Comets rolled and banked in different directions, narrowly missing the onslaught of enemy fire.

"Stay out of range of those cannons!" Howler shouted over the radio.

"They can be destroyed," Banshee said. "I took out the cannons on the Pinnacle."

"I think Howler's right," Cowboy said. "We should probably concentrate on staying clear of them for now...we're gonna have our hands full with their fighters here in a minute."

"We need to minimize that...stick to the plan and get ready to open fire on their launch bays," Lawyer said, doing his best to keep everyone focused.

Sabre had been listening, but his attention had been completely on the Polaris, and nothing else. He'd placed his focus entirely on the large square panel atop the rear portion of the Kaloian ship. That, he'd learned, was where the radar and weapons guidance systems were housed. Though it was protected with heavy armor, Amus had been confident that a well-placed hit from one of the Comet missiles would probably be enough to disable those systems.

He broke off from the rest of the group and immediately targeted the panel. Without hesitation, he fired a missile and it flew true. The projectile made a direct hit upon the panel and inflicted enough force to rip it in half. Both portions of the metal armor hurtled upward into space, exposing the fragile systems housed within it.

"Radar and weapons guidance systems are exposed," he alerted the rest of the squad.

Sabre pulled back on the stick and began a vertical climb upward. He caught sight of the floating debris that had been a result of his missile and tugged slightly on the stick to ensure that he stayed clear of it. As he continued to pull back on the stick, his craft became inverted and before long he began a descent downward and directly over the exposed panel atop the Polaris. Just as he was about to unleash another missile, a purple bolt flashed by him, nearly hitting his Comet head on. Apparently, the diamond-shaped Kaloian fighters had already launched.

Howler and Lawyer had made a beeline for the launching bays and just as they prepared to engage them, the diamond fighters began swarming out like a cloud of bees. Both pilots simultaneously unleashed their cannons and fortunately, the effort was highly effective. They looked on as dozens of diamond fighters shattered to pieces, while some spiraled wildly out of control.

"Good shooting!" Cowboy said, as he witnessed the skillful display.

"Nice job, but don't celebrate too much," Banshee warned. "Dozens more got out. Let's get to work!"

***

"Incredible," Drago said, in obvious awe. "For such a weak race, you seem to possess the hearts of a Katooian lion," he added with admiration.

"It's true," Amus agreed. "Your pilots are quite skilled."

Roger swelled with pride. "You're watching the best of the best."

Hightower leaned forward, eyeing the Polaris. "Now is our time," he said, determined. "We board now."

Amus nodded, his black helmet hiding the smile upon his face. With effortless precision he guided the small shuttle down below the heavy fighting, occasionally dodging both bullets and plasma bolts as they advanced. With as much subtlety as one could muster in such a situation, Amus quietly approached the bay opening of the Polaris from down low. As the shuttle entered the ship, they were met with oncoming diamond fighters scrambling to join the fight against the attacking Comets.

"What are those tiny fighter ships called?" Roger asked, curiously.

"They are called cutters," Amus answered. "Very small and agile crafts...but very easy to destroy."

"They're shaped like diamonds," Roger said. He paused as he considered the ship's name and then smiled.

"What?" Hightower asked, noticing his expression.

Roger shook his head. "Now I won't be able to refer to them as anything but diamond cutters," he replied.

Captain Hightower ignored the jape and returned his attention to the interior of the Polaris. The hangar area was bustling with activity. There were numerous soldiers scampering about adorned in the exact same attire as them. As long as none of them questioned the presence of their ship, it appeared that they'd be able to blend in quite easily.

"You sure they're not paying any attention to us?" Roger asked as the shuttle came to a rest.

"No," Amus answered as he unstrapped from his seat. "But I doubt it. They've basically got two operations going on at once. They're engaged in battle with your Comet fighters, and they're also still scanning the surface of Pana for any sign of the resource for their elixir. We are in a shuttle that, as far as they know, belongs to them. We are dressed like them. There does not appear to be any high ranking Supreme Regency officials in the hangar at this time because it is far too dangerous. I think it is safe for us to go, but we must go now."

Captain Hightower began to make his way toward the rear of the shuttle where the ramp began to lower. He paused and turned to Drago. "Hang tight here, we'll bring you back some armor that fits."

Drago snarled and seemed frustrated.

"We stick to the plan," Roger said, pointing at the large Bothian. "You knew this was part of the plan."

"It does not mean that I'm happy about it," Drago spat. He then crossed his arms and sat in an inconspicuous spot as the ramp finally opened all the way.

Amus, Hightower, and Roger clambered out and immediately scrambled toward a darkened corner where they could observe their surroundings for a moment.

"Okay, what now?" Roger asked anxiously.

Amus shrugged. "I think I would feel much safer if Drago was with us. I think our first order of business should be getting him a uniform."

Captain Hightower reached for his sidearm. He felt more comfortable with it in his hand. With his other hand, he pushed a button on the side of a device that was wrapped around his arm. The screen on the device illuminated to reveal a blueprint illustration of the Voyager starship. "I seem to remember seeing what appeared to be a shop...or military exchange, in that direction," he said, pointing toward the opposite wall of the hangar. "I don't think it was very far. I'm guessing we may be able to find what we're looking for there."

"That's a gamble," Roger said, leaning over to study the blueprint. "I'm not sure it's a gamble we should take. Maybe we need to look for someone with Drago's build and—"

"And what?" Captain Hightower interrupted. "Look around you, Stellick. There are soldiers everywhere. We can't exactly attack one of them without the rest of them seeing."

"The Captain is right," Amus said. "Attacking one of the soldiers to take their uniform is a larger gamble."

Roger huffed, and his shoulders slumped, though he knew what his counterparts said was true. "Okay," he said. "If we're going to do it, let's do it now while the chaos is still going on."

At that moment, the entire ship shuddered hard enough that they all nearly lost their footing. Many of the Kaloian soldiers *did* fall to the metal decking.

Roger glanced upward. "Our pilots are giving them hell," he said with a smirk.

CHAPTER 30

Sabre had been unable to finish off Polaris' radar and weapons guidance systems—at least for the time being. Currently, he was being pursued by three diamond fighters and he was wondering how the other squad members were faring. As he dove at a blistering pace he checked the radar screen and found that, amazingly, the diamond fighters continued to close in. Not surprisingly, the lead craft in pursuit began firing a furious array of plasma bolts toward the diving Comet.

Sabre grabbed the stick and quickly entered a barrel roll. As the craft turned over numerous times, the purple bolts zipped by, however, one of them skimmed across the bottom of the Comet. The impact jolted the craft slightly, and Sabre feared that it would be enough to upset his smooth trajectory and potentially cause one—or both—of his wings to break away. He was very much aware that any second, another volley of purple plasma would be fired at him, so he prepared to pull a daring maneuver that he'd heard about but had never tried.

Without further hesitation, Sabre reversed his craft's ion thrusters while simultaneously pulling back hard on the stick. The Comet's nose darted upward abruptly, and the ship's speed decreased so dramatically that Sabre momentarily wondered if his belts would be strong enough to secure him in his seat to prevent him from hurtling through the cockpit glass and into the vacuum of space. Fortunately, the belts *did* hold, and the unsuspecting Kaloian pilots had to react quickly to keep from crashing into him—and each other. As the diamond fighters streaked by, Sabre immediately released two missiles and then fired his cannon on the ship directly in front of him. Just as he'd planned it, all three ships were disposed of entirely. Sabre then throttled up his thrusters again to rejoin the rest of his squad.

Meanwhile, Banshee had taken out no less than nine fighters before turning her attention back onto the Polaris' plasma cannons; Harlan Wolfe's advice be damned. She knew if she was going to succeed, she'd have to be quick and it would take no less than four well-placed missiles to accomplish the feat.

"Banshee, what are you doing?"

It was Lawyer and he sounded genuinely concerned.

"I'm taking out these plasma cannons…it may be an important factor for the Captain and the others to get off that ship in one piece later," she said.

"Banshee, pull back," Lawyer snapped. "It's too dangerous, you need someone to watch your six."

"So, watch it for me," she replied.

"Merissa, don't be an idiot." This time it was Howler. "This isn't a time to be a hero...we are a team."

Banshee ignored him. It was apparent that they were all against her, so if she was going to do this, she'd be doing it alone.

"Guys, the shuttle has made it on board," Cowboy said suddenly. "I think it's time for us to come up with an exit strategy."

"Copy that," Lawyer replied. "Guys, let's keep fighting, but we need to begin distancing ourselves from the Polaris."

"I recommend taking the fight to the other side of Pana," Sabre chimed in. "I just took three of them south of the planet and took them out pretty easily...none of the other ships followed."

Banshee listened to the radio traffic but kept her eyes on the prize ahead. Just as she'd experienced with the Pinnacle, the plasma cannons began to illuminate blue, like the pilot light on a gas heater. Without further contemplation, she unleashed her missiles in quick succession. Each of them zipped directly toward their targets, but not before the starboard cannon fired off a ball of plasma.

Banshee jerked the stick right to evade the incoming danger, but unfortunately, she was too late. It was not a direct hit, but it was more than enough to rip the portside wing off the Comet fighter. The ship began to roll and spiral in a wild trajectory toward Pana.

"I'm hit! I'm hit!" Banshee shouted, but strangely her voice was eerily calm.

"Dammit!" Howler shouted back. "I knew it! I knew this would happen!"

"Merissa, how bad is it?" Lawyer asked. He sounded panicked.

"It's bad," she answered. "I'm—I'm spiraling toward Pana...trying not...not to black out."

"I've got a visual on her," Sabre said. He pointed the nose of his fighter after her and again went into a steep dive to pick up speed. "She's heading for Pana's atmosphere."

"Stay with her," Howler said. "Is there anything you can do for her?"

"No—I'm not gonna make it," Banshee answered for him. "Pull...pull back."

"You gotta try something," Howler said. "Can you help her get to the ground on Pana?"

Sabre was gritting his teeth and pursuing the heavily damaged Comet with a high rate of speed, perhaps even faster than he'd gone when the three diamond fighters were pursuing him. "I don't know," he muttered. "I can't catch up to her."

"Stay after her," Cowboy said. "I'd love to help, but I've got company over here."

"Do you need help?" Lawyer asked.

"I wouldn't turn it down!"

"I'm locked onto your position and headed your way," Lawyer replied.

Sabre kept the nose of his craft pointed directly after the falling spacecraft ahead of him. "Banshee, you still with me?" he asked.

No response.

"Banshee…do you read me?"

Still no response.

"She's gotta be unconscious," Howler said, somberly. "There's nothing you can do, Christian."

"Pull back," Lawyer said. "You did your best, but if you keep up that pace you're gonna lose your own craft."

"I'm getting closer," Sabre argued. He was beginning to feel lightheaded, but he kept it to himself.

"Christian, it's over," Howler pleaded. "You did your best, now pull back."

Sabre continued to watch the falling craft, unblinking. At one point, he thought he was closing in, but now it appeared she was getting further away from him. As the craft began to enter the atmosphere of Pana, he finally allowed himself to accept that it was a hopeless endeavor. She was going to crash, and there was absolutely nothing he could do about it.

"Pulling back," he said in a voice just above a whisper. "I can't keep up anymore."

"You did all you could," Lawyer said. "We'll check for a beacon and see if we can find her when we get out of here."

Sabre felt a burning sensation in his eyes and soon realized he was crying. He squeezed his eyes tightly in an effort to shut the water works down. There was still an ongoing fight and his teammates needed his help.

"I'm on my way back," he said, renewed determination in his voice.

"I'm leading them toward the back side of Pana," Cowboy said. "If they want to keep fighting, they'll have to do it out of sight of their mother ship."

The other three Comets followed his lead and before long, the remaining diamond fighters that pursued were disposed of and the dogfight ceased.

***

"Make sure you walk with purpose," Captain Hightower said, as the trio marched across the hangar.

There were still soldiers scrambling about in all directions and no one seemed to give them much attention at all. Polaris appeared to have taken significant damage and Hightower momentarily wondered if the ship would survive the assault. Roger noticed him looking around, as if he expected a huge gash to suddenly open in the ceiling above them, with the vacuum of space in turn pulling them all out to their deaths.

"I told you they could handle the job," Roger said.

Captain Hightower glanced over at him but said nothing. Amus led them to an arched doorway that opened into a long hallway. There were doors on either side with signage, but it was Kaloian and nothing Roger or Hightower could understand. Amus, however, could read it with ease.

"Right here," he said, pointing to the first door on their left.

Roger frowned as he noticed the keypad that would undoubtedly dictate who could go in or out.

"I hope you know the code," Roger said, dismayed.

Amus smiled behind his helmet. "I can handle this," he said confidently. There were multiple codes he'd gathered from President Dala's intel and he was certain at least one of them would open the door. By the time he punched in the third code on the list, the door was open, and an expansive warehouse opened before them. There were various bags, helmets, and all sorts of clothing available, so much in fact, it was a bit overwhelming.

"Okay, I'll search for a helmet, why don't you two look for the rest of the uniform," Captain Hightower suggested.

Roger nodded, and immediately set out to find a large enough jacket for Drago while Amus searched for pants and boots. After several frantic minutes, Hightower found a helmet.

"I think this one will work," he said, holding up the massive black helmet. "You guys have any luck?"

"No, unfortunately not," Roger said, obvious frustration in his voice. "All of this stuff is just too small."

"We've got to keep looking," Amus said. "We'll need Drago's help if we're going to make it through this."

Suddenly, they heard the door slide open and the heavy boots of a soldier enter the room.

"Who is in here?" a man's voice called out.

The three men immediately crouched down behind a crate and Roger readied his hand cannon.

"We have to dispose of him," Amus whispered.

Roger shook his head. "No, we wait for him to leave."

"He's here because he knows we are in here," Amus said. "He won't leave until he finds us. We've got to get rid of him before he alerts someone else."

Roger sighed. "Alright…I'll handle this."

Captain Hightower grabbed his arm. "What are you going to do?"

"I'm going to incapacitate him," he replied, holding up the hand cannon.

"We need to stop him without using that thing if possible," Hightower said. "The last thing we need is to cause a ruckus that will attract more of them here."

Without discussing the matter further Roger darted out from behind the crate and made his way around a rack stocked with helmets. He wanted to surprise the unknown assailant from behind, but as he rounded the corner, he was met with a surprise of his own. The Kaloian soldier was massive. Roger estimated that he stood at a height of nearly seven feet, and probably weighed 275 pounds. There was a plasma pistol in his right hand, but for the moment, he was unaware that Roger was approaching him from behind.

Roger took a deep breath, returned his weapon to its holster, and charged at the soldier. The large Kaloian turned as he heard footsteps approaching and pointed his weapon. Roger backhanded the pistol from the soldier's hand and immediately threw a left hook, connecting soundly with the man's ribs. The pistol flew across the room and clattered across the metal floor. The Kaloian howled in pain from the blow he'd taken to the ribs and responded by immediately throwing a punch of his own. Roger was surprised when he realized his attacker had punched him straight into his face. Though the helmet took most of the shock, the visor that went across his eyes cracked and he felt himself stumbling backwards.

The soldier seemed amused and laughed. He then reached down, grabbing Roger by his right arm and right leg, lifting him off the floor. Next the solider used his weight to spin his body around like a top. When he felt he'd gotten the momentum he was looking for, he released Roger, sending him crashing through a stack of wooden crates. His already damaged helmet jarred loose and he felt the air forcibly vacate his lungs. He'd rolled over onto his hands and knees when the soldier trotted over to him, ready to strike his unprotected skull. Roger felt the copper taste of blood in his mouth and as he desperately tried to get a gulp of air, he noticed the hulking Kaloian soldier standing over him. The soldier drew his arm back, but before he could throw a punch, Amus had snuck up behind him and put the barrel of his hand cannon into the Kaloian's back.

The soldier stopped dead in his tracks and slowly lowered his arm. "Who are you?" he asked, still sounding as if he were the one in control.

"It doesn't matter," Amus said. "But what matters next is entirely up to you. You can do what we say, or you can die…it doesn't matter to us."

The Kaloian's shoulders slumped slightly, and it was apparent that he believed what he was told.

"What do you want me to do?" he asked, his deep voice much softer now.

Roger scrambled to his feet and wiped the blood away from his mouth. Captain Hightower and Amus looked at each other simultaneously.

"We want you to get undressed," Amus said very matter-of-factly.

The soldier paused awkwardly, but then removed his helmet. His head was large and there did not seem to be any sign of a neck. His hair was blonde, and far longer than Roger would've guessed. His eyes were blue. He looked utterly confused.

"Why do you want me to undress?" he asked, his voice raising an octave.

He was now facing Captain Hightower and Amus. Before they had a chance to respond, Roger grabbed a helmet from one of the busted crates, drew back, and swung it with everything he had. The makeshift weapon connected solidly with the back of the Kaloian's head and he immediately fell forward, landing on his face.

"That was…effective," Amus said, lowering his cannon.

"Quickly, get his uniform," Captain Hightower said as he knelt to pull off his boots.

Once they'd stripped the unconscious soldier of his uniform, Amus shoved it all inside a duffel bag. "I think only one of us should take this to Drago while the other two waits here," he said, zipping the bag closed.

"I agree," Hightower said. "I'll do it."

"No," Roger said. "I don't want you taking any unnecessary risks. I'll take it to him."

Captain Hightower pondered the statement before nodding. "Are you sure?"

"Yes," Roger replied as he retrieved a new helmet to replace his damaged one. "I'll get Drago suited up and we'll be back here as fast as possible."

Amus looked over at the captain and nodded, signaling that he agreed with the plan.

"Okay, but be quick," Hightower replied.

Roger nodded and scooped up the duffel bag as he headed for the door. Once he was in the hallway, he paused and looked in both directions for any signs of Kaloian soldiers. He saw none but heard a multitude of footsteps echoing in the direction that went away from the hangar. Without wasting any more time, Roger began to walk briskly in the direction of the shuttle. Once in the hangar, he quickly noticed that many of the Kaloian diamond cutters were returning from their battle with the Comet fighters moments earlier. Roger wondered and hoped that all his pilots made it back safely, but he didn't allow his mind to ponder on it for very long. He set his sights on the shuttle and, as discreetly as possible, made his way across the hangar and to the shuttle. Along the way he noticed many of the Kaloian fighters smoking with significant damage, and several of the pilots were receiving medical attention. The abundance of commotion was exactly what he needed to make his way to the shuttle unnoticed.

Once he arrived, the rear door slowly descended, and he quickly made his way on board.

"Took you long enough," Drago said with annoyance.

Roger tossed him the bag. "Hurry up and get dressed or I'm leaving you here."

The Bothian chuckled. "You will not," he said as he removed his metallic tunic. "You need me a lot more than I need you." He dropped the tunic and it clanged loudly on the floor. He then set about putting on the black Kaloian armor. It was a struggle for him to get his head through, but finally he prevailed.

As he dressed, Roger noticed a lot of scars across his muscular torso and wondered what the story was behind them.

A question for another day...he thought.

"My feet will not fit into these boots," he grumbled tossing the Kaloian footwear aside.

"Your boots are black, they'll have to do," Roger said, anxiously. He looked out of the window and noticed things were beginning to calm down. This new development troubled him. "Hurry up," he said, turning to observe Drago's progress.

The reptilian humanoid was struggling to fasten his pants, but his waist was too big.

"Just leave them unsnapped and pull your shirt down over your waist," Roger quipped. "Get your helmet on, we need to move."

Drago snorted and snatched the helmet from the bag. Roger had to refrain from laughing as the Bothian struggled mightily to get his head inside. After a solid minute, he finally succeeded.

"I can barely move my mouth," he said, clearly struggling to speak.

"That's a good thing," Roger said, and he motioned for Drago to follow him.

They quickly made their way out of the shuttle and began the trek back across the hangar. Along the way, they met two officers coming from the hallway. Roger noticed the older men eyeing them suspiciously.

"Stop," one of them said, holding up a hand. "Where are you two going?"

Roger and Drago looked at each other and then back to the officers.

"We're just—"

But Roger never got an opportunity to finish his sentence. Drago immediately reached out and grabbed both men by their heads. He then slammed their skulls together with enough force to knock each of the men out immediately. Blood began pouring from their nose and ears.

"What are you doing?" Roger asked, panicked. He was trying his best not to shout.

"Eliminating a threat," Drago answered. "Isn't that why you brought me along?"

Roger wanted to argue the matter further but knew there wasn't any time.

"Help me," he said, as he scooped the smaller officer under the arms and began to drag him away.

Drago in turn simply reached down with his right hand and grabbed the other officer by the front of his uniform. He picked him up off the ground like he was lifting a pail of water. Roger led him to the room where Captain Hightower and Amus were still waiting.

"What is this?" Hightower asked, shocked to see the unconscious officers.

Roger dragged the man to where the Kaloian soldier he'd knocked unconscious was lying and then dropped him. He noticed that the captain and Amus had tied up the soldier.

"They were a threat and I eliminated them," Drago said proudly as he dropped his own Kaloian.

Captain Hightower whipped his head around to Roger. "What happened?"

Roger sighed and shook his head. "They confronted us on the way back and lizard-head here reacted before I could even speak to them."

Hightower marched over to the large Bothian and pointed a finger in his chest. "You told us you'd engage the enemy *when needed*," he growled. "Those were your words, correct?"

Drago's face was hidden behind the dark visor of his helmet and Roger could only imagine the expression that must've appeared across his face. He figured the captain's sudden anger and display of authority must've bewildered him, at least momentarily.

"Yes, I remember what I said," he replied.

"Then think before you act!" Hightower scolded. "We will use your brute force *when needed*...as agreed."

Drago nodded. "I understand," he said in a low grumble. "I will be more cautious."

Captain Hightower nodded. "Thank you," he said before turning to Amus and Roger. "Now, as we planned, this is the point where we split up."

CHAPTER 31

"Amus and I will make our way to the bridge," Captain Hightower said. "Roger, you and Drago will go and retrieve Ralu."

Roger nodded. However, though he knew this was part of the plan all along, something still troubled him. "Getting onto that bridge will be no easy task," he said.

Hightower glanced over at him and he wished there was no visor hiding his expression. Roger desperately wanted to read his eyes. "Stellick, let Amus and I figure that out," he said. "You and Drago focus on getting Ralu and getting back to the shuttle," he paused and glanced at Drago. "Only fight when necessary."

Drago nodded but growled softly.

"Make sure your comms are on, but keep them silent," Hightower continued. "If you're summoned, only communicate when it is safe to do so."

Amus shifted his feet and looked nervous. Roger hoped he was up for the task.

"We'll get your father," he said, trying to ease the young Avaxian's mind.

"Thank you Commander Stellick," Amus replied softly.

Hightower glanced at his watch. "Both parties need to be back at the shuttle in no more than one hour whether we complete our respective tasks or not, is that clear?"

All of them nodded in agreement. "Very well," the captain said. "Let's get this done."

Roger immediately summoned the navigational device strapped to his arm and pulled up the blueprints of the Polaris. Drago leaned in near him. "I think our best bet is to use the trash chute located at the end of this hallway," he said. "It'll be a straight shot down to the bottom deck and we will not have to worry about encountering any Kaloians."

"You lead, and I'll follow," Drago said.

"Be careful, Stellick," Hightower said as they all moved to the door.

"You too," Roger said, snapping a quick salute to his captain.

***

As soon as Sabre landed back on board the Titan, he immediately began punching his console in frustration. Deck Chief Tim Reed noticed and quickly climbed a ladder to intervene.

"That's enough," he said, grabbing Sabre's arm. "What happened?"

As he asked the question, three more Comets screamed into the hangar. Tim waited for the last one and when he realized it wasn't coming, he suddenly understood.

"Who was it?" he asked softly.

Sabre removed his helmet and tossed it out of the cockpit. "Banshee," he replied somberly. "She went down…crashed on Pana."

Tim nodded and then climbed back down the ladder. He noticed Lauren West watching from a window of the lounge area. He motioned for her to come to him. Concerned something was wrong, Lauren ran into the hangar and Tim met her halfway.

"Go to him," he whispered to her. "They lost one and he's taking it hard."

Lauren nodded as she took a deep breath. She then found herself glancing at the other pilots as they exited their own respective fighters. "What about everyone else?" she asked.

"I'll handle them," Tim answered. "You look after Sabre…do whatever you need to do to keep his head right. He could be called up again at any moment."

Lauren nodded as she understood. She moved past Tim and approached Sabre's Comet as he clambered out. When he saw her, he immediately collapsed into her arms.

Tim looked on as Lawyer, Cowboy, and Howler moved toward the lounge. All three of them looked as if they were in a trance, none of them speaking or even looking at one another. Colonel Madigan suddenly appeared from another entrance.

"They're back," he said, glancing at the recently landed Comets. "Did everyone come back?"

As he asked the question, he seemed to find the answer himself as he counted the fighters. His mouth dropped open. "Who didn't make it back?" he asked in a voice just above a whisper.

"Merissa Voight," Tim answered. "Banshee didn't make it."

Madigan sighed and closed his eyes tightly. He remained that way for several seconds before finally opening them again. The first thing he noticed was Sabre in an embrace with Lauren. He was clearly distraught. The other men were in the lounge and he could see them through the window. They were seated on chairs, their heads down, resting on the palms of their hands, elbows on their knees.

"I'll call Dr. Holtz," he said. "We'll get her down here immediately."

"I think that's a good idea," Tim said. "We've lost too many pilots lately."

"Any word on the shuttle?" Madigan asked, almost as an afterthought. "Did they make it?"

"I didn't ask," Tim said. "I guess you need to go find out, sir," he added.

The colonel again glanced toward the pilots in the lounge and nodded slowly. "I'll go talk to them," he said.

Tim watched him walk away, obvious dread with every step he took.

***

When Roger and Drago stopped at the end of the hall in front of the garbage chute, they saw a soldier watching them from another adjoining hallway. Roger offered a slight wave to the Kaloian, and he stood there stupidly, wondering if they were about to be found out before they'd really even gotten started. The soldier returned a slight wave and then turned away from them.

"Okay, we go now," Roger said, and without further hesitation, he tumbled backward through the plastic flaps that closed off the chute.

As he fell downward, he immediately pushed out his hands and feet against the walls on either side of him to slow his fall. The bottom deck was only two down from where they'd started. Within seconds he'd reached the end of the chute and he came to a smooth stop, barely making a sound on top of the vast pile of trash. He looked up and his eyes widened as he noticed the large Bothian tumbling toward him with little effort to slow his descent at all. Roger had to push his back against the wall behind him to avoid being crushed as Drago slammed into the trash with enough force to almost disappear completely.

"Are you alright?" Roger asked, as he fell to his knees to try and pull Drago from his buried state.

"Of course, I'm fine," Drago answered, and he began thrashing and tearing his way up and out of the hold he now found himself in.

The environment smelled terrible and with Drago now free, Roger wasted no time searching for the way out. The two of them had fallen into a vast pit of garbage, but as he peered across the pile, he noticed a large portion of the pit that wasn't covered in trash at all. There were windows and a door on the wall opposite of where they currently were. Roger crawled and rolled his way across the pile until he finally made his way to solid ground again. Drago followed and soon joined Roger just as he reached the door.

Roger pulled up the blueprints of their current floor and was relieved to find that the brig was only two doors down from where they currently were.

"Makes sense," Drago muttered. "They keep all of their garbage close together on the same deck."

Roger glanced at the button next to the door and considered it a moment. There was no window so there would be no way to see if there were any Kaloian soldiers on the other side. When he pushed that button, they'd be committed to advancing no matter who or what was on the other side.

"I'm going to go first," Roger said, turning to Drago. "Go ahead and pull your hand cannon in case there is trouble, but don't come out of here until I signal it's safe to do so."

Drago nodded and immediately retrieved his weapon. "I'm ready," he growled.

Without mulling the situation further, Roger pushed the button and the metal door slid away to reveal another hallway. Roger stepped out slowly and looked in both directions.

"We're clear," he said, motioning for Drago to follow.

The large Bothian returned his weapon to its holster and followed Roger further down the hallway. They finally reached the door to the bridge, and beside it there was a window with bars across it and a Kaloian soldier seated behind it. He was short and dumpy with no helmet to reveal his face. His hair appeared wet and was slicked back. There was a tiny mustache above his lips.

"Can I help you?" he asked, very non-chalantly from behind the bars.

"Yes," Roger replied, doing his best to sound official. "Due to the recent attack, the captain has requested that we transport the prisoner Ralu for questioning."

The Kaloian looked taken aback. "Transport him where?"

"Not sure," Roger answered confidently. "We were ordered to transport him to the top deck where we will hand him over to the captain's custody. There seems to be suspicion that the Avaxians were behind the attack and the captain wants to question Ralu immediately."

Roger glanced slightly to the left and noticed another guard standing behind the door. He was armed, and he was listening intently to the conversation.

"Everything you just said goes completely against every protocol I've been given with regards to transporting prisoners," the Kaloian said, and Roger looked on in horror as he reached for what appeared to be some sort of phone. "Let me call the bridge and confirm this with my superiors before I just hand him over," he said.

"No!" Roger said, a little louder than he expected.

The man glared at him, narrowing his eyes. "Who are you?" he asked, suddenly sounding very skeptical.

"Drago, there is one behind the door!" Roger shouted as he quickly reached between the bars and jerked the Kaloian forward, slamming his bare forehead hard into the metal. He immediately went limp, and Roger released him. The unconscious man collapsed to the floor.

At exactly the same time, Drago raised his large foot and pushed through the metal door with a tremendous amount of force. The door projected inward and crushed the other guard against the wall, but it wasn't enough to stop him. The armored Kaloian soldier pushed the door aside and raised his plasma rifle at Drago's chest. The Bothian leaped at him, twisted the rifle free, and then grabbed the Kaloian by the back of the head. With a quick motion he thrust the man downward, face first onto the metal floor. The Kaloian's helmet clanged loudly and bounced off the floor, but the blow was obviously hard enough to render him unconscious.

"Nice work," Roger said, placing a hand on Drago's shoulder.

He moved past him toward another door and grabbed his hand cannon. "Alright, another door…there may be more guards on the other side," he said, looking again at Drago. "You ready?"

Drago nodded, his large helmet bobbing slightly.

Roger pushed the button and as the door slid open, they encountered a corridor with four holding cells on either side. At the end of the corridor was yet another guard. As soon as he saw Roger and Drago, he raised his plasma rifle.

"Drop it!" Roger shouted.

"Who are you?" the guard shouted back, clearly confused to see individuals dressed in Kaloian armor invading the brig.

"Put down the weapon!" Roger ordered fiercely.

Drago moved past him and snatched the rifle away. He then grabbed the Kaloian by the throat and lifted him off the ground.

"Where is Ralu?" he hissed.

The guard clawed at Drago's hand, desperately trying to pull his large fingers away. He tried to speak but was unable to formulate words.

"He can't talk with you cutting off his airway," Roger said as he stood next to him.

"Excuse me," a voice called out from behind one of the nearby holding cells.

Each cell had a large door with a small opening where food trays could be given and received. The opening had a small flap over it that could be slid open. Roger noticed one of them open and a blue hand was protruding out.

"I am Ralu," the voice said.

Roger hurried to the cell door and pushed the button that opened the door. An Avaxian man that looked eerily like Amus—yet older—stepped forward and smiled, revealing two rows of pointy teeth.

"Thank you," he said. "Are you Kaloian rebels?"

Roger looked at Drago and then back to Ralu. "Who, us?" he asked. "Absolutely not...but we *are* here to help you escape."

The guard that Drago was holding continued to struggle and gasp for air.

"Drago, put him in the cell," Roger said, pointing at the open door.

Drago complied, throwing the Kaloian guard inside. He immediately began coughing and panting as he pulled his helmet off. Roger pushed the button to seal him inside.

"Well that wasn't so bad, was it?" he asked, breathing a sigh of relief.

At that moment, a thunderous blast erupted from somewhere behind him and a bolt of purple plasma whizzed by Roger's head, ultimately contacting Drago's left shoulder. The large Bothian was immediately swept off his feet and crashed down hard onto the metal floor. Ralu dropped to his side and tried to aid him.

Roger whirled his head around and was shocked to see Captain Malcolm Steiger standing at the entrance of the corridor, a smoking plasma pistol in his hand.

"Captain Steiger," Roger said, surprised.

"Remove your helmet," Malcolm spat in anger.

Roger suddenly realized he had no idea who he was. He pondered Steiger's demand but couldn't think of any other option. With great reluctance he removed the helmet.

Malcolm's eyes widened as he realized who he was looking at. "Commander Stellick," he said in amazement. "I should've known."

"Yeah, we meet again," Roger said with a mischievous smile.

Malcolm stepped forward and raised the pistol toward Roger's head. "I should kill you right where you stand," he muttered.

Roger noticed the metallic noise his legs made when he walked, and he seemed to have developed a limp of some sort.

"You betrayed us," Roger said, trying his best to sound unafraid.

Malcolm nodded. "Yes, I did," he admitted. "For the betterment of all Kaloians."

"Why?" Roger asked. "What does that even mean?"

Malcolm took another step forward and placed the barrel of his gun against Roger's forehead. The metal was still warm, and it burned his skin. Roger resisted the urge to pull away.

"I don't have to explain anything to you," Malcolm snapped. "You're an inferior race."

Roger chuckled. "If we're inferior then why have you all been losing to us ever since we entered your galaxy?"

Malcolm's jaw clenched, and Roger read his eyes. His time was up, and he allowed his instincts and training to take over. With one sweeping motion, he batted the gun away, just as Malcolm pulled the trigger. Another blast erupted and this time the bolt of plasma impacted the holding cell door to their left. It then ricocheted back and into the top of Malcolm's foot. Roger expected him to howl in pain, but instead he smiled at him. It was a shocking thing to witness and as it took Roger off guard, Malcolm took advantage of the moment. He landed a stinging right hook that made Roger stumble. Had it not been for the nearby cell wall to catch him, he'd have fallen to the floor.

Malcolm laughed. "Like I said...inferior."

He then raised a foot off the ground and prepared to stomp down on Roger's head. He rolled away just in time. The sound of metal striking metal startled Roger as he soon began to realize that Malcolm's legs were no longer his own. He glared up at his attacker, wide-eyed.

"At first, I was mortified at the loss of my legs," Malcolm said. "But you know, I think I'm starting to like my new ones."

Malcolm again raised his cybernetic foot off the floor and again prepared to stomp down on Roger. Roger prepared to dodge the new attack, but suddenly something else caught Malcolm's attention.

"Captain Steiger," a gravelly voice called out.

Malcolm immediately paused and pulled his foot back. He looked over his shoulder and noticed the monitor at the guard station was illuminated. Roger saw a man with very white skin, wearing a red robe on the screen.

"Yes, your excellency," Malcolm said as he quickly made his way toward the monitor.

Roger was amazed at how quickly he'd seemed to forget about him. Whomever was beckoning him must've been someone of great power. He began to slowly reach for his hand cannon.

"Have you subdued our guests?" the man in the red robe asked.

"I have, your excellency," Malcolm answered.

Roger continued to watch the monitor as he slowly moved the hand cannon forward.

"Are you certain of that?" the man asked.

Suddenly another man—much younger—stepped into the frame. He had an eye patch and massive scar over the top of his skull. He was also wearing a robe, but his was dark blue in color. The other man raised his hand and closed his good eye. All of a sudden, with no way to explain it, Roger was unable to move his hand any further. He seemed to be able to move all his other extremities but there seemed to be some unseen force holding his arm into place.

Malcolm turned to look back at Roger and saw the hand cannon firmly in his grip. He charged at him and furiously kicked the weapon away. Roger winced as he felt the metal foot make hard contact with his hand. Suddenly, he could move his arm again and all at once he felt a tremendous amount of pain. It was very likely that his hand was now broken.

Malcolm hurried back to the monitor. "Thank you Jado," he said to the man in the blue robe. "And thank you Potentate Shade."

Roger recognized the name *Shade*. He'd heard Malcolm refer to him soon after the Titan had followed the Pinnacle through the gate.

"Captain Steiger, I need you to ask Commander Stellick to give me the frequency so that we may contact the Earthling ship," Potentate Shade commanded.

Malcolm returned to Roger and jerked him up from the floor, dragging him to the monitor. "The potentate needs the frequency to contact the Titan," Malcolm growled at him. "Give him what he requests."

Roger glared at Malcolm and then at the monitor. He was surprised that Shade knew his name and guessed Malcolm had given it to him. Roger then stared at Romulus Shade for a long moment, and then briefly at the young man next to him, the man Malcolm referred to as *Jado*. As he observed their surroundings, he guessed they were on the bridge of a ship. *Were they on the Polaris?*

"If you're going to kill me, you may as well get it over with," Roger said, still looking directly at Shade. "I won't be giving you anything."

The potentate smiled and made a strange clacking noise with his teeth. "How brave," he said. "How stupid," he then added. Shade then looked over to his right and motioned for someone to approach. Roger looked on in horror as a Kaloian guard escorted Captain Hightower into the frame. His hands appeared to be bound behind his back. Shade looked at the captain as if he were a piece of trash and then he reached inside his robe to retrieve what appeared to be some sort of coiled whip.

"I'm going to ask again, Commander Stellick," Potentate Shade snarled. "Give me the frequency so that we may contact your ship."

"Don't give him a damn thing!" Captain Hightower shouted defiantly.

Jado immediately snatched the back of Hightower's collar, choking him off before he could say anything further. "Don't make me hurt you," he said.

Roger swallowed hard and he could feel Malcolm's eyes peering hard at him. "I told you," Roger said. "You may as well kill me because I'm not giving you anything."

Captain Hightower smiled, and he never noticed Romulus Shade uncoiling the whip behind him. Roger looked on as the whip illuminated into a hue of blue and appeared to have some sort of electrical current running through it. Shade then drew back and unfurled the whip so that it wrapped tightly around the captain's neck with a loud *crack*. Hightower's mouth opened in agony and the scream that he released was sickening and unlike anything Roger had ever heard before.

"Tell me!" Shade screamed like a madman.

Roger's eyes widened as his breathing increased significantly.

"Give him what he wants!" Ralu called out from behind him.

Roger looked back and could see that Drago was conscious but writhing in pain as he clutched his injured shoulder.

"Give him what he wants, or he will kill him," Ralu said.

Roger glanced over at Malcolm and he stared back, stone-faced. "You better listen to him," he said coldly.

"Okay, okay!" Roger blurted out. "I'll give it to you, just let him go!"

Romulus Shade immediately released Hightower and the man fell to the ground, his neck still smoking, his flesh severely burned.

"I knew you'd eventually come to your senses," Shade said, and he clacked his teeth again.

CHAPTER 32

"I-I'm terribly sorry about Banshee," Colonel Madigan stammered as he entered the pilot lounge. He took a seat at the round table in the center of the room and exhaled slowly.

"We have to launch a rescue mission," Howler said, determined. "She could've survived, and even if she didn't..."

"If she didn't, we still need to retrieve her body," Lawyer said, finishing the statement. "She'd do it for us."

The colonel glanced around the room, making eye contact with each man. "We'll obviously check for a beacon," he said. "In the meantime, as required by S.A.M.A. regulations, each of you must sit down with Dr. Holtz so she can do an evaluation."

Cowboy rolled his eyes and shook his head. He wanted to point out the fact that the colonel stopped short of making a promise that he would indeed launch a search mission for Banshee.

"I'm fine, sir," he said, rising from where he'd been seated on the sofa next to Lawyer.

"I'm sure you are," Madigan replied. "But the doc still needs to look you over, so have a seat because she's on her way. Like I said, it's S.A.M.A. regulations. If Harry were here, he would not allow you to skirt around that. I'm not either."

Cowboy reluctantly fell back into his seated position. Lawyer patted him on the back. "Relax, it's just a formality," he said.

Howler shifted uncomfortably. "I want to be involved in the mission to go find her," he blurted out suddenly.

Colonel Madigan looked over at him, somewhat surprised. "If the time comes—"

"I want to be involved too," Lawyer interrupted.

"Don't think you're gonna leave me out," Cowboy added, looking at his fellow pilots. "And sir," he said, turning to Madigan. "Respectfully, I don't appreciate your use of the word *if*."

The colonel smiled and looked away awkwardly. He was clearly uncomfortable and not ready to commit to sending out a party to search for Banshee. He believed she was most likely dead and risking more lives just didn't make sense. Suddenly, the gray metal doors slid open, and he whipped his head around expecting to see Dr. Holtz, but instead, he saw Lieutenant Hayden Carter. His face was white, and he looked extremely troubled.

"Carter," Madigan said. "What's wrong?"

"Sir, you're needed on the bridge immediately," Hayden said.

"What's the matter?" the colonel asked, rising from his chair.

Hayden looked around the room, unsure if he needed to say anymore. Lawyer noticed, and he too stood. "What is it?" he asked, his voice rising.

"Spit it out," Madigan snapped.

Hayden shook his head. "It's Captain Hightower," he said. "He's been captured and he's on the telecommunicator right now."

Madigan looked at him, confused, and all of them began sprinting to the bridge. "The telecommunicator?" he asked in disbelief. "Who in this galaxy knows how to contact us on that?"

"Obviously, the captain does," Lawyer said.

Madigan shook his head. "Harry would never give up that information—never."

"Well there isn't another explanation," Howler replied. "How did he look, Carter?"

Hayden had reached the elevator first and waited for all the other men to pile in. "He looks bad," he answered somberly. "He's injured."

Once they'd finally reached the bridge, Madigan immediately noticed the somber expressions on all the crew. Rowena Walker had obviously been crying, her glasses were lying on the console in front of her. Jake Crosby's eyes were wide as saucers, and his color was as ashen as Hayden's. In the center of the room, the table for the telecommunicator was activated, and a twelve-inch hologram of Captain Hightower, Romulus Shade, and Jado Baylor stood in high definition. Romulus Shade stood to the right of the captain, pointing a plasma pistol at his head. Hightower's neck appeared to be burned severely.

"What's the meaning of this?" Colonel Madigan roared when he saw the troubling display.

"You must be Colonel Merrill Madigan," the potentate said in a sickeningly polite tone. "Very pleased to make your acquaintance. I am Romulus Shade, the potentate of the Supreme Regency. I assume you recognize this fine man standing at the other end of my weapon?"

"Of course, I do," Madigan spat with anger. "I demand that you lower that weapon at once!"

The potentate shook his head slowly and used his free hand to remove the hood over his head. The colonel noted how incredibly pale Shade's skin was and his hair was white as snow. It was stark contrast with the red robe that he wore.

"I'm afraid I cannot comply," Shade replied. "You see, your captain, along with three others, snuck on board my ship. Their actions on board the ship are not only illegal according to galactic law, but also highly insulting to me, the final judge of said galactic law."

Madigan swallowed, and his Adam's apple bobbed as he considered what his next words would be. He wondered where Roger, Amus and Drago were. He could clearly see that the captain was staring directly at him, his eyes seemingly urging him to remain strong and in control. "What do you want?" he said finally.

Romulus Shade glared at him and clacked his teeth. "What do I *want*?" he snarled. "I want the same thing I wanted when you first came through the gate! I want you to surrender at once, and after you'll assist me in gaining the surrender of your entire planet. One way or the other, I will take it, but I prefer to do it as peacefully as possible."

"Give me my men back, and I'll consider the offer," Madigan countered.

The potentate glared at the colonel and his mood turned much darker. "You think I'm bargaining with you?" he asked, sounding utterly amazed. "This is not a request, colonel. This is a demand. And failure to comply will result in all your deaths, starting with your captain," he added, pushing the barrel of the plasma pistol tighter against Hightower's head.

Madigan felt his heart rate increase and he again stared into Hightower's eyes. The captain slowly and subtly shook his head. A clear sign that he did not want his old friend to comply with the demand.

"Can I have a moment to consider?" he asked. He didn't have any idea what he could do at this point.

"No, you may not," Shade answered coldly. "I will eventually find you, and I will eventually kill you all if you do not comply immediately."

Hayden Carter leaned near Madigan. "Colonel, I think we should consider—"

"Shut up, Carter!" Madigan snapped.

"So, you've made your decision?" Shade asked, as he watched the exchange.

Madigan took a step closer to the hologram where he could get a better look at the captain. "Harry," he said softly. "Harry, you're captain...what—"

"Fight," Captain Hightower rasped, his voice weak. "Fight and do not let them take Earth."

Madigan swallowed hard and felt a knot tighten in his stomach. At the same moment, his jaw tightened, and he stood taller. He then turned his attention back to Romulus Shade. The potentate briefly looked surprised, but quickly regained his composure.

"Very well," he said bitterly.

Captain Harry Hightower closed his eyes tightly, and suddenly a purple bolt of plasma burst through the side of his head when Shade pulled the trigger on the weapon. Everyone on the bridge of the Titan gasped and screamed in unison as Captain Hightower immediately collapsed, his lifeless body thudding loudly on the metal floor underneath him.

Colonel Madigan lunged toward the telecommunicator table, his mouth agape in total shock. He groaned a pitiful wail of agony and watched helplessly as a puddle of blood blossomed around the corpse of his dead captain.

"We will find you," Shade hissed. "You cannot hide from us forever."

The hologram then disappeared, and the communication was lost.

***

"No!" Roger screamed as he fell to his knees. He'd just witnessed the death of a man that he'd long looked upon as a fatherly figure. He couldn't blink as he watched Hightower's body drop to the floor. The potentate stood over him without a hint of remorse in his eyes. Shade made another threat and the monitor suddenly went black. Roger stayed on his knees a long moment and sobbed.

"Get up," Malcolm said.

Roger stopped sobbing as soon as he heard the Kaloian's voice. He'd almost forgotten Malcolm was even there. Suddenly, the sadness that had overtaken him began to be replaced with something else. He tightened his fists as he stood back up.

"Do not try and fight me again," Malcolm said, seemingly unconcerned. He stepped around Roger and reached to open a cell door. "You're now a prisoner here. I'm sure the potentate is on his way down as we speak." He paused and motioned for Roger to step inside.

What Malcolm didn't notice was that Drago had suddenly returned to his feet. Without hesitation, he reached forward and grabbed Malcolm by the back of his head. He then twisted his arm forcefully, and the Kaloian's neck cracked loudly in protest. Roger looked on as Malcolm's eyes widened and he screamed out in pain—and then it was over. Drago had broken his neck with little effort.

"Damn you," Roger muttered, and he kicked Malcolm's corpse.

"Come, we have little time," Ralu said. "There is an escape pod on this deck and we must find it while we are still near the planet Pana."

Roger nodded and immediately stepped beside Drago, who looked weak from blood loss. He pulled the large Bothian's arm over his shoulder to give him support. "Come on, let me help you," he said. "And thanks."

"I'm fine," Drago said, but he didn't reject Roger's assistance. "And you're welcome…I'm ashamed I was unable to help sooner."

Ralu led them out of the brig and into the hallway, immediately turning left. Near the end of the hallway, there was another door with a keypad beside it.

"I don't know the code," Ralu said, dismayed. "The escape pod is behind this door."

"Move out of the way," Drago said, still sounding weak. He drew back with his good arm and thrust his fist hard into the keypad. Sparks flew along with a wisp of smoke, and amazingly the door opened.

"You're really starting to prove your worth," Roger said, and he then dragged the Bothian forward and through the opening.

Once inside, there was another door, much smaller.

"It's the entrance to the pod," Ralu explained, and he twisted a knob in the center of the door.

There was a hiss, and immediately after, the door swung open. The three of them clambered in, and Ralu seemed to know exactly what to do. He began to work on a series of buttons located on a small console beside the door while Drago and Roger closed the pod door. Within seconds, Roger felt the eerie sensation of falling. He looked out one of the small view ports on either side of the triangular pod and realized they were now separated from the ship.

"How do you pilot this thing to Pana?" he asked, unable to hide his worry.

"The pod is designed to automatically lock on to and land on the nearest planet," Ralu explained. "We're safe for now."

"What's to keep the Polaris from firing their cannons on us?" Roger asked, as he glanced upward at the large Kaloian ship above them.

"Nothing," Ralu explained. "But I think it's highly unlikely that they'll do that. The Kaloians believe in capture and torture when they have the opportunity. They will most likely send soldiers down to search for us—assuming they notice we're gone."

Roger sighed and tried to relax as he knew there was nothing he could currently do but trust the pod to land them safely. He closed his eyes and thought of Captain Hightower as a single tear streamed down his face.

***

"We're seconds too late," Jado said as he and Potentate Shade glanced through the viewing window at the vast darkness of space below.

There had once been an escape pod behind the glass, but now nothing but space and the bright greens and browns of the planet Pana looming nearby. With the escape pod gone, the door that once led to it was now automatically locked and sealed shut.

"We must find them," Shade said. "Especially the Earthling."

"Your Excellency!" a young man in officer attire called out from the doorway of the nearby brig. It was the captain of the Polaris, Stuart Lord. "Come quickly!"

The potentate moved briskly toward the doorway with Jado in tow. Once they arrived, they discovered the lifeless body of Captain Malcolm Steiger lying in the doorway of an open cell.

"No," Jado said, his voice just above a whisper.

He moved past the potentate and kneeled beside his former captain. "His neck," he said. "It's broken."

"There are three other guards here that are injured, but alive," Captain Lord said. Some of his soldiers were attending to the guard's injuries. "We will question them as soon as they're able to talk."

"You do that," Shade quipped furiously. "And after you question them, tell them that I'll be personally questioning them also on the root cause of their obvious incompetence."

"Yes, Your Excellency," Captain Lord replied nervously.

Jado was still kneeling over the body of Malcolm Steiger.

"We'll avenge his death, Jado," Shade said, and he placed a reassuring hand on the young Kaloian's shoulder. "You'll get an opportunity to use your power to make the Earthlings pay for this."

Jado glanced up at the potentate. "Teach me everything you can. I want to use my power to the fullest," he said, determined. "I want to be a tool for our people—the tool you want me to be."

"Very good," Shade said, nodding slowly. "You and I will rule this entire galaxy together. We will bring the Kaloian race to its rightful place—the superior race that rules over all the others."

"Yes," Jado said, and he rose to his feet, his good eye narrowed. "I am your instrument of death and destruction...use me."

Chapter 33

"How are you feeling?" Lauren asked.

Sabre had just woken up from a long sleep. It had been several hours since he'd returned to the ship. He slowly sat up on the bed and wiped the sleep from his eyes.

"Much better," he said groggily.

"Good," Lauren answered. "You need to get dressed. Colonel Madigan has ordered that you get your required evaluation from Dr. Holtz immediately."

She tossed him his gray jogging pants and shirt.

"Any news on Banshee?" he asked, as he pushed his head through the shirt.

"I don't know," she answered. "I just woke up about ten minutes before you."

She watched as he got dressed and could tell he was still very hopeful that Merissa Voight was alive. She wanted to press him for more information but thought better of it. This was going to be a happy day, and the last thing she wanted to do was bring more gloom into the picture before she shared the wonderful news.

"What are you smiling about?" Sabre asked, shattering her thoughts.

Lauren's eyes widened, and her mouth immediately turned into a straight line. "Oh, nothing," she muttered. "I didn't even realize I was."

"Well you were," Sabre said, standing. He moved over to her and pulled her close. "What's on your mind?"

She looked up at him. "Nothing," she said. "Just glad you came back to me in one piece."

He stared at her and shook his head. "No," he said. "There's something else."

Lauren smiled again and looked away. Clearly, he was onto her.

"Well," she began, her head resting against his chest. "I was going to go with you to see Dr. Holtz...I wanted her there when I told you."

Sabre pulled back from her and moved his head, so he could look her in the face. "Tell me what?" he asked anxiously.

Again, she smiled, this time wider. "Oh, alright," she said. "I suppose it would be cruel to make you wait at this point..."

Suddenly there was a knock at the door. Sabre shook his head and exhaled. "Hold that thought," he said, leaning forward to kiss her on the forehead.

She nodded and strolled over to the couch to have a seat.

Sabre pushed the button to open the door and Arthur Law was standing there. He looked exhausted and appeared to still be wearing his flight suit.

"Lawyer," Sabre said, looking him over. "Have you gotten any rest? What are you—"

"Christian," Lawyer interrupted. "I'm glad you're awake. I was going to come sooner, but the colonel was adamant that we let you rest."

Sabre could sense that something very bad had happened. "Tell me," Sabre said. "What's wrong?"

Lawyer took a deep breath and released it slowly. He then made his way into the room. "I have news," he said. "But before I tell you, you have to go sit down beside Lauren."

***

Colonel Merrill Madigan was seated at Harry Hightower's desk. He was staring at a photo of both he and Hightower from way back when they were in the academy together. Madigan had given it to Hightower for his birthday three years ago. It was a token of his appreciation for the friendship Hightower had given him ever since they'd first met in their early twenties—a moment in time captured in the photograph. He then turned his attention to a bottle of bourbon he'd swiped from Ray Compton's stock and took a long pull from the bottle. Then be began to sob.

He remained in that condition for half an hour, when a sudden knock at the door startled him.

"Come in," he grumbled, leaning back in the chair. He quickly wiped the tears away from his eyes.

"Sir, you're needed on the bridge," Hayden Carter said as he stepped into the room.

Madigan shook his head and waved him off. "Not now, Carter," he groaned. "Leave me be for a while. I've got to decide what our next move will be, and I want to do it alone."

Hayden drew near the colonel and put a hand on his shoulder. "Sir, this is a huge burden for you to bear and you shouldn't have to bear it alone."

"No," Madigan said, shoving Hayden's hand away. "I *have* to do it alone, I promised Harry I'd do the job and I'm going to do the job."

Hayden looked at him, perplexed. "Sir, you don't understand," he said. "You will not have to do this alone. You need to come to the bridge at once."

"What? Why?" Madigan asked again, this time a hint of anger in his voice.

"I was ordered not to say, sir," Hayden replied. "Please, just come to the bridge at once."

"Ordered?" Madigan said, and he suddenly stood from behind the desk, his eyes blazing with fury. "I'm in command of this ship! You take orders from me!"

Hayden was suddenly very uncomfortable. "Sir, I'm afraid that's not the case anymore. You *really* need to come to the bridge at once."

Madigan shook his head and cursed. He then snatched up the bottle of bourbon and took another long pull before slamming it back onto the desk. Some of the amber liquid sloshed out and wet his hand. Madigan cursed again and wiped the alcohol off on the front of his uniform. He then stormed past Hayden and made his way toward the bridge. When he arrived, he was surprised and angered to see that someone was seated in the captain's chair. Madigan could only see the back of the man's head, but something about the dark hair looked very familiar.

"What's the meaning of this?" Madigan growled. "Who do you think you are?"

The chair slowly spun around to face the colonel and what Madigan saw made him rub his eyes in disbelief. The Asian man was short, middle-aged, and wore black horn-rimmed glasses. He stood from the chair and smiled.

"Good to see you colonel," he said. "I want to personally thank you for your leadership during this difficult time, however, I think the moment has arrived for me to take command."

"Yes, Mr. President," Colonel Madigan said, awestruck. "But how…" he paused. "How…where did you come from?"

President Akagi Hiro chuckled and clasped his hands together. "We have much to discuss," he said. "But first things first. We need to devise a plan to rescue Commander Roger Stellick."

SC Titan Officers and Notable Crew

Captain	Harry Hightower
Executive Officer	Colonel Merrill Madigan
Commander	Roger Stellick
First Lieutenant	Hayden Carter
Chief Medical Officer	Dr. Phoebe Holtz
Helmsman	Rowena Carter
Communications	Jake Crosby
Deck Crew Chief	Tim Reed
Physical Fitness	Lauren West
Bartender	Ray Compton
Deck Hand	Charlie West

Comet Fighter Pilots & Squadrons

ALPHA SQUAD	CALL SIGN	ECHO SQUAD	CALL SIGN
Roger Stellick	Ice	Merissa Voight	Banshee
Daniel Miller	Wrench	Franklin Fuller	Bull
Zebulon Ryder	Blackout	Simon Richardson	Shadow
Harvey Sears	Subzero	August Johnson	Waldo
Gentry McNevin	Cowboy	Steven Hunt	Hogie

BRAVO SQUAD	CALL SIGN	FOXTROT SQUAD	CALL SIGN
Christian Smith	Sabre	Robert Drake	Tombstone
Charity Price	Covergirl	Noah Fisher	Jaws
Eldon Walker	Rough Rider	Nathan Carmichael	Moondog
Morgan Cross	Moose	Warren Pickett	Spike
Wilson Collins	Popsicle	Thad Watson	Top Dog

CHARLIE SQUAD	CALL SIGN
Tobias Bancroft	Shephard
Calvin Reynolds	Tinker
Moses Ward	Pope
Parker Stevens	Phantom
Peyton Kelly	Ruffles

GOLF SQUAD	CALL SIGN
Vincent Hunter	Spade
Maggie Shaw	Scarlet
Simon Owen	Deep Dive
Nicholas Cox	Neo
James O'Connell	Lucky

DELTA SQUAD	CALL SIGN
Howard Scofield	Hotwire
Amelia Turner	Sunshine
Jesse Foster	Jinx
Arthur Law	Lawyer
Silas Griswold	Grizzly

HOTEL SQUAD	CALL SIGN
Harlan Wolfe	Howler
Georgia Clarke	Peach
Cooper Jenkins	Cyclops
Ben Foster	Bones
Garrett Butler	Romeo

CHECK OUT OTHER GREAT
SCIENCE FICTION BOOKS

SALVAGE MERC ONE
by Jake Bible

Joseph Laribeau was born to be a Marine in the Galactic Fleet. He was born to fight the alien enemies known as the Skrang Alliance and travel the galaxy doing his duty as a Marine Sergeant. But when the War ended and Joe found himself medically discharged, the best job ever was over and he never thought he'd find his way again.

Then a beautiful alien walked into his life and offered him a chance at something even greater than the Fleet, a chance to serve with the Salvage Merc Corp.

Now known as Salvage Merc One Eighty-Four, Joe Laribeau is given the ultimate assignment by the SMC bosses. To his surprise it is neither a military nor a corporate salvage. Rather, Joe has to risk his life for one of his own. He has to find and bring back the legend that started the Corp.

SERENGETI
by J.B. Rockwell

It was supposed to be an easy job: find the Dark Star Revolution Starships, destroy them, and go home. But a booby-trapped vessel decimates the Meridian Alliance fleet, leaving Serengeti—a Valkyrie class warship with a sentient AI brain—on her own; wrecked and abandoned in an empty expanse of space. On the edge of total failure, Serengeti thinks only of her crew. She herds the survivors into a lifeboat, intending to sling them into space. But the escape pod sticks in her belly, locking the cryogenically frozen crew inside.

Then a scavenger ship arrives to pick Serengeti's bones clean. Her engines dead, her guns long silenced, Serengeti and her last two robots must find a way to fight the scavengers off and save the crew trapped inside her.

CHECK OUT OTHER GREAT SCIENCE FICTION BOOKS

FURNACE
by Joseph Williams

On a routine escort mission to a human colony, Lieutenant Michael Chalmers is pulled out of hyper-sleep a month early. The RSA Rockne Hummel is well off course and—as the ship's navigator—it's up to him to figure out why. It's supposed to be a simple fix, but when he attempts to identify their position in the known universe, nothing registers on his scans. The vessel has catapulted beyond the reach of starlight by at least a hundred trillion light-years. Then a planetary-mass object materializes behind them. It's burning brightly even without a star to heat it. Hundreds of damaged ships are locked in its orbit. The crew discovers there are no life-signs aboard any of them. As system failures sweep through the Hummel, neither Chalmers nor the pilot can prevent the vessel from crashing into the surface near a mysterious ancient city. And that's where the real nightmare begins.

LUNA
by Rick Chesler

On the threshold of opening the moon to tourist excursions, a private space firm owned by a visionary billionaire takes a team of non-astronauts to the lunar surface. To address concerns that the moon's barren rock may not hold long-term allure for an uber-wealthy clientele, the company's charismatic owner reveals to the group the ultimate discovery: life on the moon.

But what is initially a triumphant and world-changing moment soon gives way to unrelenting terror as the team experiences firsthand that despite their technological prowess, the moon still holds many secrets.

CHECK OUT OTHER GREAT SCIENCE FICTION BOOKS

IN PERPETUITY
by Jake Bible

For two thousand years, Earth and her many colonies across the galaxy have fought against the Estelian menace. Having faced overwhelming losses, the CSC has instituted the largest military draft ever, conscripting millions into the battle against the aliens. Major Bartram North has been tasked with the unenviable task of coordinating the military education of hundreds of thousands of recruits and turning them into troops ready to fight and die for the cause.

As Major North struggles to maintain a training pace that the CSC insists upon, he realizes something isn't right on the Perpetuity. But before he can investigate, the station dissolves into madness brought on by the physical booster known as pharma. Unfortunately for Major North, that is not the only nightmare he faces- an armada of Estelian warships is on the edge of the solar system and headed right for Earth!

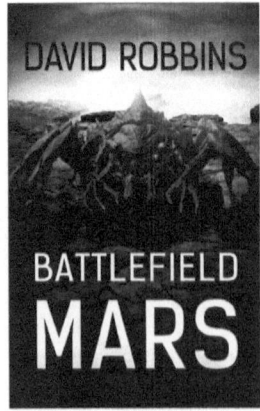

BATTLEFIELD MARS
by David Robbins

Several centuries into the future, Earth has established three colonies on Mars. No indigenous life has been discovered, and humankind looks forward to making the Red Planet their own.

Then 'something' emerges out of a long-extinct volcano and doesn't like what the humans are doing.

Captain Archard Rahn, United Nations Interplanetary Corps, tries to stem the rising tide of slaughter. But the Martians are more than they seem, and it isn't long before Mars erupts in all-out war.

www.ingramcontent.com/pod-product-compliance
Lightning Source LLC
Chambersburg PA
CBHW031947170626
46807CB00006B/2381